THE UNVEILING

The Unveiling

Age Of Faith: Book One

Tamara Leigh

ISBN: 1942326033
ISBN 13: 9781942326038

Splitting Harriet, 06/15 (ebook), 2007
(print): RandomHouse/Multnomah
Faking Grace, 09/15 (ebook), 2008 (print): RandomHouse/Multnomah

Southern Discomfort: A Contemporary Romance Series
Leaving Carolina: Book One, 11/15 (ebook), 2009
(print edition): RandomHouse/Multnomah
Nowhere, Carolina, 2010 (print): RandomHouse/Multnomah
Restless in Carolina, 2011 (print): RandomHouse/Multnomah

OUT-OF-PRINT GENERAL MARKET TITLES
Warrior Bride, 1994: Bantam
*Virgin Bride, 1994: Bantam
Pagan Bride, 1995: Bantam
Saxon Bride, 1995: Bantam
Misbegotten, 1996: HarperCollins
Unforgotten, 1997: HarperCollins
Blackheart, 2001: Dorchester Leisure

*Virgin Bride is the sequel to *Warrior Bride*
Pagan Pride and *Saxon Bride* are stand-alone novels

www.tamaraleigh.com

1

Lincolnshire, England, October 1149

A NIGHTMARE SEIZED him from sleep, turned around his throat, and filled his mouth so full he could not cry out. Desperate for air, he opened his eyes onto a moonless night that denied him the face of his attacker.

By all the saints! Who dares?

He struck out, but a second attacker appeared and pitched him onto his belly. Though a foul cloth had been shoved in his mouth, the loosening of hands around his throat permitted him to wheeze breath through his nose. Then he was yanked up from the blanket on which he had made his bed distant from his lord's tent.

Too late realizing the error of allowing dishonor to incite him to isolation, he thrust backward and nearly found his release.

Hands gripped him harder and dragged him toward the wood.

Who were these miscreants who spoke not a word? What did they intend? Would they beat him for a traitor? Worse?

A noose fell past his ears. Feeling death settle on his shoulders, he knew fear that surpassed any he had known. He shouted against the cloth, struggled to shrug out from beneath the rope, splayed and hooked his useless hands.

Lord, help me!

The cruel hands fell from him, but as he reached for the rope, it tightened and snapped his chin to his chest. An instant later, he was hoisted off his feet. He flailed and clawed at his trussed neck but was denied even the smallest breath of air.

Realizing that this night he would die for what he had intended to do…for what he had not done…for Henry, he would have sobbed like the boy he ever denied being had he the breath to do so.

Unworthy! The familiar rebuke sounded through him, though it was many months since he had been called such.

Aye, unworthy, for I cannot even die like a man.

He turned his trembling hands into fists and stilled as the lessons taught him by Lord Wulfrith numbered through his mind, the greatest being that refuge was found in God.

Feeling his life flicker like a flame taking its last sip of the wick, he embraced the calm that settled over him and set his darkening gaze on one of his attackers who stood to the right. Though he could not be certain, he thought the man's back was turned to him. Then he heard the wheezing of one who also suffered a lack of breath.

A mute cry of disbelief parted his lips. Of all those who might have done this, never would he have believed—

Darkness stole his sight, swelled his heart, and brought to mind a beloved image. He had vowed he would not leave her, but now Annyn would be alone.

Forgive me, he pleaded across the leagues that separated them. *Pray, forgive me.*

As death tightened its hold, he could not help but weep inside himself for the foolishness that had sent him to the noose.

His body convulsed and, with his last presence of mind, he once more turned heavenward. *Do not let her be too long alone, God. Pray, do not.*

Castle Lillia

Annyn Bretanne lowered her gaze from the moonless mantle of stars. "Jonas…" She pressed a hand over her heart. Whence came this foreboding? And why this feeling it had something to do with her brother?

Because you were thinking of him. Because you wish him here not there.

"My lady?"

She pushed back from the battlements and swung around. It was William, though she knew it only by the man-at-arm's gruff voice. The night fell too black for the torches at the end of the wall-walk to light his features.

He halted. "You ought to be abed, my lady."

As always, there was a smile in the title he bestowed. Like the others, he knew she was a lady by noble birth only. That she had stolen from bed in the middle of night further confirmed what all thought of one who, at four and ten, ought to be betrothed—perhaps even wed.

Though in such circumstances Annyn was inclined to banter with William, worry continued to weight her.

"Good eve," she said and hastened past. Continuing to hold a hand to her heart, she descended the steps and ran to the donjon. Not until she closed the door on her chamber did she drop her hand from her chest, and only then to drag off her man's tunic.

Falling onto her bed, she called on the one her brother assured her was always near. "Dear Lord, do not let Jonas be ill. Or hurt. Or…"

She turned aside the thought that was too terrible to think. Jonas was hale and would return from Wulfen Castle. He had promised.

She clasped her hands before her face. "Almighty God, I beseech Thee, deliver my brother home from Wulfen. Soon."

2

THERE WAS BUT one way to enter Wulfen Castle. She must make herself into a man.

Annyn looked down her figure where she stood among the leaves of the wood. And scowled. Rather, she must make herself into a boy, for it was boys in which the Baron Wulfrith dealt—pages who aspired to squires, squires who aspired to knights. As she was too slight to disguise herself as a squire, a page would be her lot, but only long enough to assure Jonas was well.

Still haunted by foreboding, though it was now four days since it had burrowed a dark place within her, she dropped her head back against the tree beneath which she had taken cover and squinted at the sunlight that found little resistance in autumn's last leaves. If only her mother were alive to offer comfort, but it was eight years since Lady Elena had passed on. Eight years since Annyn had known her touch.

A thumping sound evidencing the wily hare had come out of the thicket, Annyn gripped her bow tighter and edged slowly around the tree as her brother had taught her.

Though the scruffy little fellow had not fully emerged, he would soon. She tossed her head to clear the hair from her brow, raised her bow, and drew the nocked arrow to her cheek.

The hare lifted its twitchy nose.

Patience. Annyn heard Jonas from two summers past. Would she hear his voice again?

Aye, she would see him when she journeyed to Wulfen Castle where he completed his squire's training with the mighty Baron Wulfrith, a man said to exercise considerable sway over the earl from whom he held his lands.

Annyn frowned as she pondered the Wulfrith name that brought to mind a snarling wolf, her imagining made more vivid by the terrible anger the man was said to possess. Since before William of Normandy had conquered England, the Wulfrith family had been known England to France for training boys into men, especially those considered seriously lacking. Though Jonas's missives spoke little of that training, all knew it was merciless.

The hare crept forward.

Hold! Jonas's voice, almost real enough to fan her cheek, made her smile, cracking the mud she had smeared on her face as her brother had also taught her to do.

She squeezed her eyes closed. Thirteen months since he had departed for Wulfen. Thirteen months in training with the feared Wulfrith who allowed no women within his walls. Thirteen months to make Jonas into a man worthy to lord the barony of Aillil that would be his as Uncle Artur's heir.

The hare thumped.

Annyn jerked, startling the creature into bounding from the thicket. *Follow, follow, follow!*

She swung the arrow tip ahead of the hare and released.

With a shriek that made her wince as she did each time she felled one of God's creatures, the hare collapsed on a bed of muddy leaves.

Meat on the table, Annyn told herself as she tramped to where her prey lay. Not caring that she dirtied her hose and tunic, she knelt beside it.

"Godspeed," she said, hoping to hurry it to heaven though Father Cornelius said no such place existed for animals. But what did a man who did not know how to smile know of God's abode? She lifted the hare and tugged her arrow free. Satisfied to find tip and feathers intact, she wiped the shaft on her tunic and thrust the arrow into her quiver.

She stood. A catch of good size. Not that Uncle Artur would approve of her fetching meat to the table. He would make a show of disapproval, as he did each time she ventured to the wood, then happily settle down to a meal of hare pie. Of course, Annyn must first convince Cook to prepare the dish. But he would, and if she hurried, it could be served at the nooning meal. She slung the bow over her shoulder and ran.

If only Jonas were here, making me strain to match his longer stride. If only he were calling taunts over his shoulder. If only he would go from sight only to pounce upon me. Lord, I do not know what I will do if—

She thrust aside her worry with the reminder that, soon enough, she would have the assurance she sought. This very eve she would cut her mess of black hair, don garments Jonas had worn as a page, and leave under cover of dark. In less than a sennight, she could steal into Wulfen Castle, seek out her brother, and return to Aillil. As for Uncle Artur...

She paused at the edge of the wood and eyed Castle Lillia across the open meadow. Her disappearance would send dread through her uncle, but if she told him what she intended, he would not allow it.

She toed the damp ground. If he would but send a missive to Wulfen to learn how Jonas fared, this venture of hers need not be undertaken. However, each time she asked it of her uncle, he teased that she worried too much.

Movement on the drawbridge captured Annyn's regard. A visitor? A messenger from Wulfen? Mayhap Jonas once more returned for willful behavior? She squinted at the standard flown by the rider who passed beneath the raised portcullis and gasped. It belonged to the Wulfriths!

Though the men on the walls usually called to Annyn and bantered over her frightful appearance, her name did not unfurl any tongues when she approached the drawbridge.

Ignoring her misgivings, she paused to seek out the bearded Rowan who, as captain of the guard, was sure to be upon the gatehouse. He was not, but William was.

She thrust the hare high. "Next time, boar!"

He did not smile. "My lady, hasten to the donjon. The Baron Wul—"

"I know! My brother is returned?"

He averted his gaze. "Aye, Lady Annyn, your brother is returned."

So, neither could the renowned Baron Wulfrith order Jonas's life. She might have laughed if not that it boded ill for her brother's training to be terminated. Though of good heart, he had thrice been returned by fostering barons who could no more direct him than his uncle with whom he and Annyn had lived these past ten years. Thus, until Uncle Artur had sent Jonas to Wulfen Castle, brother and sister had been more together than apart. Soon they would be together again.

Silently thanking God for providing what she had asked, she darted beneath the portcullis and into the outer bailey, passing castle folk who stared after her with something other than disapproval. Telling herself her flesh bristled from chill, she entered the inner bailey where a half dozen horses stood before the donjon, among them Jonas's palfrey. And a wagon.

As she neared, the squire who held the reins of an enormous white destrier looked around. Surprise first recast his narrow face, then disdain. "Halt, you!"

She needed no mirror to know she looked more like a stable boy than a lady, but rather than allow him to mistake her as she was inclined to do, she said, "It is Lady Annyn you address, Squire."

Disdain slid back into surprise, and his sleepy green eyes widened further when he saw the hare. "Lady?" As if struck, he looked aside.

Annyn paused alongside Jonas's horse and laid a hand to its great jaw. "I thank you for bringing him home." She ran up the steps.

The porter was frowning when she reached the uppermost landing. "My lady, your uncle and Baron Wulfrith await. Pray, go quick 'round to the kitchen and put yourself to order."

Baron Wulfrith at Lillia? She glanced over her shoulder at the white destrier. How could she not have realized its significance? The baron must be angry indeed to have returned Jonas himself. Unless—

William's unsmiling face. The lack of disapproval usually shown her by the castle folk. The wagon.

Not caring what her appearance might say of her, she lunged forward.

"My lady, pray—"

"I will see my brother now!"

The porter's mouth worked as if to conjure argument, but he shook his head and opened the door. "I am sorry, Lady Annyn."

The apology chilling her further, she stepped inside.

The hall was still, not a sound to disturb God and His angels were they near.

Blinking to adjust to the indoors, she caught sight of those on the dais. As their backs were turned to her and heads were bent, she wondered what they looked upon. More, where was Jonas?

The hare's hind legs dragging the rushes where the animal hung at her side, she pressed forward, all the while telling herself Jonas would soon lunge from an alcove and thump her to the floor.

"'Twas an honorable death, Lord Bretanne," a deep voice struck silence from the hall.

Annyn halted and picked out the one who had spoken—a big man in height and breadth, hair cut to the shoulders.

Dear God, of whom does he speak?

He stepped aside, clearing the space before the lord's table to reveal the one she desperately sought.

The hare slipped from her fingers, the bow from her shoulder. Vaguely aware of the big man and his companions swinging around, she stared at her brother's profile that was the shade of a dreary day. And there stood Uncle Artur opposite, hands flat on the table upon which Jonas was laid, head bowed, shoulders hunched up to his ears.

Annyn stumbled into a run. "Jonas!"

"What is this?" the deep voice demanded.

When Uncle's head came up, his rimmed eyes reflected shock at the sight of her. But there was only Jonas. In a moment she would have him up from the table and—

She collided with a hauberked chest and would have fallen back if not for the hand that fastened around her upper arm. It was the man who had spoken. She swung a foot and connected with his unmoving shin.

He dragged her up to her toes. "Who is this whelp that runs your hall like a dog, Lord Bretanne?"

Annyn reached for him where he stood far above. He jerked his head back, but not before her nails peeled back the skin of his cheek and jaw.

With a growl, he drew back an arm.

"Halt! 'Tis my niece."

The fist stopped above her face. "What say you?"

As Annyn stared at the large knuckles, she almost wished they would grind her bones so she might feel a lesser pain.

"My niece," Uncle said with apology, "Lady Annyn Bretanne."

The man delved her dirt-streaked face. "*This* is a woman?"

"But a girl, Lord Wulfrith."

Annyn looked from the four angry scores on the man's cheek to his grey-green eyes. *This* was Wulfrith? The one to whom Jonas was entrusted? Who was to make of him a man? Who had made of him a corpse?

"Loose me, cur!" She spat in the scratchy little voice Jonas often teased her about.

"Annyn!" Uncle protested.

Wulfrith's grip intensified and his pupils dilated.

Refusing to flinch as Jonas had told her she should never do, she held steady.

"'Tis the Baron Wulfrith to whom you speak, child," her uncle said as he came around the table, his voice more stern than she had ever heard it.

She continued to stare into the face she had marked. "This I know."

Uncle laid a hand on Wulfrith's shoulder. "She is grieved, Lord Wulfrith. Pray, pity her."

Annyn glared at her uncle. "Pity *me*? Who shall pity my brother?"

He recoiled, the pain of a heart that had loved his brother's son causing his eyes to pool.

Wulfrith released Annyn. "Methinks it better that I pity *you*, Lord Bretanne."

Barely containing the impulse to spit on him, she jumped back and looked fully into his face: hard, sharp eyes, nose slightly bent, proud cheekbones, firm mouth belied by a full lower lip, cleft chin. And falling back from a face others might think handsome, silver hair—a lie, for he was not of an age that bespoke such color. Indeed, he could not have attained much more than twenty and five years.

"Were I a man, I would kill you," she rasped.

His eyebrows rose. "'Tis good you are but a little girl."

If not for Uncle's hand that fell to her shoulder, Annyn would have once more set herself at Wulfrith.

"You err, child." Uncle Artur spoke firm. "Jonas fell in battle. His death is not upon the baron."

She shrugged out from beneath his hand and ascended the dais. Her brother was clothed in his finest tunic, about his waist a silver-studded belt from which a sheathed misericorde hung. He had been made ready for burial.

She laid a hand on his chest and willed his heart to beat again. But nevermore. "Why, Jonas?" The first tear fell, wetting the dried mud on her face.

"They were close." Uncle Artur's low words pierced her. "'Twill be difficult for her to accept."

Annyn swung around to face those who stared at her with disdain and pity. "How did my brother die?"

Was Wulfrith's hesitation imagined? "It happened at Lincoln."

She gasped. Yesterday they had received tidings of the bloody battle between the armies of England's self-proclaimed king, Stephen, and the young Henry, grandson of the departed King Henry and rightful heir to the throne. In spite of numerous skirmishes, raids, and deaths, it was told that neither man could claim victory at Lincoln. Nor could Jonas.

"Your brother squired for me. He was felled while delivering a lance to the field."

Despite her trembling, Annyn held Wulfrith's gaze. "What felled him?"

Something turned in his steely eyes. "An arrow to the heart."

All for Stephen's defense of his misbegotten claim to England.

She sank her nails into her palms. How it had pained Jonas to stand the side of the usurper when it was Henry he supported. And surely he had not been alone in that. Regardless of whose claim to the throne one supported, nobles vied to place their sons at Wulfen Castle. True, Wulfrith was Stephen's man, but it was said there was none better to train knights who would one day lord. If not for this silver-haired Lucifer and his thieving king, Jonas would be alive.

"He died an honorable death, Lady Annyn."

She took a step toward Wulfrith. "'Twas for Stephen he died. Tell me, Lord Wulfrith, what has that man to do with honor?"

As anger flared in his eyes, Uncle Artur groaned. Though Uncle also sided with Stephen, he had been aware of his nephew's allegiance to Henry. This, then—his hope of turning Jonas to Stephen—among his reasons for sending his nephew to Wulfrith.

Amid the murmuring and grunting of those in the hall, Annyn looked to Wulfrith's scored flesh and wished the furrows proved deep enough to mark him forever. And of Stephen who had pressed Uncle to send Jonas to Wulfrith? Whose wrongful claim to England had made the battle that took Jonas's life?

"Again, were I a man, I would kill your beloved Stephen."

While his men responded with raised voices, out of the darkness of his accursed soul, Wulfrith stared at her.

"Annyn!" Uncle strangled. "You do not know of what you speak."

"But I do." She turned her back on him and gently swept the hair off her brother's brow.

"Pray, Lord Wulfrith," her uncle beseeched, "do not listen——"

"Fear not. What has been spoken shall not pass from here."

Annyn looked over her shoulder. "My uncle is most grateful for such generosity from the man who bequeathed a grave to his heir."

Wulfrith's lower lip thinned with the upper, and his men objected more loudly, but it was Uncle Artur's face that stayed her. His torment pushed past the child in her and forced her to recognize it was not Wulfrith who staggered beneath her bitter words. It was this man she loved as a father.

She swallowed her tears. She would not further lose control of her emotions. After all, she was four and ten winters aged—a woman, though her uncle defended her as a girl. If not for his indulgence, she might now be wed, perhaps even with child.

She closed her eyes and drew a deep breath. When she lifted her lids, Wulfrith's harsh gaze awaited hers. "We wish to be alone," she said.

He inclined his head and looked to Uncle. "Lord Bretanne."

"Lord Wulfrith. Godspeed."

Despising the baron's ample shoulders and long-reaching legs, Annyn stared after him until he and his men passed through the door held by the porter.

"You should not have spoken as you did," Uncle said, though the steel in his voice would forge no sword.

Jonas's death had aged him, had stolen the breadth of shoulders on which he had borne her as a young girl.

Pressing her own shoulders back, she stood as tall as her four feet and some inches would stretch. "I know I have shamed you, and I shall endeavor to earn your forgiveness."

He mounted the dais and put an arm around her. "All is forgiven." He turned her to Jonas.

As she looked at her brother, a sob climbed up her throat. Reminding herself she was no longer a girl, she swallowed it.

"An honorable death."

Uncle's whispered words struck nearly as hard as when Wulfrith had spoken them. Though she struggled to hold back the child who incited words to her lips, she could not.

"Honorable! Not even eight and ten and he lies dead from serving a man who was more his enemy than—"

"Enough!" Uncle dropped his arm from her.

"Can you deny Jonas would be alive if not for Stephen's war?"

Anger met weariness on his brow. "Nay, as neither can I deny he would yet breathe if Henry, that whelp of Maude's, did not seek England for his own." He reached past her, ungirded Jonas's belt, and swept up his tunic. "Look!"

She did not want to, longed to run back to the wood, but that was the girl in her. Jaw aching at the force with which she ground her teeth, she dragged her gaze to the hideous wound at the center of her brother's chest.

"What do you see?" Uncle asked.

"A wound."

"And whose army do you think shot the arrow that put it there?"

Henry's, but—

"Whose, Annyn?"

Henry's, but Stephen—

"Speak it!"

She looked to her quaking hands. "Henry's."

He sighed, bent a finger beneath her chin, and urged her face up. "Stephen may not be the king England deserves, but until a worthier one appears, he is all there is. I beseech you, put aside Jonas's foolish allegiance to Maude's son. Henry is but a boy—barely six and ten—and unworthy to rule."

Unworthy when he led armies? Unworthy when—

She nodded.

Uncle stepped back. "I must needs pray."

As she ought to herself, for Father Cornelius told it was a long way to heaven. The sooner Jonas was prayed there, the sooner he might find his rest. "I shall join you shortly."

As her uncle turned away, Annyn saw the captain of the guard step out of a shadowed alcove. Had he been there when she entered the hall? Not that any of what had been said should be withheld from him, for he also had been like a father to Jonas. Did Uncle know of Rowan's presence?

She looked to her uncle as he traversed the hall and saw him lift a hand to his chest as if troubled by the infirm heart that beat there.

Panged by the suffering of the man who had been good to her and Jonas—far better than his brother who had sown them—Annyn silently beseeched, *Please, Lord, hold him hale.*

A moment later, she startled at the realization that she called on the one who had done nothing to protect her brother. Thus, it was not likely He would answer her prayers for her uncle.

When the old man disappeared up the stairs, Annyn drew nearer the table and reached to pull Jonas's tunic down. However, the V-shaped birthmark on his left ribs captured her gaze. Since it was years since the boy he had been had tossed off his tunic in the heat of swordplay, she had forgotten about the mark.

She closed her eyes and cursed the man whose charge of Jonas had stolen her brother from her. Wulfrith had failed Jonas. Had failed her.

When Rowan ascended the dais, she looked around.

The captain of the guard stared at the young man to whom he had given so many of his years, then a mournful sound rumbled up from his depths and he yanked down Jonas's tunic.

For fear she would cry if she continued to look upon Rowan's sorrow, Annyn lowered her face and reached to straighten the neck of her brother's tunic. If not for that, she would not have seen it. Would never have known.

She looked closer at the abraded skin deep beneath his chin. What had caused it? She pushed the material aside. The raw skin circled his upper neck and, when she traced it around, it nearly met at the back.

Understanding landed like a slap to the face. Wulfrith had lied. An arrow had not killed Jonas. Hanging had been the end of him. Why? Had her brother revealed his allegiance to Henry? More, who had fit the noose? Wulfrith who stood for Stephen? It had to be. And if not him, then surely he had ordered it.

Annyn whipped her chin around and saw that Rowan stared at what she had uncovered.

Bile rising, she stumbled past him and dropped to her knees. When the heaving was done, she wiped her mouth on her sleeve. "What will Uncle say of Wulfrith and Stephen now 'tis proven Jonas was murdered?"

Rowan sank deeper into silence, and she realized that, though Uncle's heart might abide the honorable death of one he had loved, Jonas's murder would likely ruin it, especially as he had sent her brother to Wulfrith in spite of Jonas's protests.

If not that she loved her uncle, she would have hated him. "Nay, he must not be told." Feeling as if she had aged years in these last moments, she stepped past Rowan and pulled the misericorde from her brother's belt.

Frowning over the pommel that was set with jewels to form the cross of crucifixion, she wondered whence the dagger came. She would have noticed such a splendid weapon had Jonas possessed one. Was it of Wulfen? It mattered not. All that mattered was revenge.

Vengeance is not yours, Annyn. Jonas's voice drifted to her from six months past when he had come home for three days. *Vengeance belongs to God. You must defer to Him.*

Her anger at the visiting nobleman's son who had set one of her braids afire had faltered when she heard Jonas speak so. He, who had so often shrugged off God, had found Him at Wulfen. Considering Baron Wulfrith's reputation, it had surprised her. And more so now, having met the man and discovered his lie about Jonas's death.

False teachings, then. A man like Wulfrith could not possibly know God. At that moment, she hardly knew Him herself. For days, she had prayed He would deliver Jonas home. And this was His answer.

She squeezed her fists so tight that her knuckles popped.

How she ached to make Wulfrith suffer for the bloodguilt of her brother's death. She knew vengeance was God's privilege, but she also knew it had once been the privilege of surviving family members.

Would God truly strike her down if she turned to the ways of the Old Testament? Revenge *was* the way of the world—certainly the way of men. Revenge begat revenge, as evidenced by the struggle for England's throne.

She nodded. How could God possibly deny her, especially as He was surely too busy to bother with such things himself? Were He not, He would not have allowed what had been done to Jonas.

Splaying her fingers on her thighs, she glared at the ceiling. "Vengeance is *mine*, and You shall just have to understand." A terrible, blasphemous thought crept to her tongue, and she did not bite it back. "If You are even there."

"Annyn?"

She looked to Rowan whose talk had turned her and Jonas to Henry's side—Rowan who would surely aid her. If it took a lifetime, Wulfrith would know the pain her brother had borne. Only his death would satisfy.

It had been necessary. Still, Garr Wulfrith felt the stain of young Jonas's death.

He reached for the hilt of his misericorde and too late realized he no longer possessed it. *That* had *not* been necessary.

Berating himself for the foolish gesture, he lifted a hand to his cheek where Jonas's shrew of a sister had scored his flesh. So the girl who looked and behaved like a boy had also turned. Though Artur Bretanne remained loyal to Stephen, somehow his brother's children had found Henry. For that, Jonas was dead. And hardly an honorable death as told.

Remembering what he had done the morning he found his squire strung from a tree, he told himself it was better that the truth of the betrayal die with the betrayer. No family ought to suffer such dishonor, not even a family that boasted one such as Annyn Bretanne. Thus, he had falsified—and now felt the brunt of God's displeasure.

Save me, O Lord, from lying lips and deceitful tongues, his mother would quote if she knew what her firstborn had done.

For this, Garr would spend hours in repentance and pray that this one lie did not breed, as lies often did—that after this day, he would know no more regret for having told it.

He looked over his shoulder. Though it was the receding Castle Lillia he sought, Squire Merrick captured his gaze. A promising young warrior, if not a bit peculiar, he and Jonas had served together in squiring Garr. At first there had been strain between the young men who both aspired to the standing of First Squire, but it had eased once Jonas was chosen. In fact, the two had become as near friends as was possible in the competitive ranks of the forty who sought knighthood at Wulfen Castle. But, as Merrick now knew, friendships often had false bottoms.

Garr shifted his gaze to Castle Lillia. He pitied Artur Bretanne. The man would be a long time in ridding himself of his niece, if ever, for who would take to wife that filthy little termagant who had but good, strong teeth to recommend her?

Of course, what man took any woman to wife other than to get an heir? Women were difficult, ever endeavoring to turn men from their purpose. However, as with all Wulfrith men who preferred warring over women, especially Garr's father, Drogo, Garr would eventually wed. Forsooth, he would have done so three years past had his betrothed not died of the pox.

He turned back to the land before him. Once Stephen secured his hold on England, Garr would find a wife of sturdy build whom he could visit a half dozen times a year until she bore him sons to raise up as warriors—men who stood far apart from ones like Jonas.

An image of the young man's death once more rising, he gripped the pommel of his saddle. How could he have been so wrong? Though he had sensed Jonas's allegiance to Henry, he had used it to put heart into the young man's training. After all, how better to make a man than to give him a powerful reason for becoming one? The aim was not to turn one's allegiance, though sometimes it happened. The aim was for the squire to give his utmost to his lord, which was of greatest importance in battle.

But the strategy had failed with Jonas—fatally. A mistake Garr would not make again.

Telling himself Jonas Bretanne was in the past, dead and soon buried, he released the pommel. As for Annyn Bretanne, she would put her loss behind her. All she needed was time.

3

Castle Lillia, Spring 1153

CASTLE LILLIA WAS taken, blessedly without loss of lives. From his bed, Uncle Artur had ordered the drawbridge lowered to admit Duke Henry's army. Now they were within, wafting their stench upon the hall and sounding their voices to the rafters.

Holding the high seat on the dais was Henry himself. However, it was not the vibrant man who carried Annyn's gaze time and again. It was the squire who sat at a lower table.

The talk of the hall was that, though destined for the monastery, the deaths of his brothers in the wars between Stephen and Henry had made the boy heir. Of a family strongly opposed to Henry's claim on England, he had been captured by the duke's army a sennight past while en route to Wulfen Castle. Such hopes his father must have that Wulfrith could turn him from a sickly pup into a wolf, but it would not come without much effort and pain. And now that he was to be held at Lillia, it might not come at all.

Annyn peered closer. He was slightly taller than she, who had risen to five feet three inches in the four years following Jonas's death, and his hair was nearly as dark as hers. There was not much to his build, as there was not much to hers.

"My lady," a warmly familiar voice spoke at her elbow.

She met Rowan's gaze. Regardless of the years that aged his eyes, there was something more to them than she had ever seen. The man he would have sit on England's throne had been let into Lillia. "Rowan?"

"The Duke requests your attendance."

Henry would see her? During his three hours at Lillia, he had not acknowledged her though she directed the servants and had done her best to look the lady of the castle.

Bitter humor tugged at her. Lady of the Castle, and yet beneath her mother's chainse and bliaut—dragged on as Henry came into Lillia—she wore tunic and hose. And for it she perspired.

She tugged the bodice off her moist skin. "I am presentable?" she asked in a voice that was more husk than the scratch it had been four years earlier.

"As presentable as a boy turned lady can be."

Wishing there was time to work her mess of hair into braids, she blew breath down her small-breasted chest. "Then to Henry I must go." She started past Rowan but halted. "Pray, hasten abovestairs and tell my uncle I shall attend him shortly."

Hoping Uncle Artur, who had been abed these past months, did not fret his failing heart over the happenings belowstairs, she traversed the hall. As with an increasing number of those who had long sided with Stephen, the intervening years were wrought with disenchantment for her uncle, though more for fear of the king that Stephen's son, Eustace, would one day make.

She settled her gaze on Henry. *Poise befitting a lady*, she reminded herself, *small steps, small smile, small gestures, small voice, small talk.* While inside, her heart beat large.

She ought to have been born a man. No matter how she tried for Uncle, it was not in her to be a lady. Would it ever be? If Jonas had lived, perhaps, but his murder left little for the woman's body into which she had been given.

Lifting her skirts, she sidestepped the sots whose bellies sloshed with Uncle's wine and ale. As she ascended the dais, Henry paused over the rim of his goblet and regarded her with large grey eyes.

She curtsied. "My lord." When she straightened, a faint smile lifted his freckled cheeks above his beard. He was handsome, though on other men such a square face and feverish red hair would be less pleasing.

"The lady Annyn." He gestured to the bench beside him. "Sit."

Realizing her skirts were still hitched to her ankles, Annyn dropped them and came around the table. As she lowered to the bench, Henry studied her with such intensity she feared he saw beneath her bliaut and chainse to the tunic, hose, and—

She gasped.

Wafting the scent of wine, Henry sat forward. "Something is amiss?"

Feigning a cough, she wiggled her toes beneath her skirts. She had forgotten to exchange her worn boots for slippers. Had anyone seen?

She tucked her feet beneath the bench, summoned an apologetic smile, and patted her neck. "A tickle, 'tis all."

He eased back into the high seat. "You are not uncomely, Lady Annyn."

Though his words were unexpected, she maintained an impassive expression. What response did he seek? She could agree she was not uncomely, but neither was she comely. Plain was the better word for one whose face was unremarkable beneath pale freckles, whose breasts were not much larger than apple halves, and the span between waist and hips was nearly unchanged.

"Why are you not wed?"

She flinched and immediately berated herself for failing to conceal her feelings. Jonas would have been disappointed.

"Be assured, Lady Annyn, though you are of an age, I shall find a fitting husband for you when I am king. One who will lord Aillil as it ought to be lorded."

Though her anger was more for his plan to wed her away from the freedom she was allowed, neither did she like being spoken of as if she were an old woman at eight and ten. Old women did not swing swords, tilt at quintains, or hunt. And they certainly did not wear men's garments. Perhaps Henry would not make a good king after all.

He chuckled, and she realized she had revealed herself again. "Ho, you do not like that!"

Careful, he shall soon be your king. Still, she could not acquiesce as Uncle would have advised and Rowan would have desired. She retrieved a small smile befitting a lady. "Do you wish the truth, my lord, or a lie?"

Henry grinned. "That is all the answer I require, Annyn Bretanne. Now, where does your loyalty lie?"

She released her tight smile. "You have my fealty, my lord."

"As I had your brother's, eh?"

Feeling the color pull from her cheeks, she asked, "You knew of Jonas's stand?"

Though he shrugged, she glimpsed in his eyes what looked like plotting. "A good king knows his subjects, Annyn Bretanne, and a good king I shall be."

And no more would he speak of Jonas. She clenched her hands. "I am certain you shall, my lord."

Henry grabbed a loaf of bread and wrenched off a bite. "What does your uncle think, Annyn Bretanne?"

It was curious, but he had not ordered Uncle Artur from his bed, nor gone abovestairs to confront the lord of the castle. It was as if Uncle was of no consequence. And perhaps he was not. Not only had he stood down from Henry, but he would not be much longer in this world. That last made her ache.

"Annyn Bretanne?"

Though she had never found her name offensive, it vexed that he was intent on speaking it in its entirety. She lowered her gaze. "Though I cannot speak for my uncle, is it not enough that he did not subject Castle Lillia to siege?"

Silence, and the longer it grew, the more fearsome it was felt.

Wondering where she erred, she looked up.

Henry's face was flushed. "'Tis not enough."

She swallowed. "What would be enough, my lord?"

"From his own lips he shall renounce his allegiance to Stephen."

And if he did not? "As you know, my uncle is infirm. If you ask this of him, I fear it will break a heart already broken in many places."

"You would have me depart Aillil with its lord still firm to Stephen? I did not enter here merely to quench my thirst and hunger, Annyn Bretanne. I came to take this barony from Stephen."

To whom it had not belonged for several years, though Uncle could not bring himself to foreswear the false king. Again, Annyn wondered if she had erred in supporting the duke, but that would mean Jonas had erred. And that was not possible.

"There is another way, Annyn Bretanne."

"My lord?"

"Aye, and most satisfactory. You shall wed a man of my choosing."

Realizing he did not refer to her marrying once he was king, but sooner, Annyn's booted feet stuttered out from beneath the bench.

"And for it, your uncle may hold to Stephen if that is what he would do. We are agreed?"

As if it were so simple. As if she had a choice. But though she hated it, marriage was inevitable. As Uncle's heir, she must wed; as Henry's subject, she must make an alliance with one of his own.

"Agreed. You shall send word when a suitable husband is found?"

"The bargain I make is that you wed on the morrow."

She startled. "The morrow?"

His eyes sparkled, and she realized this proposal had not come upon him suddenly.

Perhaps none is worthy to wear the crown of England, she seethed before chastising herself for judging him solely on how his ascension affected her. For all that was told of Henry, and by his acts, he would make a worthy king—better than Stephen and far better than Stephen's brutal son, Eustace.

"I shall have your answer now, Annyn Bretanne."

She looked to the occupants of the hall, one of whom Henry would choose to make of her mere chattel—a possession, a servant who directed servants, a body for spilling a man's lust, a womb for breeding. It was all she would become to one of these drunken sots. Worse, it meant her brother's death went unavenged and Wulfrith would never know Jonas's pain. She struggled but turned from the dark desire. She would not have Uncle Artur suffer further.

"I accept your proposal, my lord, but were I a man, such terms would not be acceptable."

He laughed. "Were you a man, Annyn Bretanne, for naught would I put such terms to you."

Under cover of the ridiculously long sleeves of her mother's bliaut, she clasped her hands tighter and rebuked herself for speaking with a child's tongue.

Henry reached for his goblet. "'Tis settled. On the morrow you shall wed." He swept his gaze around the hall as if in search of the groom, and his eyes settled on one farther down the lord's table. A baron, she believed, and young, mayhap a score and five.

Though she knew she ought to be grateful he was not decrepit—indeed, he was handsome—he appeared to love his ale, as evidenced by the weave of his head and the stain on his tunic. If there was one thing Annyn detested, it was an excess of drink. Her mother had suffered the weakness, and though Annyn had been quite young before Lady Elena's passing, the raucous laughter often followed by wrenching tears was well remembered.

Henry grunted and drained his goblet. "I shall make my decision on the morrow. Good eve."

Annyn stood. "Good eve, my lord."

"Annyn Bretanne."

"My lord?"

He thrust his goblet toward a serving wench. "Henceforth, there will be no more swordplay, no more tilting, no more hunting."

He knew. Something inside her shriveled. Not yet wed and already she was bound. Nothing left to her but the tedious chores of ladies, of which she could do few. "Aye, my lord."

"Too, my dear wife, Eleanor, would advise that slippers are the better choice beneath a lady's skirts."

She curled her fingers into her palms, her toes in her boots. "And she would be quite right, my lord. Is there anything else she would advise?"

"That is all."

She knew she ought to remain in the hall to direct the servants, but she could not. She would attend Uncle Artur, then withdraw to her own chamber.

When she was halfway across the hall, Henry's prisoner once more fell to her regard. The squire was slumped on an upturned hand, oblivious to the clamorous escort who had been taken with him. If not for his capture, it would be Wulfrith's hall in which he sat, Wulfrith to whom he answered, Wulfrith—

She must think only of Uncle Artur.

Shortly, she entered the solar. It was aglow, the fire in the hearth painting the walls orange and yellow. Though there was no place in all of Lillia as warm and vibrant, the bargain struck with Henry numbed her to it.

She looked to where Uncle lay in the postered bed, then to Rowan who sat in the chair alongside. "He sleeps?"

Before he could answer, Uncle's lids lifted. "Annyn."

She hastened forward, sank onto the mattress edge, and kissed his brow. "I am here."

"You...look the lady."

As she so rarely did. "I have tried."

He touched her sleeve. "I remember the last time your mother wore this gown. Such a beautiful woman."

It was how all remembered Elena Bretanne. Unfortunately, or perhaps fortunately, Annyn fell short of the woman who had borne her.

Uncle Artur sighed. "Aillil is Henry's now."

Though it was as Annyn wished, she felt little satisfaction. "'Tis."

"My Jonas was right. A better king Henry will make."

Annyn cupped his face. "Rest, Uncle."

"A better baron Jonas would have made."

If not for Wulfrith.

His lids trembled downward. "And a better husband I would have made...your mother."

She startled and glanced at Rowan who also jerked with surprise.

"We loved," her uncle breathed.

Annyn shook her head. "Uncle?"

Rowan issued a short, bitter laugh. "So that was the way of it."

Annyn met the gaze of the one who had first been her father's knight, ever near to comfort away bumps and bruises regardless of whether they were accidental or meted out by his lord's terrible temper.

She winced in remembrance of the bad humor that had not been spared their mother. Though Father Cornelius would have pronounced Annyn and Jonas evil, they were relieved upon the death of the one who had sired them. Shortly afterward, they had come with their mother to Lillia, and Rowan had brought them. There was none Annyn trusted more. All he had taught her: horses, hawking, the sword, the lance, the bow. Never would she know him as Jonas had known him, but he was a friend.

He squeezed his temples. "He was the one."

Annyn stared at him. What pained him so? Aye, he had cared for her mother, but...

She sought backwards and pried at memories of her mother and Rowan. There was not much to draw upon, other than that Rowan had been ever near and kind. And how grateful her mother had been for his unfailing attendance. But why had Rowan cared so much? Had he more than cared? As, it seemed, her uncle had done?

She knelt before the knight. "Did you love her, Rowan?"

He dragged a hand down his face. "What man did not? Even your father, for all his cruelty, loved Elena."

"Ah, Rowan." She laid a hand to his jaw. "I did not know."

"'Twas for none to know."

"Not even my mother?"

"She knew, and for a time I believed she felt for me, but she did not." Face darkening, he looked to Uncle. "It seems 'twas Artur she cared for."

Annyn followed his gaze to where her uncle lay silent. She had been but six when her mother died, unaware of what went between men and women. Had Elena returned Artur's love?

As Annyn stared at her uncle, longing for him to awaken that she might know her mother's secret, she was struck by the utter rest upon his face.

She looked to his chest and waited for it to rise. It did not. She twisted around and pressed an ear to Uncle's chest, but no matter how she strained, a heart that no longer beat could not be heard. She gasped and looked to Rowan. "He is gone."

He stared.

Annyn sank back on her heels. Her mother lost to her, then Jonas, now Uncle. If not for Rowan, she would truly be alone. She hugged her arms to her. Though she told herself she would not cry, tears wet her cheeks.

She did not know how long she sat wrapped in misery, but finally Rowan laid a hand on her shoulder and said softly, "Aillil is yours now."

What did it matter? Though she loved Aillil and its people, even if the latter shook their heads when she passed, she had none with whom to share it. And come the morrow, it would all be taken from her. "Nay. Aillil belongs to one of Henry's men."

Rowan's eyebrows clashed. "Of what do you speak?"

Accursed tears! Good for naught but swelling one's eyes. "I am to wed on the morrow." She stood, crossed to the window, and unlatched the shutters. "I agreed to it that Henry would not force Uncle to renounce Stephen."

Though Rowan rarely betrayed his emotions, she felt his anger. It surprised her, for though she knew he held her in affection, he was Henry's man.

"Who would he have you wed?"

As the cool night air emptied the oppressive heat from her, she said, "Even he does not know. He shall decide on the morrow."

"But your uncle is dead."

"And you think that changes anything?" She gasped. It changed everything. She had agreed to Henry's terms to spare her uncle pain, and pain he could no longer feel. But did she dare? If not for her ache, she might have smiled. Aye, Annyn Bretanne dared.

She turned to Rowan. "I shall leave Lillia."

"Where will you go?"

To where she had longed to venture for four years. "Wulfen Castle."

He drew a sharp breath. "We have spoken of this, Annyn. You must put aside your revenge. Naught good—"

"Will you take me? Or do I go alone?"

Never had she seen him struggle so, for if he agreed, he would betray his future king. Though she knew she should not ask it, she needed his help. "You also want Jonas avenged. Do you deny it?"

"I cannot." His voice cracked. "But though I would have vengeance on Wulfrith and render it myself if I could get near him, what you intend could mean your death."

Then it was fear for her that stayed him. She crossed to his side. "Do you think I will not be dead if forced to wed?"

"You speak of blood upon your hands."

"The blood of my brother's murderer!" Regardless of whether it was Wulfrith who put the noose to Jonas or he'd had another do it, through him her brother had died. "Whether or not you aid me, I will do this."

He scrabbled a hand over his bearded jaw. "How?"

"You will aid me?"

He slowly inclined his head.

Then she would have her revenge. "There is a squire in the hall who was traveling to Wulfen when he was captured by Henry," she said.

"Jame Braose."

Then he had also heard the talk. "I shall need his papers and to learn all there is to know of him."

He understood what she intended, but rendered no more argument. "I shall take ale with him and his escort."

"We leave the hour ere dawn."

"I shall be ready." He crossed the solar.

"Rowan?"

He looked over his shoulder.

Annyn steepled her hands beneath her lips and whispered, "I thank you."

With a dip of his chin, he departed.

Pretending she did not feel the misgivings that sought to weaken her resolve, Annyn told herself she would do this thing, and when it was done she would know peace.

Vengeance is not yours, Jonas insisted.

"You are wrong." She looked to Uncle who, it seemed, had loved and been loved by her mother.

She struggled with the desire to pray for him that vied with the fear of attempting to gain God's ear when her heart was so corrupt. In the end, she stepped forward and touched her lips to the old man's cheek. "Godspeed, good uncle."

Had Artur been the one? Rowan halted on the stairs, turned to the stone wall, pressed his palms to it, then his forehead. Though he longed to never again return to the darkness, he peeled away a score of years and once more saw that night.

Artur had also been there, having arrived hours before Drogo Wulfrith and his entourage stopped at the castle to request a night's lodging—a night when Elena's husband had yet to return from London. Though Artur had never revealed his feelings for his brother's wife, nor she for him, perhaps he *had* been the one. Yet all these years Rowan had believed it was Drogo Wulfrith. And hated him for it.

That night in the hall, the renowned maker of knights was unable to move his gaze from Elena. And, curse her, she who was inclined to partake of too much drink had played to him.

They had bantered, quaffed goblet after goblet, laughed until jealousy so fiercely gripped Rowan he forgot to whom Elena belonged.

Rowan dragged his hands down the stone wall and wrenched his head side to side to escape memories of the unpardonable thing he had done in believing Drogo—

But it might have been Artur. Indeed, it likely was. Jealousy found fuel in the man Rowan had served since bringing Elena and her children to Lillia. How he had hated the name of Wulfrith, and now, it seemed, for naught. Still, there was the bloodguilt of Jonas's death that the Wulfriths bore. And for Rowan, a need to finally avenge that death.

Though a part of him urged him to find a way to turn Annyn from her course, a young man he had loved had been murdered. A young man who had been as a son to him. Though never could he love Annyn as he had loved Jonas, he cared for Elena's daughter. Whatever the cost, Drogo's son would pay in kind.

But only if Annyn could kill. Of that Rowan was not certain. Forsooth, was she even prepared for the training she must endure to draw near Wulfrith?

As she had asked, Rowan had trained her and tried to make his time with her a balm to his loss of Jonas; however, he had not demanded of her all he would have required of a boy aspiring to manhood.

Fortunately, it was unlikely much had been required of Jame Braose, destined as he had been for the church. Thus, Annyn Bretanne as Jame Braose would not be expected to know much of arms and squiring. All she must know was where best to sink a dagger so that its victim would not rise again. And that Rowan could teach her.

4

The woods of Wulfen Castle, England

STARING AT HER distorted reflection, Annyn waited for the water disturbed by her hands to still and return her face to its familiar planes. When it did, she felt assured that none would know what was concealed beneath loose tunic, hose, and braies—the latter padded at the groin lest the hem of her tunic carried up.

She fingered the black hair she had cut to her jaw two nights past. Of all she had done to look the boy, this contributed the most. However, she was not overly saddened by the sacrifice of the greatest proof of her femininity. Indeed, her hair had too often proved a hindrance.

She filled her lungs with crisp air. Spring. Awakening from the death of winter, it made the world over and gave hope to those who had none. It soothed, leaving behind the old and painful and giving rise to the new and joyful. For some.

Trying not to think of Uncle who was in the ground by now, and Henry who surely fomented over her disappearance, she ran her fingers across the new shoots of grass alongside her boots. The blades were reborn, as she was into this man's world.

When Rowan's reflection appeared over her shoulder, she saw he wore the colors of the family she had taken for her own and shaved his beard, the latter making him appear younger and assuring he would not be recognized.

He met her gaze in the pool. "Are you ready, Jame Braose of Gaither?"

She stood. "I am."

"Still I see the woman."

"Because you know the woman." She tugged at the bindings that bound her small breasts beneath the tunic.

"Perhaps." He settled a cap on her head. "As much as possible, wear this. And take care with your voice. 'Tis a squire you pretend, not a page."

Though her natural huskiness lent to the pretense, a lower pitch was required. "I shall." She plucked at the bindings.

"And refrain from that."

She made a face. "Considering I am not much bigger in the chest than a boy, is it truly necessary for me to be bound?"

His brow lowered. "Is it necessary for you to do this thing?"

He knew it was, though since their departure from Lillia she had felt his disquiet deepen. "It is."

"Then you must needs be bound." He strode toward the horses.

'Twill not be for long, Annyn consoled herself, certain that, within a sennight, she would find an opportunity to avenge Jonas.

Vengeance is not yours.

She pushed aside her brother's words and touched the misericorde bound at her thigh. The great vein in the neck, Rowan had told.

"Come!" he called.

Thrilled with fear, she hurried after him and mounted her horse. They maintained silence to the edge of the wood, beyond which lay Wulfen Castle.

Annyn's first glimpse of the darkly imposing structure perched firmly on a hillock made her swallow. It was high and wide, walls washed in dark grey, red flags as blood upon it.

"You would stay the course?" Rowan asked.

Wishing there was another way that would not cost him his allegiance to Henry, she sat straighter. "I would."

He nodded and spurred his mount forward. "Godspeed," he shouted as they hurtled across the land.

Not until they slowed midway did Annyn see what transpired to the left of the castle. Four score men swung swords, tilted, and grappled hand-to-hand on a training field more vast than any she had seen. Its perimeter fenced, the interior crossed by yet more fences, the field was sectioned in such a way that each activity was separated from the other.

When thunder arose from behind, Annyn turned in her saddle to watch as five armored riders advanced on them. They were of Wulfen, their red surcoats emblazoned with charging wolves. Stomach tossing, she reined in alongside Rowan.

"Do not forget who you are, *Jame Braose,*" he warned.

Meaning this young man torn from the priesthood had not likely more than laid eyes to arms. But that did not mean he could not learn quickly.

Wulfrith's men drew around her and Rowan, and Annyn saw they were not quite men. Only a few sprouted whiskers, and then without much enthusiasm. They were all young men, squires approaching knighthood.

"Who goes?" demanded the one who sported a darkly fuzzed chin.

It seemed she was not alone in trying to sound like a man.

"I am Sir Killary," Rowan rendered in the superior voice of one who ranked above another. "This is Jame Braose of Gaither. Baron Wulfrith expects us."

The young man urged his horse nearer. "Your papers."

Rowan withdrew the parchment from his saddlebag and slapped it in the squire's palm.

The young man unrolled it and scrutinized the words that Annyn had put to memory. "Ride," he said and jutted his chin in the direction of the castle.

Though Annyn expected the activity on the training field to cease as they neared, there was no break in the fierce battles between those who struggled toward knighthood, nor when Wulfrith's escort halted them before the field.

Young men were everywhere, grunting and perspiring. Among them moved older men who shouted direction and demonstrated technique. However, the one who captured her gaze was a large figure engaged in hand-to-hand combat.

Silver hair bound at his nape, the back of his tunic dark with perspiration, Wulfrith lunged and dropped his young opponent with a clip to the jaw.

A shudder went through Annyn. The baron was not to be bested by a boy.

But I am a woman. And this woman will put him *to ground*—into *the ground.*

As the young man regained his feet, Wulfrith said something and showed a fist. The squire nodded and Wulfrith turned away.

The face Annyn had first seen four years past topped a body that looked even more powerful in simple garments. A moment later, those arresting grey-green eyes landed on her.

Breathe! She held his stare as he traversed the training field, secure in the knowledge gleaned by Rowan that Wulfrith had never met Braose. As for Annyn Bretanne, four years had changed her, and the one time they had met, her face had been crusted with mud. He would not recognize her. But would he see the woman beneath the man's garments?

Continuing to hold her regard, he halted two paces to her left.

Her insides rattled. Was her nose large enough for a man? She flared it. Teeth too even? She seamed her lips. Shoulders too narrow? She pushed them back. Chest too—?

"The papers, Squire Philippe," Wulfrith ordered.

The darkly fuzzed one stepped forward. Only then did Annyn realize he and the rest of their escort had dismounted. Should she and Rowan?

"'Tis Jame Braose of Gaither, my lord."

Wulfrith unrolled the parchment and lowered his gaze, but no sooner did Annyn draw a breath of relief than he looked up. "You are late."

She struggled with throat muscles that were tighter than they needed to be. "I fear——"

"This is all the escort your father provided?"

"My lord," Rowan said, "I am Sir Killary, in service to Baron Braose. En route to Wulfen, we were set upon by Henry's army. Though all were captured, the boy and I had the good fortune to escape two nights past. We came directly to Wulfen."

Wulfrith stared.

Did he see through her and Rowan? *Please, God——*

Sacrilege! Father Cornelius castigated from afar. God would not aid in her revenge. And though Annyn excused her plans by telling herself she was aiding God, she knew death for death would not be forgiven. To hell she would go, that dark place often preached by Father Cornelius.

"Why do you wait?" Wulfrith demanded.

"My lord?" Annyn nearly choked on the title.

His nostrils flared. "Such musing will see you dead, Braose. I say again——"

Again?

"——dismount. Your training begins now."

"But I have only just arrived."

He moved so suddenly it was as if by sorcery he appeared at her side. Gripping her boot, he jerked her out of the saddle.

She landed on her back. As she fought for breath, she looked up at where he stood over her with legs spread. It was good she did not quickly refill her lungs, for the words to which she longed to give breath would surely prove her undoing.

At last catching air, she looked to Rowan. Though warning fell from him, there was struggle in his eyes that told of the effort he exerted to keep from setting upon Wulfrith. As for their escort, their mouths were still, but their eyes spoke as loudly as Rowan's. Not with warning, but amusement.

"Gain your feet," Wulfrith ordered.

She stumbled upright and snatched her cap from the ground. As she jammed it on her head, she turned. Though four years had put her closer to Wulfrith's height, still a foot stretched between the top of her head and his.

Cunning and stealth, she reminded. What he did not see would give her revenge.

"Lesson one," he said, "when spoken to, listen well."

She tightened her throat muscles. "Aye, my lord." *Never* her lord!

"Lesson two, never question me."

"Aye, my lord." *Miscreant!*

"Lesson three, act when told to act."

I shall act, all right. "Aye, my lord."

"Lesson four, keep your eyes on your opponent."

"Aye, my lord." *Cur!*

"Now get to the field."

As dearly as she longed to look to Rowan, she knew it would not be tolerated. Lesson three, was it not? Or was it four?

As she stepped away, Wulfrith addressed Rowan. "Tell your lord his son is received."

Rowan was leaving? Surely Wulfrith would extend one night's hospitality? She looked over her shoulder—a mistake.

"'Round the field ten times, Braose!" Wulfrith ordered.

Curse him! And she did, over and over until she was halfway around the field and again caught sight of Rowan. As she watched him ride from Wulfen, she ached. She had not even been allowed to wish him Godspeed. But, then, men did not bother over farewells.

On her fourth turn around the field, she saw the last of Rowan from sight. But he would be near, and when Wulfrith met his fate, Rowan would see her safely away.

Trying to turn back her woman's tears, she lowered her gaze to the ground. Six turns more, she told herself as she perspired into her tunic, and she did not doubt Wulfrith would know if she cut it by one.

She searched him out and found him head and shoulders above a squire whose height made *her* look tall.

She frowned. A page? Aye, and there were more of smaller stature, some looking as young as seven or eight. Though it was not unusual for pages to train alongside squires, Annyn was surprised that Wulfrith trained the young boys himself.

By the time she made the last turn of the field, her tunic and bindings were damp and the latter chafed. Remembering Rowan's warning, she clenched her hands to keep from picking at her discomfort. When she reached the entrance to the training field, she gripped her aching sides and bent forward.

She had thought herself more fit. Though nearly every day she exerted herself, either by chasing game through the wood or learning weapons with Rowan, this hurt.

Yielding to the need to sit—for a moment only, she vowed—she dropped to the ground, only to yield again and lay back on the scrubby grass.

Panting, she looked side to side. Her mount was gone. Had it been taken to the stables? What of the pack containing her scant possessions?

She curbed her worry with the reminder that neither was of consequence, closed her eyes, and listened to her breathing that, according to Rowan, was the surest way to calm it.

A cloud moved across the sun, offering sweet reprieve from its heat.

"You are not very fast," said a dread voice.

Not a cloud, but Wulfrith. She peered up at him.

His eyes were reproachful. "You will have to do better if you are to don armor. Get up."

Thinking him every foul name she could call to mind, she staggered upright and followed him to the training field.

Though those she passed tipped her senses with potent perspiration and made her long to cover her mouth and nose, she suffered through it to the center of the field where quarterstaffs were piled.

Wulfrith swept one to hand. "Choose."

He would test her himself? She ground her teeth. To plant a dagger in him was what she wanted, not to play at fighting.

"Braose!"

She grabbed a staff and turned. "You are to train me, my lord?"

He put a two-handed grip to his quarterstaff. "All start with me. All end with me."

"And in between?" She placed her hands too near as Jame Braose might do.

Wulfrith's gaze fell to them. "When you have proven yourself worthy to train at Wulfen, you will be assigned a knight to serve." He stepped forward, gripped her right hand, and pushed it down the quarterstaff.

His touch jolted, and it was all she could do not to wrench away.

"Hold it so." He jutted his chin. "Now show whether you are a boy or a man." He raised his staff, lunged, and was on her before she could counter.

She bent beneath the blow to her shoulder and grunted out her pain. Though Wulfrith had surely exercised restraint, it was not gratitude she felt but a deepening desire for revenge.

"Not worthy," he taunted. "Come again."

Forgetting the inexperienced young man she was, she lunged.

This time their staffs met at center, but as Annyn congratulated herself on deflecting his blow, he arced his staff and slammed it against the knuckles of her left hand.

She cried out, loosed the quarterstaff, and hugged her throbbing hand to her chest.

Curse his black soul! Curse his loins that they might never render forth another like him. Curse—

"Not worthy. Arm yourself!"

She retrieved the staff, fended off his next assault, and became the attacker. The staffs crashed between them, but Wulfrith was solid. Nearly chest to chest with him, assailed by his strong, masculine scent, she looked up.

He looked down. "Not worthy. You fight like a girl."

Fanned by the hot breath of revelation, Annyn forgot her pain. *Did she fight like a girl? Did* he see Annyn Bretanne? Or was this part of her training? Surely the latter, for she hardly fought like a girl. Indeed, she had forgotten Jame Braose and put Rowan's training to good use.

"I fear I am at a disadvantage, my lord, for surely you are two of me."

His lips curled. "Mayhap three." He thrust her back.

Affecting the untried person of Jame Braose, she staggered before coming at him again. However, further pretense was unnecessary when next their staffs met. For all of Annyn's training, her skill was as water to his wine.

He turned his staff, met hers, pushed back, met again, pushed again, and knocked her so hard to the ground that the staff flew out of her hands.

Bottling her cry of pain, Annyn dropped her head back and showed him her hate.

"We will use that," he said. "Anger makes a man strong."

As it was said to make him strong?

"You but need to learn when to use it and to what degree, little priest."

His reminder of who Jame Braose was cooled her expression of hatred.

"Now the pel." He turned.

The pel? And what else?

As Annyn rose, she saw the field had emptied. Gauging by the lowering sun, the supper hour neared. And she was alone with Wulfrith—of certain advantage were she capable of working vengeance without stealth.

"Braose!"

Muttering beneath her breath, she tramped after him.

He stood before a wooden post set in the ground. "Your sword." He extended the one he held.

Her fingers brushed his as she turned them around the hilt, and she felt her blood rush. How curious hate was—

The tip of the sword hit the ground, and she stared down the blade's length before realizing she had been given a blade twice the weight of others. Though she knew such swords were used to develop muscles and grow one accustomed to wielding weapons, Rowan had never pressed her to swing one.

"Are you hungry, Braose?"

Dare she hope he might forego this exercise? "Indeed I am...my lord."

"Then the sooner you take the pel to ground, the sooner you may fill your belly."

All the way to ground? Though she supposed she ought to be grateful the post was not thick, she hated Wulfrith more.

She took a step back, closed her other hand over the hilt, and heaved the sword up. It was not the pel she struck once...twice...a dozen times. It was the image she summoned of Wulfrith. She hacked until her arms trembled. And still the post was not halfway felled.

Throat raw from labored breath, she lowered the sword.

"You have much anger for one promised to the church," Wulfrith mused.

She looked to where he leaned against the fence. How was she to respond? As Jame Braose. "Were your own destiny snatched from you, you would also be angered."

He arched an eyebrow. "So I would." He strode from the fence and advanced on her. "Finish with the pel and come to the hall. You will pour wine at table this eve."

When was *she* to eat?

She thought he meant to pass behind her, but he paused at her back, leaned in, and said, "I promise you, Jame Braose, we will turn that anger of yours to good."

His warm breath on her skin made her shiver. *Her* good, not his.

She heard his footsteps retreat. When she was fairly sure he was gone, she looked over her shoulder. Only she remained on the training field, and somewhere out there, Rowan.

With a grunt, she raised the sword and swung. The blade bit, causing the wooden post to shudder and chips to fly. If it was a pel Wulfrith wanted, a pel she would give him.

Across the darkening of day, Garr looked down from the battlements to the young man on the training field. Though Braose's arms and shoulders surely raged, he continued to swing the weighted sword.

He was not as expected. Though years from a man's body, he was not fragile and fought well for one who had received little training in arms. And the anger that colored his eyes!

It reminded Garr of the anger he himself had known as a boy. But Braose's seemed to go beyond his loss of the church. Indeed, it was as if directed at Garr himself. Because Garr stood Stephen's side and the little priest turned heir had gone to Henry's side? *That* the young man's father had not told in the missive sent two months past beseeching that his son be accepted at Wulfen.

As for Jame's impertinence, he dared mightily when it had been told he was acquiescent. As for face, he was nearly pretty, his skin smooth and unblemished and lacking any evidence that a beard might soon sprout.

There was something else about him that bothered. Though Garr was trained to the eyes, that well of emotion more telling than men's lips, something dwelt in the young man's hate that could not be read. But soon enough he would come to it, Garr hoped, for his reading of men's eyes had failed him once. Only by God's grace had it not cost hundreds of lives.

He shoved a hand through his hair. Though nothing was certain in life, there was merit in going to the eyes to truly know a person—rather, a man, for could one truly know a woman? And would one wish to?

Bothersome creatures, his father, Drogo, had often said. But they were useful, for without them there would be naught, Garr conceded no more than his father and grandfather had done. Still, truth be known, he had never come nearer a woman than through the ease of his loins, and only with harlots.

At the age of four, Drogo had taken him from Stern Castle to begin his training at Wulfen. It had been the same for the two brothers that followed, never knowing much of their mother or sisters beyond the once, sometimes twice-a-year visits. Women were a bad influence, Drogo had told. They weakened a man's heart when it needed to be strong. Thus, as it had been for the generations before Garr—men who knew women only for the lusting and getting of heirs—so it would be for the generations to follow.

Garr looked one last time at Jame Braose. Whatever it was about the young man, he would discover it. Silently cursing that he was late to prayer, he swung away.

When the irony of his blaspheming struck, he raised his eyes. "Forgive me, Lord." Such was the difficulty of even putting one's thoughts to women. Always they turned a man from his purpose.

5

H OT AND STICKY from her bindings out, gait unbalanced by the pel beneath her arm, Annyn stepped into the great hall.

She paused at the sight that did not greet her: slopping tankards, overturned benches, filth-strewn rushes, facedown drunkards, dogs warring over bones. There were none of these things that ought to abound in a place absent of women.

Squires and pages moved quietly among the tables as they served peers and superiors. As for the manners of those who partook of the meal, spoons did not drip above trenchers and food did not color the beards of those whose faces were of an age to bear whiskers. Voices were tempered, and, unlike Annyn, all those within wore freshly laundered tunics and hose and their heads were bare of caps.

It was hard to believe these were the same ones who had labored on the training field. Hard to believe this was of Wulfrith's doing. But they were and it was. Unless she had sweated herself into a hallucination, Wulfrith's hall was refined, though Uncle had always said—

She pushed past the pang of loss. He had said that, without women, men were an uncivilized lot destined to run with the beasts. But the same could not be said of those in Wulfrith's hall.

A prick in her side, she pinched the bindings through her tunic before remembering Rowan's warning. Lowering her arm, she settled her gaze on Wulfrith who filled the lord's chair—a squire over his shoulder, a knight seated to his left, a priest seated to his right.

A priest at Wulfen? Certain as she had been that Wulfen was the devil's lair, she had not considered it would boast a man of God. But then, it *was* at Wulfen that Jonas had found his faith. From this man?

The splintered pel nicking her through her tunic, she regretted her impetuous decision to deliver its remains to Wulfrith. She would be on show for all, not just the one she had expected to find amid disarray.

She glanced over her shoulder at the squire who stood as porter before the doors. His face had reflected surprise when he saw her burden. Now his eyes danced.

"Squire Jame," the dread voice put an end to retreat, "what do you bring into my hall?"

Why could Wulfrith not have been blind a few moments longer?

She pulled the cap from her head and shoved it beneath her belt. Though she felt watched by all, it was Wulfrith's gaze that drew hers. Standing taller, thighs and calves aching as much from her feud with the pel as her traversing of the hall, she ascended the dais.

A movement over Wulfrith's shoulder drew her attention to the squire at his back. The young man's presence signified he held the coveted position of First Squire, the same as Jonas before his murder.

The pain of his passing never far, she looked to Wulfrith. "My lord, the pel has been taken to ground." She stepped forward and unloaded her burden. It rolled over the tablecloth and settled against a platter of viands.

Displeasure darkening his eyes, Wulfrith lowered his goblet and clasped his hands before him. "Your word would have sufficed."

"But you hardly know me, my lord." *And never you shall.* "For what would you believe a stranger?"

"For what?" he snapped. "That my fine table not be fouled."

Longing for the cover of her cap, she said, "Apologies, my lord. 'Twas not meant to offend." *Liar.*

His lids narrowed in agreement with her silent slur. "Your completion of the task is noted."

Annyn hefted the pel.

"Set it on the fire, then take yourself to the kitchen and remain there 'til I send for you."

No doubt, her presence offended—a shriveled apple among polished. But better the kitchen than here. Still, she had to ask, "You would not have me pour wine?"

His nostrils flared. Though she had sought to move him toward anger, she was stung with apprehension.

"And imperil my good health?" His voice was too level for comfort.

'Tis your own doing, Annyn berated herself. Not only would such conduct make her time at Wulfen more difficult, but it could become a barrier between her and revenge. She must get nearer Wulfrith, and inciting him was not the means to do so.

"I shall await your summons, my lord."

As she turned, her eyes met those of the knight beside him who was also tended by a squire—as were all the knights seated at the high table. The man bore a resemblance to Wulfrith. A relation?

With somber grey-green eyes, cleft chin, and tightly compressed lips, he had to be, though he was somewhat younger and the color of his hair could not be known as it was scraped from his scalp. Surprisingly, the next knight also bore a resemblance, though his hair was dark brown and showed no bit of silver. In contrast to the man beside him, his eyes sparkled as he struggled to maintain the stern set of his face.

Brothers? She did not remember it being said that Wulfrith had any.

Tightening her grip on the pel, she considered the next man. Though she expected him also to bear a likeness, he was well removed with a narrow face and sleepy green eyes. Still, he was strangely familiar, and that familiarity shoveled fear through her.

Where had she seen him? Might he recognize her? If so, it did not show in the eyes that swept her before returning to his trencher.

She stepped from the dais and met the stares of squires, pages, and knights as she lugged the pel across the hall. They watched her progress, countenances reflecting disapproval tempered by amusement. How they must long to laugh, but they kept their humor to their eyes and twitching mouths.

Annyn heaved the pel atop the blaze, then wiped her hands on her tunic and turned to the corridor that, she presumed, led to the kitchen. But there were two corridors. Unfortunately, she had paid no attention to the squires and pages with their platters of viands, and, for the moment, none came or went.

She rubbed her sore flesh through the bindings. Which corridor would deliver her to the kitchen? She decided left, but as she entered it, a squire bearing steaming meat pies came at her.

"Wrong way!" he snapped.

She hugged the wall as he passed. Both corridors led to the kitchen, then? One for outgoing, one for incoming? She had never heard of such.

Shortly, Annyn entered the kitchen. Great cauldrons hung over fires, shelves of foodstuffs coursed the walls, barrels and vats stood about, a dozen tables were laden with viands, and working those tables were squires and pages.

"For what do ye come to my kitchen?" someone barked.

She easily located the corpulent man who stood to the right. Fists on hips, mouth pursed amid an orange-red beard, the cook stared at her.

"Lord Wulfrith sent me."

"Like this?" He swept a hand down to indicate her manner of dress. "Ye'll not dirty my food, ye won't."

Then they were of a mind, for the thought of being set to work, especially in this heat, did not bear. "I am to await Lord Wulfrith's summons."

"Then sit by the garden door and touch naught."

As she started around him, her belly rumbled.

His lowering brow told he had heard. "You may partake of bread and milk, but first wash yourself." He pointed to the back wall where a table held a large basin.

Bread and milk. She grimaced and, as she passed a table spread with tarts, was tempted. If not for the page who arranged the glistening sweets on a platter, she would have snatched one.

Annyn hooked her feet beneath the stool's upper rung and propped her elbows on her knees and her chin in her cupped palms. How long since Wulfrith had sent her from the hall? An hour? Two? As she succumbed to the weight of her eyelids, a loud clatter fell upon her ears.

"You keep our lord waitin'," the cook said as she squeezed him to focus.

Clumsily, she unhooked one foot and followed with the other. If not that the cook slapped a bloated hand to her arm, she would have taken the stool to the floor with her.

"Thank you," she murmured.

He stepped back. "Be quick now."

Yawning, she started past him.

"Are ye forgettin' something?"

She followed his gaze to the pails at his feet, the source of the clamor that had denied her more than a ten-count of sleep.

"Go on, fill 'em and get ye to the lord's solar."

Fill them? For what? And why did he speak of the lord's solar? She slid her gaze to the steaming cauldrons over the fires, and her insides twisted at the realization that she was to bear her enemy's bath water.

This was her punishment for disgracing Wulfrith's hall? As a lady, though often in title only, she had never hauled bath water. Always it had been borne to her. But her hesitation went beyond the toil. To bathe meant one must disrobe, and that meant she would likely be pouring water into a tub filled with an unclothed man.

She drew a deep breath. Never had she seen a man full in the flesh, and she certainly did not wish her first glimpse of one to be of Wulfrith.

"He be waitin', lad."

She surveyed the kitchen. Except for the two of them, it was empty. "Surely 'tis not intended for me to do it alone?" Two, sometimes three servants had conveyed water for her bath, all the sooner to assure it arrived hot.

"Aye, two pails at a time." The immense man scrubbed at his rosy nose.

Did Wulfrith seek to weary her spirit? "Then a chill bath he shall have," she griped.

The cook's eyebrows jumped. "And a long night ye shall have."

Meaning if she dallied, she would be the one to suffer. She pulled the cap from her belt, set it on her head, and grasped the pails. Even empty, they were not light. Would she be able to lift them when they were filled?

She crossed to the nearest cauldron that spit and blew moist heat. Steeling herself, she lowered the first pail into the cauldron and winced as it sucked water to its depths. When it was filled, she had to throw her weight back to lift it free—foolish, for the boiling water splashed the back of one hand and wet her tunic. She cried out and released the pail.

"There!" the cook shouted. "What have ye done?"

Annyn waved her scalded hand and pulled at her tunic with the other.

He grabbed her wrist, hurried her to a table, and plunged her hand into a pitcher of milk. Though hardly cold, it was soothing.

"Foolish lad." He pulled her hand out. "Mayhap 'twill not blister."

Though flushed, her skin did not look as if it would shrivel or scar. But it stung.

He reached to the hem of her tunic. "Let me see yer chest."

"Nay!" She jumped back. Was it suspicion that carved ruts in his face? "I…" She patted her chest. "I am fine." And she was, the bindings having deflected most of the heat.

"Then get ye to the lord's bath." He lumbered opposite. "I'll fill the pails, ye lug 'em."

Annyn blinked. "Thank you."

As she had sunk the first pail to the bottom of the cauldron, he retrieved another. Shortly, both were filled.

"Make haste, lad, and take care you do not slop more on ye."

It hurt to close her hand, but she turned it and the other around the handles.

"Get yer arse beneath ye!"

She tucked and lifted with her legs. The strain was almost too much, but she unbent her knees.

Flinching with each slop of the pails, she traversed the kitchen. When she reached the threshold of the right-hand corridor, she was struck by the possibility that a score of stairs lay ahead. She looked over her shoulder. "The lord's solar is abovestairs?"

The big man shook his head. "Abovestairs be where the knights sleep. Lord Wulfrith makes his solar in the chamber behind the dais."

She was grateful, but how strange that Wulfrith placed himself near pages and squires when more privacy and comfort could be had higher up.

Upon gaining the hall, she saw that its occupants had bedded down for the night, muted torchlight the only movement, snores and dream mutterings the only sounds.

In the dim light, Annyn picked out a path that would not require her to weave among the many who made their beds on the floor. Unlike in Lillia's hall, those who slept in Wulfen's hall did so in orderly rows to the left and right of the dais. Fortunate, for if she had to lug boiling water among them, she might not be the only one scalded.

Shoulders aching, wrists burning, she refused the temptation of rest for fear she might not get her "arse" beneath her again.

Her ascension of the dais caused her knees to quake, but she made it. As she negotiated the length of table, she glanced at the curtain behind. Bare light filtered through, so either the curtain was thick, or little light shone within. She hoped for the latter—shadows in which to conceal herself and not be forced to look upon Wulfrith if he was, indeed, unclothed.

As she came around the table, she noted the sleeping figure who made his pallet just outside the solar—one of Wulfrith's squires, no doubt, and there was an empty pallet beside his. She halted before the curtains. "My lord," she called in her man's voice, "I bear water for your bath."

The curtains parted, causing light to tumble into the hall. However, it was not Wulfrith who stood before her, but the squire who had been at his lord's back during the meal.

"Be quick about it, lazy urchin!" He threw the curtain wide.

Annyn felt her tongue unwind, but there was no stopping the words that spat off it. "Lazy? Who carries the water?"

"Braose!" Wulfrith thundered.

She returned the squire's glower and stepped past him. At least the pails did not slop, she congratulated herself and glanced down. But then, they had done most of their slopping through the hall, as evidenced by the absence of water several fingers below the rims.

Wulfrith sat at a long table against the wall, head bent to quill and parchment, silver hair reflecting the light of three torches and a fat tallow candle, figure wrapped in a robe.

Relieved he did not look around, she scanned the solar.

It was neither large nor small, the postered and curtained bed placed center and back, a tapestry behind, a chest at its foot. To the right was a chair and small table, nearer right a brazier, and before the latter a tub. Thankfully, it was of a smaller size than what she had enjoyed at Lillia, though how a man of Wulfrith's height and breadth found comfort in it, she did not know. Regardless, it would mean a dozen trips to the cauldrons. She traversed the solar and lowered the pails before the tub.

"The water grows cold," the squire said, appearing at her side.

Annyn lifted the first pail. What did he mean cold? Still there was steam—if one squinted hard. Sucking her tongue to the roof of her mouth so it would not speak words she would regret, she emptied both pails into the tub.

"Make haste!" the squire ordered.

Each successive trip was more difficult than the last, her shoulders, arms, and legs protesting, her hand stinging. On her sixth return to the solar, she was appalled to feel the prick of tears.

Looking toward Wulfrith, she saw he was no longer at the table where he had not once looked up during her previous trips. A moment later, she faltered at the sight of bare shoulders above the rim of the tub and startled when she ran into Wulfrith's impatient gaze.

"I wait, Squire Jame."

Seeing his squire knelt alongside the tub soaping his lord's back, she hurried forward and averted her eyes so she would not be made to look upon Wulfrith's nakedness. She was pleased to discover that the water had risen considerably with his bulk, meaning two or three more trips ought to suffice.

"In my solar," Wulfrith said as she poured water at his feet, "you will show respect by removing your cap."

She set down the first pail and swept the cap from her head. Though she felt his gaze beckon, she kept her eyes down. "'Tis to be another lesson, my lord?"

"Does it need to be?"

"Nay, I shall remember." She poured the second pail of water, but as she turned to go, his large fingers closed around her wrist.

She gasped, dropped the pail, and looked up. The sight of his chest rolled with muscle making her heart knock as if to be let out, she dragged her gaze higher.

He regarded the back of her hand. "You have burned yourself."

Was that concern? Surely not.

He turned her palm up and pressed a thumb to its center. Though it had escaped the boiling water, his touch caused something curious to twist inside her.

"Squire Warren, go into my chest and bring my salve."

"Aye, my lord."

Though Annyn longed to wrench free, she felt like a hare trapped before a thicket too thick to grant refuge.

Wulfrith's grey-green eyes returned to her. "You lack grace."

Then she did not behave like a girl? Though pleased with her fit of Jame Braose, a part of her took offense. When the occasion warranted, she wore grace well enough. She pulled her hand free. "Of what use is grace to a man?"

He raised an eyebrow. "For one who ought to have been learned in respect, at least of the Lord, you know little of it, Braose."

What had respect to do with grace? Before she could catch back Annyn Bretanne's words, she said, "All I have learned of respect, my lord, is that it is earned."

His eyebrows gathered.

Annyn, you fool!

"Lesson five," he growled.

Another?

"Speak only when spoken to."

"But you did speak to me, my lord."

"I spoke, but a conversation I did not seek. There *is* a difference, and upon my vow to make you a man worthy to lord over Gaither, you shall learn it."

"Aye, my lord." She looked down, plucked at her bindings, and stilled. Had he seen?

"Squire Warren."

The young man stepped from behind Annyn and handed her a small pot.

"Tend your hand," Wulfrith ordered.

"Now?" She was too surprised to consider whether a response was appropriate following his latest lesson. From his lowering brow, it was not.

"You shall know pain at Wulfen, Braose, but pain that teaches and is earned."

She lowered her gaze and was immensely grateful that the water lapping Wulfrith's abdomen was fogged by soap. She averted her eyes. "What of your bath water?"

"We are not conversing, Braose!"

Silently, she berated herself. She did not lack wit—could read, write, and reckon. If not for her training with Rowan, she could even have kept Uncle's books. However, in Wulfrith's presence she struggled and fumbled as if slow-witted.

Surprisingly, the salve smelled pleasant and soothed when she smoothed it in. She refit the stopper and extended the pot to the squire where he again stood behind his lord. "I thank you."

"Keep it until your hand is healed," Wulfrith said.

She opened her mouth but closed it with the reminder that he did not seek to converse. She was learning.

She spread the strings of the purse on her belt, dropped the pot into it, and grabbed the pails. Only a few more trips—

"Your task is finished," Wulfrith said, beginning to rise from the tub.

She jerked her face aside that she not be made to look upon him.

What had he said? Her task was done? Aye, but why when more water was needed? Surely not because of her hand. He was not so merciful. Perhaps he was merely tired. Or disliked baths.

Regardless, she was dismissed. Heartened by imaginings of a soft pallet, she turned away.

"Stay, Braose."

Keeping her gaze down, she came back around. "My lord?"

"We must needs speak further."

Didn't he mean *he* must needs speak and she listen? What other lesson was there to learn at the middling of night? She ventured a sidelong glance and was relieved to find he had donned his robe.

"Sit." He swept a hand toward the table.

She lowered the pails, adjusted her tunic, and crossed the solar. Settling in the chair farthest from the one he had earlier occupied, she was dismayed when he pulled out the chair beside hers.

"What is the highest honor, Braose?"

She considered his thick column of throat. A pulse beat there, evidence of his humanity. And mortality.

"The..." She deepened her pitch. "The highest honor, my lord?"

"What is it?"

Had Rowan spoken of it? Father Cornelius? Though something told her she knew, Wulfrith was too near. So near she could feel the heat of his body.

"You do not know."

"It escapes me, my lord."

"That with which one is unfamiliar cannot escape." He poured a goblet of wine and settled back to watch her as he drank. Finally, he lowered the goblet. "The highest honor, Jame Braose, is to serve others."

As she knew. What was wrong with her? It had to be fatigue.

"And that is your sixth lesson—that you serve others. Do you think you can?"

"Aye, my lord. For this I was sent to Wulfen."

"You were, but if you do not prove yourself within a fortnight, you shall be returned to your father."

Surely Jonas would be avenged before then. "I shall not disgrace him," she spoke for Jame Braose. "This I vow."

"Lesson seven, do not make vows you cannot keep."

That she assuredly knew, for a vow made four years past had brought her to this moment and place. "Aye, my lord."

"Your training at Wulfen will be the most difficult thing you have endured, especially as it must needs be accelerated for your previous lack of training."

She sat straighter. "I am prepared, my lord."

"Of that we shall see." He thrust his legs out as if he intended to stay for a time. "For a fortnight you shall serve me beneath First Squire Warren and Second Squire Samuel."

Samuel being the one on the pallet outside the solar?

"And to both you shall answer and show respect. In that time, if you prove worthy to pursue knighthood, you will be given in service to Sir Merrick for the remainder of your years at Wulfen. During your final six months, you shall come again to serve me as Squire Warren and Squire Samuel serve me. If I determine you are honorable and capable, you shall be knighted."

As Jonas was to have been. Annyn squeezed the feeling from her fingers.

"You wish to remain, Braose?"

"I do."

He put the goblet aside and sat so far forward there could not have been a foot between their noses. "Then I can be assured you will bring no more spoils to my table."

The pel. To her dismay, warmth rushed her cheeks, but in the next instant she felt the blood drain from them as she peered closer at the left side of his face. Scarring? Aye, four faint lines to attest to Annyn Bretanne's hatred when this man had brought Jonas home four years past. As she had longed for, he was marked as her brother's murderer.

"Speak lesson one, Squire Jame."

She was to have committed them to memory? "Lesson one..."

"When spoken to, listen well," he snapped.

"'Tis as I was about to say, my lord."

His eyes did not believe her. "Then I can be assured?"

"I shall bring no more spoils to your table." She held her breath.

"Good. Now tell how a young man trained to God knows the sword and staff."

As Rowan had warned against revealing her facility with weapons, she had fumbled and stumbled, but not before revealing something of her true skill.

"Braose!"

"'Tis a conversation you seek, my lord?" She knew it sounded impertinent, but her hesitation might otherwise be interpreted for the deceit it was.

His face darkened. "Your father told that you knew little of weapons."

His wine-scented breath made her heart beat faster. "My father presumes that where there is God there is naught else." Believable?

"What else do you know, Braose?"

"I have hunted."

"Deer and boar?"

She shifted on the chair. "Aye."

"Do your arrows land?"

It was true she had once felled a boar as it charged her, but always it was Rowan who took deer to ground. Though she had sighted them many times, always she wavered. They were so beautiful with their large, unblinking eyes and the grace with which they bounded through the wood. But one day she would put venison on the table.

Realizing that in making Wulfrith wait she violated a lesson, she hastened, "I have taken hares and a boar, my lord, but not yet a deer."

"You shall." He sat back. "Seek your rest, Braose."

Hastening to her feet, she silently groaned over her aching muscles. "Your pallet is beside Samuel's."

Then she was to sleep on the empty pallet she had earlier noted—near Wulfrith as was necessary for what she had come to do. Feeling the press of the misericorde strapped to her thigh, she said, "Sleep well, my lord."

She turned to where Squire Warren stood stiffly before the curtains. To get to Wulfrith she must get past this young man who, as First Squire, slept at the foot of his lord's bed. Or perhaps beside it.

She pinched the bindings through her tunic and would have rubbed at her flesh if not for the realization she was watched. Quickly, she retrieved the pails and stepped through the curtains.

When she returned to the kitchen, Cook was gone, no doubt having determined that Wulfrith's bath was sufficient. However, he had left a wedge of cheese on the table nearest the corridor. As all foodstuffs were locked away at night, she silently thanked him for another kindness as she chewed through it on her return to the hall.

She found her pack at the head of her pallet beneath a folded blanket. As was habit, she started to disrobe, but Wulfen was not a place to sleep unclad. Odd though it would appear to the others who were certainly without clothes beneath their blankets, she could not risk it. They would simply have to think modesty bade her to wear garments to bed. But then, Jame Braose *was* to have been of the Church.

She settled and spread the blanket over her, but for all her weariness, sleep was yet one more task to complete.

6

"Up, Braose!"

The command did not fully penetrate her dreams. A kick to her backside did.

"Get up," snapped the one whose boot had roused her.

Suppressing sharp words, Annyn sat up. It was not Squire Warren, but that other one, Samuel. Though tall and possessing broad shoulders and muscled arms, he was thinly set, his face and the flaxen hair curved around it proving that some men could be called beautiful.

"Squire Jame!"

Annyn lurched to her feet. Not only did her arms and shoulders ache from her battle with the pel and carrying Wulfrith's bath water, but she was weak. She had not eaten or slept nearly enough.

Squire Samuel frowned. Though she knew he wondered at her reason for sleeping clothed, he said, "Put your pallet and pack with the others, then get to the chapel."

There was to be morning mass? She ought to have guessed it from the priest's presence. As for Wulfrith, he was likely still abed and probably never threw his shadow where the Lord lit. "Aye, Squire Samuel."

He turned and started across the hall that was dim only for lack of sunlight, a dozen or more torches giving light to those who pulled on tunics, rolled on hose, tugged on shoes, and carried pallets to a far corner.

Annyn fingered the cap beneath her belt but decided against it. She would just be made to remove it upon entering the chapel.

As she gathered her pallet and belongings, she scraped the back of her injured hand. The burn had lessened, but it still pained.

She smoothed Wulfrith's salve into her skin, then crossed to where the others had piled their pallets high and packs deep. Unburdening her arms, she discovered she was watched by a young man whose face was decidedly unattractive despite being set with the deepest blue eyes she had ever seen. He seemed familiar and she realized he was the squire who had stood behind one of the knights at Wulfrith's table on the night past—the dark-haired knight who resembled Wulfrith.

"I knew your brother," the young man said.

Be calm. 'Tis Jame Braose's brother of whom he speaks. Remember that which Rowan told. Hoping the squire had not met Jame, she said, "You speak of Rhys?" The eldest. Pray, let it be the eldest, for she could not name the second brother.

"Nay, Joseph."

That was it. "How is it you knew him?"

He stepped nearer. "We served together under Baron Vincenne. He was a squire when I was yet a page." A sad smile touched his lips. "Your brother taught me much of the sword."

"I see. What is your name?"

"I am Charles Shefield, First Squire to Sir Abel, soon to be Sir Charles Shefield, one day Baron Shefield of West Glenne."

At least he knew his destiny. "I recognize the name." Jame Braose might have, mightn't he?

"Your brother spoke of me?"

She ought to have pretended ignorance. After all, one schooled for the priesthood did not necessarily engage in discourse over knightly training, especially with a brother one rarely saw. "He did."

His wide mouth curved, then fell. "I was aggrieved to hear of his death and that of your older brother."

Annyn wondered at the flush of sorrow she felt. It did not belong to her but the young man held by Henry. It must be because of Jonas. As Jame Braose knew the loss of a brother, so did she—though for him it had been *two* brothers.

Set as she was on revenge, she had given little consideration to what Jame might feel. He had been but an opportunity. This, then, the reason God claimed vengeance for his own? That one not be made unfeeling? Was that what she had become? Callous? Indifferent? It seemed so, and it made her doubt herself. Mayhap—

Four year old anger curled her fingers into fists. Jonas had been murdered and God had done nothing to punish Wulfrith. Even if it cost her soul, justice would be done.

"If we do not make haste," Charles said, "we will be late for mass."

Annyn started to follow him but paused at the heaviness of her bladder. "I..." She felt heat seep her face. A man would not be so uncomfortable!

Squire Charles looked over his shoulder.

"I must needs relieve myself." Was she blushing as deeply on the outside as the inside?

He inclined his head. "The chapel is on the floor above at corridor's end."

She sighed as he bounded up the stairs. One thing was certain: if she wished to remain Jame Braose, she must avoid Charles.

When she stepped off the stairs a short while later, the priest's voice met her ears. Mass had begun.

Though she was prepared for a small place of worship, as at Lillia, there was nothing small about the place she stepped into. It was so large there was room for all—pages, squires, and knights each provided a space that did not crowd one with another. The furnishings were costly, from the ceiling to floor tapestries that depicted the Lord on Earth and in His Heavens, to the ornate altar set with relics. But most surprising were the wide shoulders and bowed silver head at the front of the chapel.

So Wulfrith *did* throw his shadow where the Lord dwelt.

How was it possible? How did such a man stand here where he no more belonged than fallen angels? It had to be pretense. Nothing at all to do with godliness. The one responsible for her brother's murder acted a part. For those in training? The priest?

She looked to the latter. Forehead gathered with annoyance, the priest stared at her as he continued to speak the mass.

Annyn stepped to the left. Grateful to be at the rear that she might be spared further disapproval, she bowed her head with the others. But there was no solace in the false obeisance of one whose heart beat so vengefully she refused to heed not only her brother's warning about vengeance, but that of God who often enough whispered it to her. Thus, throughout the mass, all she could think was how sacrilegious it was for her to be in the house of the Lord.

As much as Annyn longed to hasten from the chapel when the priest dismissed them, it emptied from front to back. Thus, as she would likely fall beneath Wulfrith's regard, she dragged fingers through her hair and tugged her tunic straight.

He was the first down the aisle behind the priest and, true enough, his gaze found her. From his lowered eyebrows and pressed lips, he was displeased.

He knew—not only that she had come in last, but late. How? She had not seen him look around. Regardless, he would have another lesson for her. How many would that make?

Wulfrith passed from the chapel, followed by his brothers and the knights of Wulfen, then squires and pages.

Imagining the chapel sighed as it expelled her from its hallowed depths, Annyn followed the others along the corridor and down the stairs to the hall.

At Lillia, one always broke fast at table, but at Wulfen there were only sideboards. Though their surfaces evidenced they had been laden, the last of the meal was being taken up by stragglers, the others having traded the hall for the outdoors. Not even dawn and training had begun.

Annyn's belly groaned. Knowing she would have to tighten her bindings if she did not eat better, she hastened to the nearest sideboard and seized a scrap of cheese and an end slice of bread. Though there was a slop of ale in one of the pitchers, there were no clean tankards. She shrugged, put the pitcher to her lips, and gulped the meager contents.

As she stepped into the dark that was dotted with stars and swept by a chill breeze, she popped the cheese in her mouth. By the time she reached the outer drawbridge, she had swallowed the last of the bread.

The training field was lit by torches that showed the others had formed orderly lines before it. Seeing Wulfrith and his knights at the fore, Annyn slipped into the back of the nearest line.

"A half hour!" Wulfrith shouted. "If you have not returned in that time, you and those of your group will run it again."

Annyn sagged. Anything but running rounds of the training field.

"To belts!"

Pondering his meaning, she followed the others to where they gathered belts from a cart. Not wishing to be last, she pushed her way forward and seized one. It was heavily weighted. Whereas at Lillia a squire's muscles and stamina were developed by running in old armor, pieces gradually added until a young man was able to support an entire suit, at Wulfen belts hung with sacks of rocks were used.

As Annyn had never run weighted, she was unprepared. With trembling arms, she stretched the belt between her hands. And was hauled back by the neck of her tunic.

"I've another lesson for you, Braose—forsooth, two."

Have mercy!

Wulfrith released her and stepped in front of her. "Lesson eight, make mass on time."

She looked into his torch lit face. "Aye, my lord." *Beast!* "And the other lesson?"

"Methinks you can tell it yourself."

She swallowed. "Lesson nine, do not come late to the training field."

"Good. Do not forget."

Certain he would question her later, she put both lessons to memory as he lifted the belt from her.

"Wrong cart," he pronounced. "Wrong line."

"I do not understand, my lord."

"You are to join Sir Merrick's line when you come to the field. 'Tis he who oversees those recently elevated to squire."

"Did you not say it would be a fortnight ere I served under Sir Merrick?"

His mouth tightened. "Aye, but still you will train at arms with him."

She nodded. "Which of these knights is Sir Merrick, my lord?"

He looked across the field. "There, at the quintain."

Though the mix of dark and torchlight divided Squire Merrick's features, she realized he was the one who had seemed familiar on the night past—and whose familiarity had frightened her. Where *had* she seen him? Or did his narrow face and sleepy eyes merely favor someone she knew?

"Be of good speed," Wulfrith said, "or you and the others under Sir Merrick shall run twice."

As they were to be given a half hour for the exercise, it was not around the training field they would run, for it took perhaps two minutes to circle once. Meaning she faced something greater. But she was determined she would not do it twice, especially as others would suffer for her straggling.

She darted past Wulfrith and retrieved a belt from the cart alongside Sir Merrick. Blessedly, it felt half the weight of the first.

"You are late!" Sir Merrick snapped.

"Apologies, my lord." She slung the belt around her waist, but before she could fumble with the fastening, he thrust her hands aside and fastened it for her.

"Do not disappoint me, Braose." Though it was a warning, Annyn thought she glimpsed encouragement in his heavily-lidded eyes.

She hurried to the end of the line where the others awaited the signal—most of them her height or shorter. As the belt settled to her hips, Wulfrith's shout resounded and the squires and pages burst forth.

Annyn stayed with the mass as they rushed the downside of the hillock on which Wulfen was built. Though the rocks suspended from her belt glanced off her buttocks and hips, making for keen discomfort, she did not slow. Whatever lay ahead, she would overcome. However, her determination wavered when she entered the wood. It was dark, moonlight barely parting the shadows from the trees and the young men ahead.

As she strained to see, someone knocked against her and caused her to drop to a knee. She shot back to her feet. Then another passed her, a large figure whose pale hair set him apart from the others. The squire lunged left, right, certain of his path as if he had run it many times. Though all of her ached, she stayed with him through the wood.

What was their destination? Would she make the half hour? She tugged at her bindings and was grateful for the dark that allowed her to ease the discomfort that had grown with the need to fill her constricted lungs. Would it truly imperil her if she removed the bindings? Her tunic was full and—

Nay, a squire's training included wrestling, and if she were grabbed about the chest it was best that she remain bound. She touched the misericorde at her thigh. When would it set her free?

Free to wander the path to hell, Father Cornelius whispered as an elbow struck her shoulder and a foot landed atop hers. Without apology, the offender shot ahead and melted into the darkness.

"Curse you, Wulfrith," she spat, putting the blame where it belonged. "Curse your black soul!" Determinedly, she resettled her gaze on the large shadow that was her beacon through the wood.

When the sound of falling water reached her, dawn had turned the sky from black to deep blue, the towering sentries to trees, the shadows to squires and pages, and the one ahead to a man. It was Wulfrith, the pale hair that had held her to him not flaxen as supposed, but silver.

She swerved and nearly collided with another squire. The young man shouted, but she was too intent on distancing herself to make sense of his words. Staying to the right of the group, she glanced over her shoulder. There were perhaps a dozen behind her, meaning there were thrice as many ahead. Would she make it back to the training field before time was called?

A waterfall came into view, along with squires and pages who negotiated stones across its width. Annyn looked down at the pool into which the water poured and saw it was a steep ravine she ran alongside. And she was at its edge.

She tried to alter her course, but a foot fell from beneath her. She cried out and slapped her hands to the ground. Down she slid through the mud and undergrowth that clung to the side of the ravine, each hand-hold leaving her grasping uprooted vegetation.

She glanced over her shoulder. The deep water pool below was banked, so she would not find herself immersed. But then she must climb out of the ravine. Worse, she would have to make it back to the training field before the last minute of the half hour—only possible if she could fly. And no bird was Annyn Bretanne.

Muddied from the slide, bruised from the rock belt and sticks and stones encountered during her descent, she found purchase near the bottom of the ravine.

Rolling onto her back, she drew a breath against her bindings and skipped her gaze across the pool's tumultuous surface to the opposite side of the ravine. It was also sloped, though not as steeply. Unfortunately, to make it to the other side would require getting soaked.

She glanced overhead. Better wet, even if chilled to the bone, than to try and climb out.

She struggled to her feet. Knowing the weighted belt would sink her if the water proved too deep, she peered down the pool and saw it let into a river scattered with stones. It seemed she might not have to wet more than a toe. Not that she didn't need a bath.

Though the bank was slippery and she fell once, she soon hopped to the first of the stones that would deliver her across the river. With their moss and mold, they were precarious, but she reached the other side.

As she glanced at the lightening sky that would steer her toward Wulfen, a voice pronounced, "Not worthy!"

She gasped and looked to the left.

Leaning against a tree, arms crossed over his chest, Wulfrith stared at her from beneath the silver hair fallen over his brow.

How long had he watched? And had she revealed anything? She had not tugged at her bindings, had she? The wily churl! Could she make no blunder without him catching it? Such a man would not be easy to sink a dagger into.

"Why did you stray from the path?"

There was no path, but she would not violate a lesson by arguing it. "I vow, 'twas not my intention, my lord."

He scrutinized her muddy figure and pushed off the tree. "'Tis a pity you and Sir Merrick's other squires must needs run the exercise again."

It was dreadful enough that *she* must do it, but the others? She pressed her shoulders back. "The half hour is not done, my lord."

He halted before her. "You cannot make it."

Regardless how she ached, she would prove him wrong. "I can."

"Not if you stand here arguing."

As she stepped around him, a thought struck her. "Pity you must also run it again, my lord."

His lips skewed into a smile that nearly disarmed her for how it transformed his face.

Stirred by something never before felt, she bounded away. Not that she couldn't guess what this feeling was, for she had ears to hear the things spoken between servants. Too, there was the eve she had come upon a knight and chamber maid as they met against a wall in the hall. Though she had been but ten and three, their mutterings and fumblings required no explanation. Aye, what she felt was the stuff of men and women. And she despised herself for it.

The press of the secreted misericorde suddenly urgent, Annyn grudgingly conceded the time was not right. No revenge would be had without considerable advantage over Wulfrith. And so she ran.

Following close behind Jame Braose, Garr looked to the sky. If the squire had any chance of making it before the half hour was gone, he would require more speed.

He drew alongside Braose. "You will fail!"

The young man reached his legs farther.

It was a challenge Garr had known he would accept as so many before him had done, including Garr whose father had always asked more of him than he had asked of others. No man wanted to be told what he could and could not do. And in that lay a well of strength from which one might not otherwise draw.

Garr dropped back but stayed near Braose. There was much to be gained from an opponent's breath on one's neck.

The young man wound the woods, bounded over logs and streams, surely burned in every muscle, but he did not slow. When he broke from the trees, the battlements of Wulfen Castle were touched by the rising sun.

If the half hour was not upon them, it would soon be. "You waste your breath," Garr called.

Braose gathered more speed, running as he had not likely known he could.

Those upon the training field grew larger with each reach of the legs, and Garr knew the others watched and likely believed Braose could not do it. But they were wrong.

"Unworthy!" Garr reached deep inside the young man.

Braose grunted and, shortly, burst upon the training field. Gasping for breath, he glared at Garr who had halted ahead of him.

Garr looked to Sir Merrick. The knight held up the water clock that could not have more than a drop of water remaining.

Murmurs of relief rose from the squires gathered around him.

Though Braose surely longed to drop to the ground, he propped his hands on his thighs and bent at the waist.

"To your stations," Garr commanded the others.

As they swelled toward pels, quintains, swords, and lances, Garr strode toward Braose who watched his advance through the hair fallen over his brow.

"It seems you have learned lesson ten on your own." Garr halted before him.

Braose tilted his head back.

Garr let him wait that he might ponder it, then said, "Let no man make your way for you."

Annyn blinked. His goading was meant to drag strength from her? To push her to a place she had not known existed? As much as she preferred to believe it had been of cruel intent, it seemed not. And she told herself she hated him more for not fitting the man his murdering hands cast him to be.

She pushed off her thighs and straightened. "Then I am worthy, my lord?"

"That I did not say."

Insufferable knave! What she would not give for one moment to stand before him as Annyn Bretanne who had every right to gush hatred at him. "When will you say it, my lord?" Not that she required it.

"When 'tis so." He delved her eyes as if to read her through them.

She lowered her gaze. "Then I shall endeavor to further prove myself."

"If you wish to remain at Wulfen, you will. Tell me, what is lesson four?"

"It is…" Which lesson had she violated? Ah, but she hadn't truly violated it, had she? She forced her gaze to his. "Lesson four is to always keep one's eyes upon one's opponent, my lord."

"Yet time and again you look away from me."

To hide from him, and he knew it. "At the moment, we are not in opposition, my lord."

"Are we not?"

More than he could know. His nearness and words making it difficult to breathe, she gulped another breath. "Are we, my lord?" *I sound like a poltroon!*

"Aye, Jame Braose, you war with me. As if I have wronged you."

He saw too much. "Wronged me, my lord? How can that be?"

His smile was full of falsehood. "I know not, but I shall."

When a dagger was the end of him.

"Remove your belt and get to Sir Merrick."

Swept with relief when he strode away, Annyn looked to where Sir Merrick led his squires in the thrusting of swords.

"Squire Jame," Wulfrith called.

Ordering her countenance, she looked over her shoulder. "My lord?"

"How do you know my soul is black?"

Annyn nearly convulsed. How did he know what she believed of his soul? She had not— Aye, when she had run the wood, unaware Wulfrith was her beacon, she had cursed him. But had she truly spoken aloud?

She shrugged. "'Twould seem only one with a black soul would make young men awaken ere the sun's rise, don weighted belts, and seek an obstructed path through the darkness…my lord."

"Indeed."

This time, Annyn indulged in relief only when he was gone from sight. Blowing a breath up her brow, she reached to the belt and unfastened it.

"Braose!" Sir Merrick called.

She hastened to the cart and dropped the belt atop the others. When she turned, the knight was before her.

"You nearly earned my wrath," he said.

But she had not disappointed as he had warned against. "I am aware of that, my lord."

He turned on his heel. "Come, we are at swords."

Annyn followed. Though the five squires who served and trained beneath Sir Merrick said nothing, she felt their vexation long before she stood in their midst. For her mistake, they had nearly been punished. Fortunately, she did not require their acceptance. She was at Wulfen for one reason only.

7

S WORDS, PELS, AND more pels. The morning droned on until Annyn was certain Wulfen was but another name for hell. If not for her woman's body and that she would not be staying, she might indeed be a man at the end of her time here—a formidable one.

Shoulders bent, she entered the hall amid the others and sighed at the smell of Cook's efforts for the nooning meal. Sideboards were crowded with various dishes that put a haze upon the air, and the tables were laid with crisp, white cloths.

"Hands!" a page called.

Impatient to stuff up the hole in her belly, Annyn tensely awaited her turn with the pages who held basins of water and towels to bathe away the filth of the training field. Finally, the tepid water was poured over her fingers and her hands wiped dry. She turned toward the tables and there, before her, stood Wulfrith's second squire, Samuel.

"You are to pour wine at the lord's table." He thrust a pitcher at her.

Annyn stared. If she did not eat soon, she might collapse, and it was no exaggeration, for twice in past years it had happened when she had gone too many hours without sustenance.

She moistened her lips, only to cringe at the feminine show of tongue. Had the squire noticed? Nay, he was too busy frowning over her absent response.

She cleared her throat with a manly grunt. "Surely I am to be allowed to eat first?"

"After you pour. At the half hour, another shall relieve you so you may eat."

Such generosity! Accepting the pitcher, she clenched the handle so tightly that had it not been fashioned of pewter it might have snapped.

She advanced on the high table where Wulfrith sat, gaze impatient, the stem of his goblet caught between his fingers. As she ascended the dais, she ticked through the lessons and found one that served.

"Lesson three, Braose," Wulfrith said.

She inclined her head. "Act when told to act. Apologies, my lord." *Wretch!*

He thrust his goblet forward, and she filled it to the rim—a mistake, though it was too late to remedy.

His shoulders rose with waning patience. "A finger's width below the rim, Braose."

"Aye, my lord." She moved to the man beside him, talk on the training field having told that he and the other were Wulfrith's brothers, Sir Everard and Sir Abel.

Light from the upper windows shining on Sir Everard's shaved pate, the tight-mouthed knight bent his ear to something his younger brother said.

Annyn filled his goblet to a finger below the rim, then Sir Abel's goblet.

"Better, Squire," the younger murmured.

Annyn looked at him, but his dark head was once more turned to Everard. At least the Wulfriths were not all uncivilized.

Feeling another's gaze, she looked to the squire who stood at Sir Abel's back. Charles Shefield inclined his head.

Stiffly, Annyn acknowledged him in kind. Somehow, she must avoid him.

Next was Sir Merrick. As if she did not obstruct his sight, he stared through her as she poured. He was a strange one, offering little encouragement on the training field, though what he had spoken seemed genuine. It was as if he dwelt more inside himself than out and liked it well enough to stay there.

Annyn moved on to those who sat on the other side of Wulfrith. As she poured, squires brought viands to the table, the smell causing her stomach to gurgle. Never had she been so hungry.

Let the half hour be of good speed, she sent up a prayer. However, as testament to the deaf ear God turned to her, the minutes dragged and her hunger pangs increased.

"Squire!" Wulfrith called.

As she hastened to replenish his drink, her head began to unwind. *Ah, nay. Not here!*

Wulfrith's face warped and gathered darkness around it.

Annyn slapped a hand to the table to steady herself and gulped air, but it was in vain. She heard the pitcher topple a moment before darkness swept over her.

It was not the first time a young man had collapsed, but something about the horror in Jame's eyes struck Garr deep. Ignoring the wine that poured into his lap, he stood and skirted the dais as a murmur rose from the tables. Silencing it with the slice of a hand, he dropped to a knee beside Braose.

The young man breathed, his chest rising in spurts and his face nearly as white as the tablecloths.

Garr smacked Braose's cheek. "Braose!" Had hunger felled him? Exhaustion? Mayhap he suffered the same ailment of breath that—

Braose gasped, but did not open his eyes.

"To your meals!" Garr reproached when the murmurings began again. The humiliation Braose would suffer was great enough without adding to it.

The young man coughed and dragged another breath.

Why did he have such difficulty breathing? Garr reached to the hem of the young man's tunic and began to draw it up.

Braose sat up so suddenly his head clipped Garr's jaw.

"By faith!" Garr barked.

The young man clapped a hand to his head, the other to his tunic. "Apologies, m-my lord."

Garr stood. Though Braose could not be sufficiently recovered, if he was to salvage his dignity, he must rise on his own. "Gain your feet, Squire."

Braose's eyes widened when he saw the stain darkening Garr's tunic. "My lord, I am sorry. I—"

"Rise!"

Fear recasting Braose's features, he reached to the table and pulled himself up. His face, waxen moments before, flushed. "I know, my lord." He gripped the table's edge. "Not worthy."

It was not what Garr intended to speak, but he nodded. Ignoring the impulse to send Braose from the hall, as it would only add to his shame, he said, "Clear the wine and refill the pitcher."

Surprise flickered in the squire's gaze as if he had expected severe punishment. Still, Garr was allowed to see no more than that and, again, was bothered by the depth he could not delve. Secrets would be revealed if ever he saw beyond the veil the young man cast over his eyes. And he would.

"Aye, my lord." Braose reached to the pitcher.

Garr strode around the table and tossed back the curtain of his solar where Squire Warren waited with a fresh tunic.

Though Garr could have quickly returned to the high seat, he lingered in order to give Braose the time needed to set the table aright. And it *was* aright when Garr returned.

Regaining his seat, he reached across the fresh tablecloth and lifted his goblet. It was filled as bid. As he quenched his thirst, he watched Braose at the far end of the dais. The boy was pale, but appeared recovered. Less than a quarter hour more and he could sit down to meal. Hopefully, he would endure and his faint would be sooner forgotten.

"I say he shall be sent from Wulfen ere the fortnight is done," Everard spoke at Garr's shoulder.

Garr considered his brother who had been birthed two years after him. "Why do you say that?"

"He is a long time from a man. Too long."

Abel turned his head to the conversation. "Methinks you are wrong. Forsooth, I wager it."

Everard looked to the youngest. "I accept," he said in a taut voice.

Abel looked to Garr. "What do you think?"

What *did* he think? It was rare he did not know the outcome of those sent to him, but the young man was elusive. Though there was much to recommend him, the little priest did not seem to have the heart of a man. And yet neither did he have the heart of one promised to the Church. "I do not know yet, but he is determined."

Abel's eyebrows jutted. "What do you mean you do not know?"

"Naught that will help you determine the odds of wagering."

Abel shot a grin at Everard. "Still I will wager you."

"And I shall empty your purse."

Garr turned from their negotiations and again settled on Braose. Who would win? Everard or Abel?

Feeling Wulfrith's gaze, Annyn looked down the table. Did he require more wine? Nay, his goblet was set before him, meaning he likely pondered what had happened, as had she when consciousness returned and she had felt his slap. Her heart had lurched to find him above her. And nearly burst when he drew up her tunic.

By the grace of God, though why God would aid her she did not know, she had not been revealed. By the grace of Wulfrith, though why one so cruel had not beat her and sent her from the hall she could not fathom, she had been allowed to gather her scattered pride. If she looked deeper on it, she feared it might be concern Wulfrith had shown her. And that did not fit.

A young squire rose from a lower table and gained Annyn's side. Grateful, she relinquished the pitcher and descended the dais. As she dropped to a bench, a trencher was brought to her. Never had food so pleased.

Impossible. And even *if* possible, for what?

Annyn slid her tongue over the backs of her teeth as she watched Sir Merrick lead the horse around the enclosure. As the animal tossed its great head and snorted, Sir Merrick halted at the center of the enclosure. "Who shall be first?"

Stand a bareback horse? Not she. It was not natural.

"Braose!"

Mercy! "My lord?"

He waved her forward. "First you."

"I have not done it before."

"For that reason you shall be first."

Squire Bryant, who had glared at her throughout the morning and now the afternoon, leaned near. "Coward."

It was not the first ill remark he had made since her collapse in the hall, but it was the first spoken directly to her. She had ignored the laughter and sly glances roused by his words, but no more.

She considered the chapped flesh of his upper lip before casting aside a twinge of sympathy. "*This* coward shall stay aloft longer than *this*"—she poked a finger to his chest—"leach."

His color rose, but before he could retort, Sir Merrick called, "You keep me waiting, Braose."

Annyn made strides of her steps as she crossed the enclosure. She could do this, just as she had done several years ago when Uncle had placed a chess piece atop her head and made her walk around the hall until she could do it without toppling the ivory queen.

Her chest tightened at one of many memories that was all she had left of the man. How many times around had it taken to prove she could move with a woman's grace? Twenty? Thirty? More. But she had earned Uncle's approval, and thereafter been reproved when she came to the hall without that same grace that Wulfrith said she did not possess.

She halted before Sir Merrick where he held the reins. "I am ready, my lord."

"Then mount."

"I should remove my boots?"

"Nay."

She was not to have the benefit of gripping with her toes. She stepped past him and faltered. No saddle, thus, no pommel. How was she to gain the horse's back? There was only the mane, but she had never used such. Hoping it would not pain the horse, she gathered a handful, put her other hand to the animal's back, and boosted herself atop. The horse did not seem to mind.

Annyn sighed, though her relief was cut short by the large figure who entered the enclosure.

Would Wulfrith be so available when it came time to sow her dagger?

He strode opposite where the squires awaited their turn, put a foot on the lower rung of the fence, draped an arm over the top rung, and awaited her humiliation.

Hoping to redeem herself for what had happened in the hall, she looked to Sir Merrick.

"Put your knees to him," he said.

She braced her hands to the horse's shoulders and pulled one knee up, then the other.

"Now your feet."

She slowly raised a knee, positioned her foot on the horse's back, then the other.

"Now stand."

She splayed her fingers on the horse's shoulders, but as she lifted a hand, the animal shifted. Gripping him, she waited for him to settle, then tried again. She lifted one hand, the other, and tucked her backside. Holding her breath, she slowly straightened.

Find your center. She felt her arms out to shoulder level, tilted them up to steady herself, then down, until she stood erect. Threading breath between her lips, she looked to Wulfrith.

His eyebrows were raised as if he considered it a miracle she had made it this far—as if to say she would go no further. But she would prove him *and* Squire Bryant wrong.

"You are steady?" Sir Merrick asked.

"Aye, my lord."

He stepped ahead of the horse and urged the animal forward.

Annyn flapped an arm up, the other down, the former down, the latter up. Though the soles of her boots were between her and the horse, she clenched her toes. Any moment now, she would fall and land hard on her pride for all to chortle over. And Wulfrith would find her unworthy.

Reminding herself of the poise she had learned from her uncle, she bent her knees slightly to offset the jarring gait, loosened her hips to better move with the horse, and slowly drew her outstretched arms nearer. It seemed to work, though still she felt as if she would plummet. How she would love to look upon Wulfrith's face, his arched eyebrow met with the other in wonder. Surely Squire Bryant was also astonished.

With a snort, the horse surged forward, threatening to ride out from under her and causing her to once more thrust out her arms.

Sir Merrick led the animal around the enclosure once…twice…and like a miracle poured from God's palm, Annyn remained aloft. On the third time around, she smiled. She had done it! Regardless of what the remainder of the day held, her chin would ride high.

The horse halted, and Annyn gripped air that slipped through her fingers. Realizing there was only one way to avoid the ground, she threw her hands out, opened her legs, and slammed to the horse's back with a leg on either side. Though jolted hard enough to snap her teeth on her tongue, she landed upright. Blood in her mouth, tears wetting her eyes, she looked to Wulfrith.

Garr stared. How had Braose done it? Though Garr had been fairly certain the young man would lose the horse's back in setting off around the enclosure, and quite certain of it when Sir Merrick increased the pace, Braose had held as if it was not the first time he had attempted the exercise. It was unusual for one of little or no training to exhibit such deftness—such grace—but more curious was that Braose was not bent over and clutching his manhood. His eyes were moist, but that was all. Indeed, the slight turn of his lips bespoke satisfaction. Mayhap he had not hit so hard or had taken the brunt to his backside.

"Well done, Braose!" Sir Merrick conferred rare praise.

The squire looked to him. "I thank you, my lord, but may I pose a question?"

"You may."

Braose threw a leg over the horse and dropped to the ground. "Of what use to stand upon a moving horse?"

The knight turned to the others. "Squire Bryant!"

"My lord?"

"Why do we endeavor to stand upon a moving horse?"

As Garr watched, the young man slid a tongue over his top lip, a nervous gesture that caused the lip to be perpetually chapped and scabbed. "For control and balance, my lord, that in battle one can maneuver a horse with naught but the knees."

"What else?"

The tongue again. Though Squire Bryant, who had been at Wulfen for nearly a year, affected mettle and daring, he was still fearful. But by the end of his training, that would be gone. Already, much of it was.

"That when engaged in foot battle, one knows well his balance in order to better stand the ground."

Sir Merrick looked to Braose. "Your question is answered."

"Thank you, my lord."

Garr pushed off the fence and followed Braose to where he placed himself back from the others. "Well done."

Eyes sparkling, Braose said, "You are surprised, my lord?"

"Aye, 'twould seem you are gifted with grace after all."

The young man averted his gaze. "Grace is required to walk the House of the Lord without disturbing others at prayer."

"Ah." Garr had not considered that. Still, the explanation was lacking.

He eyed Squire Bryant who had gained his feet on the horse. He did not possess the poise of Braose, as evidenced by his fall shortly thereafter. Nor did he possess the good fortune, for his attempt to land astride the same as Braose had done ended on a howl of pain. Clutching himself, he slid from the horse's back.

When Garr looked back at Braose, he saw the young man gripped his bottom lip between even teeth.

"Withdraw, Squire," Sir Merrick clipped, then called, "Squire Mark!"

Garr leaned near Braose. "Do you think Squire Mark will be able to stay atop?"

Braose slid his lip out from between his teeth. "I do so hope, my lord."

"If not this day, then the next," Garr said, "and if not that, soon thereafter. All knighted at Wulfen stand the horse's back at no less than a trot."

Braose's eyes grew large. "A trot, my lord?"

"Aye."

The young man considered Squire Mark whose knees were on the horse's back. "Can you do it, my lord?" He looked back at Garr, challenge shining from his eyes. However, the window into the young man's mind closed before it could be breached.

Garr crossed his arms over his chest. "I do not ask of any what I cannot do myself."

"Then all are measured by you?"

The puck! He goaded as if an equal. A reminder of lesson two, that Braose should never question him, rose to Garr's tongue, but he withheld it.

"Though 'tis true all men are different," he said, "each endowed with distinct gifts of which they are capable of attaining their own level of mastery, still they are men. Or shall be."

Braose shifted his weight.

"Men are providers," Garr continued. "They are defenders. Thus, each must attain the highest level possible for himself. As you and the others are sound of body and firm of mind, 'tis required that you pull yourselves up, clawing and scratching if needs be, to attain your fullest. This exercise and others will train you to manhood that will make you worthy of being called a man. But if you do not make it past the fortnight, you need not worry on it."

Braose's head came up. "I shall make it past the fortnight."

"Mayhap." Garr looked to Squire Mark. Though it was a struggle for the young man to remain upright, he fared well and dismounted a few moments later. With an open-mouthed grin and pride in his stride, he crossed to where the others awaited their turns.

Squire Merrick scanned their ranks and lit on Garr. "You would like to demonstrate, my lord?"

For this he often came to the enclosure, though this time Braose had drawn him. It was usual for Garr to stay near those newly arrived at Wulfen to determine whether or not they would remain, but the young man continued to unsettle him like a riddle aching to be answered.

Shortly, Garr's booted feet were firm upon the horse's back, the reins held loosely in his right hand. Nodding Sir Merrick aside, he set the horse to motion.

Annyn stared with the others. Before Wulfrith was fully around, he had the horse at a trot. How was it possible for so large a man to become one with a horse? Astride, aye, but standing? Were he not so hated, he would have her respect.

She looked from his silvered head to his broad shoulders, his tapered back to his hips, his muscled calves to his balanced feet. Through bone and sinew he was a warrior. Skilled in death, but slow to die. A man who saw things others did not. A man who missed little.

Reminded of her drop to the horse's back, she clenched her hands. Though a woman, still there should have been discomfort—minor, compared to a man's—but the hose stuffed in her braies had provided a relatively soft landing. Not until Squire Bryant had himself landed astride and bent to the pain had she realized her error. Excepting her bitten tongue that had caused tears to rush her eyes, she had shown nothing. Hope though she did that Wulfrith had not noticed, she would be a fool to believe it. She must leave Wulfen soon, meaning the deed must be done sooner.

She closed her eyes against the sight of the big man who could overpower her with one hand, but he rose behind her lids. Telling herself he was better outside her mind than in, she opened her eyes wide.

When Wulfrith dismounted and turned his attention to a group of older squires who had donned armor for sword practice, Annyn was grateful and watched as the others took their turns on the horse's back.

A half hour later, Sir Merrick shouted, "To swords!"

Again? It was not easy to be a man.

As she followed the others across the field, Sir Merrick drew alongside her. "You learn quickly, Braose."

Praise? "I would not wish to find ill favor with you, Sire."

He looked sidelong at her and again she wondered where she had seen his face. "As for Squire Bryant, he and the others will push you, but it is the same for all. 'Tis how men are made."

Which was the reason they were so uncivilized. Though Annyn had often wished she had been born male, in that moment she was glad she had not been. That thought was followed by another. How civilized was *she* to come to Wulfen with a dagger bound to her thigh?

It was different where vengeance was due, she told herself.

Nay, Annyn, Jonas's voice drifted to her. *Vengeance belongs to God.*

"Methinks you shall do fine, Braose." Sir Merrick clapped Annyn on the back, lengthened his stride, and left her behind.

Perspiration from the exercise causing her bindings to cling and chafe, she tugged at them as she followed the knight. However, as she passed the armored squires, her gaze met Wulfrith's.

Lowering her arms to her sides, she cursed her foolishness. If she was not careful, the bindings would reveal her. On that thought, she set her mind to what lay ahead. Would this be the night? Before dawn, might she be away from Wulfen? Of course, if she was caught…

She would not think on that. Regardless of the consequences, it would be done.

It could not be done. Not this night.

Annyn lowered the tray to the table before which Wulfrith sat and glanced at Squire Warren who stood over his lord's shoulder.

Nay, not this night. Not only was it exceedingly late and she exceedingly tired, but Wulfrith and his squire were exceedingly awake.

Though a part of her sank, another part was relieved. Fatigue, she explained it, the demands of the day causing her arms and legs to quake and lids to spasm for want of closing. In the morning, she would be tenfold sore.

She lifted the goblet of wine from the tray and was grateful for the finger's width below the rim that offset her trembling hands. Setting the goblet before Wulfrith, she asked, "Is there anything else you require, my lord?"

"Nay." He did not look up from his ledgers. "Take your rest."

Discomfort twinging her ribs, she picked at the bindings and reached for the tray.

"Lesson eleven," Wulfrith growled.

Annyn met his gaze. "My lord?"

"Cleanliness. When did you last bathe?"

Did she smell? She lowered her hand to her side. "I..."

"Have you fleas?"

Repugnant though the thought was, she would have embraced the filthy vermin over the woman's body that threatened to reveal her. "Nay, my lord, 'tis merely an itch I suffer."

He swept his gaze down her. "See to it."

"I shall, my lord." She reached again for the tray.

His hand gripped her forearm, causing nettles to prick her skin. "Now."

Dread wound through her.

He jutted his chin toward the table near his bed. "You may use my basin."

"Your basin?" The moment the words squeaked from her she regretted them. Not only did they hardly compare to the voice she had affected these past two days, but surprise swept away much of the husk that was hers. The woman was showing.

And Wulfrith was looking straight at her with a questioning brow.

Did he see Annyn Bretanne? She put a hand to her neck and gruffly cleared her throat. "I would not impose, my lord."

The intensity with which he regarded her caused her toes to cramp in her boots. "You impose with your scratching. A few minutes at the basin will make it no worse."

Did he intend for her to bare herself? A male among males was not likely to balk over the removal of his tunic, but for her it would be ruinous.

"Do it now," Wulfrith's voice rose, "else I shall do it for you."

Annyn crossed to the basin. There, she glanced over her shoulder and saw Wulfrith's back was to her and his head bent toward his ledger. Squire Warren remained unmoving near his lord.

Would either look around? No matter. She would simply reach under her tunic and wipe at her bound chest. And the sooner done, the sooner she could leave.

An ache spreading across the backs of her eyes, she dipped a hand towel in the cool water. Another glance over her shoulder assuring her that all was well, she raised the hem of her tunic and wiped her underarms, then made a pretense of scrubbing her bound chest.

"What is lesson seven?" Wulfrith asked.

Annyn stilled. Was it about making vows? If so, what had it to do with bathing?

"Lesson seven," Squire Warren said, "is make no assumptions, my lord."

Then it was to his first squire that he put the question. It seemed she was not the only one forced to recite lessons. More surprising was the realization that the lessons were different for each. Wulfrith had to be of good intellect to remember the multitude of lessons and the sequence for each squire to whom they were issued.

Annyn wet the towel again. As she wiped her face, a scent wafted to her that made her pause. It smelled of earth and something not entirely unpleasant, though she would guess it tasted of salt.

"Find the error," Wulfrith said.

It was *his* scent. He had used the towel before her. The realization inciting another stirring, Annyn drew a sharp breath.

"I shall, my lord," Squire Warren said.

At the sound of the ledger being pushed across the table, followed by the scrape of a chair, Annyn glanced over her shoulder. Though Wulfrith leaned back in his chair, his attention remained on the ledger.

She thrust up her tunic sleeves and wiped her arms. Deciding that would suffice, she folded the towel and laid it alongside the basin, then crossed the room and retrieved the tray.

"Modesty is a virtue honorable in a priest, Braose," Wulfrith said, "and women, but unbecoming in a warrior."

Though Annyn knew she ought to be relieved that her discreet bathing was attributed to Braose's priesthood training, she was struck by the realization that each moment with Wulfrith put greater distance between her and revenge—that all she did might prove for naught. Especially as it seemed nothing got past him.

She gripped the tray tightly and met his gaze. "Have you another lesson for me, my lord?" Inwardly, she winced at the scorn she was unable to keep from her voice.

He delved her face and, too late, she looked away.

"Whoever loves instruction, loves knowledge," he said, voice so level it sent a tremor of fear through her. "He who hates correction is brutish. And a fool, Squire Jame."

It was the same verse Father Cornelius had often used during his attempts to instruct Annyn in the behavior expected of Christian women. How was it Wulfrith knew the words?

"Proverbs," she breathed, knowing such a response was expected from a young man who had been given to the Church.

"Aye."

Fearful Wulfrith might ask her to number the verse, she said again, "What other lesson do you have for me, my lord?"

With eyes that continued to seek inside her, he stared. And somehow she managed to not look away.

"Lesson twelve, a warrior is bold, not modest. Though it is good for you to know scripture, Braose, the Church is no longer your destiny."

"I shall endeavor to remember that, my lord."

He inclined his head. "Take your leave."

She hurried from the solar to the dim hall that was settled by sleeping men. When she finally lay down on her pallet, fatigue lay down with her—as did worry. How was she to get to Wulfrith? When? Before the fortnight was gone, the deed must be done, for thereafter her menses would begin, and that she could not risk. There were twelve days remaining, but surely in all that time...

There would be an opportunity. She could wait.

8

STILL SHE WAITED. A sennight at Wulfen and naught but fierce training that made her first days seem facile. If it was not Wulfrith wanting more from her, it was Sir Merrick, if not Sir Merrick, Wulfrith's squires. The burden was unlike any she had carried, and she often cursed Rowan for not better preparing her. He had treated her too well.

Nearly as trying was Charles Shefield, the squire who had known Jame's brother. Any spare moment Annyn had, rare though it was, she spent avoiding him. He spoke of too many things on which she could not converse, asked too many questions she could not answer. What a fool she had been to claim that Jame's brother had spoken of him!

"There!" Sir Merrick rasped, bringing her back to the wood. "You see it?"

She peered through the mists. Aye, and a fine deer it was. Having silently chanted throughout the hunt that she could do this, Annyn raised her bow. "I see it." She swallowed against the sore throat that worsened with each day of straining her voice toward a man's.

The horse shifted beneath her, sending a whisper of warning through the trees that caused the deer to lift its antlered head.

"Slowly," Sir Merrick hissed.

She glanced at where he sat his horse alongside hers.

"'Tis yours, Braose. Bring it to ground."

Grateful it was he who instructed her and not Wulfrith who watched with the others a short distance away, she drew the string to her cheek.

Sight, Jonas came to her, causing chill bumps to course her flesh. *Steady.*

She sighted the deer down her arrow shaft, held steady.

That's it, Annyn.

"Aye," she breathed, but still she held when the release of her arrow was all that stood between life and death.

Release!

"Now!" Sir Merrick rasped.

She clenched her teeth, but wavered at the moment of release. The arrow flew through the wood, gusting the air that was all it would pierce this day.

"Not worthy!" Wulfrith shouted as the deer bounded away.

Cur! Seething as a derisive murmur rose from the dozen squires in his midst, Annyn lowered her bow.

Though disappointment was on Sir Merrick's brow, no condemnation shone from his eyes. Hard though he pushed her, these past days had shown her that he was not the beast Wulfrith was. Indeed, were things different she might like him.

"We shall try again on the morrow," he said.

As they had tried again this day after Annyn missed her mark two days past. She slid the bow over her head and settled it on her opposite shoulder.

Wulfrith thundered forward. "*This* day we try again." He halted alongside. "Come up behind me, Braose."

At her hesitation, he gripped her upper arm and wrenched her toward him, giving her no choice but to straddle the small space behind his saddle.

"Hold to me!" He jerked the reins and the horse lurched, nearly sending her off its back.

Annyn wrapped her arms around Wulfrith. Through the woods she clung to him, cheek to his mantled back, his muscled chest flexing and tensing beneath her hands, his body emanating heat that, when the sky began to weep its promise of rain, drove the chill from her. And, curse her wayward senses, there were those stirrings again. Of hate, she told herself. After all, she sought his death, did she not?

It was then she remembered the misericorde and realized here was the opportunity she awaited. They were alone in the wood, his back to her, and Rowan was surely near. She could be done with it and gone from Wulfen this very day.

Loosing a hand from Wulfrith, she pressed it to her thigh. The misericorde had shifted higher on her leg, but though she had only to lift her tunic to retrieve it, she clenched it through the material.

The large vein, Rowan had said. She raised her gaze to Wulfrith's sinewed neck above the collar of his mantle. Four years she had prepared for this, and yet she quaked. But she could do it.

Just as you could loose your arrow on the deer?

The horse veered right, causing her to slip sideways.

"Hold to me!" Wulfrith shouted.

She whipped her arm around him and tightly clasped her hands.

Shortly, Wulfrith reined in. "Off!"

She threw a leg over and dropped to the ground. Though the clouds had yet to issue the torrent they promised—still no more than an inter-mittent drizzle—the absence of Wulfrith's heat poured discomfort through her. How she wished she had thought to wear a mantle as he had done.

He appeared at her side. "Nock an arrow."

Annyn lifted the bow over her head and reached to her quiver. Was the deer near? Surely the chase would have sent it farther afield. She fit an arrow to the string and trailed Wulfrith through the woods.

He slowed and glanced over his shoulder. "Your prey is near. Be ready."

Hoping she would not fail again, she looked to her bow. Seeing the arrow had ridden up the string, she refit it.

Wulfrith bent low, darted forward, and halted behind an ancient oak.

Annyn crept to his side.

"Go." He jutted his chin.

Moving slowly as Jonas had taught her, she peered around the tree. There, a pool, but where—?

There, but she would have to draw nearer.

"Lesson three," Wulfrith hissed.

Act when told to act. She put a foot forward but was halted by a hand on her shoulder. Did she err again?

She looked around, but rather than disapproval, there was encouragement in Wulfrith's grey-green gaze. Strangely moved, she looked away.

"You can do this," he spoke low.

"I shall not fail you, my lord." Pray, let her not fail him. She would rather—

What was wrong with her? This she did for herself, not her brother's murderer! Which reminded her of the misericorde. Mayhap once she brought down her quarry...

She turned from Wulfrith and eyed the deer. Providing she stayed upwind of her prey, she would not fail. She slipped from behind the tree and on to the next. Tree by tree she advanced, acutely aware of the man who watched.

When the deer was within arrow's reach, she raised her bow, pulled the string to her cheek, and sighted her quarry where its head was bent to the pool.

You can do this. With a startle, she realized this voice was not Jonas's. It was Wulfrith who encouraged her as she did not wish him to do.

She fixed on the deer. A perfect kill. As little suffering as possible. Drawing a deep breath of moist air, she drank in the taste beget by rain upon the wood.

You can do this.

"Leave me be!" she whispered.

The deer lifted its head, exposing its chest.

You can!

Where was Jonas? It was his encouragement she wished.

You can!

And she did. The arrow ran the chill wood and found its mark.

The animal lurched, stumbled, dropped to its forelegs, and heaved sideways.

"Worthy!" Wulfrith shouted.

Was she? She swung around and searched his gaze as he advanced. Approval was there, and though she tried to deny the sensation that shuddered through her, she was heartened. And more so when he loosed a smile from that firm mouth of his.

Again struck by how comely he was, Annyn looked to the ground.

Wulfrith clapped a hand to her back. "It seems we shall have fresh meat for the table after all. Well done, Braose."

"Thank you, my lord."

He prodded her forward. "Come, let us see your prize."

She matched his stride, though only because he did not reach his very long.

As they circled the pool, the drizzle turned to rain—large, brisk drops that flattened Annyn's hair to her head and made her fear it might also flatten her tunic to her chest. Bound though she was, a thorough dousing might reveal her if any peered near enough.

Looking to the man beside her, she saw his hair was becoming drenched though he could easily cover it with the hood of his mantle. As she watched, a bead of rain slipped from his brow, ran the curve of his nose, and settled on the bow of his upper lip. For an unguarded moment, she longed to brush it away, to feel the curve of his mouth beneath her fingertips. But then he looked down at her.

She wrenched her gaze to the fallen deer and silently cursed the weakness of her sorry soul.

As they drew near the animal, the sight of blood pooled around it caused her throat to constrict. God had put animals on earth to feed man, Father Cornelius told. It was meant to be. Still, as she stood over the deer, staring at the arrow shaft she had put through it, her eyes moistened.

Before she could turn, Wulfrith looked up from where he knelt over her kill.

"I know," she snapped and swung around, "lesson thirteen: men do not cry."

He rose at her back. "But men do cry. Of course, 'tis best done when no others are present."

Had she heard right? Had this man who so often pronounced her unworthy said it? She looked over her shoulder but found no evidence of mockery on his face. Her loathing for him floundering, she turned back to him. "You also cry, my lord?"

"I am far older than you, Braose."

Not as far as he believed.

"I have learned to command my emotions. Still, I am not without being moved on occasion. Of course, that is when I seek refuge in God."

Annyn felt as if slapped. He sought refuge in God? This man who was responsible for her brother's death professed to know God? Aye, he attended mass and was not unfamiliar with Proverbs, but she knew that for what it was. At least, she thought she did.

Brow furrowing as if he were suddenly uncomfortable with the conversation, Wulfrith swept a hand to the deer. "Look to your prize and be gladdened. This night it shall feed hungering bellies."

She stepped toward the deer.

"I knew you would not fail me."

She lifted her gaze. "And if I had?"

"Then I would have to teach you better."

She saw that he nearly smiled again. Where was the beast in him? The one who had put Jonas to the rope? Who was this man who spoke of God with such ease and familiarity? Though she knew she ought to leave off, she asked, "And if still I failed you, my lord? What price, then?"

The light swept from his face, and he was once more a trainer of knights. "Throughout your stay at Wulfen, you will fail many times. Did you not, of what use would be my training? However, for he who is unable to rise above a weak mind and body, the price is dire. To him falls dishonor. He is returned home."

Sometimes dead? Remembrance caused Annyn to shiver.

Wulfrith swept the mantle from his shoulders and onto hers. "Worry not, young Braose, methinks you are not among those destined to return home in dishonor."

Though the fortnight was only half done, already she had proven herself? "Truly, my lord?"

"We shall see." He dropped to his haunches alongside the deer.

Disconcerted by his confidence in her, the unexpected kindness he showed in relinquishing his mantle, and his talk of God, Annyn fingered the collar of the garment that gave his heat to her.

"We shall put the deer over my horse and walk it out of here." Wulfrith issued a shrill whistle that resounded through the wood and called his mount to him.

Though Annyn helped as best she could, it was Wulfrith's strength that put the deer over the horse's back, Wulfrith who bound it, Wulfrith who—

What *was* his Christian name? Surely he had one, though she had not considered it. He was simply Wulfrith. It was all she had ever heard him called.

As they left the pool behind, Annyn berated her pondering, though only because of Rowan. It was his face she glimpsed through the veil of rain before he slipped behind a tree, his questioning felt across the distance.

Wulfrith drew his sword. "Make haste, Braose. We are not alone."

How did he know? Were his senses so honed?

As she hurried after him, Rowan's questioning returned to her: Why had she not killed Wulfrith?

There was no opportunity, she silently defended herself. But there had been. If not the dagger, she could have turned the arrow on him.

What must Rowan think? Was he disappointed? Of course he was. Though Wulfrith had finally pronounced her worthy, she was not—yet.

Despite her churning and her brother's warning about revenge, she silently vowed Jonas would be avenged. *I give you my word, Rowan.*

A score of men were mounted before the raised drawbridge, their flaccid pennants showing the colors of England's future king, and on either side of them, Wulfrith's men.

Fear uncoiling, Annyn halted alongside Wulfrith at the edge of the wood. Had Henry come for her?

"By faith!" Wulfrith growled.

"Who comes to Wulfen, my lord?" she feigned.

It was a long moment before he spoke. "Henry's men."

Not Henry himself? "Why do they come?"

His shoulders rose with a deep breath. "To make of me an ally."

He was certain of it? Mayhap he was wrong and they came for her. But if not, *would* Wulfrith turn from Stephen? Go to Henry's side? "Will they succeed, my lord?"

As if she had not spoken, he tugged the reins with which he led his horse and strode forward. "Come!"

Annyn glanced behind. No Rowan, but he was there. Somewhere.

Resisting the longing to flee to the wood, she drew the hood of Wulfrith's mantle over her head and hastened after him. As they neared, evidence of Wulfen's reputation as a formidable stronghold became apparent. Though most of those who stood on the walls were but squires, they were weapon-ready to defend their lord's castle. Would it be necessary?

Annyn looked to the scabbard on Wulfrith's belt. He had returned his sword to it as they came out of the wood, and there it remained. If he anticipated trouble, it was not apparent. Of course, his sword could be put to hand in an instant.

True enough, it was not Henry who awaited the lord of Wulfen, but a nobleman Annyn recognized as the one the duke had longest considered as a husband for her. As the hooded man nudged his mount over sodden ground to meet Wulfrith, she silently beseeched her heart to calm. She had the cover afforded by the hood, and even if she came out from beneath it, the man would not likely recognize her. Of course, he surely knew Jame Braose who had arrived with him and Henry at Lillia. If any called her by name, she would be revealed.

"Lord Wulfrith," he shouted above the fall of rain. "I bring you tidings from the duke."

Though the man did not appear drunk where he sat astride an ivory destrier, he presented as somewhat older than she had first thought. *Was he older, or was it an excess of drink that aged him?*

Garr halted and considered the man. So, Henry had sent Geoffrey Lavonne to do his bidding. Interesting choice, for not four years ago, Garr had himself knighted Lavonne alongside Sir Merrick in a ceremony that had been absent Jonas Bretanne.

Pressed heavily by memories of the young man he had returned to Castle Lillia in a cart, he put them from his mind.

In matters of warfare, Lavonne had proven himself worthy of knighthood. Forsooth, he had surpassed most, though never Jonas Bretanne. However, his imperious bearing caused him to be disliked. He was boastful, antagonistic, and inclined to drink. Too, though his family supported Stephen's rule, Garr had sensed the young man's lean toward Henry. Now that Geoffrey was a baron, he had turned to Henry's side. And regardless of his training at Wulfen, it would have no bearing on what his new liege had sent him to do. A man's body could be trained in the ways of service and honor, but his heart did not always follow.

Garr glanced to where his brother, Everard, was mounted to the left of Lavonne, behind him a half score of squires. Standing guard on the other side of Henry's men was Sir Merrick, also bounded by squires. And center upon the wall was Abel and the others. Arrows trained on those who had come uninvited to Wulfen, they would easily fell any who raised a sword.

With such numbers, Henry's men would not dare. Of course, without they likely would, which once more returned Garr to the presence he had sensed in the wood. It had to have been one of Lavonne's men.

Garr wiped the moisture from his brow. "Deliver your tidings, Lord Lavonne."

Out of the corner of his eye, he caught Braose's startle at the name of the man who had come to Wulfen. Did they know each other?

"Tidings are best relayed over a tankard of ale"—Lavonne shifted in his saddle—"a platter of venison"—he jutted his chin toward the deer—"and a warm fire."

"Indeed." Garr looked to those accompanying the baron. A dozen knights, a half dozen squires. Too many to allow within. "Then come inside, Lord Lavonne, and relay your tidings." He signaled for the drawbridge to be lowered.

The baron turned his horse and nodded to his entourage.

"Choose three to accompany you," Garr called as the chains of the drawbridge let out.

Lavonne jerked his horse around, kicking up mud that further befouled Garr's boots. "Three?" he bellowed

Garr looked to his boots, back to Lavonne. "Two."

The man threw off his hood. "What do you think? That I shall put a knife to you in your own hall?"

Beside Garr, Braose shifted.

Lavonne swept up a hand. "In the presence of your *men?*"

It was a taunt, but if Lavonne did think to steal upon him, he would soon recall that the squires of Wulfen were more worthy than most knighted elsewhere.

"Two," Garr repeated.

Lavonne's lips thinned. "With this weather, we shall require a night's lodging."

"If I grant it, you shall be given a chamber. As for the others, they may raise their tents outside my walls."

The baron's jaw bulged, but he bit, "Two 'tis," and chose his knights.

With a final groan, the drawbridge met the ground. As Garr crossed over it, Squire Jame trailing, the weight he had carried these past years settled more heavily on his sodden shoulders. It was time to choose between England and loyalty. Either way, blood would be let.

Squire for Baron Lavonne? That arrogant, insolent sot whose voice had time and again risen from the solar during the three hours he had spent behind its curtains with Wulfrith? Who had been content with naught at Wulfrith's table during the evening meal? Who had made full show of his vainglory even as he showed himself to be a fool with each swill of ale?

Annyn sighed. At least he did not disappoint, for he was exactly as his reputation told—a reputation that had chilled her when he had sent a missive to Uncle a year past suggesting a marriage between him and Aillil's heiress. As his lands adjoined Uncle's, he had sought to improve his lot. Fortunately for her, his recent siding with Henry had caused Uncle to reject the offer and they had not been introduced. Unfortunately, that new alliance had nearly gained him the wife Uncle had refused him.

Curse him! And curse Wulfrith for offering "Squire Jame"—thankfully, he had not spoken the surname—for the duration of his stay. Not only had Annyn's dislike of Geoffrey Lavonne trebled since his arrival, but there remained the possibility he might recognize her from Uncle's hall.

Pray, let me not be made to undress him, she silently pleaded as she mounted the stairs with her pallet and blanket beneath an arm. *Let him be drunk asleep on the bed.* It *was* possible considering the effort required for him to cross the hall a short while ago.

"Squire Jame!"

She looked around. Though Sir Merrick was only two steps down from her, she had been too chafed to hear his approach.

"Sir Merrick?"

He opened his mouth, but closed it as if to rethink his words. Finally, he said. "Sleep light. The one you serve this eve is not to be trusted."

There was depth to the warning, as if…"You know the baron, my lord?"

His lips compressed and brow lowered above his sleepy eyes. "If one can truly know such a man, aye. He and I were knighted together four years past."

Then the baron had trained under Wulfrith. Four years past…

Finally, Annyn grasped what had eluded her. Sir Merrick was the squire who had attended Wulfrith in bringing Jonas home, the same who had mistaken her for other than a lady. Had he served alongside Jonas? He must have, or at least known her brother. But why had he remained at Wulfen? Were not all those who trained here destined for lordships? Surely there were lands that Sir Merrick ought to be administering.

He heaved a sigh. "Sleep lightly, young Jame."

"I shall."

Annyn stared after him as he descended the steps. Did he know anything of Jonas's death? Might Lavonne? He had also been present during Jonas's training. Of course, what was there to be told that she did not already know? Jonas had been murdered, and surely Wulfrith was responsible. Had to be. Didn't he?

Cease this senseless pondering! Though Wulfrith might be capable of showing kindness, it did not make him incapable of murder. Still, she was afflicted by doubt. Grumbling, she turned and climbed the last of the stairs.

As she paused on the landing, the chapel at the end of the corridor drew her gaze, it being the only room abovestairs that she had previously entered. Though the doors were closed, a flicker of light shone from beneath. As at Lillia, candles were kept lit before the altar.

Annyn sighed. Too soon she must drag from her pallet and hasten to make mass on time to avert Wulfrith's wrath. Too soon she must choke down bread and cheese on her way to the training field. Of course, with the day's rainfall—

Nay, still they would run as they did every morning. *War does not wait for good weather,* she imagined Wulfrith making a lesson of it. Hopefully, the rain would cease during the night.

She crossed to the chamber that Squire Warren had told her belonged to Wulfrith's brother, Everard, and which Lavonne had been given for the night. The baron's companions were in the next chamber that belonged to the youngest of the Wulfriths, Sir Abel. Unlike Lavonne, they had not been given a squire to tend them.

Annyn dropped her pallet to the left of the door where she was to sleep "lightly" and knocked.

"Enter!" Lavonne shouted.

Annyn pushed the door open.

From his chair before the brazier, the baron waved her forward and slurred, "Come quick ere all the heat escapes, fool!"

He will not recognize you. If he once lifted his gaze beyond his tankard at Lillia, 'twould have been much. And, once again, he is full up in his cups. She closed the door behind her. "My lord, I am to serve you."

"Aye, now be the good little man Wulfrith has taught you to be and see me out of these filthy clothes."

Suppressing a groan, she started toward the bed. "I shall first turn back the covers."

"You shall first undress me!"

She met his fiery gaze. "Aye, my lord."

She would start with his boots. Though she had yet to perform such service, it was surely the place to begin, especially as he looked to have no intention of prying himself out of the chair.

When she tugged off the first boot, a sour odor assailed her and she dipped her head to conceal a grimace. The second boot proved as base.

"You have not been long at Wulfen, have you?" Lavonne asked.

She set the boots before the brazier to dry. "A sennight, my lord."

"I am given a squire with but a sennight's training?" He pushed on the arms of the chair as if to lever up, but immediately collapsed.

Annyn stood. "I am sure Lord Wulfrith's choice was not meant to offend," she rushed to defend a man who could well defend himself. "I vow, Lord Lavonne, I am capable—"

"Enough!" Glowering as if he were a child refused a sweet, he turned his face to the brazier and muttered, "Never was I worthy enough."

"My lord?"

"Leave me!"

Annyn hastened to the door lest he call her back. There, she glanced behind.

Lavonne's head hung on his chest, but not in sorrow. He was no longer conscious.

In the corridor, she spread her pallet and, as she did each night, removed only her boots. However, no sooner did she settle a shoulder to her pallet than the light at the end of the corridor tempted her. The flicker of candlelight shone not only from beneath the doors of the chapel, but the seam where the two doors did not quite meet. Someone had entered.

She tossed the blanket aside and padded to the chapel to peer through the narrow opening between the doors.

It was Wulfrith. Silver head bowed, he knelt before the altar. Seeing the proud warrior humbled made new doubt ripple through her and caused the vow she had made Rowan to stagger. She should not be here.

Feeling a presence at his back, Garr opened his eyes. Braose? Though fairly certain it was the young man whose pallet he had seen alongside Lavonne's chamber minutes earlier, he flexed his prayerful fingers in anticipation of bringing his dagger to hand. This night, men who would become his enemies if he did not join them were within and without his walls.

A moment later, he caught the sound of retreat and lifted his head. "Why do you come to my back?" He settled his gaze on the relics upon the altar.

The door whispered wider and the young man answered, "'Tis I, my lord, Jame Braose."

— 99 —

Garr eased his mind from the dagger. "Come within."

"It is late. I—"

"Lesson three!"

"Act when told to act," he begrudged. A few moments later, he stood beside Garr.

"I have another lesson for you, Braose."

"My lord?"

"Thirteen: be quick to show respect in the house of the Lord."

Though Braose was surely groaning inside, he dropped to his knees. Garr closed his eyes and returned to his prayers.

"My lord?"

Gripping patience, Garr looked to the young man.

"For what do you pray?"

For more than he could tell. Three hours he had spent with Lavonne as the man droned on about England's heir and what would be required of the Wulfriths in Henry's England. Through it, all Garr could think was what a pity it was that Henry did not better choose men to speak for him. But why was Braose so forward? "Why do you ask?"

The young man looked to his clasped hands. "I am never certain what to pray for, especially as it seems that all I ask for is denied me."

"Do you not ask that Henry be king?"

The young man's head snapped up, and there was no mistaking the fear in his pale blue eyes, fleeting though it was. "You do not know that is what I ask."

"But I do." Garr smiled derisively. "In sending you to me, no doubt your father thinks to turn you to Stephen's side."

Braose looked to the altar, and the silence grew until, finally, he conceded, "*Can* you turn me to Stephen?"

Garr studied his profile—a pretty one that, hopefully, would become masculine with maturity. He frowned. What was it about Braose that continued to niggle at him? Strangely, the answer felt within reach, as if it might be unveiled if only Garr would take hold of it.

Braose met Garr's gaze. "Can you, my lord?"

If only he could read the young man's eyes, but they remained largely closed to him. Still, one thing was clear. Garr shook his head. "Henry is strong in you. But others have turned. Not that it is expected. If it happens, so be it and the father is either well-pleased or greatly displeased. Regardless, he has a son worthy to administer and defend his lands."

"You say you do not try to turn them?"

"What is lesson ten, Braose?"

"Let no man make your way for you."

"Aye. Those who leave Wulfen would not be worthy of knighthood if they allowed another to choose their allegiance."

After a long moment, Braose said, "You have not told me what you pray for, my lord."

Garr returned his regard to the altar where he came when troubled. Here he sought answers as his mother had first taught him to do. "I pray for England, young Jame. I pray for all that is best for our land. I pray it once more prosper and war be buried with the dead."

"And you think Stephen and Eustace are best for England?"

How bold he was! But rather than rebuke him, Garr said, "Though loyalty holds me to Stephen, naught could hold me to his son."

Surprise rose in Braose's eyes. "For what have you to be loyal, my lord?"

Aye, for what, especially now that there was Eustace? It was the same Garr had asked himself time over, and always the answer was, "Stephen saved my father's life when they were young men. My father vowed ever to be his man."

"Then 'tis for him, a ghost, that you remain loyal to Stephen." Braose shook his head. "What of lesson ten: let no man make your way for you?"

Garr's anger pricked. "'Tis not only loyalty that holds me to Stephen. He is a good man—at times weak, but good."

"Not good enough for England."

His anger surged. "When he took the crown there was none better, only that blustering Maude. In her hands, England's present suffering would be ten-fold."

"Even so, now there is someone better, England's rightful heir. But still you will let another make your choice."

Garr's anger snapped, violating the first lesson his father had taught him. "Enough!" He surged to his feet. "I shall not allow a whelp to speak politics to me!"

Braose rose. Though uncertainty flickered in his eyes and caused him to clasp his hands before him, still he dared. "You are right, my lord. Far better to listen to a ghost than a lowly squire."

Garr clenched his hands as he warred with emotions that a man should never allow to consume him. But there was so much fuel for them: the meeting with Lavonne, the knowledge that what the arrogant man spoke was true, the realization that loyalty had no place in determining England's future, that this land would soon boast another king.

Garr swung away. "I do not know what makes me allow you what I allow no other."

"Mayhap 'tis because I speak true, my lord. Henry *will* be king."

Garr swept his gaze to the doors at the rear of the chapel. "Aye," he begrudged. "It seems that all you ask for when you go to prayer is not denied after all." He looked over his shoulder.

The young man frowned, then blushed. "So it seems, my lord."

"Good eve."

As Annyn watched Wulfrith pass through the door, she laid a hand between her bound breasts and wondered at the ache in her heart. She hurt for Wulfrith's struggle.

He is responsible for Jonas's death!

She shook her head. "I am getting too near him to see clearly," she whispered. And suddenly she knew. It must be done this night or it would not be done at all.

9

SQUIRE SAMUEL SLEPT. Had he also been instructed to sleep lightly?

Feeling the weight of the blood coursing through her, Annyn slipped behind the curtain and into near darkness. As expected, the two hours since midnight had doused the torchlight within. Still, the narrow slits on either side of Wulfrith's bed allowed the moon's clouded light to penetrate the oilcloths, but only enough to differentiate between shades of black.

Annyn gripped the misericorde tighter and told herself she could do what needed to be done. *Stay left to avoid Squire Warren who sleeps right,* she recited, *a dozen steps to the foot of the bed, four more to the head, a single sweep of the blade.*

Standing just inside the solar, she strained for sounds of sleep from Wulfrith and his squire.

There was one breath, deep and softly snoring, but the other could not be heard. Likely, the former was too loud. That must be it.

She peered through the dark and picked out Wulfrith's figure in the center of the bed.

Be done with it! For Jonas, for Rowan, for you!

As she put a foot forward, chill bumps coursed her arms and legs.

No different from stalking a deer.

But there was no place to hide, no oaks to peer out from behind, and if she was seen, Wulfrith would not simply bound away. Indeed, it might be *her* blood that choked the mattress. And would she truly know peace if he died by her hand? Though in that moment she knew she would not, it had to be done.

And if 'twas not he who put the noose to Jonas? her conscience protested. *Even so, he is responsible! Why else would he lie about Jonas's death?*

As her inner voices warred, Annyn measured her footfalls across the solar, grateful the rushes were so fresh they did not snap and rustle. It also helped that she had left her boots abovestairs, her hose better serving to muffle her movements.

Mouth and throat as dry as parchment, she halted alongside the bed and looked upon Wulfrith's dark figure. The pale of his silver hair showed where his head lay. And drew a clear path to his neck.

She had but to lean forward, make a sweep of it, and be gone. Far from here. Far from Lillia. Far from Henry's plan to make of her mere chattel.

Though she longed to swallow hard, Annyn denied the lump in her throat lest it awaken Wulfrith. Hand quavering, she began to raise the misericorde above the man who did not fit a murderer…who had given her salve for her hand…who had not beat and humiliated her when she spilled wine on him…who had not berated her for tears shed over a fallen deer…who sought God even when no one was watching…who prayed for what was best for England…

He killed your brother!

Jonas…

Vengeance is not yours, Annyn. Vengeance belongs to God. You must defer to Him.

She struggled a moment longer, then stifled a whimper. She could not take another's life.

Strangely, it felt as if a burden was lifted from her. Shoulders slumping, she silently beseeched, *Lord, forgive me. Pray, forgive me.*

Knowing she must leave Wulfen Castle this night, she lowered her hand that held the misericorde.

In the next instant, steel slammed around her wrist.

Clamping her teeth to keep from crying out, she strained back. Wulfrith tightened his grip, causing her fingers to spasm and release the misericorde. Then he dragged her forward.

Behind, Annyn heard Squire Warren's startled voice, though what he spoke as he lurched up from the floor and what Wulfrith answered, she could not have said.

Desperate, she dipped her head and bit the hand that held her.

"Lord!" Wulfrith bellowed.

It was only a slight loosening, but enough to slip her small hand free. Annyn jumped back and felt the brush of Wulfrith's fingers over her arm as he thrust up from the mattress. She spun about and made it across the solar only to meet with Squire Samuel's entrance.

God must have forgiven her for what she had not done, for He gave her wings. She darted left, evaded both squires, and pushed through the curtains.

The fray in the solar having awakened those in the hall, most had risen from their pallets to search out the cause. Fortunately, it was to Annyn's advantage. As the weak torches threw too little light to identify her, and the young men were muddled by the unexpected awakening, she slipped unnoticed among them as Squires Warren and Samuel came through the curtain. But she could not stay here when she was to have spent the night abovestairs.

"Our lord has been set upon!" Squire Warren shouted. "The knave is among you!"

Annyn pushed on, praying the torches would not be lit prior to her reaching the stairs and she could make it to her pallet before those who kept chambers above rushed down to the hall.

She made it past the others and, at the stairs, glanced over her shoulder. There was still not enough light to put faces to any, but she knew it was Wulfrith who had come out of the solar. Though she allowed herself only the one glance before taking the stairs two at a time, she was struck by his stance. It lacked urgency, as if he had not come near death, as if he knew his assailant, as if he knew where to find him—rather, *her*.

Voices above, followed by the thump of feet, halted Annyn's ascent. Willing her heart to stay in her chest, she swung around and descended the stairs in hopes of appearing to have made it down ahead of the others.

Staring out across the darkened hall, Garr ran a finger over the impressions in the back of his hand and, when the torches rose to flame, lowered his gaze. Teeth. Not a warrior's weapon. Indeed, those trained to knighthood would first use a fist or draw another dagger. Unfortunately, that expectation had caught him unaware and allowed his assailant to escape.

Berating himself for the error, he narrowed his gaze on the marks. Small, even teeth, as of a young page, which did not surprise him, for the figure had lacked stature.

Amid the clamor of the hall, he turned his hand and opened his fingers to reveal the dagger meant to sever his life. And stopped breathing.

He swept his gaze to the pommel where crimson jewels were embedded to form a cross. It was a ceremonial dagger awarded only to those knighted at Wulfen—excepting one who should never have been given the honor. But he was dead.

So to whom did this misericorde belong? Of those present, only Garr's brothers, Wulfen's knights, and Lavonne possessed one. Though the latter was most likely responsible for the attack, it was certainly not he who had brandished the weapon. Of course, some of the young men here had fathers knighted by Garr's father, Drogo, grandfathers knighted by Garr's grandfather, and further back.

What irony if he had been felled by a Wulfen dagger! Not that there had been any possibility of that, for he had heard his assailant enter the solar. He had lain unmoving, feigning a soft snore to coax the young man near. If not for those vicious teeth, this moment he would have the miscreant at his feet. But there would be no escape for him.

Looking out across the hall, Garr wondered which of the young men's heart beat with fear. Whose brow perspired? Hands trembled? Who had so strongly stood the side of Henry that he would murder for the man who would be king?

"You are well, Brother?" Abel asked as he and Everard gained Garr's side, both wearing skewed tunics donned in haste.

Garr searched those in the hall. The one who captured and held his gaze was Lavonne where he stood near the stairs, a knight on either side. The baron's clothes were rumpled as if he had slept in them, face red-nosed and squint-eyed. However, his only surprise at being awakened so early was surely that it was not for the reason expected—to look upon the death of the one who had trained him to knighthood. So which of these young men had he set to do the deed?

Garr tightened his robe and stepped to the edge of the dais. "Silence!" All turned to him.

He contemplated each, many of whom had teeth so crooked they were easily eliminated along with those too tall and stout. He paused on Braose where the young man stood not far from Lavonne. As was known to be his preference when he settled on his pallet, he was fully clothed, unlike the other squires and pages who either hugged blankets about themselves or had hastily donned tunics.

Might it have been Braose? Garr held the young man's gaze. Not only was he small of stature, but he was Henry's side. Too, this eve he had squired for Lavonne. But behind those unreadable eyes, could he murder? Remembering the deer in the wood, the tears in Braose's eyes when he looked upon the slain animal, Garr concluded it was not possible. Braose could hardly kill, let alone murder.

Garr considered the next squire, but dismissed the young man who was not only tall, but lacking a front tooth. Still, among the many were possibilities, and one belonged to the misericorde.

Garr raised the weapon and stepped forward. "To whom does this belong?"

There was interest, but no one claimed it. Not that Garr expected his assailant to reveal himself. Fortunately, there was a way he might draw the young man out, providing he had any honor about him.

Garr descended the dais and strode through the rift that opened before him as the young men stepped aside. He passed Braose, halted before his *guest,* and lifted the misericorde. "You recognize this, Lavonne?"

The man's brow puckered. "Why do you ask?"

"You know this dagger?"

"Of course I do. 'Tis the same as you gave me the day of my knighting, the same given to all knighted at Wulfen."

Garr held out his other hand. "I would see yours."

The baron sputtered. "You think I carry it on my person?"

"No longer, for this night you gave it to another to put through me."

As outrage darkened Lavonne's face, the baron's knights on either side set hands to their swords.

"I would not," Everard spoke in a deep rumble. He, Abel, and Sir Merrick had slipped behind Lavonne and his men. Swords drawn, they stood ready.

"What is this?" Lavonne demanded. "You think me so fool as to try to kill you whilst I lie beneath your roof?"

"I do."

Lavonne glanced left and right. "Upon my word, this night I did not seek your death."

Though Garr detected no lie in the baron's eyes, he doubted his judgment as he had done many times since Jonas—

He did not want to think there. Meeting Everard's waiting gaze, he nodded.

Everard laid the edge of his sword to Lavonne's throat. The man's knights were helpless to aid him as Abel and Sir Merrick were too soon upon them.

Fear peeling away arrogance, the baron demanded, "What do you intend?"

Very soon they would know whether or not the assailant had honor. Garr slid the misericorde beneath the belt of his robe, folded his arms over his chest, and considered the man before him long enough to cause a sheen of perspiration to form on Lavonne's upper lip. "What I intend is to return you to Henry on the morrow, drawn and quartered."

Behind, a sharply drawn breath rose above the murmurs of pages and squires. Braose?

"You would not dare!" Lavonne roared.

Garr waited for the assailant to drag honor from fear, but when he did not, nodded. "I would. After we hang you."

"Nay!" Braose cried in a voice pitched higher than Garr had ever heard it. "'Twas not he."

Disgusted at having been so blind, angered that he should be so betrayed as he had vowed never to be again, Garr strode to the young man who stood with chin high and hands clenched at his sides. "It seems the baron shall not be alone in paying the wages of treachery."

Braose swallowed, and when he spoke his voice was hardly familiar—husky, but lacking depth. "He has done naught to warrant your vengeance. 'Twas I and no other."

"See now!" Lavonne yelped. "I demand recompense for the injustice done me!"

Garr could almost believe Braose was alone in this. Ignoring the baron, he pulled the misericorde from his belt and thrust it before the young man's face. "Is this not Lavonne's?"

"Nay, it belonged to my brother."

His brother... Something about the young man's voice and the accusation in his eyes wrenched Garr far from Wulfen.

It could not be. He looked again to the misericorde, turned it, and found the initials that, newly knighted, he had scratched into the blade beneath the hilt: G. W.

It was. The filthy urchin who had so hated him with her eyes, who had marked him with her nails, and now her teeth, had become a woman.

Anger coursed through Garr, once more testing the first lesson his father had taught him. Before he could dam the emotion, it flooded him and he caught the front of his assailant's tunic. Staring into her startled blue eyes, he slashed the dagger down through the material.

A cry parted bowed lips and showed straight, even teeth.

Garr stared at the bindings revealed between the edges of the rent tunic. And he was not the only one to see the truth of Jame Braose.

Amid shock that parted mouths and put tongues to voices, Garr returned to the face he had never truly seen. A pretty face. The face of a woman, and one whose chin did not fall, whose eyes were wide with an anger that challenged his own.

He dragged her near. Not until her face was inches from his, and no less defiant, did the full impact of her presence hit him. A woman within Wulfen's walls where there had never been one. A woman! And one not unknown to him.

Were I a man, I would kill you. Were I a man...

Garr put his face nearer hers and dared her to hold his gaze. Though something flickered in her eyes—fear, he thought, though with women one could not be certain—she did not look away.

"A woman at Wulfen!" Lavonne jeered. "Tell, Lord Wulfrith, who is this foul creature who has made a fool of you?"

Still Garr waited for her to look away. "The *lady's* name is Annyn Bretanne."

Despite the unveiling, she did not even blink.

Lavonne choked, spluttered, and demanded, "What do you say?"

"This is Lady Annyn Bretanne of Aillil," Garr repeated, the hand with which he held her aching to batter flesh and bone. Praying Lavonne would give him a reason to turn his anger from the woman to whom he could not put a fist, he looked to the baron.

The horror in Lavonne's eyes turned to rage. "Unhand the termagant!" From the color that rose on his face and the spasming of his right eye, he did not demand the Bretanne woman's release that he might offer her his protection. "Unhand her I say!"

Garr twisted her tunic in his fist, bringing her so near he could feel her breath on his jaw. "She is my prisoner."

"Nay, she is my..." Lavonne drew a rattled breath. "...betrothed."

The grudging pronouncement stunned Garr, as it also seemed to stun the woman who gasped and breathed, "Nay."

"This *termagant*," Garr bit, "the same who tried to murder me, is to be your *wife*?"

Lavonne raised his seething gaze. "By order of Duke Henry. But do not think I knew what she intended, for until this hour she was unknown to me. Nine days past she and her man, Rowan, fled Castle Lillia. None knew she was destined for Wulfen, and certainly none knew she had donned men's clothes to pretend herself a man."

Though Garr was unconvinced Lavonne was blameless, for the moment he was done with him. He looked to Everard, Abel, and Sir Merrick, and momentarily wondered at the unease wreathing the latter's face. Did his breath trouble him again?

"Clear the hall!" Garr shouted. He would have none lend an ear to his dealings with the Bretanne woman. He dragged her toward the dais.

"Lord Wulfrith," Lavonne called, "I demand—"

"Remove the baron!" Garr shouted over his shoulder.

Despite Lavonne's protests, his voice quickly faded from the hall.

Garr pulled the woman around the high table, thrust the curtain aside, and propelled her ahead of him into the solar. If not for the table she stumbled against, she might have lost her footing. He almost wished she had. Such anger he felt to once more know betrayal at the hands of a Bretanne!

Annyn returned the stare of the man whose death she had denied herself. Now it was surely she who would die, for regardless that Henry had promised her to the detestable Lavonne, Wulfrith would not deny himself.

Though fear made her long to clutch her tunic closed, she found strength in knowing her destiny. Laying her hands flat on the table behind, she raised her chin.

Still holding the misericorde that had waited four years to bleed him, Wulfrith strode toward her.

Annyn steeled herself for his assault.

He halted before her. Eyes so cold it was as if an icy wind swept the solar, he slid the misericorde beneath his belt. "You have made a fool of me, Annyn Bretanne."

Though she longed to sidestep and put the room between them, she stretched her chin higher. "I would think you pleased that I did not make a corpse of you."

A muscle in his jaw leapt, but the anger that had pulsed from him in the hall had diminished as if he were gaining control of it. "Were you a man, you would kill me, hmm?" he repeated the threat she had made upon seeing Jonas laid out at Lillia.

She squeezed the table edge. "It is what I said. It is what I meant." *But what I could not do.* Did he know? As no sooner had she forsaken her vow to Rowan than Wulfrith had seized her, she could not be certain. "My brother's death was no mishap as you told—as you lied. He was murdered." She gave a short, bitter laugh. "Did you truly believe the rope burns around his neck would go undiscovered?"

Wulfrith's jaw strained, his only reaction to learning she knew the truth.

"Honorable death!" Were she a man, she would spit.

"I kill when 'tis necessary to defend home, land, and my people," Wulfrith growled, "but I am no murderer. No innocents fall to my sword."

"Do they not? You were ready to hang, draw, and quarter Lavonne!"

He smiled grimly. "Was I?"

Had his threat to the baron been only that—meant to reveal the one whom Wulfrith believed Lavonne had enlisted?

"In one thing you are right," Wulfrith conceded. "Your brother's death was not honorable. Forsooth, 'twas most *dis*honorable."

The admission, could it be called that, took Annyn's breath. She waited for more, but he strode to the cool brazier.

"How dishonorable?"

He looked around. "Where is Jame Braose?"

Then he would not tell her of Jonas's death. Very well. Murder was murder regardless how it was done. Still, to know…

"Did you and your man Rowan, whom I presume is the one who calls himself Sir Killary, murder him?"

"Murder!" Annyn pushed off the table. "I am no mur—" She lowered her gaze. From what had passed this night, he would believe her capable of murder. He need never know of her failing.

She met his gaze. "Jame Braose is at Castle Lillia where he was brought after Duke Henry captured him and his escort. I took his name and place. That is all."

Wulfrith traversed the solar and once more placed himself over her. "Nay, Annyn Bretanne, that is not all."

Though he seemed to have gained control of his emotions, still there was anger in him, anger for her daring to enter a place forbidden to women, for disguising herself as a man, for the dagger that had sought his blood, for the fool she had made of him. Would her death satisfy?

"Is my fate to be the same as my brother's? Will you hang me?"

She heard his teeth snap and would have looked away if not that her fate could be no worse than that which she had already accepted. However, she was unprepared when his large hands settled around her neck, causing a small cry to burst from her.

With his thumbs, he pressed her chin higher. "Though 'twould be within my rights to put you to the noose and none would call it murder, there are better means of punishment."

Why could she not breathe when his hands were not so tight as to prevent it? Though she swallowed, still she could not open her throat.

"'Twas Rowan in the wood, was it not?" he asked.

Sliced by fear for the man who had stood by her when there was no other, she lowered her gaze so Wulfrith would not see her weakness. Glimpsing his chest revealed between the edges of his robe, she looked lower and lit upon the misericorde. It was within reach.

"You wish to try again?" Wulfrith challenged. "To fail again?"

She hated him for knowing the course of her thoughts.

"Aye," he said, "it was Rowan in the wood, though what I do not understand is why you did not turn the arrow on me."

Finally, breath stuttered through her. Defiance all that held her head above fear, she said, "I should have."

Slowly—purposefully—he drew his thumbs downward, but did not stop at the base of her throat. Hands splaying her collarbone, he continued to the upper edge of her bindings and hooked his thumbs beneath.

Would he tear them from her? Make her suffer greater humiliation than when he had revealed her in the hall? Ravish her? This last jolted, for she could not believe it was something he would do.

Poltroon! shrilled the darkness within. If he could murder, he could violate. Still, she remembered the chapel and the man on his knees praying for England. Could that man murder? Ravish?

The uncertainty, the warring between past and present, and her body's response to his touch, made her long to scream.

"I shall find this Rowan," Wulfrith broke through her turmoil.

So few words for so great a threat! For her, Rowan had sacrificed his allegiance to Henry. And now, perhaps, his life. She would rather die ten times than have him suffer for her ills.

"He has done naught. Though I convinced him to assume the person of Sir Killary, still I would have come had he not agreed. He did it to protect me."

"Protect you?" Wulfrith dropped his hands from her. He turned, put a stride between them, and came back around. "Where is he now that you are in need of protection—*dire* need of protection?" He pointed to the outside wall of the solar. "He cowers in yon wood waiting for you to murder a man he also wishes dead."

He did not know that. Did he?

"I am right, hmm?"

Annyn took an entreating step forward. "Pray, do not—"

"You are lovers?"

She drew a sharp breath. Truly Wulfrith must think her base to believe such when he, her enemy, had been more intimate with her than any. Of course he could not know his was the first man's body she had seen unclothed. "Rowan should not be made to answer for what I did. Pray—"

"Pray! Aye, that you should do. And do not stop 'til you've no more breath."

Then there was nothing she could say or do. Her revenge was now his and he would not turn from it.

Annyn stiffened her spine and crossed her arms over her chest. "I have naught else to say to you."

"That is good, but there is one thing more I need to know." He came to her again. "Raise your arms."

"For what?"

He stepped nearer and slid his hands beneath her arms and down her sides.

Annyn strained away, but he gripped her sides.

"What are you doing?" she demanded.

"Have you more weapons?"

"Only my teeth."

His lips thinned, but rather than speak the words surely on his tongue, he continued his search. Less gentle, though still impersonal, his hands at her waist caused the fine hairs along her limbs to stand erect. And when he ventured up again, one hand curving around to her back, the other passing over her belly, she tried again to evade him.

He placed a hand against her lower ribs and sought her gaze.

"I have no more weapons," she said through clenched teeth.

His hard eyes did not believe her. "If you wish me to spare you further humiliation, you will remain still." He dropped to his haunches, turned a hand around each ankle, and slid upward.

Trying to put her mind anywhere but here, Annyn looked to the ceiling.

He felt her calves, her knees, her thighs. She trembled. He swept her hips, brushed the hose tucked in her braies. She shuddered.

"Hose?" he rumbled.

"Aye." She steeled herself for further degradation, but he straightened and swung away.

"We leave within the hour."

She felt as if dashed with chill water. "Leave?"

He halted before the curtains. "I will not have Wulfen further befouled by a woman."

As if women were all the ill of the world when they were the life and breath of it as her mother had told. "Where are you taking me?"

"Away." He swept the curtain aside. "All of Wulfen is known to me, Annyn Bretanne," he warned, then strode from the solar.

Leaning back against the table, she dropped her chin to her chest. She had failed, and now punishment would be hers. Unless…

Though there was no escaping Wulfen, once they left she might find an opportunity. But if she escaped Wulfrith, where would she go?

She shook her head. Later she would worry on it. If later came.

10

Now that Annyn Bretanne was unveiled, her deception revealed, where *would* he take her? Garr halted in the center of the hall. More, once he delivered her, what was to be done with this woman who had tried to murder him?

Hands remembering the feel of her, her trembling when he had searched her, he was disturbed as he did not wish to be.

He turned his hands into fists, but it provided no ease, and the anger he had pushed down found a foothold and climbed back up. This time, however, it was more anger for himself than Annyn Bretanne. During the past sennight, she had shown herself—in the unreadable eyes of a woman, her unease at viewing his man's body, that she had slept fully clothed, the instances of a pitched voice he had told himself was between a boy's and a man's, and a grace unknown to young men. But perhaps the greatest evidence was when she had dropped to the horse and not been pained.

Remembering the hose in her braies, Garr growled. Though there were times he felt unworthy of lording Wulfrith lands, there had been none as great as this—unless one included Jonas Bretanne's betrayal and subsequent death shortly after Drogo ceded the barony to Garr.

Garr returned to memories of that morning at Lincoln when he had looked upon the young man's lifeless form swinging from a tree. He had cut Jonas down and, that afternoon, following a bloody contest between Stephen's men and Henry's, had begun the journey to Castle Lillia.

What he had not expected was to be met by a girl who looked more a boy and who blamed him for her brother's death as if she saw through his lie. What he had hoped was that Jonas, in his finest tunic and hose, the ceremonial misericorde of Wulfen girded—the same dagger awarded to Garr the day of his knighting—would be set in the ground without any discovering the rope burns around his neck.

To spare the girl and her uncle shame, he had lied. A good reason, he had believed, but the marks of hanging had been revealed and, thus, his lie. He should not be surprised that the discovery added to Annyn Bretanne's belief he was responsible for her brother's death. What he had never expected was for her to make good her vow that were she a man she would kill him.

Grudgingly, he acknowledged what anger had previously held from him: *were* Annyn Bretanne a man, her attempt at revenge would be warranted—though not in God's eyes—by the unveiling of his lie. Truly, her only trespass was in taking another's name and disguising herself as a man to enter Wulfen.

"By faith!" Garr touched the scores on his cheek left by the young Annyn Bretanne. They were so faint he could not feel them, but they were there. He pushed a hand back through his hair. What was he to do with her?

"Brother?" Abel peered around one of the great doors that granted passage to the inner bailey and smiled apologetically. "'Tis a chill night and there are yet two hours of sleep to be had ere rising."

This the reason Garr had left Annyn Bretanne to herself—to return those of Wulfen to their beds. He beckoned for the men to enter.

Lavonne was among the first to clamber through the doorway. The night air striping his cheeks pink, he surged toward Garr. "I demand to speak with her!"

Her, not *my betrothed*, not *Lady Annyn*. "For what?"

"Henry gave her to me. 'Tis my right."

Garr made him wait while he silently ticked through the preparations to be made before departing Wulfen. Finally, he said, "Your rights ended when she raised a dagger to me. But if ten minutes will suffice, I shall grant it."

"Ten minutes!" Lavonne's nostrils flared, mouth twisted, and color went from pink to crimson.

Though the man before Garr was one only glimpsed during his years of training at Wulfen, he had always existed. If not that Garr's father had put loyalty before sense, the same as he had done with King Stephen, Lavonne would not have been allowed to complete his training here. But Drogo had insisted, placing the Wulfriths' one hundred year ties with the Lavonnes above Wulfen's reputation for turning out honorable men.

Loyalty! Garr silently scoffed at his father's failing. Admirable, but only where due. He ground his teeth and silently begrudged that Drogo was not alone in that failing. He himself struggled with it as if it had been passed through the blood from father to son. England was in dire need of a worthy king, and neither Stephen, nor his son, was or could be that.

In that moment, Garr accepted the answer to prayers he had long prayed. Though it wrenched his gut, it was time for him to join Henry.

He focused on the man sent by the one who would be king. "Ten minutes or naught."

Lavonne drew a harsh breath. "Very well."

As he strode toward the dais, Everard stepped alongside Garr.

"It seems you have won your wager with Abel," Garr said.

Though Everard had to be pleased, there was no gloating on his face. "You are taking her from here?"

"Within the hour. I shall leave Wulfen in your care."

His brother inclined his head. "I will not disappoint."

"This I know." Garr looked around the hall, caught Abel's gaze, and motioned him forward. "I regret you shall not gain the two hours of sleep you desire. You will accompany me from Wulfen."

"I knew 'twould be me." Abel sighed. "And our destination?"

Garr looked again to Lavonne as the man tossed the curtain aside and entered the solar. "We go to Stern."

"Stern?" both brothers exclaimed.

To that place where Garr had been birthed and been but a visitor since leaving it as a young child. He did not wish Annyn Bretanne among his mother and sisters, but there was no other place—at least, until he determined her fate.

He breathed deep. "Aye. Stern."

It was Wulfrith she expected, not the man who strode toward her with the unsure step of one still suffering the effects of too much drink.

Annyn rose from the chair she had lowered into moments past, and with one hand gathered her parted tunic together. "Lord Lavonne."

He halted within an arm's reach, stared a chill wind through her, and swept the back of a ringed hand across her cheek.

With a muffled cry, Annyn dropped into the chair.

He slammed his hands to the arm rests and thrust his face so near hers she knew not only his deepest pore, but the depths of his sour belly. "I, Baron Lavonne, betrothed to a woman who runs from me, then disguises herself as a man?"

Denying herself the comfort of pressing a hand to her throbbing cheek, Annyn held his gaze. *Naught to fear. He can do no worse than Wulfrith.*

"Do you know how they laugh at me?"

She narrowed her lids. "The same as Lord Wulfrith, I presume."

He caught a fistful of her hair and forced her deeper into the chair. "Witch!"

Though tears burned her eyes, she held his gaze.

Abruptly, he released her and turned away. "Why?"

She knew what he wished to know, but though inclined to deny him, she decided it could do no harm. If nothing else, he might reveal something that would allow her to see Jonas's death more clearly, especially considering his drunken state. She gathered her tunic closed. "Retribution for my brother's murder."

Lavonne chortled and looked around. "Wulfrith did not murder your brother, fool woman!"

Then she was wrong about Wulfen's lord? Chest filling with what felt like relief, she asked, "If not Wulfrith, who murdered Jonas?"

He put his head to the side and winced as if pained by the movement. "No one murdered him. Your brother hung himself."

Annyn's relief withered as Wulfrith's words returned to her: *Your brother's death was not honorable...most dishonorable.*

All of her rejected what both men told. Jonas, never sure of anything more than he was of himself, would not commit suicide, especially after he had found God. Either Lavonne lied or someone had told him a lie.

"How do you know this?" she asked in a voice so strained she hardly recognized it.

He shrugged. "All who were there that day at Lincoln know it. Wulfrith merely put the wound to Jonas to spare your family shame."

She could hardly breathe. "What shame?"

"That your brother sided with Henry."

"The same as you, Lord Lavonne."

"The same as I do *now*."

She wondered about that. "Very well, but what has that to do with his death?"

"Everything. He stole a missive delivered from Stephen to Wulfrith that revealed plans of attack against Henry's army. Fortunately for Stephen, it was found in your brother's pack ere he could deliver it across the lines."

Another lie. Or was it? Annyn's hands trembled on the chair arms. Jonas had to have loathed squiring for a man allied to Stephen, but would he have betrayed Wulfrith? Had he, it would have given Wulfrith cause to hang him.

"For his treachery," Lavonne continued, "Wulfrith intended to send him home, but the shame was too much for your brother and he hung himself."

Annyn sprang to her feet. "You lie!"

Lavonne gripped her arms so fiercely she would surely be marked. "Unhand me!"

He jerked her forward, causing her to fall against him. "You are mine, Annyn Bretanne, as is Aillil. I shall have you both."

She dropped her head back. "There is naught that would convince me to take a drunk for a husband."

He released her, but only to once more raise a hand to her.

Annyn threw up an arm to deflect the blow, but it did not land.

With a strangled cry, Lavonne released her.

Warily, Annyn lowered her arm.

Pain shone beyond the fury contorting the baron's face. Right hand clasping his left forearm against his body, blood running between his fingers, he stared at the misericorde that protruded from his upper arm—Jonas's dagger.

"You and your men are leaving Wulfen now," Wulfrith said from where he stood before the curtains.

"See what you have done to me!" Lavonne cried as he dripped crimson on the rushes.

"Surely you remember lesson eight, Lavonne."

The baron bared his teeth. That a man so comely could turn so unbecoming was frightening.

"I am no longer your pupil, Wulfrith."

"As you should never have been. Now gather your men and be gone from Wulfen."

The baron pointed at Annyn. "She belongs to—"

"Now!"

Lavonne sneered. "Henry shall hear of this."

"I expect so, and when he does, tell him that if he wishes to speak to me he should send a grown man."

As Lavonne sputtered, the curtain parted to admit Sir Everard with a sword in hand.

Resisting the longing to probe her tender cheek that his gaze paused upon, Annyn clutched her torn tunic together.

"Baron Lavonne is leaving," Wulfrith said. "See that he does not tarry."

Sir Everard eyed the man. "Will you require a cart to convey you from Wulfen, Lavonne?"

The bloodied man traversed the room. As he neared the curtains, Wulfrith proffered a hand. "The dagger."

"I shall bleed to death!"

"Then you had best remove yourself quickly from Wulfen that you might tend your injury."

With a grunt of pain, Lavonne wrenched the misericorde free and glanced at Everard who tensed in readiness. Muttering an oath, he turned the misericorde hilt first and slapped it in Wulfrith's palm. "My blood upon you, Wulfrith. Next time, it shall be yours upon me."

"Only if by foul means," Wulfrith demeaned the man's honor.

Lavonne stared at him for what seemed time interminable, then stepped to the curtain. Everard followed him into the hall.

Feeling Wulfrith's gaze for the first time since he had entered the solar, Annyn averted her face and dropped to the edge of the chair.

She heard Wulfrith's feet on the rushes, and out of the corner of her eye she saw him cross to the small table beside the bed. He set the misericorde on it, dipped his hands in the basin, and wiped them on a towel. Next, he strode to his chest and produced a key to the lock she had attempted to open before Lavonne had entered the solar.

As he searched the chest, Annyn stroked beneath her right eye. Not only was it tender and beginning to swell, but Lavonne's ring had drawn blood at the corner.

A shiver crept over her as memories of her mother's bruises returned. Annyn's father had been such a man as Lavonne, the kind she had vowed she would never marry. And she would not. She was almost grateful her end lay with Wulfrith.

Once more struggling to put down his anger, Garr dragged a white tunic from the chest, crossed to Annyn Bretanne, and dropped it in her lap. "Don this." He would have turned away, but what he glimpsed on her face made him look again. However, she dropped her chin before he could confirm what he had seen.

Anger spreading as if his first lesson had never been taught him, he caught her chin. She allowed but another glimpse of the injury before jerking free.

Aching for a sword to hand, Garr turned. And stopped two strides short of the chest. *The woman tried to murder you. What do you care what Lavonne did to her? She is no better than he. Worse.*

Or was she? She believed her brother was murdered.

Garr eyed the chest where his sword lay. Though he longed to twist a blade in Lavonne's gut, he denied himself. Were Lavonne and his men not already gone from the castle, they would soon be.

He returned to the chest, pushed aside his sheathed sword, and lifted out the salve that Brao—Annyn Bretanne—had returned to him.

When he looked around, he saw she had risen from the chair. Keeping her back to him, she pulled the tunic over the one he had put the misericorde through and smoothed it down her hips. A woman's hips—slightly flared for the making of children.

Why Garr allowed his mind to wander so, he did not understand. He traversed the solar, but though she surely knew he was at her back, she did not turn. He caught her arm, but before he could pull her around, she gasped and wrenched free. Lavonne again?

"Sit," Garr ordered. When she warily complied, he dropped to his haunches before her.

Though he thought she would hide her face again, she looked up.

Why had he not seen the woman in her? Though it had struck him that Jame Braose was pretty, he had pondered no deeper in spite of the squire's peculiarities. Had a man ever been so blind?

In spite of her shorn hair and the blow to her cheek, she *was* pretty. Not beautiful, but comely with a pert nose, delicately arched eyebrows, bowed mouth, softly curving jaw, and large, pale blue eyes—eyes that, if ever they smiled, might melt a man.

"Are you quite finished?" she snapped.

Berating himself, he looked again, but this time as one assessing a prisoner. There was no self-pity in those eyes, not even hatred. Indeed, if there was a name for what braced her, it would be determination. She had endured a sennight of knighthood training, had her plans for revenge wrested from her, been revealed for a woman, and suffered Lavonne's assault. Yet she did not succumb to despair. Unlike most women Garr had met, Annyn Bretanne was strong. If not for her purpose at Wulfen, he might admire her. Or perhaps in spite of it, he did.

He offered the salve to her. Though she didn't flinch as she smoothed it across her cheek, her jaw tightened.

"Your arm as well," he instructed.

She hesitated before pushing up a sleeve to reveal the darkening bruises made by Lavonne's cruel fingers.

"I would not have had him harm you," Garr said tightly.

"Would you not?" She smoothed the salve into her skin. "I did try to murder you, Lord Wulfrith."

He did not need to be reminded of that. Or perhaps he did. "A man should never strike a woman."

"Then you would not raise a hand to me?"

Her unreadable woman's eyes did not say it, but he knew what she asked: what was to be her punishment if not something physical? As he had yet to determine that himself, he ignored her question. "That a man should never strike a woman is a lesson you would have learned were you Jame Braose."

A bitter smile caught up the corners of her mouth. "A lesson your student, Lavonne, did not learn."

Garr needed none to tell him that, especially this woman who was the most unworthy of all.

She sighed and pushed up the opposite sleeve.

Though Garr should have known she would be marked on both sides, he tensed further.

When she finished with the salve, she held out the pot.

As he had done a sennight past when she had burned her hand, he said, "You shall need it." He straightened.

She looked up, the salve on her cheek emphasizing Lavonne's blow, the hard set of her jaw making her appear no less weary for the night's revelation. Indeed, if he could read her eyes, he would likely see a woman struggling against collapse.

"You are certain?" She turned the pot in her hand. "'Tis nearly as good a weapon as teeth."

She was proud of that. And she ought to be, considering something so impotent had afforded her escape, brief though it had been. "Keep it." He turned away.

"Do not say I did not warn you."

Behind, he heard the creak of the chair as she stood. "I am ready to leave."

Once more before his chest, Garr considered the tunic he had removed for the journey to Stern Castle. As there were two hours of sleep to be had before all of Wulfen Castle arose to the new day, he decided to delay their departure. Though he told himself it was best that they not ride through the dark while Lavonne and his men were out in it, it went beyond that. And he did not wish to know where.

He removed rope from the chest. "We are not leaving. Not yet."

She eyed the rope as he strode forward.

"Sit, Annyn Bretanne."

11

GARR GLANCED AT Annyn where she rode alongside him. She was silent, as she had been throughout the ride, as she had been the two hours she had sat in the chair in his solar staring into the dim.

Though he had intended to sleep that he might be rested for the long ride to Stern, he had watched her from the shadows drawn around his bed. Throughout, her only movement had been the one time she tested the ropes that bound her to the chair. Though his judgment of her may have gone astray, he *did* know how to tie a knot.

He looked to the sun that was now perched past noon. The horses could not go much farther without being watered and rested, which meant leaving the open countryside for the wood. He did not like it, for there was the possibility they did not travel alone. Of course, considering Lavonne's injury, he and his men had likely removed themselves from Wulfrith lands. And the Bretanne woman's man, Rowan? He numbered only one. There was naught he could do against a dozen well-trained men. Still, Garr would be a fool not to wield caution.

He captured Abel's gaze and nodded toward the wood. They veered left, and Annyn Bretanne heeded the change of course as if she made the determination herself.

When they slowed to enter the wood, they drew their swords. The vigilance of each man tangibly felt, they guided their horses to the stream.

Garr dismounted. "Sir William, Sir Merrick, Squire Samuel," he called, "stand guard."

As they turned to search out stations that would afford the best vantage, Squire Warren appeared at Garr's side. The young man did not look away, but Garr knew he was shamed—as was Squire Samuel—not only for Annyn Bretanne's breach of the solar, but that she had escaped. The shame was earned, though Garr knew it was more his blame than theirs. He had not better prepared them, but that would be remedied.

He passed the reins to Squire Warren and strode around his destrier, only to find the Bretanne woman had already dismounted. As if he were not an obstacle in her path, she pulled the reins over her mount's head and brushed past Garr to lead the horse to the stream.

Wondering what thoughts occupied her, Garr stared after her. Did she hope Rowan would deliver her?

"She troubles you, this sister of Jonas Bretanne," Abel said as he came alongside.

Garr scowled. "She is a troublesome woman."

"That is all?"

It was not, which was the reason she was so troublesome. "That is all." Garr returned his attention to where she stood before the stream that yesterday's rain caused to overflow the banks.

"You have told her the truth of Jonas's death?"

Garr pressed the heel of his palm to his sword hilt and kneaded it. That day at Lincolnshire, Abel and Everard had been there, and both had aided in making Jonas's death appear honorable. "She knows all she needs to know."

"Are you sure it is enough?"

Not for Annyn Bretanne, but it was for the best. "Aye."

"She is unlike any woman I have met," Abel murmured, then grumbled, "She lightened my purse a goodly amount."

He spoke of the wager paid before their departure this morn. Regardless that Braose was revealed to be Annyn Bretanne, Everard would not let it keep him from collecting on his bet.

"I have warned you against wagering him," Garr said. "He rarely loses."

"And then only to you."

"Which is the reason he no longer wagers me. You ought to learn from that, Abel."

He grimaced. "Then what pleasure would be afforded me?"

Garr knew to what he referred—the long stretches without a woman that suited neither Abel's lusty bent, nor Everard's, the civility of the hall, the discipline. But they were Wulfriths, and this was their destiny. Once wed, the administration of the lands they were given would regularly take them from Wulfen, but still they would return to train boys to men.

"What pleasure?" Garr mused. "The pleasure of being the master of your coin." He stepped past.

"I thank you for that," Abel called, then slyly added, "and your consideration of the Lady Annyn that granted me two hours of sleep I had thought were to be denied me."

That last pricked. Abel liked to think he understood people better than they understood themselves. But if that were so, he would not wager Everard.

At the sound of Wulfrith's approach, Annyn hugged her short mantle nearer and stared harder up through the trees.

He halted at her back, causing her to stiffen though she tried to appear unmoved. "You require something, Wulfrith?" Just as she no longer affected a deeper pitch, neither did she afford him the title she had so loathed.

"I ponder what you are thinking, Annyn Bretanne."

She turned. Though she knew his use of her full name—meant to deny her title—was a small thing, it reminded her too much of her audience with Henry when he had played her as a wooden soldier, moving and controlling her as he pleased. Resentment warming her bruised face, she said, "I am thinking I would have you cease calling me that."

He peered at her through narrowed lids. "Surely you do not ask that I call you Jame Braose?"

She glared. "I ask that you not call me by my full name. I do not like it."

"You would have me call you Lady Annyn?"

It did sound strange on his lips, especially considering this past sennight, that she continued to wear men's clothing, and that she denied him his own title, but it was as she had always been called. "I do not doubt 'tis as displeasing to you as the drone of Annyn Bretanne is to me, but it is what I prefer."

"Very well. Now tell me, Lady Annyn, what are you thinking?"

Of the tree from which Jonas was hung, of the lie Lavonne had told that had denied her rest before leaving Wulfen, of what Wulfrith would say if she confronted him with it. He would say nothing, she concluded. He would simply name Jonas's death "dishonorable" as he had done on the night past.

"I was thinking which evil I would choose given the opportunity— the ill end you have planned for me or marriage to Lavonne."

His dark eyebrows rose. "And?"

"I fear one may be as bad as the other."

"That does not speak well of Lavonne."

She drew a hand from beneath the mantle and touched her cheek. "Nor does this."

A muscle twinged near his eye. It angered him. Regardless of his statement that striking a woman was something men should not do, she had yet to understand why he should care that the baron had struck her. After all, her attempt to kill Wulfrith made her more his enemy than Lavonne.

"Come." He turned away.

Alarm leapt through her. Now he would mete out punishment? "Where?"

He looked over his shoulder. "You have been hours astride, Lady Annyn. 'Twill be night ere our journey's end."

Relieved her punishment was not at hand, grateful he was not more blunt about the need to relieve herself, she inclined her head. "Of course, but I can see to my own needs."

"You cannot."

He thought she would run. And he was right. Somewhere Rowan lay in wait, though how she was to take advantage of that with Wulfrith over her shoulder, she did not know. As she followed him away from the others, she met Squire Charles's hard stare. She had made a fool of his lord. Thus, she had made a fool of his squire. And he resented it. If she could apologize, she would.

Wulfrith's hand fell to his sword hilt as they left the others behind to pass deeper into the wood. "There." He nodded to a thicket.

Though it offered adequate privacy, Annyn was warmed by embarrassment. Averting her face, she hastened behind the cover.

When she emerged, he was scanning the wood. Did he sense Rowan? If he was near, a better chance of aiding her escape was not likely to appear. But that realization gave rise to fear. Though Rowan was skilled in arms, he was not the warrior Wulfrith was. A contest between the two men would likely see Rowan dead.

Annyn quickened her step to Wulfrith's side. "Still you have not said what is to be my punishment," she attempted to draw his regard.

"I have not."

"I ask again, is it to be the same as my brother's?"

He gave her the regard she sought, though she would have preferred to be spared its wrath. "I did not hang him, Annyn Bretanne."

She ignored the loss of title. "Then who did?"

He did not answer.

"This morn you said his death was dishonorable. I would know *how* dishonorable, and do not dare tell me he hung himself!"

His grey-green eyes narrowed. "I do dare, Annyn Bretanne."

He lied. Four years of anger, hatred, and helplessness flooding her, she struggled to keep her hands at her sides, but one broke free. She drew it back and landed a slap to his cheek.

Color suffusing his face, he regarded her with eyes so chill she feared he would strike her as Lavonne had done.

With a sharp breath, she turned to run, but he seized her shoulder and dragged her back around.

"I have suffered your claws, Annyn Bretanne, your teeth, and now your hand. I have endured your trespass, your lies, your attempt on my life, and your false accusations. But no more."

With his great hands pinning her body to his, never had he seemed so large, nor more a beast. Fear threatening to overwhelm her, she summoned defiance, but it did not answer. A tremor betrayed her, then another.

Why did he wait? Why did he not beat her and be done with it?

His nostrils flared with a deep breath. "Though I wished to spare you and your uncle the truth of your brother's death, and for that I lied, I shall tell you all that we may speak of it no more."

He was not going to strike her? Of course he was not.

"Though I know you do not wish to believe it, your brother did hang himself."

"He would not!"

He jerked her shoulders. "At Lincolnshire, I received a missive from Stephen that laid out plans of attack against Henry."

The same as Lavonne had told.

"It was discovered missing. All those who were known to be sympathetic to Henry were searched, though not Jonas until he was the only one who remained. As my First Squire, I trusted him and was certain he would not betray though we stood on different sides. I was wrong. The missive was found in his pack."

Something inside Annyn teetered. Though she did not wish to believe it, a voice within said it was possible. But even if Jonas had betrayed, it was not possible he had hung himself.

"He admitted to taking the missive," Wulfrith continued, "but said that afterward he realized he could not betray me."

It sounded like Jonas—reckless, yet true of heart. *Was* it Jonas?

"Though more severe punishment was warranted, I determined the shame of being returned to your uncle would suffice." The rest of Wulfrith's anger seemed to empty as something else rushed in to fill him. "And there again I misjudged. I believed him to be stronger and never considered he would take his life."

Though Annyn longed to deny that Jonas had died by his own hand, she knew Wulfrith was not done with the telling. And she would hear all of it.

"For that you may fault me with his death, but do not name it murder. I would not have had him die."

"Jonas did not hang himself."

"You were not there. You do not know his shame."

She put her chin higher. "I knew my brother and would wager my very breath he would not end his own life."

"Then you would also lie dead."

A memory of Jonas laid on the high table ached through Annyn. The rope burns around his neck, the wound at the center of his chest... "'Twas you who put the arrow through him?"

His eyes momentarily closed. "It was a dagger. I did it to spare your family."

All these years of not knowing the truth and now...Still she did not know all of it, for nothing Wulfrith could say would convince her Jonas had hung himself. He had been murdered. But not by Wulfrith.

Her breath caught as she finally acknowledged the truth she had refused to accept though it had been presented time and again. Wulfrith could not have murdered her brother. Another had made it appear Jonas had taken his own life.

As she stared into Wulfrith's eyes, she awakened to another truth. Something had happened that should not have. She had come to feel for this man. And being so near him now caused those emotions to deepen. But it went beyond the senses, beyond this strange awareness of him. It was as if she was leaving behind the girl who had lived for revenge and turning toward the woman who had denied her that revenge—a woman she did not know.

She dropped her chin. *Dear God, who am I?* Where was Annyn Bretanne who had seethed alongside Duke Henry nearly a fortnight past?

"I am sorry I could not spare you the truth, Annyn," Wulfrith spoke low, his familiar use of her name causing her to shudder. He released her shoulders and urged her chin up.

Hating that he saw her tears, despising the first that fell, she pressed her lips together.

"More," he said, softer still, "I am sorry I did not foresee what your brother would do." His gaze followed the tear's path to the corner of her mouth. He laid a thumb to it and swept it beneath her lower lip.

That so simple a touch could loose such flutterings was more than frightening, but though Annyn knew she should pull free, she could not.

Wulfrith sought her gaze again and, for those few moments, it was as if the world stopped, as if all behind and before them had never been and would never be. There were two—naught else in all this vastness—and as they stood in that great alone, awareness breathed between them. Then his head lowered.

His mouth covered her untried lips, asking something of her that she struggled to understand. What was it? And why did he kiss her? With her shorn hair and men's clothes that concealed all evidence of femininity, she was hardly pretty. More, she had sought his death.

He deepened the kiss and, when she did not respond, turned his arms around her and drew her up to her toes.

Ignoring the voice that protested what she allowed, she parted her lips.

Wulfrith groaned.

Hearing the breath pant from her as if from a distance, she slid her hands up his chest. The muscles beneath were thick, and she wanted—

What did she want?

Wulfrith drew a hand up her side, but the tunic and bindings denied his seeking. And reminded her that Jonas was the reason she was here.

Shame washing over her, Annyn pulled her head back. "Do not!"

Realization darkened his eyes and firmed the mouth that had covered hers.

"Unhand me!"

He unwound his arms from her only to grip her where Lavonne had bruised her.

When she winced, he placed his hands on her shoulders. "Forgive me, I should not have done that."

Nor should she have allowed it. She was no better than the chamber maids who let the castle guard toss up their skirts. "Release me!"

"Aye!" a startlingly familiar voice shouted. "Release her!"

Annyn whipped her head around.

Rowan stood alongside a tree, arrow nocked and ready to fly.

Rebuking himself for his desire for a woman no man ought to want, Garr tightened his hold on her. Not that he would use her as a shield. A man did not take cover behind a woman.

"I say again, release her!"

Annyn met Garr's gaze. Though one could not be certain with women, he thought there was pleading in her eyes. "Do not shed blood over me. 'Tis better spent elsewhere."

Who had watch over this part of the wood? Where was the man whose incompetence permitted Rowan to creep near?

God in His heavens! First his squires allowed Annyn Bretanne to seek a dagger to him, now this. It seemed his father had been right—as long as Garr allowed God so prominent a place in his training of young men, they would not attain the worthiness of those trained by previous generations of Wulfriths. But God was all Garr had taken of his mother from Stern Castle, and only because He was not something Drogo could lay a hand to. How his father would scorn his oldest son were he alive.

"Wulfrith!" Rowan barked.

Garr considered the bow. If the arrow were loosed, it would clear Annyn and strike him high in the chest and to the right.

"I beg you," she whispered.

He looked into her face, and in that moment knew the answer he had sought since discovering she was a woman. He would let her go. His lie had given her a reason to seek his death, and for that no punishment was due.

Whether Drogo had made Heaven or been banished below, he was surely shaking his head, for he would never have spared the Bretannes the shame of Jonas's death. Indeed, he would have lifted it up for all to know how great the regard for receiving knighthood at Wulfen. And the consequence of betrayal.

Garr released Annyn.

"It is done?" she whispered. "You will not seek revenge?"

He wondered that his hands had never felt so empty. But this was the best end to Annyn. "Vengeance is not mine. It belongs to God." One of the hardest lessons a man must learn. "Aye, Lady Annyn, I yield to Him above."

As if what he said was a revelation, she stared. But then, considering what she had come to Wulfen to do, perhaps it *was* a revelation.

"You?" she breathed. "'Twas you who taught Jonas that?"

Garr frowned. "It is as I aspire to teach all who seek knighthood."

"I—"

"Make haste, Annyn!" Rowan shouted.

Annyn? Not *Lady* Annyn? Garr would have sworn she was untried, that no man before him had tasted her. Had he been wrong? Was he right in first believing she and Rowan were lovers?

She held his gaze a moment longer, then turned and ran.

The best end, Garr told himself again. However, as she neared Rowan, he caught the bow's movement and saw the arrow was now centered on his chest. He lunged to the left and reached for his sword, but before he could pull it, the arrow burned a path through his flesh and staggered him back.

He looked to his blood-splattered sleeve and the shaft piercing his sword arm, then jerked his gaze to Annyn.

She stood beside Rowan, eyes large in her face, but the words she spoke to her man fell beyond Garr's reach.

Rowan reached for another arrow. "That which we came to do," he snarled as he fit the string.

Arm protesting, Garr swept his sword from its sheath and started toward them.

A shout to his left—Sir Merrick?—tore across the wood.

Annyn grabbed Rowan's arm. "We must go!"

The man narrowed his eyes on her bruised face, then turned his seething gaze one last time to Garr before fleeing with her.

Blood coursing the back of his hand to coat his sword hilt, Garr gave chase. The two stayed out of reach, winding the trees and jumping debris, unhindered by the pain that slowed their pursuer. Then, ahead, was the horse that awaited its lord's return.

Rowan mounted, reached a hand to Annyn, and swung her up behind. With a jab of the spurs, their departure scattered leaves before Garr.

"God's blood!" he shouted. He glared at the sky, then again at the arrow piercing the shoulder of his sword arm. Not God's blood, but his, and too much of it. He snapped the arrow shaft near its entrance, then looked to where Annyn and Rowan had disappeared. Nay, it was not the end.

"My lord," Sir Merrick called, nearly breathless as he reached Garr's side.

Garr swung around. "What happened to your watch?"

Brow furrowing at the sight of Garr's wound, the knight said, "Apologies, my lord. I fear I lost my breath."

It was several years since the man had experienced such trouble, though Garr had glimpsed instances of its effects since Annyn's arrival. Still, Merrick had failed, but that would be dealt with later. What was needed now was a horse.

As he stepped past Merrick, Abel arrived. He reined in and dropped to the ground. "Bloody rood! She did this to you?"

"Her man, Rowan." Garr sheathed his sword, pushed past Abel, and put a foot in the stirrup of his brother's mount. As he swung into the saddle, four more of his men halted their horses alongside.

"Whose watch?" Abel demanded.

Garr looked to Squire Warren. "Give me your bow and quiver."

The young man hurriedly passed them to his lord.

"Your wound must be tended," Abel protested.

Garr jabbed his heels to the horse.

"Do not give your life for her!"

The woods sped past in a blur of greens, browns, and bits of blue sky, but Garr could not have said if it was the horse's speed that melded the colors or his straining consciousness.

Blood wet him shoulder to fingers, and though he knew the wound should be tended, his anger—that which his father had many times warned would send him young to the grave—would not be quieted. He would have Annyn and her Rowan.

Shortly, he glimpsed white among the green of the wood. There they rode, the tunic he had given Annyn visible beneath the short mantle flying from her shoulders.

As he pushed the horse harder, his consciousness dipped. Grinding his teeth, he drew deep breaths and pushed on. Though his men could bring them down, he would do it himself and return ten-fold the wrong done him.

Topping a rise, he reined in, all the while keeping his prey in sight as they rushed the wood below.

"My lord?" one of his knights asked as he halted his horse alongside.

Garr nocked an arrow, lifted the bow, and grunted as he forced his arm to pull the string as it cried it could not do. But it did, and trembled for it. He sighted Rowan.

And if his quaking muscles caused him to strike Annyn?

Then he would nock another arrow!

With a growl, he swung the bow ahead of his quarry and released. Without pausing to see if he made his mark, he pulled another arrow and let it fly. There was no time for a third. Fortunately, both buried themselves deep in the chosen tree. Would their combined strength—one tight alongside the other—suffice?

A moment later, the protruding shafts caught Rowan high in the chest and knocked him and Annyn off the horse's backside.

"Never have I seen such!" one of his men exclaimed.

Garr lowered the bow and eyed the two where they sprawled. Consciousness receding, turning his breath shallow, he nudged the horse forward and down the rise. He wanted to see their faces, for them to see his and know the dire mistake made in seeking his death. His consideration to allow them to escape was no more, but both understood revenge—except where it was and was not warranted. *That* Garr understood.

With his approach, Annyn roused, sprang to her knees, and bent over her man. "Rowan!" She shook his shoulders.

He was not dead. Garr was sure of it. Had he wished an immediate death, he would have aimed higher on the tree so the arrows would collapse Rowan's throat. The breath was merely knocked from him.

As Garr neared, Rowan convulsed and wheezed. Annyn murmured something, looked up, and slowly straightened.

Though, previously, Garr had only glimpsed her fear, it now filled her eyes. Never had he read a woman more clearly. But then, never had one elicited more emotion from him. Gesturing for his men to halt their advance, he continued to where Annyn stood.

She looked to his shoulder. If not that she had tried to murder him, he might have said it was concern on her bruised face.

Garr stiffened to counter the sway that threatened to unhorse him. As he had earlier warned Lavonne to tend his wound, so must he. An instant later, he was struck by the bitter irony that he and the baron should both suffer injury over this woman. However, Garr had not sought to harm her. Too, his injury was more serious than Lavonne's. His sword arm was nearly all that he was, and if he left it much longer, it might mean his death. He should never have touched her.

"Again I have you, Annyn Bretanne, and now your man, Rowan."
He glanced at the knight who was struggling to sit upright. "I shall take
pleasure in meting out judgment."

She stepped toward him. "I am to blame. Rowan did not wish me to
come to Wulfen."

Darkness dragged at Garr. "Did he not? 'Twas he who put an arrow
through me though I yielded what he asked. Your man is without honor,
Annyn Bretanne—unworthy, and for that he shall pay in kind."

"Murderer!" Rowan spat, a hand to his chest where he had crossed
the arrow's path. As he bent forward and coughed, Annyn dropped to
her knees alongside him.

Garr stared at the two and struggled to pull himself out of the grey
light that was expanding to black. He had given too much blood.

Hearing Abel's shout, he looked to the blur riding toward him. It
seemed his brother had taken another's horse—*his* destrier, Garr realized as he slid sideways and crashed to the floor of the wood.

All he could think as he lay bleeding was what his father had said
of women—that they turned a man from his purpose and made him
vulnerable. And so he bled out his life for one taste of a woman no man
should want. And still he tasted her.

Annyn stared at where Wulfrith lay with eyes closed, face devoid of
color, and the sleeve of his tunic bled through.

Vengeance is not yours, she heard the lesson she knew Jonas had
taken from Wulfrith. And here was the reason vengeance belonged to
God. With a cry strangled by the din that rose from Wulfrith's men, she
scrambled around to his side. "Wulfrith!" *Lord, what is his Christian name?*

He was still, as if no longer of this world.

"Stand back!" Sir Abel shouted.

She pressed a hand to Wulfrith's chest, seeking the beat of his heart.
It was there.

Feeling Rowan's hard, accusing gaze, she looked to Wulfrith's
wound. The blood must be stanched. She swept up the hem of the tunic
he had given her and tore a strip from it.

Dear Lord, do not let him die, she silently pleaded as she reached to his shoulder. *Deliver him. I ask it in Your holy name.*

When she had first come to Wulfen, never would she have believed such a prayer would cross her heart. Nor would Rowan have believed it. When he had shot Garr and she had cried out, his eyes had looked through her as if she were no longer known to him.

Hardly had Annyn begun to wrap Wulfrith's wound than she was dragged upright.

"I said stand back!" Sir Abel bit. Gone was the good humor that had set him apart from his older brothers. Before her now was a distant, hard-hearted Wulfrith. But then, his brother had been injured, perhaps mortally. And she was to blame.

He shoved her back. "If he dies, so shall both of you." He dropped down beside his brother. "Squire Charles, Squire Warren, I give these two into your care to be bound and kept full in your sight until we arrive at Stern."

"Aye, my lord."

For the first time, Annyn looked to those gathered around. Wrath stared at her—hatred for what had been done to their lord.

As Squire Charles advanced with a rope, Rowan rose and glared at her. "Never would I have believed you would betray," he rasped.

She cringed at his condemnation. She could not blame him, though, for she would feel the same if she had not known Wulfrith as she had this day. "This I know." She turned to Squire Charles.

He despised her, and as she could not fault Rowan, neither could she fault this young man. She put her wrists together. While he bound her, so tightly she would surely lose feeling, Squire Warren seized Rowan's sword and dagger.

Annyn turned and watched as Abel wrapped his brother's wound with the linen of her tunic. Would Wulfrith make it to Stern? How many leagues?

The pound of hooves announced the arrival of the remainder of Wulfrith's men, and at their head was Sir Merrick. He drew near, looked upon Wulfrith, then met Annyn's gaze. But the anger she expected was not there. Sorrow, regret, and something else, but not anger.

Why? What set him apart from those who looked at her as if they longed to do to her as Lavonne had done? Merrick was loyal to Wulfrith, she did not doubt, and yet it was as if he was divided. By what? Between whom? And what did it have to do with her?

She frowned. Perhaps it had nothing to do with her and all to do with Jonas. He *had* squired with her brother. Her breath caught. Could it have been he—

Nay, but perhaps he knew who.

12

Only as a young boy longing for home had Stern seemed so distant.

Garr meandered in and out of consciousness, never long enough to more than bring the speeding ground to sight and revive his anger with remembrance of who had turned him from his purpose. Where was she? If his men allowed her to escape...

As he was lifted and carried, torchlight pried at his lids. Passing through the doors of Stern's great hall, he opened his eyes and saw his mother, Isobel, dressed entirely in black as she had dressed every day since wedding Drogo thirty years ago. Yet for all that dark, she smelled of roses. She hurried alongside him, her anxious face aging her years beyond the last time he had seen her.

"Garr," she gasped when she saw he had returned to consciousness.

He closed his eyes and opened them again. "Where is she?"

His mother shook her head.

Abel leaned into sight, showing it was he who bore Garr's upper body. "She and her man are imprisoned in the outer tower."

That dark, filthy ramble of cells that—

"Of whom do you speak?" Isobel asked, her voice softly rolled with accent.

"Once Garr is put to bed," Abel said, "I shall tell you all of it, Mother."

Isobel bit her lip and nodded. "The solar. He shall have my bed."

"What of the physician?" Abel asked as they repositioned Garr to convey him up the winding stairs.

Isobel stepped back to allow them to precede her. "I sent for him when your messenger arrived an hour past. He ought to return soon."

As they began the climb, Garr looked to his shoulder. It was bound with linen, the blood on it dried. He would not die as his brother feared, he told himself, his training of men proving time and again the power of belief. He had lost a goodly amount of blood, but it was stemmed. However, that did not mean he would regain full use of his arm to wield a sword as all Wulfriths must do.

The strength of his anger dimming his consciousness, he once more succumbed to darkness.

Annyn tucked her legs tighter beneath her. Under cover of her mantle, she flexed her hands that were slow to regain feeling from Squire Charles's rope. Of course, the terrible dank and chill of this place did not help.

She swept her gaze around the dim that the single torch in the corridor outside the grated cell failed to light. Rowan sat in the opposite corner. Though she could barely see his shadow, she knew he watched her. What to say now that they were alone? Was there anything?

Aye, but would he believe it? For years they had blamed Jonas's death on Wulfrith, but now...

"Why did you not kill him in the wood?" Rowan's voice shot across the cell.

He spoke of yesterday when they had tracked the deer. "The time was not right."

"Not right?" She heard him lurch to his feet. "I was there—waited for you to do what you vowed you would do. And you did not!"

She huddled deeper in her corner, but pulled away when the moisture weeping the walls penetrated her clothes. "'Twas simply not right."

"Did you lie with him?"

"I did not! He thought me a man 'til last eve when—"

"Had I not come for you, *would* you have lain with him?"

It was she who had ended the kiss—a kiss that had done unspeakable things to her. Quivering with remembrance, she pulled her mantle nearer and wished it were longer so she could gather more warmth about her.

Rowan came across the cell. "I saw you in his arms. You put him from you, but not ere first you gave to him."

She had prayed he had not seen that much. Though she knew she ought to preserve the little heat left to her, she stood. "I would not have lain with him."

"Then he would have ravished you had I not come."

All of her protested. Though once she might have believed Wulfrith capable of forcing his attentions on a woman, she no longer did.

She met the glint of Rowan's gaze from beneath her hood. "I shall endeavor to forget you spoke such to me."

"The same as you have forgotten what Wulfrith did to your brother?"

She drew a deep breath. "He did not do it, Rowan." She pushed her shoulders back to brace for his response.

"Did not do it?" he bellowed. "Just as he did not put that bruise on your face?"

Annyn touched the tenderness. "Just as he did not. 'Twas Baron Lavonne who struck me, the one to whom Henry would see me wed."

Rowan was silent a long moment, then demanded, "If Wulfrith did not hang Jonas, who did?"

"I do not know, but I tell you it was not he."

"Fool woman! Your brother lies dead and you allow Wulfrith to lay the same hands to you that killed Jonas."

"Nay, I was wrong. We were wrong. It was someone else. It had to be."

"It had to be because you *wish* it to be!" He shoved his face near hers. "When you let him touch you, did you think to ask about the rope burns on Jonas's neck that he hid from us?"

"He believes Jonas hung himself, but I—"

Rowan's hands descended to her bruised arms. "Never would he have killed himself. You know it, Annyn!" He pushed her back against the weeping wall. "And yet you believe Wulfrith's lies for want of giving yourself to him."

She was sick unto death of being ill-used. "Believe what you wish," she snarled, her tone so cutting its jagged edge sliced even her. "I no longer care."

With a gust of breath, Rowan released her and turned away. "I do not understand how you can so easily forget Jonas and the evil done him."

She pushed off the wall. "I have not forgotten him. He was my brother!"

Rowan swung around. "As he was my——"

Silence snapped up the rest of his words, his pain transcending Annyn's anger and meeting her own that had yet to find its release.

Longing to cry, she dropped her chin to her chest. Of course Rowan despised her championing of Wulfrith, just as she had despised Uncle Artur's refusal to believe Wulfrith was guilty of wrongdoing.

She lifted her head. "I know Jonas was as a son to you, and you were as a father to him, but so much has changed, so much I do not understand." She laid a hand to his shoulder, and he tensed beneath it. "I do not know what our fate is to be, but while we wait, let us be at peace with one another." Would he allow it? Or would he leave her utterly alone?

After what seemed minutes, Rowan heaved a sigh. "Let us be at peace. Come, 'tis bitter cold." He guided her to the corner of the cell from which she had risen.

Side by side they huddled, near enough to draw heat from one another, though not enough to warm them that they might find rest after so many hours in the saddle. When Rowan's arm finally came around her, drawing her closer than she had ever been to him, Annyn was grateful. Still, it was hours before she slept, but not a single minute did she waste as she gave herself over to prayer as she had not done in years.

Seeking refuge in God as Wulfrith had told her he did, she prayed for forgiveness for what she had intended to do, prayed for Rowan to see past revenge as she had done, prayed for those at Wulfen harmed by her deception, but mostly prayed for the man who lay bleeding somewhere beyond these walls.

"I would see those responsible for my son's injury."

The accented voice brought Annyn awake. She lifted her head from Rowan's shoulder and realized he was rigid where he held her against his side.

"But my lady," a guttural voice protested, "Sir Abel ordered that none were to enter without his leave."

"Ah? A mother must seek permission from the whelp she bore?"

Annyn startled at the realization of who came to them.

"I say now and not again, open the cell!"

Wulfrith's mother was Scottish, Annyn realized, though the lilting accent had obviously gone soft after many years among the English.

"Aye, my lady." The light of a torch breached the dim of the cell.

Rowan withdrew his arm from around Annyn and stood. Though every muscle in her protested, she also rose.

The guard peered through the grate at them and, satisfied, fit the key in the lock. The door swung inward to reveal the broad figure of their jailer and the torch that brought the light of the outside in.

Annyn put up a hand to shade her eyes from the glare.

"Lady Isobel of Stern be here to see ye. Give her no trouble and I'll give ye none." The jailer stepped to the side and rested a hand on his sword hilt.

Lady Isobel appeared. Dressed in black, from her veil to her slippers, she stepped into the filth. Her pale face beautiful despite the age and sorrow etched there, she looked from Rowan to Annyn before continuing forward.

"Ye ought not go so near, my lady," the jailer warned.

She continued forward until she was a stride from them. She measured them, though for what Annyn did not know. All she knew was that never had she felt so far from a woman than at that moment when she stood before one who would not look a man even if she sheared her hair, donned men's clothing, and wore filth upon her as Annyn did.

"You are Lady Annyn?" the lady finally spoke, her eyes lingering on Annyn's bruised cheek.

Annyn lowered her hand from her eyes. "Lady Annyn Bretanne of Castle Lillia upon the barony of Aillil." She nodded to Rowan. "Sir Rowan, Castle Lillia's captain of the guard."

Lady Isobel denied him acknowledgment. "My son, Abel, has told me what transpired at Wulfen Castle and during the journey to Stern." Her gaze traveled down Annyn and up again. "Incredible as it seems, I see 'tis true." Her lips pressed to a thin line.

"I am sorry, Lady Isobel. What happened should not have." Beside Annyn, Rowan stiffened further, still firm in his belief that Wulfrith had killed Jonas.

"It should not have happened?" The woman tilted her head. "Was it not my son's death you sought, Lady Annyn?"

"It was, but—"

"Then you ought to be satisfied, hmm?"

Annyn felt as if speared. Had Wulfrith died? "Does your son yet live, Lady Isobel?"

Though the woman's eyes turned moist, the accusation there did not soften. "Aye, Wulfrith lives."

Relief swept Annyn, followed by bewilderment. Even Wulfrith's mother called him by that name. Perhaps he did not have another.

"But if infection sets in..." The lady drew a breath and turned away. "I must needs pray."

As Wulfrith had done the night Lavonne came to Wulfen. Had he learned it from his mother?

Lady Isobel swept past the jailer. "See they are given pallets and blankets and better than bread and water."

"But, my lady—"

She halted in the doorway. "When my sons are gone from Stern, to whom do you answer?"

The man's jowls jerked. "I shall do your bidding, my lady."

Then it was she who kept Stern Castle? Most peculiar—and enviable.

In the corridor, Wulfrith's mother looked back and fixed on Annyn. "Though 'tis true my son has a terrible anger, I need none to tell me 'twas not he who struck you, just as I need none to tell me he did not murder your brother." Her dark eyebrows rose. "But this you already know, Lady Annyn." Then she was gone.

Their jailer followed with a huff, a creak of the door, and a click of the lock.

Once more in darkness, Annyn looked to Rowan who pivoted and returned to the corner. She lowered beside him, but he did not offer his warmth again. And so the day—or night—wore on. Eventually, pallets, blankets, and passable foodstuffs were brought to them, but no further word did Rowan speak.

13

FOUR DAYS LOST to him, four days of hardly knowing dream from reality, four days of thundering pain and heat.

Garr stared at the ceiling of the solar his father had occasionally shared with his mother and breathed in the scent of mint-strewn rushes as his thoughts went to the woman who besieged his dreams. Where was she? The outer tower? It was what Abel had told.

"Garr?"

He followed the voice to the chair alongside the bed. His mother's smile, that never quite met her eyes, greeted him.

Wafting the scent of roses, she stood and laid a palm to his forehead. "The fever has passed," she pronounced as she had less than a quarter hour ago when he had first awakened—spoken once more as if to convince herself the danger was over.

She bit her lower lip. "I feared."

"You feared wrong, Mother." He had not been going to die, and certainly not from an arrow to the shoulder, regardless how much blood and infection it had let. He looked to his bandaged wound. It was clean and dry.

His mother stepped back. "You are right, of course. God would not allow it." She who had given all of herself those first four years of his life to make him a godly man, lowered to the chair's edge.

Garr shifted his gaze to the ceiling that was patterned with fleur de lis, closed his eyes, and sent thanks heavenward. His arm was spared, the fear of awakening and finding it severed having haunted his dreams. Then there was Annyn who had come in and out of them…

"Abel told me of Lady Annyn," his mother said, "and the reason for her and her man's imprisonment in the outer tower."

It was to be expected, and likely Abel had left nothing unspoken. Determining he would not be drawn into a conversation about the woman, Garr flexed his shoulder. Though it pained him, it was no longer agonizing. He would be swinging a sword within a fortnight, would gain back what was lost—he prayed.

"I went to see her."

"For what?" Garr demanded.

"To speak with her, of course." She frowned. "The woman is not as expected."

Garr felt his anger swell. "What did she say?"

"Little. Though, forsooth, I did not give her much leave to do so." Isobel sank deeper into the chair. "What she did say was that she would not have had happen to you what did. Curious, hmm?"

Garr chafed. Though the physician had warned him not to move from his back, he pushed up to sitting and drew a deep breath against the pain.

"You should not." Isobel protested. "The physician—"

"I know what he told, Mother, and I tell you: Annyn Bretanne is a deception. You shall not speak to her again."

She narrowed her gaze, a portent of things to come as when Drogo had lived. Though deeply religious, she had often been at heads with the husband she had not wanted and who had made seven children on her, of which five had survived to adulthood. For all the warrior Drogo had been, and though he had never put his Scottish bride first, she had often come close to turning him from his purpose. And all dissension had begun with her incessant wearing of black to witness the darkness cast upon her by a forced marriage when her heart was given to another. Though Drogo was dead, she continued to wear the color.

Still, for all the years of having borne witness to his father's bitterness, for which none could fault Drogo, Garr felt for Isobel Wulfrith. She had been a good mother those few years before her husband had, in turn, taken each of their sons to Wulfen, the love she denied Drogo given all to her children.

Nevertheless, in the deepest reaches of Garr where the boy had been banished, dwelt resentment, and not only toward her. Though it was customary for a boy to begin his page's training at the age of seven, Drogo retaliated against Isobel by taking their sons from her upon their attainment of four years and made them train alongside others far older. And no quarter had he given.

"She ought to be moved from the tower," Garr's mother returned him to the present.

He laid a hand on his bandaged shoulder and applied pressure to its throbbing. "Nor would I have you speak *of* the Bretanne woman."

Isobel clasped her hands in her lap. "I have prayed about this. Though by this woman your life was beset, she is still a lady and, it seems, given good reason to seek revenge."

Abel *had* told all. "Enough!"

"The outer tower is no place for her. 'Tis chill, damp, and abounding with sickness."

"I say again, speak no more of—or to—her."

Isobel's lips parted, but she quickly pressed them inward.

"We are of an understanding, Mother?"

She lowered her lids, raised them. "As far as my son can be understood."

Garr ground his teeth. "Do not test me."

"I would not think to."

Aye, she would.

She stood and heaped the pillows at his back. "If you insist on disregarding the physician's orders, you ought to at least be comfortable."

She turned away. "I shall send for your sisters. They are anxious to see how you fare."

"First I would have you send for Abel." Gaenor and Beatrix, whom he hardly knew, could wait.

His mother did not look around until she reached the door. "I have done so. He shall be here soon." As she pulled the door open, puzzlement creased her face. "Several times during your fever, you spoke her name."

Why did his mother persist? "To curse her, I am sure."

"It did not sound a curse to me. But as you wish." She stepped into the corridor and closed the door.

Garr clenched his jaws and leaned back against the pillows, but as he closed his eyes, he heard a murmur of voices from the corridor. The one that answered his mother belonged to Squire Warren.

The young man entered a few moments later. "Is there anything you require, my lord?"

"That I be left alone!"

The squire's eyes widened. "Aye, my lord." He hastened from the solar.

Garr lifted his aching arm and opened and closed his fingers. Though he knew the greater fault of the injury lay with him for having allowed Annyn Bretanne to distract him, Sir Merrick had much to answer for. Regardless whether it was his loss of breath that had made his guard vulnerable to Rowan's presence, or a case of negligence, the man could no longer serve as a senior knight. But then, what was left to Merrick? He could not take up his lands, for upon attainment of knighthood he had relinquished them to his younger brother. A knight-errant, then. There were worse things.

The outer tower is no place for her, his mother's voice came again, *chill, damp...abounding with sickness.*

Garr raised his hand before his face—open, close, open, close. His arm but needed healing and exercise.

She is still a lady...given good reason to seek revenge.

As he had concluded, but that was before he had taken an arrow for her—when she had turned him from his purpose.

The door opened. "Lo!" Abel exclaimed, a smile large on the face he stuck around the door. "You are returned to us." He stepped inside and closed the door. "And from what Mother tells"—he leaned a shoulder against the curtained post at the foot of the bed—"you are as a hungry bear too long at slumber."

Abel had been tumbling a wench in the stables, as evidenced by the scent of hay and the fibers overlooked in brushing off his clothes.

Continuing to flex his hand, Garr lowered his arm. "Mother tells too much, as do you."

"Ah, Annyn Bretanne." Abel's smile turned chagrined. "I told her. If she were to lose a son, it seemed she ought to know the reason."

"Then you did not expect me to live."

"Of course I did, the same as I expected to win my wager with Everard." Abel chortled. "Mayhap my lot is changing, eh?"

"In this. Still, were I you, I would guard my coin. Now tell, are there tidings of Lavonne or Duke Henry?"

"All is silent."

Still, one or both would come, not only for Annyn Bretanne, but the alliance England's future king sought with the Wulfriths. And for that, Garr must make a swift recovery.

"Sir Merrick seeks an audience."

As Garr had known he would. "Later."

"I told him so." Abel slapped a hand to his thigh. "Now you wish to speak of Annyn Bretanne."

Did he? Though piqued that his brother knew him so well, Garr said, "Mother tells that she and her man, Rowan, remain in the outer tower."

"They do, and are most comfortable with the pallets and blankets she ordered delivered there. And the foodstuffs."

Not even a curtained bed and the finest venison would make comfort out of that place. The outer tower of Stern that stood reinforcement for the castle's exemplary guard was a warning to any who thought to come against the Wulfriths. Though most nobles kept their captives better, some even in luxury, Stern was known throughout England as a place one did not wish to be taken prisoner. Thus, its enemies were content to hate from afar—excepting Annyn Bretanne and her man.

"Four days," Garr said. "How do they fare?"

"The jailer tells they are quiet. Indeed, they do not even speak one to the other."

Garr's first thought was that they were plotting, but realization thrust it aside. "They share a cell?"

"You surprise me, Brother. If I recall correctly, and I do, you said she was but a troublesome woman. Mayhap she is more?"

Garr clenched his hand on an illusory hilt. "Regardless of the wrong she did, she is still a lady, and a lady does not share quarters with a man who is not her husband."

Abel's eyes sparkled. "A lady? One could not tell it from looking at her."

But one knew it to hold her—

By faith! Why did he allow Abel to draw him in? More, what did he care whether Annyn slept alone or made a bed with Rowan? It was his sword arm he ought to set his mind to.

He met his brother's waiting gaze. "Our conversation is done."

Abel pushed off the post. "I quite agree."

He lied. There was more, and upon reaching the door he said, "I shall have her brought to the donjon."

Grudgingly, Garr inclined his head. "Her man, Rowan, remains."

"Of course." Then Abel was gone, leaving his grin hanging on the air.

Garr berated himself for whatever allowed his youngest brother to know him. It was a mistake to release Annyn, but it was one he would have made regardless of whether or not Abel had taken it upon himself to do so. The outer tower was no place for her. But neither was the donjon.

Sleep pressing him down, he closed his eyes. But then Gaenor and Beatrix entered. Fifteen and thirteen respectively, they twittered their way into the solar and hovered on either side of the bed until he opened his eyes.

He sighed. Though he was nearly a stranger to them and certainly did not invite their attention, they were fond of him. He drew the coverlet up his bared chest.

"Gaenor," he acknowledged the older one who had grown taller since his last visit and appeared more awkward than before. For this had her betrothed's family broken the betrothal six months past? Or had that been Isobel's doing? She had not liked the young man Drogo had chosen for their eldest daughter.

Gaenor dimpled both sides. "Greetings, Brother."

He inclined his head and looked to his younger sister who was impossibly delicate in comparison. "Beatrix."

She grabbed up her skirts and hopped onto the mattress. "At last you are returned."

And, it seemed, would be staying longer than the three or four days he usually kept at Stern.

Gaenor shifted foot to foot and eyed the empty space beside Garr.

Reconciled to foregoing sleep, begrudging that a woman had once more turned him from his purpose, he said, "Sit, Gaenor. You are causing me to strain my neck."

Hurt flitted across her face, and too late he remembered how it bothered her that she should be so tall.

He forced a smile. "Come, I am certain you have much to tell."

"She does," Beatrix exclaimed. "Another has offered for her—Lord Harrod of Banbrine."

With measured movement that bespoke of Gaenor's effort to appear less awkward, she lowered beside her brother. "He is forty and three years aged!" Tears sprang to her eyes.

More than old enough to be her father. Garr knew he should not care, as such marriages were made every day. Still, he said, "Aye, too old."

With a trembling smile, she said, "I thank you, Brother."

"Still you shall wed, Gaenor."

Her smile flattened. "And who will want me other than old men whose eyes are dim?"

Where was Mother? This was not something a man should have to deal with. "There will be many. You shall see."

As though he had made her a promise certain to be kept, she smiled again, a pretty smile that gave him hope he had not told her wrong.

The light of day blinded greater than the torch that had delivered her from the tower.

Annyn halted, fumbled the musty hood of the mantle over her head for the shade it offered, then took a deep breath of a day that was approaching noon. How sweet the air, how pure the taste!

"You are coming?"

She peered at Sir Abel who stood strides ahead, an impatient bend to his mouth. It was the first he had spoken to her since the jailer ushered her from the cell. "Where are you taking me?"

"To the donjon."

She longed to ask the reason but knew her question would go unanswered. Was Wulfrith improved? She prayed so. Was it he who had summoned her? If so, would he see her? He must, for there was pleading to be done for Rowan who had thus far been spared retribution by Wulfrith's illness. Of course, Wulfrith had but to leave Rowan where he was and the end would be the same. He was ailing, the cough that began yesterday growing more raw in the dank cell. Then there was the wheezing.

"I grow impatient," Sir Abel snapped.

Of course he did. He was a Wulfrith. Swallowing, she winced at the sting that had begun in her own throat hours earlier and stepped forward.

He led her across the outer bailey to the inner drawbridge. She was watched, and when she followed the strongest of the sensations, her squinted eyes found Squire Charles where he paused outside the stables. A moment later, Squire Samuel, leading Wulfrith's destrier, appeared.

Nose running, Annyn sniffed and turned her eyes forward as she passed beneath the portcullis.

The inner bailey provided her first view of Stern's donjon lit by daylight. Though simply designed, it was majestic and more immense than any she had seen. Indeed, two of Castle Lillia's donjons could fit into it.

The steps were treacherous, though not because of disrepair. Rather, her eyes continued to struggle with the light she had been too long denied.

At the great doors, the porter shot Annyn a questioning look as he stepped aside to allow Sir Abel and her to enter.

The fresh scent of mint that contrasted sharply with the fetid odor of the cell, struck Annyn before she set foot within. Though she had never been fond of using the herb to scent the rushes at Castle Lillia, it now appealed. Entering the hall, she breathed it deep and wished Rowan was with her. He had hardly spoken to her for however many days had passed, but she longed for the friendship he had extended all these years. However, her discourse with Wulfrith's mother had turned him again and she was once more the betrayer.

Annyn looked around the hall where a half dozen servants set out trestle tables for the nooning meal. As the exterior of the donjon was simple, so was the interior, but it did not lack for warmth. The ceiling to floor tapestries were woven of muted colors, the furnishings sparse but solid, the stairway of modest size. Indeed, the only excess, could it be called that considering the size of the hall, was the massive stone fireplace that reached to the ceiling.

Longing to stretch her hands to the flames, she lowered her hood and followed Sir Abel. As they neared the stairway, a figure dressed in black halted on the bottom stair.

Startled eyes evidencing she had not known her son's prisoner was summoned, Wulfrith's mother looked to her youngest son.

He shrugged. "Wulfrith ordered it."

Then he *had* summoned her. Meaning he was recovered? *Thank you, Lord.*

"'Twill not do," Wulfrith's mother said as she assessed Annyn, from her disheveled hair to her begrimed boots. She waved her forward. "Something must needs be done."

"What say you, Mother?"

The woman turned a sour eye on her youngest boy. "Prisoner or no, I do not allow such filth in my home. It attracts fleas and rats."

Annyn could not take offense. She *was* horribly fouled.

"Come, Lady Annyn, let us see what can be done."

She followed Lady Isobel up the stairs, as did Sir Abel.

The woman must have heard his footsteps, for she swung around. "Go back to your wench in the stables. I do not require your attendance."

"You should not be alone with her, Mother."

Her hands fell to her hips. "Has she a weapon?"

"Nay, but—"

"Go—unless you wish to carry her bath water."

Annyn blinked. She was to have a bath? Ah, mercy! To wash away the filth, to smell clean again.

"He will not like it," Sir Abel said.

"That we shall know soon enough."

He grunted, turned, and descended the stairs.

The lady of Stern resumed her ascent. Though the winding stairs continued upward, she turned off the first landing.

The realization that Wulfrith was likely behind one of the four doors made Annyn's heart skitter. As she passed the first, the laughter of girls sounded from the chamber. He could not be there.

His mother traversed the corridor to the end and pushed open a door.

The chamber was of a good size despite the enormous bed that sought to diminish it, but as with the hall, it was simply furnished.

"My son's chamber when he is at Stern," Lady Isobel said, then muttered, "which is far too rare."

It was Wulfrith of whom she spoke, but where was he if not here? The solar? Aye, his mother had given it up that he might know greater comfort.

"I shall send for the tub and water," the lady said.

The door closed, and when Annyn turned, she was alone. But she would make no trouble. Not only was she chill and ailing, but she must speak with Wulfrith about Rowan. She crossed to the brazier that glowed softly from earlier use, meaning Wulfrith's mother had likely taken the chamber for herself while her son recovered.

Though the warmth spread through her fingers, it came nowhere near the chill at her center. Shivering, she wondered how long it would be until the hot bath was delivered.

She glanced at the bed and imagined crawling beneath the heavy coverlet. However, not only would it be inappropriate, but she would sully the bed. In fact, though fatigue pressed her to sit, she didn't dare settle her filth onto the chair.

The tub, borne by two servants, arrived within a few minutes. As Wulfrith's mother directed that it be set before the brazier, Annyn stepped aside.

Shortly, a hand touched her shoulder. "Sit, Lady Annyn."

She met Lady Isobel's steady gaze. "I am fine, my lady."

"You are not." She pressed Annyn toward the chair. "Worry not. The chair will clean."

Why was Wulfrith's mother so kind to one who had sought to kill her son?

"Sit," the lady's accented voice turned more firm.

Annyn lowered herself. "I thank you."

The woman turned as the first buckets arrived.

Annyn watched the maid servants carry them within and remembered when she had lugged water for Wulfrith's bath. It seemed so long ago.

"Josse," Lady Isobel addressed the pretty young maid who next entered the chamber, "add coal to the brazier, then assist Lady Annyn in the removal of her garments."

"Aye, my lady." When the young woman approached Annyn, her lips were pressed as if to hold back a smile and her eyes danced. Doubtless, she had never assisted a lady who looked as Annyn did with her bruised face, shorn hair, and the filthy clothes of a man. "If you would stand, my lady, I shall make you ready for your bath."

Beneath Lady Isobel's gaze, the mantle was lifted from Annyn's shoulders, next the tunic that Wulfrith had given her. She shivered.

"What is this?" Lady Isobel took the white tunic from Josse and ran fingers over the ragged edge from which Annyn had torn the strip for Wulfrith's shoulder. "'Tis what bound my son's injury?"

How had she guessed? The fine linen? "Aye," Annyn said, "the blood needed to be stanched."

The woman considered the modest embroidery around the neck. "It belongs to him."

Then it was surely she who had made the stitches. "He gave it to me when…" Annyn put a hand to the cut tunic that revealed the bindings she would have removed if not for the additional warmth they provided. "He gave it to me when my own was…torn."

Lady Isobel's eyes lowered to the bindings. "So that is how you did it. Clever." She stepped forward and peered into Annyn's face. "Still, I do not understand how Wulfrith—or any other—did not see you. I would have instantly known you for a woman."

She would have? It was not as if Annyn possessed the beauty of her mother or Lady Isobel that easily proclaimed their femininity.

"But then, I am a woman and they are not." A bitter laugh parted Lady Isobel's lips. "How blind men are, especially those of the warrior class who are far too busy searching out war to look near upon the small and precious things of life."

The lady hurt, Annyn realized, something in her past weighing upon her.

"But that is the way of men." She beckoned Josse forward.

As the servant removed Annyn's tunic, Lady Isobel turned away. "I shall return ere long." She crossed to the door and paused. "Mayhap later you will tell me how your own tunic was rent."

That her son had put a dagger through it?

The lady closed the door.

Josse flung the tunic onto the chair and grimaced over the bindings. "I shall have to unwind you." When Annyn's chest was finally bared, she exclaimed, "Oh, my lady, see what you have done!"

Annyn's flesh was angry, especially where the upper and lower edges of the bindings had rubbed. But she hardly felt it, she was so cold. Looking to the bath that wafted steam and the scent of roses, she reached to her braies.

Josse pushed her hands aside. "'Tis for me to do."

When Annyn finally settled into the tub, she moaned as the water gave its heat to her. Closing her eyes, she reveled in a pleasure that had only ever seemed a chore. She hardly felt the hands rubbing soap into her skin, the water streaming over her head, the fingers scrubbing her scalp, but too soon the bath cooled.

As Josse ushered her into a towel, Lady Isobel reappeared with a bright blue bliaut, white chainse, head veil, and hose and slippers.

Strangely, Annyn was not disappointed that she would once more don lady's clothes. More than ever, including when she was a very young girl and had still dreamed of being the beauty her mother was, she longed to look the lady. For what reason, she did not care to admit.

Lady Isobel considered Annyn's scrubbed face and bare shoulders above the towel. "As expected, you are pretty."

Truly? The nearest she had come to such a compliment was when Duke Henry had condescended to pronounce her "not uncomely." "Thank you, Lady Isobel."

The woman eyed Annyn's arms. "The Baron Lavonne is also responsible for these bruises?"

Then she knew it was he who had struck her face, likely told by Abel who would have learned it from his brother. "He was angered by what I said to him."

Lady Isobel put her head to the side. "Angrier than you made my son?"

It took Annyn a moment to decipher the woman's message that her son was not a beast. But Annyn already knew that.

Lady Isobel sighed and looked to Josse. "We must needs make haste. Lord Wulfrith grows impatient."

Josse lifted the armful from her mistress. "Come, Lady Annyn." She stepped to the bed and laid out the garments.

It felt strange to be dressed by a maid, for Annyn had not liked the close attentions of the woman that Uncle had given in service to her at Castle Lillia—the tittering over her choice of clothes, the muttering over the grime caused by her training with Rowan.

"It has been four days since you arrived at Stern," Lady Isobel spoke from the chair Annyn had earlier occupied.

It seemed twice as many. Wishing she had a towel with which to wipe her nose and that she could shake the chill that had returned to her, Annyn sniffed and looked up from the bliaut Josse had pulled over her head.

"And yet," Lady Isobel said, "you have not asked how my son fares."

Annyn's heart jerked. He was recovering, was he not? "I assumed that, as he sent for me, he must be healing." She caught her breath as Josse pulled in the side laces of the bliaut that fit a bit too snug. "He is, is he not?"

"Aye, he heals."

Thank You, Lord.

"Lady Gaenor's gown is a wee tight." Josse stepped back to assess Annyn. "But it will do."

Who was Lady Gaenor? Annyn looked from Josse to Lady Isobel, but neither enlightened her. Whoever the woman was, and for whatever reason she kept clothes at Stern, Lady Gaenor was tall. Even with slippers, the bliaut's skirt would trail—not only in back as was intended, but in front as was not. If Annyn was not careful, she would go sprawling. But at least the sleeves falling from her wrists did not sweep the floor as her mother's had—a style no longer in fashion.

"Very good, Josse," Lady Isobel said. "Now her hair, and be quick."

Josse put her head this way and that to determine what could be done. In the end, the only thing for it was to brush it out, drape the veil over it, and fit a circlet of silver. "There now. None will know your hair is shorn, my lady."

"You may leave us," Lady Isobel said.

The maid curtsied and met Annyn's gaze. "*Now* you look the lady." Her mouth no longer suppressing its smile, she withdrew.

Lady Isobel stepped before Annyn. "Are you ready to stand before Wulfrith?"

Again struck by her use of his surname as if he was hardly known to her, Annyn asked, "Was your son not given a Christian name, my lady?"

"Of course, but as it has always been, when the Wulfrith heir takes his place as baron, from that day forward he is known as Wulfrith and his Christian name used only by intimates, and then never in public. 'Tis a matter of respect, especially suited for those who train at Wulfen."

As much as Annyn longed to know his name, she was not an intimate. Or was she? She touched her lips, remembered his kiss, and told herself the shiver that shook her was only a chill. Nay, surely those few moments in his arms did not qualify her as an intimate. He had meant nothing by it.

"Do not fret," Lady Isobel said, "for methinks he shall soon enough tell you the name his father gave him."

How did she know?

Wulfrith's mother stepped back and circled Annyn. "Aye," she said, "you shall make a passable wife for my son."

14

"Wife? What do you say, Lady Isobel?"

The woman clasped her pale hands against her black skirts. "What you heard, Lady Annyn."

"I do not understand. I am your son's enemy. I tried to—"

"But you did not."

How did she know that when not even Wulfrith knew she had turned from revenge?

"Thus, you are no longer his enemy." Lady Isobel crossed to the chest and lifted the lid. "And that"—she turned with a kerchief in hand—"is what we must convince my son."

Annyn did not know what to say. Regardless that it was Rowan who had sent the arrow through Wulfrith, she was to blame. "I do not understand that you would wish me for a daughter. And even if 'tis so, surely you know it is not possible."

The lady extended the kerchief. "I am mistaken in believing your heart has turned to my son?"

In that she was not completely wrong, but it was not as the lady believed. It could not be. "You are wrong, my lady." Annyn accepted the kerchief and dabbed her nose. "As I now know your son could not have murdered my brother, I regret what happened. But 'tis only regret I feel for the terrible wrong done him. Naught else."

Lady Isobel's gaze narrowed. "Even if he cared for you?"

She nearly laughed. "Truly, Lady Isobel, after all that has happened, the last thing your son feels for me is care."

The lady turned on her heel. "We shall see. Come."

Insides aflutter, Annyn stared after her.

Finding herself alone at the door, Lady Isobel said over her shoulder, "As you surely know, he does not like to be kept waiting."

As Annyn stepped into the corridor, her gaze clashed with Squire Warren's where he stood erect outside the second door. His brow furrowed as he stared at her, but a moment later recognition flew across his face. Then disbelief.

Was she so transformed? Could a bath and bliaut effect such?

He recovered, as evidenced by eyes that were no more kind than Squire Samuel's or Charles's when she had been brought from the tower.

"My lady," he greeted Wulfrith's mother.

"Squire Warren. Wulfrith is alone?"

"Nay, Lady Gaenor and Lady Beatrix yet attend him."

Gaenor, to whom belonged the bliaut Annyn wore. Something painful sank through Annyn, something Rowan would not like.

"You may announce us," Lady Isobel said.

Squire Warren turned and knocked.

"Enter!"

Wulfrith's voice, strong and sure as if he had not suffered these past days, made Annyn's heart jump. Telling herself it was time to put aside pride and plead for Rowan, she pressed her shoulders back.

Squire Warren pushed the door inward. "My lord, your lady mother calls and brings with her Jame—er, Lady Annyn Bretanne."

Silence.

Annyn looked to Lady Isobel, but the woman's eyes were forward. Would Wulfrith not see her?

"Bid them enter."

A chill coursed Annyn, but it was more than the cold she had yet to fully warm away. Praying she would not shiver when she stood before

Wulfrith, hoping Lady Gaenor was not terribly beautiful, Annyn followed Lady Isobel into the solar.

Garr was unprepared for the woman who entered behind his mother, who sought his gaze with those same eyes that had looked through his dreams at him. Though he had kissed her, even acknowledged she was pretty, Annyn Bretanne clothed and presented as a lady made a dry pit of his mouth. And caused his resentment to root deeper.

The transformation to lady was what had delayed her. What was his mother thinking? Here was the one who sought his death, who was responsible for an injury that could lame him for the remainder of his life, and yet she dressed Annyn in finest as if she were not a prisoner.

"She is the one?" Beatrix whispered where she sat to his left. "What ill befell her face?"

Her observation jolted Garr, for he had not noticed the bruise. Though it was more yellow than the purple it had been when last he had looked upon her, it remained distinct. But he had looked past it.

Gaenor shifted beside him, and when he glanced at her he saw she also stared. However, she held her tongue as her sister did not know how to do.

Though Isobel drew alongside the bed, Annyn halted at the center of the room, looked to Garr's sisters where they sat on either side of him, then gave her stiff gaze to Garr.

Stiff because of his partly bared chest, he realized, remembering how she had avoided looking upon his body when she was disguised as a squire. For that, he nearly drew the coverlet higher. But she ought to be ill at ease.

Gaenor gasped. "She wears my bliaut! That vile creature wears my bliaut!"

It seemed she did *not* know how to hold her tongue.

"Aye, Daughter," Lady Isobel said, "it is the same you were to wear to receive Lord Harrod who offers for you. Pity you cannot do so lacking a proper gown, hmm?"

That cooled Gaenor. Still, it was obvious she resented the woman in their midst. And neither was Beatrix pleased, though her pique was tempered by youthful curiosity.

Garr waved to the door where Squire Warren lingered. "Out! All of you!" He narrowed his gaze on Annyn. "Except you."

Gripping a kerchief, she remained unmoving as Gaenor and Beatrix exited the chamber ahead of their mother.

"Mother!" Garr called.

She looked around.

"We shall speak on this."

She inclined her head and closed the door.

Silence swelled between Garr and Annyn when their eyes met again. Finally, she stepped forward. "I would speak to you of Rowan. He—"

"—is to know no mercy, just as he knows no honor."

She halted at the foot of the bed. "Jonas was as a son to him. All these years he has believed, as I did, that 'twas you who killed him."

As she had done? No longer did? Telling himself he did not care what she thought, he sat forward, causing the coverlet to fall to his waist. "For the last time"—he winced at the pain that lanced his shoulder—"I say your brother was not killed. Shame was his end."

"You are wrong. I—" She snatched the kerchief to her mouth, turned her head, and coughed into it.

Was she ill? When she looked back, Garr saw the whites of her eyes were red and her cheeks flushed. And her cough had been nearer a bark.

She wiped her nose. "Upon my word, you are wrong."

He should not have allowed Abel to hold her in the tower. As his mother had warned, she was a lady. Of course, no lady he had known could have endured what Annyn had at Wulfen.

She came around the bed. "Pray, Lord Wulfrith—"

"I will not argue it."

"But he is ill."

And she was not? It bothered that she should care so much for the man, and again he wondered if her relationship with Rowan was one of lost innocence. True, her mouth had seemed untried, but that did not mean the rest of her was.

He drew a breath and caught the scent of roses. Shot with a desire to breathe more deeply of her, he berated himself. "'Tis for yourself you ought to plead."

She stepped nearer—within reach. "Then you would have him die there?"

"If that is what the Lord wills."

Anger brightened her eyes. "The Lord did not place him in that... abyss of inhumanity."

Once more, Garr turned his aching hand around an imaginary sword. "He did not, just as He did not make your Rowan loose an arrow on me!" Lord, why did he allow this conversation?

"That I have already explained. I can say no more on it."

"Then do not."

Her eyes sparkled. "Was it truly from you that my brother learned revenge belonged to God? Impossible, for you are without heart, Wulfrith who does not even bear a Christian name—with good reason I am sure."

Garr knew he should let her retaliation pass, but the first lesson taught him refused to hold with this woman. Arm protesting, he clamped a hand around her wrist, dragged her forward, and slapped her hand to his bared chest. "I have a heart, Annyn Bretanne," he bit inches from her face, "though your Rowan would have had it be otherwise."

He heard her sharply indrawn breath, felt its trembling release on his face. In her eyes that he should not be able to read, he saw she remembered the last time they had been so near. As if no ill stood between them, as if her beauty were unsurpassed, as if she were warm and willing to lie down for him, his body stirred to the beat of his heart against her palm.

"Aye"—she slipped a tongue to her lips to moisten them—"but of such a heart one should not boast, Wulfrith."

Garr released her. "I am done with you, Annyn Bretanne."

She straightened. "For how long?"

"For however long it pleases me."

"And then?"

"Then you shall see. Squire Warren!"

The door swung inward and the young man stepped inside.

"The lady is to be allowed the reach of the donjon, and only the donjon. This task I give you and Squire Samuel that you may redeem yourselves. Other than the garderobe, she goes nowhere without attendance."

Dismay flickered in the squire's eyes. "'Twill be done, my lord."

"If she escapes," Garr continued, "your time at Wulfen and Squire Samuel's will be done." He looked to where Annyn stood alongside the bed. "Take your leave and do not trouble my men overly much."

She smiled tightly. "I would not think to."

It vexed Garr that it was the same his mother had replied when he had earlier warned her against testing him, especially as she had then done so.

Annyn crossed the solar and stepped into the corridor.

"Be of good care," Garr warned Warren.

"I assuredly shall, my lord." He closed the door.

Garr sank back against the pillows and squeezed his shoulder. Had he torn the stitches when he seized Annyn? He looked to the bandages. God willing, there would be no seepage, for if he was to recover before Henry descended upon Stern, he could not waste even a day.

Annyn leaned back against the wall for fear she might crumble before Squire Warren. He would like that, but even if it was his due, she would not yield. She pushed off.

"Come." He stepped past her.

Where? Of course, did it matter when her audience with Wulfrith had only gained her scorn? Though she, who had set to motion all that transpired, was once more made a lady, Rowan weakened in that horrible cell. And it seemed there was nothing she could do.

"Lady Annyn!"

She met the squire's impatient gaze.

"Lady Isobel said you are to take the nooning meal with her, and it has begun."

Though Annyn tried to ease the scratch in her throat by swallowing hard, it did not aid. As she followed the squire to the stairs, she coughed into the kerchief and knew she sounded nearly as bad as Rowan.

The mood of the hall altered with her arrival as all pondered and judged her. Still, she did not falter as Squire Warren guided her to the high table where Lady Isobel was seated with her daughters. And farther down the table sat Sir Merrick who allowed her no more than a brooding glance before looking elsewhere.

What was it about him? What did he know? When might she speak with him?

"Sit beside me, Lady Annyn," bid the lady of the castle.

Skirting the table, Annyn looked to Gaenor and Beatrix whose eyes bored through her, then lowered to the bench beside Lady Isobel.

The woman leaned near. "Worry not. God shall deal with my son."

"To what end?"

"Methinks that depends on you." Wulfrith's mother dipped her spoon into the steaming trencher, the contents of which would have made Annyn's mouth moist were she not struck by the realization that the lady might be a valuable ally.

Though Annyn was not allowed to leave the donjon, there was nothing to prevent Lady Isobel from doing so. But how to convince her to aid the one who had nearly killed her son? For whatever reason she had pardoned Annyn—an incredible stretch—surely it would not extend to Rowan. Still, it was his only hope.

Ignoring Gaenor and Beatrix who continued to watch her from the other side of their mother, Annyn scooped stew from the trencher that had appeared before her. For the first time in days, the food she spooned into her mouth was hot, but though it warmed a path to her belly, her guilt that Rowan was not here to savor it bade her to lower her spoon.

"Lady Isobel," she spoke low, "if I could speak to you about Sir Rowan?"

The woman's eyes narrowed. "You press my generosity too far."

Of course she did. "Apologies, my lady." Annyn rolled the spoon's handle between thumb and forefinger while the woman continued to glare at her. Finally, Lady Isobel returned to her meal, but Annyn could not.

She coughed into the kerchief. How her throat ached, first from affecting a man's voice, now from malady. But surely it did not compare to what Rowan suffered in that filthy, dank cell.

Annyn turned again to Lady Isobel. "I am beset with fatigue. If 'twould not offend you, I would seek my rest."

Concern flitted across the woman's face, and she looked to Squire Warren. "See Lady Annyn to Wulfrith's chamber. It shall be hers for the duration of her stay."

The protest that rose to Annyn's lips died with the realization it was not the solar of which the woman spoke, but the chamber in which Annyn had bathed.

Once Annyn was clear of the hall, she breathed out relief. However, at the landing she fell beneath Squire Samuel's regard where he stood outside the solar.

The young man's becoming face was made unbecoming by the scorn that bent his mouth and made slits of his eyes. "My lady," he mocked as she drew even.

Annyn halted and let the spark in her light a fire. "I *am* a lady," she said with her chin high. "A lady that you, with all your training to become the consummate warrior, were too blind to see. A lady that you allowed to steal past you and compromise your lord's safety."

His brow grooved so deeply it nearly made him appear elderly.

"Good eve, Squire Samuel." Annyn stepped past. "Sleep light." She met Squire Warren's livid gaze where he stood a stride ahead. Though her words had not been directed at him, it had fallen as heavily. She did not care. A man might be dying and all the discomfort these two suffered was pricked pride.

As Squire Samuel sputtered at her back, she strode past Wulfrith's first squire.

"Were you the least bit pretty," Samuel's convulsing tongue finally formed words, "you could not have done what you did."

He struck harder than he could know, nearly taking her breath for all these years of knowing she could never measure against her mother's comeliness. Now, finally, someone had spoken it—worse, for the young man was not even comparing her against her mother's profound beauty. Not even pretty...

Annyn's spirit awakened and found good in it. At the door to her chamber, she turned and smiled. "I shall take that as a compliment, Squire Samuel, for if that is all that held this lady from being revealed, it recommends that I, a mere woman, am equal to men as they would not have me believe. Thank you."

Mouths slackening, the young men stared.

Annyn shouldered into the chamber that wafted blessed heat, closed the door, and crossed to the small table beside the bed. She lifted the hand mirror that lay alongside the basin.

The face reflected back at her was one she had always known, though these past years she was less inclined to look upon it— oval, set with dark eyebrows above pale blue eyes that were a bit too large, a small nose flecked with freckles, and an unremarkable mouth.

Pretty, Lady Isobel had said, but she had only been kind.

Annyn spread her lips. Her teeth were her best feature, white and evenly set. The only real difference to be found since last she had looked upon her reflection was the bruise on her cheek. The swan that Uncle Artur had years ago assured her she would become had yet to materialize, meaning it would not.

As she set the mirror back, a tickle rose in her throat. She coughed, wiped her nose, and eyed the bed. She would rest, and in the morn perhaps she would think more clearly on Rowan.

When she curled beneath the coverlet, the cough turned more insistent and summoned an ache between her eyes. Burying herself deeper beneath the covers, she groaned. Such misery!

"What is this?" Garr frowned at the folded garment tossed into his lap.

As eventide deepened, Isobel perched on the mattress edge. "Do you not recognize the tunic over which your mother toiled though she detests needlework?"

What was she plotting? He lifted the garment and saw it was the one he had given to Annyn. "I know it. Why do you bring it to me?"

"Look to the hem."

He did. It was torn, and he was momentarily swept with fury at the possibility one of his men had assaulted Annyn. But Abel would not have allowed it.

"What would you have me see, Mother?"

"From that tunic was taken the cloth that bound your shoulder. Lady Annyn herself tore it to stanch your bleeding."

Annyn who had run with Rowan after the man had put an arrow through him. Garr dropped the garment. "Why do you champion her?"

"When I sought her out in the tower, 'twas with an angry heart, but something…" She shook her head. "She is not as expected."

"Just as she is not Jame Braose." He made no attempt to lighten his loathing. "The woman is a deceiver. She will say and most certainly do whatever best serves her."

Isobel leaned near. "She knows you did not murder her brother, though she has but the evidence of her heart to tell her."

"Heart!"

Isobel laid a hand over his. "You have been too long without prayer. I bid you, go to it and find comfort. Anger will be torn from your eyes that you may see more clearly."

He pulled away from her, and when he spoke, his voice was chill. "Does a bed not await you, Mother?"

Disappointment thinning her mouth, she stood. "Do not let all I taught you ere you were stolen from me be for naught, Garr. Now more than ever you need—"

"I know what I need!" He flexed his stiff fingers. "A sword to hand and an arm to swing swift and sure."

"But going before it must be forgiveness."

He thrust off the pillows. "You dare speak to me of forgiveness when for how many years did you war with my father? Still you wear black when he is dead and buried and can no more be eaten by your longing for another man."

Her eyes dulled as if whatever nibble of light was in her had gone out.

"God's patience," he growled and dropped back onto the pillows. He was once more the young boy whose father had tested his anger and corrected it time and again. He had hurt his mother, and it was wrong, whether by Drogo's law or God's.

"You are right," Isobel said softly. "Thus, who better to advise you to forgive than one who did not and now lives in deepest regret?"

Garr frowned.

She nodded. "Though the day I wed Drogo I vowed to wear black until death parted us, only when he was gone did I realize the wrong I had done him. For that, my son—not revenge—I continue to wear black to remind me of my unpardonable error."

It was the most she had ever spoken of her relationship with his father. Though Garr knew it was not for a Wulfrith to care about such things, he hungered to understand what had happened between the two who had conceived him in bitterness.

A knock sounded, causing his mother to startle. "The physician." She hurried to the door as though she fled the devil himself.

Garr ground his teeth. His injury had waited this long for the man to return from attending an ill villager earlier in the day. It could wait longer. "Mother!"

She pulled the door open and swept past Squire Samuel and the physician.

Tempted as Garr was to vault after her, he knew one could not make a woman talk unless she wished to. And even if one could, it would be wrong to press Isobel further. The little she said had cost her much. If more were to be told, it would have to save for the day of her choosing.

"Your color is better," the physician said as he approached the bed. "How does your shoulder fare?"

"It does not pain me."

The man set his bag on the bed. "Let us see if the stitches hold."

Throughout the examination and redressing of the wound, Garr experienced a restlessness so great he was beseeched a dozen times to be still. A quarter hour later, the physician pronounced that the injury was healing well and withdrew.

Garr looked to the torches and followed their convulsing light that reached to the torn tunic. Was it true Annyn no longer believed him capable of murder? It was as she had alluded when she came to the solar, but perhaps she had said it only to soften him toward Rowan. But if it was true, what then?

He groaned. Mother was right. He was in need of prayer to battle the terrible emotions that threatened to drag him farther and farther from God. He thrust the coverlet back and dropped his feet to the rushes. Though he felt a lightening of the head when he stood, it passed, and he retrieved his robe.

"My lord!" Squire Samuel exclaimed when Garr pulled open the door. "What do you require?"

"Naught." Garr stepped past him. As the chapel was on the floor above, he started for the stairs, but he had not taken two strides when the sound of coughing reached him. He looked around. Only then did he notice Squire Warren outside the chamber that was Garr's when he came to Stern.

His mother had put her in *his* chamber? In the order of things, especially as Annyn was hardly an esteemed guest, it was where Isobel ought to bed for the night.

Garr strode back and halted before Warren who stood with a stiff back and erect chin.

Before Garr could speak, the coughing came again, so raw it struck him with unease. "How long has she been thus?"

The young man shifted his weight. "She was quiet for a time, my lord, but has begun again."

The tower had done it to her. When she had been brought to the solar this morning, he had seen she was ailing, but it had not seemed as serious as the cough now indicated. "The physician has seen her?"

"I think not, my lord, certainly not since she was given into my charge."

Garr glared at the young man. There was still much to be taught him before he earned his spurs. He motioned Squire Warren aside and opened the door.

The brazier was well laid, for it still warmed the chamber, its glow lighting the bed and the lump that was its occupant.

The cough came again, sounding ten-fold worse now that the door was no longer a barrier. Of such things men and women died.

"Send for the physician, Squire Warren." Garr stepped inside and closed the door. As he tread the rushes, the cough subsided. Not until Garr drew alongside the bed did he realize that Annyn was entirely beneath the covers, not a glimpse of dark hair to be seen.

"Annyn?" He strained to catch the rise and fall of her breath, but either there was not enough light to show it, or...

He snatched the covers back and bared the woman who curled in on herself on the same mattress that, in the past, had taken his weight. The thin chemise that damply conformed to her body revealed slim legs, smooth thighs, rounded hips.

Denying the desire that rose in him, Garr bent near, but no nearer did he get.

Annyn coughed so hard she shook, then threw out a hand as if seeking the coverlet.

Lest she open her eyes and construe his presence as concern for her well-being—or an attempt to ravish her—Garr stopped himself from turning the covers over her. Not only was it exceedingly warm in the chamber, but she could retrieve them herself. No sooner did he step back than her lids lifted.

With a cry, she flew up like birds scattered from a thicket, grabbed the coverlet, and dragged it against her chest. "What do you here?" she demanded in a graveled voice.

Garr did not need the light of torches to know her fear. He saw it by the brazier's glow that lit her wide-eyed countenance—felt it in the space that throbbed between them.

She thought he had come to take revenge in her bed. Though he knew he should not fault her, especially considering his reaction to the sight of her, it rankled that she would think it. Never had he taken a woman by force.

Shoulder aching, he crossed his arms over his chest and supported the injured one with a hand beneath. "I am not here for what you believe." And yet still he stirred. Could she not also cover her legs? Not only were her delicately arched feet visible, but her stretch of calves…

She clutched the coverlet up to her chin and tucked her legs beneath so the only bare flesh remaining was of her arms—arms that could draw a man in and hold him tight.

"For what did you come?"

Aye, for what? Not concern. Certainly not that.

She coughed, the terrible sound breaking from deep inside her chest. Bending forward, short dark hair falling over her face, she struggled to clear the sickness from her lungs.

When her heaving subsided, Garr was so tense from forcing himself to remain still he felt as if cast of iron.

Annyn tossed her head back and, eyes teared from the strain of coughing, waited for his answer.

"I came for all the noise you make," he said. "'Tis enough to awaken the dead."

Indignation flashed across her face, but as brief as lightning in the sky, it cleared. "Though you ought to hate me, I do not think you do, Wulfrith."

His ire flared. "You err in trying to know me." He strode across the chamber and slammed the door behind him.

Annyn sighed. Deny it though he did, she felt sure that concern had brought him to her chamber—and desire had held him to it, though, according to Sir Samuel, she was not even pretty. So what was there to tempt Wulfrith? And what had he seen when she lay uncovered?

She pushed a foot out from beneath the coverlet, a calf, a lower thigh. It was a nice enough leg, well-turned, smooth, and proportioned to the rest of her. But as for the rest of her...

She lowered the coverlet and eyed her small chest. Though it was certainly not a boy's, neither was it anything near the bosom her mother had not passed on to her.

Annyn blew out a breath that ended on a cough, fell back, and stared at the ceiling. Concern Wulfrith felt for her, but his desire was surely of a man too long without a woman. And it made her ache.

A knock sounded.

She whipped the covers back over her and lifted her head as a tall, slim man entered.

"My lady, I am physician to the Wulfriths."

Annyn nearly smiled. The man who claimed she could not know him had sent her a healer.

Garr straightened from the wall outside Annyn's chamber and met the man's tired gaze. "Speak."

The physician scowled. "The first I shall speak is that you ought to be abed, my lord."

In prayer was where he ought to be, but from here he would go there. "The Lady Annyn?" He was in no mood to sweeten his demand, especially after his encounter with the woman who claimed to know him.

The physician repositioned his leather bag beneath an arm. "'Tis good you brought her from the tower. Had she remained, she would have…" He shrugged. "'Twould not have boded well."

To Garr's right, Squire Warren shifted. In the quarter hour since the physician had entered Annyn's chamber, he and Squire Samuel had been fed additional lessons that had made their cheeks flush out to their ears.

"The chill has gone to her chest," the physician continued, "but it ought to resolve provided she rests and takes the medicinals I gave her. Of course, 'twould speed her healing if I bled her—"

"You shall not." Healers and their leeches! One of the few things Garr remembered of the past four days was when he had awakened to find worms sucking at his flesh. He had raged until they were removed. Despite the certainty of so many, he did not believe there was benefit to leeching, especially when one had lost as much blood as he had done.

The man inclined his head. "As you wish, my lord. Is there anything else you require?"

"Nay. Good eve."

The physician started to step around him, but paused. "The lady asked that I attend her man who is yet in the tower."

Far too loudly, Garr said, "Should I further require your services, Physician, I shall tell you."

"Aye, my lord."

As his tread receded, Garr silently berated himself for what he must do. But first, prayer.

15

WULFRITH LEFT HER no choice. As for Squire Warren—or was it Samuel who had the guard this morning?—Annyn's regrets were deepest for him. If she succeeded, he would bear Wulfrith's wrath. But better that than a man die.

Three nights past, when the physician left her and she had heard Wulfrith's voice in the corridor—further evidence he was not cold to her—she had been hopeful only to have hope dashed. Though it had been a strain to hear much of the conversation, Wulfrith's refusal to send the physician to Rowan came clear through the door, his anger clear through her heart. Rather than yield to tears, she had made Rowan a promise. And this promise she would keep. Now that an opportunity presented itself and she was fairly recovered, it was time.

She looked to the table on which sat the second of two vials the physician had given her—a sleeping elixir. She glanced at where Josse lay with the coverlet drawn up to her ears. Three days it had taken to gain the young woman's trust, three days of imploring her to accept a goblet of tainted honey milk.

Hating that she'd had to deceive her, Annyn turned. The first vial, concealed beneath the bodice of the garment that Annyn had borrowed from the maid, was a medicinal given to clear her throat and lungs. In anticipation of this day, she had taken only half doses, certain Rowan would need it more than she, praying it was not too late.

She smoothed the brown bliaut to her hips. Fortunately, Josse was nearly as tall as she. Unfortunately, the young woman was gifted with exceptional breasts that required the stuff of hose to make the bodice fit. The irony made Annyn smile bitterly, for once again she took another's identity.

She adjusted the simple circlet on the head veil one last time, swept up the tray of viands that Josse had delivered a half hour earlier, and crossed to the door.

As Squire Warren turned to her, she swept around and closed the door. Head lowered, she hurried past the young man and Squire Samuel where he stood outside the solar, praying neither would ask anything of her, praying she would not tip the tray's contents, telling herself she only imagined the bore of their eyes.

Robert Beaumont had turned, just as Garr had known he would. As formal acknowledgment of Henry's right to the throne, the earl had placed more than thirty fortified castles at the Duke's disposal. It did not bode well for Stephen.

Garr worked his fingers into his temples as the tidings delivered this morning once more distracted him from Stern's journals. He knew what he must do. Had known since that night at Wulfen when Annyn, disguised as Jame Braose, had come to him in the chapel. And Garr's overlord, the indecisive John Newark, from whom the Wulfriths held their barony, awaited the determination. This day, Garr would send a missive.

"My lord!"

Garr looked up from the journals that had suffered his divided attention these past two hours. Squire Samuel's expression saved him the sharp rebuke for not having knocked before entering the solar.

Garr thrust up from the table. "She has escaped?"

"Nay, though she attempts to."

Garr strode forward. "What do you mean?"

Squire Samuel retreated to the corridor to avoid being trod upon. "Squire Warren bid me to tell you that he follows her so you might know her end."

Redemption. Though it would have been easier for Warren to halt whatever she planned, he remembered the lesson that, before acting, one gather as much information as possible about an opponent's intent. Assumptions could be deadly. Of course, so could Annyn's disregard for the physician's order that she stay abed. Fool woman!

"Your mantle, my lord?"

"Nay!" Fortunately, Garr had dressed fully despite the physician's order that he stay abed. "How did she get past?" He descended the stairs with Samuel close behind.

"In the clothes of Lady Isobel's maid, my lord."

First Jame Braose, now Josse. But did it mean Josse betrayed? Nay, Annyn must have overpowered the young woman. "Return to Lady Annyn's chamber and aid Josse in whatever she requires."

"Aye, my lord."

There was an expectant quiet about the hall when Garr stepped into it, and he realized its occupants knew something was afoot. They had seen what Annyn had not—Warren following her.

Isobel rose from the hearth with her daughters. "'Twas she?"

"Aye." Garr strode hard across the hall.

"Your shoulder!" she called.

Garr grunted. His injury was healing fine—would support his sword arm before the fortnight was done.

The porter swung the door wide, and Garr stepped onto the landing. In a moment, his eyes found Squire Warren. Allowing the figure of Annyn Bretanne a lead of thirty feet where she passed beneath the inner portcullis, the young man held alongside the well, then crept after her.

Garr overtook Squire Warren as the young man neared the portcullis.

"My lord, I—"

"I am pleased with you. Now return to the donjon."

"But—"

"I shall follow." Garr watched as Annyn moved through the outer bailey trying to look as if she belonged among the many who worked the stables, the smithy, the carpenter's shop, the piggery, but she did not belong, even garbed in simple clothing.

Knowing she would be called to account for herself before she reached her destination, Garr waved an arm to draw the gaze of a man-at-arms on the outer wall. Gaining it, he pointed to Annyn and shook his head.

When she veered toward the outer tower, Garr was surprised only in that she believed she could escape with Rowan. Even with her training, she could not possibly think to knock the guard senseless, but it seemed so. Not that she would be given the opportunity, for there was no longer a guard over the outer tower.

Feeling like a hunter about to gain his prey, a thrill shot through Garr. However, when Annyn suddenly stopped, he had only enough time to gain the cover of the falconry before she swung around and peered up from beneath the head veil.

Annyn held her breath as she considered the workers in the bailey and the men on the walls who continued on as if her presence was of no consequence. Did she merely imagine being watched?

Praying so, she turned back to the outer tower. As she neared, she dug the vial from her bodice. The guard would likely be in the room at the base of the tower. If all went well, he would ask no questions when she told him the physician had sent her to deliver medicine to the prisoner. If all did not go well, a rock would serve. She gripped tighter that which she had scooped from the inner bailey. Unfortunately, the tower's guard was a large man and one thump to the head might not suffice, but it ought to rattle him enough for her to strike a second time.

When she entered the tower, the guard room was empty. Where was the man? Surely not delivering Rowan victuals, for it was two hours before the nooning meal. With foreboding, she considered the stairway that wound to the bowels of the tower where she had shared a cell with Rowan. It was no longer lit by torches.

Refusing to believe what whispered through her, she carefully picked her way down the steps that, unlit, soon turned to pitch. Hands to the walls, she stepped off the first landing and felt her way down the corridor to the cell where Rowan waited.

"Rowan?" She directed her voice through the grate set high in the door. "'Tis I, Annyn."

No answer, and though she strained, she heard no movement. No breath.

"I have brought you something." She pulled out the vial. "Come to the door and I will hand it through."

Silence. Refusing to listen to the whispers gathering voice within her, she shook her head. "Pray, Rowan, be quick ere someone comes."

Mayhap he was asleep? She dropped the rock and thumped a hand on the door. "Rowan?"

The door creaked open.

No longer whispers, the voices told what she could not bear. "Nay," she breathed. The guard was remiss in his duties, that was all. When she stepped inside, the stench was as bad as when she had passed those first days here.

A scuttle to the left brought her head around. "Rowan?"

The scuttle came again. Blindly, she followed it to the corner where Rowan had laid his pallet. When the straw mattress came underfoot, she dropped to her knees and felt across it. Something warm and furred brushed her fingers and, with a squeak, scampered away.

The slender thread of delusion snapping, Annyn grasped at the frayed ends and told herself Rowan must have taken her pallet for himself since the walls on that side of the cell did not weep as badly. She crossed the cell on trembling legs, but when she lowered to her knees again, she found the pallet was gone.

She sank back on her heels, dropped the vial, and put her face in her hands. While she lay abed in a warm chamber, being fed fine food, her ailments tended by a physician, Rowan was dying. All because of her, because of what she had asked of him. For her he had forsaken his allegiance to Henry, escorted her to Wulfen, and suffered this cell. For her he had died, for one who had betrayed him.

"Forgive me," she gasped. "Pray, forgive me, Rowan."

"You must love him very much," said a harsh voice.

Wulfrith had followed her, but she did not care. Not any more. Though she longed to strike out at him for putting Rowan here, it was she who had done it.

She scrubbed at her damp eyes and opened her lids onto the light of a torch that told the whole truth of the hideous cell.

"Aye." She looked over her shoulder at where Wulfrith filled the doorway, a torch in hand. "I loved him." And she did not care how he construed that.

His eyes narrowed, and on his face was something she would have named jealousy were it cast by any other. "Come."

She looked to her hands in her lap. "When did it happen?"

She heard the rub of the torch as it was placed in the sconce beside the door. Raising her gaze to the wall on which Wulfrith's shadow moved, she saw things in the oozing cracks that would have made all of her creep if not for grief. First Jonas, then Uncle, now Rowan.

Wulfrith halted at her back. "You should not be here."

She turned her head and peered up his imposing figure. "If you recall, I *was* here, as was Rowan."

"And now he is not. Come."

She drew a deep breath. "If you can find it in your heart, and I know you have one, I would ask that you allow me to be alone."

A muscle in his jaw jerked. "You need to see what I have to show you." He reached a hand to her.

She looked at his large palm and fingers and hated herself for remembering the feel of them in so terrible a circumstance.

"Now, Annyn."

Resenting that he should deny her such a small thing, she ignored the hand he offered and stood. As she turned to face him, her foot sent the vial rolling across the floor.

Wulfrith picked it from the filth. "'Twas for this you came to the tower? To bring him medicine intended for you?"

Incensed that he should begrudge Rowan relief—a chance of survival—she stepped forward. "You speak God, you pray God, but do you live God, oh mighty Wulfrith?"

His nostrils flared and lips thinned, but she did not care. Why should she when there was nothing left in this world to care about?

"Do you?" she demanded.

She felt his breath on her face, the air trembling between their bodies as if it feared to be near them.

"Answer me!"

Black was the color of his eyes, the grey and green having fled in the wake of anger. But he said nothing.

She slapped a hand to his chest. "Are you in there?"

Still as stone. Would one more push unhorse him? Two? "A warrior," she scorned. "Nay, a man who allows others to choose his path."

That should loose him, but it did not.

She squeezed her hands into fists and pounded his chest.

He stood through her assault as if it was her due. However, when her fist struck his shoulder and he jerked, she realized what she did. Cheeks wet as if she had turned her face up to rain, she blinked at where he hunched with a hand to his shoulder.

"I . . ." What words would not sound hollow? She shook her head. "It seems I do harm to all I touch. Pray, forgive me. 'Tis grief that makes me behave so."

He lifted his hand from his shoulder and considered it.

Was there blood? Had she caused his wound to open?

"You have naught to grieve," he said, cold as the dead, "not this day."

What did he mean? That Rowan was not worth grieving? Or . . .

"What do you say?" Annyn called as he strode from the cell, but he did not answer.

She hastened after him, not realizing she should have brought the torch until she was on the darkened stairs. Hand to the wall, she felt her way up and found light at the top.

Wulfrith was not there. She hurried past the guard room into the bailey where he strode toward the drawbridge of the inner bailey, his large form moving past the others as if he was the only man among boys. Then he passed from sight.

Ignoring those who stared after her, Annyn ran. As she came out from beneath the portcullis, she caught sight of Wulfrith, but only for a moment before he disappeared into one of two towers flanking the drawbridge. She entered moments later and drew up short before a man-at-arms whose broad face was spread with a nose nearly as broad.

"The topmost floor, my lady," he said, stepping aside.

She snatched up Josse's skirts and mounted the stairs.

It was four floors to the top, four that made her weakened lungs nearly breathless. And there was Wulfrith alongside the guard who had stood watch over her and Rowan in that hideous cell.

"See for yourself." His voice was nearly emotionless.

She looked to the door that lay to the left of him. "Truly?"

He stared.

She hurried forward and pushed the door inward. The room was dim, though compared to the cell, it glowed. A glimpse was all that was required to see it was comfortably settled with fresh rushes, table and basin, a chair, and a bed.

"Rowan," she breathed and crossed the room.

He slept, his face turned to the narrow window from which the oilcloth had been removed to let in fresh air.

She touched his brow. It was cool, meaning the fever had passed. Realizing her prayer was answered, she shuddered. God had not denied her—had moved Wulfrith to bring him out of the cell as she had asked. Had she any remaining doubts about Wulfrith's innocence, they blew away like leaves in the wind. He was a man of honor. A man who, in spite of the anger she provoked, lived God as she had told he did not.

Tears squeezed out from beneath her lids. She had wronged him, from the beginning had put sins upon him that, if they belonged to any, belonged to her.

"Annyn?"

She opened her eyes.

Gaze muddied from sleep, Rowan said, "The physician told me you were well. I am...pleased to see it."

Then he had put aside his anger over her betrayal? She pressed her lips to his weathered cheek. "How do you fare, old friend?"

"Better than I did in that accursed cell."

"I am also pleased." She reached to the gaping tunic that fell off his shoulder, but when her gaze fell upon a familiar mark beneath his collarbone, she stilled and touched the V-shaped mark of birth.

"Do not!" Rowan thrust her hand aside and dragged the tunic over it.

Annyn took a step back, blinking as the past sprang to the present, all that was known to her scattering such that she feared she might never know it again.

"Ah, nay," she breathed. Mere happenstance that Jonas had also carried the mark? Only a fool would believe that. She met Rowan's urgent gaze. "You and Jonas? My mother?"

Chest rising and falling rapidly, he stared.

It had been there all along—in Rowan's utter devotion to her brother, his love for Jonas that had come no nearer her than kindness, his jealousy over Uncle's feelings for her mother, his feelings for her mother revealed, the arrow he had put through Wulfrith as a father would have done to one he believed had murdered his son.

Rowan groaned, and the hand holding his tunic to his throat flopped to the mattress. "'Tis true."

Beyond Rowan, she saw the doorway fill with Wulfrith, but it was Rowan who held her, Rowan who had known her mother as Annyn's father had known her, Rowan who had sought Lady Elena's attentions and, it seemed, never received more than a grateful nod. But at least once he had lain with her.

She retreated until the backs of her knees came up against the chair. Clenching her hands, she said, "I do not understand."

He momentarily closed his eyes. "You do not understand because your mother, like you, never knew."

"How could she not?"

"Always she drank too much, all for love of a man denied her by marriage to your father."

"Uncle Artur."

"Aye," Rowan growled. "And none knew, none but your mother and him." He rubbed a hand across his face. "Do you know how long I have hated the Wulfriths?"

What had they to do with this? Annyn glanced at the doorway from which Wulfrith had not moved. Did Rowan know they were not alone? That the one of whom he spoke listened? Likely not, for the bed was positioned such that he would have to turn his head to see Wulfrith. And his attention was all on her.

She reached behind and gripped the chair with one hand.

"I have hated them since Drogo—and Artur—came to the castle that long ago winter day while your father was absent." He looked to the window beyond her and cleared his throat. "Time and again, Elena called for her goblet to be topped, leaned near Drogo, smiled and laughed, touched his sleeve. I was near mad with jealousy, and so I also drank."

He fell silent, and time interminable passed. Finally, tears wetting his eyes, he said, "That night I went to the solar to tell her of my love, but ere I could raise a hand to the door, I heard her laughter—and Drogo's, I thought."

Annyn felt herself into the chair.

"Telling myself she was but a harlot, I returned to the hall and filled my tankard, how many times I do not know." He jerked his gaze to Annyn, causing a tear to slip onto his cheek. "I was drunk when I did it."

Lord, not that. Pray, not that. "What?"

"I returned to kill Wulfrith for having her as only a husband should." Gaze imploring, he pushed to sitting. "But when I entered the solar, she was alone. She was smiling in her sleep, and it was then I...determined to have her myself."

Not Rowan who had cared for her, protected her, soothed her fears, taught her to hunt, to ride, to swing a sword. Not Rowan whom she loved as she had not loved her own father.

"I put out the torch and went to her." His voice was muffled where he spoke behind the hand gripping his face. "She whispered words of love that I told myself were for me." He braved her gaze. "She never knew, Annyn, and I never told, not even when Jonas was born bearing the mark that most males of my family bear."

Annyn felt ill, her mouth so dry it was a long time before she found her voice. "You violated my mother."

Regret turned down his mouth. "I did, and I have lived every hour of every day repenting."

Had she the strength, Annyn would have fled, but she did not. All lies, nothing to hold to in a storm. She squeezed her arms against her sides. Only minutes ago, such gratitude she had felt to discover God had answered her prayer for Rowan, that He *did* hear her. But for this? That she might know such pain and loathing?

"Though I hated myself," Rowan broke into her thoughts, "I exalted in knowing Jonas was mine, that the strength of my manhood had surpassed the all-powerful Wulfrith."

"But not Drogo Wulfrith," Annyn spoke low. "Uncle Artur."

"Aye, Artur who must have believed all these years that Jonas was his."

Rowan and Artur, Artur and Rowan, both loving Elena, both loving Jonas. "Did my brother know?"

Rowan's eyes snapped. "And have him look at me as you do? I could not have borne it."

As she was to bear all that was revealed this day. She considered her hands in her lap.

Refuge in God, she reminded herself, though she longed to rail at Him, even to deny Him. *The Lord is my light and salvation.*

"Now you know why I could not love you as I did Jonas."

Aye, and wished she did not. She lifted herself out of the chair.

"I pray you will not hate me too long," Rowan choked. "That one day you will forgive me."

She looked to Wulfrith who watched her. Was that pity in his eyes? Whatever it was, it made her long for his anger.

"Annyn?"

She returned her gaze to Rowan whom she should hate, but could not if she were to hold to God who was all that might keep her tattered raft from sinking. "I am done with hating, Rowan. There is no good in it. Only pain." And what pain! She stepped around the bed.

"You will come again?"

At the doorway where Wulfrith stood, she looked around and glimpsed Rowan's distress at realizing his confession had an audience of two. "Methinks it best that I do not." She turned back before she was made to further suffer Rowan's pain. Finding Wulfrith had stepped aside, she averted her gaze and crossed the threshold.

The guard was no longer outside the room, and she guessed Wulfrith had sent him away when Rowan's tale began. Grateful, she stepped onto the stairs and began her descent that seemed to mirror the descent of her soul.

Garr stared after her. *Curse Rowan!* However, when he looked to the man, Rowan's shame and misery pulled at him, especially now that Garr understood the reason he had taken the arrow. Any father would want punishment given to the one believed to have murdered his child.

Grudgingly, Garr inclined his head. "This shall go no further."

Rowan stared.

Garr closed the door and strode to the stairs. Just down from the second landing, he nearly trod on Annyn where she sat tight against the wall. She surely knew she was no longer alone, but she gave no indication of it.

Garr lowered himself onto the step beside her. "Annyn?"

She clasped her hands tighter.

He knew she suffered, and he told himself he should not concern himself, but he could not walk away. He caught her chin and urged her face around. Though she lowered her gaze, he glimpsed pain that carved him up like a pig to slaughter. How could this woman, whom he had longest known as a man, do such to him? It was not for a warrior to be so affected.

"Your wounds will heal," he heard himself say.

When she looked up, there were tears as he had known there would be. "As your wounds heal?"

The injury done him by Rowan was not all to which she referred. Indeed, it was as if she saw through him to the young boy torn between mother and father, and he was struck by the realization that they shared a past of being born to a loveless marriage. But then, marriages were first made of alliance. Few were made of love.

"Eventually," he said, "all wounds that do not kill, heal, though the scarring may be unsightly."

She caught her bottom lip between those neat white teeth that had marked him all those days ago. "I have wronged you. Still I say my brother was murdered, but I know 'twas not you who did it."

From her own lips, the words he had not known he longed to hear.

"For that, and the injury done you, I am sorry, but I will not burden you by asking for your forgiveness after all that has happened."

As she could not forgive Rowan, so she believed Garr would be unable to forgive her. He leaned nearer. "What *will* you ask of me, Annyn?"

"But one thing. Nay, two."

"Tell me."

She searched his eyes. "Release me."

He should have known. "And the other thing?" he asked too gruffly.

"And Rowan as well."

Then she forgave the man for what he had done to her mother? "Why Rowan?" Though he now knew she and the knight were not intimate, still it gripped him that she cared for the man.

She smiled bitterly. "You hold him for something of my doing. As for his sins, they are of the past, and for them he should not be held accountable to you."

She could not have spoken truer, though it surprised Garr that at least a portion of the vengeance that had set her to taking his life did not now turn to Rowan. But then, she had said she was done hating. "If I give you what you ask, you will leave here with Rowan?"

"Nay, I will go alone."

Because she *was* alone. These past weeks had nearly broken her. Now the only things left to her were Duke Henry's anger and marriage to Lavonne. And Garr did not need to know her better to realize that not even for the comfort of home and privilege of the nobility would she give herself to them. "Where would you go?"

"I do not know."

He would give her coin and an escort to see her safe to wherever she chose to flee, he determined. Their quarrel was done.

"Will you grant me this, Wulfrith?"

It was near his lips to agree, but he could not say it, not with her skin so soft beneath his calloused fingers. "I shall think on it."

The glimmer in her eyes extinguished. "Then still you will revenge yourself upon me?"

"Nay, Annyn. The tale has been full told, and though you do not ask for my forgiveness, I give it and accept responsibility for the lie that began it."

"Then why will you not release me?"

"Lesson fourteen—be slow to make decisions of great import."

Indignation flared in her eyes, proof that all she had learned this day had not broken her. She pulled her chin from his grasp and began to rise. "I am no longer your pupil, Lord Wulfrith. There is naught else you can teach me that I need to know."

Better she was angry than beset—at least, that was what Garr told himself to excuse what he did next. He stood, caught her arm, and pressed her back against the stairwell wall. "Is there not?"

She jerked her head back, causing the circlet to slip from her head veil and ring stair to stair on its descent. "Let me go!"

He had heard that before and made the mistake of yielding, which had seen an arrow put through him. He looked to her mouth and remembered it as if it were only yesterday he had first tasted its sweetness. "Is that what you truly wish, Annyn? For me to let you go?"

Her gaze wavered.

Garr drew the skewed veil from her hair, pushed a hand through the silken black strands, and gripped the back of her head. The moment his lips touched hers, she shuddered and gave her breath to him.

He tilted his head to more fully possess her, and beneath the urging of his mouth, she parted her lips and whispered, "Wulfrith."

It was not what he wished to hear. He wanted her to call him as no woman he had known had called him. "I am Garr," he said.

"Garr," she whispered, then slid her hands up his chest, wound them around his neck, and urged him nearer with a desperation that should have given him pause. He wanted her more than he could remember wanting any woman, even his first who had cost him—

Opening his eyes, he saw Annyn's lashes were moist with tears. And cursed himself for taking advantage of her battered emotions. She was no harlot. She was a lady, albeit unlike any he had met. And certainly he had never touched any lady as he now touched Annyn, having always slaked his need on those whose profession it was to pleasure a man.

When she finally opened her eyes, he raised a hand to her bruised cheek and gently swept the moisture from it. "You are right, you ought to be alone," he acceded what he had denied her when she had believed Rowan was dead.

He pulled her hands from his neck, stepped back, and stiffly bowed. "Once more, I apologize for my behavior. It seems I have been too long without a woman."

He could not have said anything more hurtful. Pained by what she perceived was regret at having lowered himself to one as undesirable as she, Annyn swung her palm against his cheek. "Then find yourself one and do not touch me again."

Jaw convulsing, Garr said, "As you wish, my lady."

Choking down the knot in her throat, she turned and somehow made it to the base of the tower without putting her heels over her head.

As she started for the doorway, the jailer stepped out of the shadows and offered the circlet that had fixed her veil in place—the same veil that now lay somewhere upon the stairs. "Yours, my lady?"

Embarrassment warming her for what he must think—nay, what he knew—had happened, she snatched the circlet and hastened outside.

As she traversed the bailey to the donjon, Rowan's sins, beget by her mother and uncle's sin of cuckoldry, drove a pike through her. Though her mother had often been distant, absorbed by something not understood until now, and she had been unable to hide her favoring of Jonas, Annyn had loved her. No arms comforted more, no words soothed better. But the lie Elena had lived, the deceit...

It hurt a deep path through Annyn. Was all the world made of such people? Were there none who lived a straight course? Who spoke true?

Not that she was one to judge, Annyn chastened herself for the guile she had worked at Wulfen. Indeed, it seemed she was spun of the same thread as those whose falsehoods now burdened her. Yet, at that moment, what she would not do to crawl into her mother's lap and bury her face against Elena's breasts.

Rising above the memory of the last time those elegant arms fit around her, Annyn's gaze fell to the horses before the steps, the reins of which were held by a single squire.

She faltered, causing the dirt to cloud up around her skirts. Someone had come to Stern, meaning she must go past them to gain her chamber.

Scrubbing the back of a hand across her cheeks as she neared the steps, she wondered whence the tears had come when Garr—Wulfrith!—had kissed her. Her tumultuous emotions that had first mourned Rowan?

Her revulsion for him shortly thereafter? The benevolence of Wulfrith's forgiveness? Her frustration when he had put another lesson to her? The passion, desire, turning and churning of once more knowing his touch?

All these things and more, though the tears that now threatened were for his rejection. Her mother's daughter she might be, but none would know it to look upon her.

Hearing Garr call to his men, Annyn quickly ascended the steps. However, he must have taken them two at a time, for no sooner did she step past the porter than he appeared at her side.

"Your veil." He thrust the material at her.

She accepted it, but did not settle it atop her head. It was too late, for she had already fallen beneath the regard of most in the hall, including Lady Isobel, her daughters, Sir Merrick, and Squires Warren, Samuel, and Charles.

Garr lengthened his stride, distancing himself from her as he crossed to the dais before which two men stood.

"Here now," Abel said, stepping past the men, "the Baron Wulfrith is returned."

Who were they? Dreading the answer, Annyn halted before an alcove and tightly gripped the circlet and veil.

"My lord," the tallest of the visitors said when Wulfrith stood before them, "I am Sir Christienne, come with Sir Drake to deliver tidings from Duke Henry."

Annyn hardly dared breathe.

"Sir Christienne," Garr acknowledged, "Sir Drake, what are these tidings?"

No offer of drink, nor of a seat to ease the ache of their long ride. Doubtless, they noticed the lack of hospitality. But then, until Garr decided which side he would join, they were the enemy.

"Duke Henry shall arrive at Stern in a fortnight," Sir Drake answered. "He bids us to tell you there are three things he requires."

"First?" Garr clipped.

"Your allegiance, my lord."

"Next?"

"Sir Rowan, who is to bound up as a traitor for aiding Lady Annyn Bretanne in her flight from Castle Lillia."

Annyn clenched the circlet so tight the metal gave. In spite of Rowan's confession that had so reviled, she would not have him suffer more. She looked to where Garr stood with his back to her.

"Last?" he prompted.

"That you deliver Lady Annyn Bretanne who has been given to be Baron Lavonne's betrothed."

Though Annyn was not surprised, she felt as if a dagger rent her innards. Garr had said he would think on letting her go, but in that moment she knew he would not. Those who held against Henry's rule would lose everything once he came to power.

Ignoring Lady Isobel's gaze, Annyn awaited Garr's acquiescence.

"Tell Duke Henry that the Baron Wulfrith grants him leave to come unto Stern Castle."

Annyn caught her breath at so bold a message to one who would soon be his overlord. His king.

Sir Christienne stepped forward. "That is the message you would have us deliver, my lord?"

"Exactly as spoken."

Finally, the knight said, "Aye, my lord. Now what do you say to the Duke's demands?"

"That I shall give answer myself when he arrives."

"But my lord, Duke Henry would know—"

"Exactly as spoken, Sir Christienne!"

The man inclined his head. "As spoken, my lord."

Garr motioned to a serving wench who hovered near a sideboard. "Ale for these men that they might refresh themselves ere their return journey a quarter hour hence."

Annyn startled. A quarter hour? That was all he gave? Of course it was. They had served their purpose and he was done with them.

She stared at Garr's profile, but as the memory of his kiss sought her out, she retreated to the stairs. Halfway up, she realized she was not alone and, looking around, saw that Squire Warren followed.

With a self-satisfied smile, he raised an eyebrow that told how Garr had learned she had gone missing. Had she fooled Warren, he would not be so light of mouth. "What was it that revealed me?" she asked.

He pointed to the hem of her bliaut. "Though Josse is not a lady, she would not allow her ankles to show."

But Annyn Betanne, who had pretended to be a man, had no such qualms. Worse, on the stairway she had allowed Garr—

How was it that having known and thought of him all these years as "Wulfrith" she so suddenly accepted his Christian name? Because of a kiss he would have given any harlot?

"Too"—Squire Warren glanced at her bodice—"her...uh, Josse bounces when she walks."

As the hose could not do. She smiled tightly. "Most observant, Squire Warren. I am pleased that some good came of my having outwitted you and Squire Samuel at Wulfen."

As his humor paled, Annyn turned up the stairs. It was time to return Josse's bliaut.

16

SHE WOULD NO longer hide in her chamber. Knees sore from kneeling amid the rushes, hands cramped from clasping them hard before her, throat tight from all the words she had given to God's ear, she gripped the bed post and pulled herself up.

She glanced heavenward. "I lay it at your feet, Lord. At least, I shall try." Pained that her faith was not stronger, she crossed the chamber. When she opened the door, Squire Samuel frowned over her.

"There is something you require, my lady?"

She smoothed the bodice of Gaenor's bliaut that fit better than Josse's and tried not to think on the maid's indignation that had awaited her upon her return to the chamber. "Aye, you may see me to the hall for supper."

"A tray is to be brought to you."

Though tempted to turn back, she stepped past him. "You are coming?"

He muttered something and followed.

Conversation was at its height when Annyn entered the great hall, but when attention turned to her, a hush fell.

Advancing on the high table where Garr reigned, she briefly met his narrowed gaze before searching out a place for herself. A bit of bench was between Beatrix and Sir Merrick, but as she settled between the two, Beatrix scooted nearer her sister. And not likely out of kindness.

Keeping her chin up, Annyn clasped her hands on the table edge to await the arrival of her trencher.

"You may share mine," Sir Merrick offered. He pushed it between them and motioned to a serving wench.

Once more bothered by the feeling he knew something of Jonas's death, she said, "I thank you."

As the din of the hall was slow to resume, she looked to the nearest of the lower tables and met the stare of a man there. He shifted his gaze to the trencher he shared with another. That man also looked away, and the next. By the time the serving wench delivered a spoon to Annyn and a goblet of wine, nearly all feigned an interest in something or someone else.

"You are much improved, my lady?" Sir Merrick asked as she scooted her spoon around the trencher.

She nabbed a piece of venison. "I am. How do you fare, Sir Merrick?"

"Well."

And yet the deep shadows beneath his eyes told otherwise. As he searched out the trencher, she wondered how best to broach the subject of Jonas. Straight on. "Did you kindly regard my brother, Sir Merrick?"

His spoon paused above the trencher.

"Ah, you did not." Hopefully, that would move him.

He lowered his spoon. "Aye, I did. We squired together under Lord Wulfrith."

She forced herself to dip her spoon again. "Then you were at Lincolnshire with him."

"Why do you ask, Lady Annyn?"

She met his gaze. "That I might know how he died."

He returned his attention to the trencher.

"Do you know, Sir Merrick?"

"Lord Wulfrith did not do it," he finally spoke.

She laid a hand on his arm. "Nor did Jonas."

"In that you are right."

He knew! She waited for the rest, to finally learn who had murdered her brother, but he resumed his search of the trencher.

Annyn gripped his arm. "Will you tell me?"

"I cannot tell what I do not know, Lady Annyn."

"But you said—"

"I did, but that is all I have to tell." He took another bite of stew before returning his gaze to her. "As Lord Wulfrith is not one to murder, neither was your brother one to take his own life. One need not have been present at the hanging to know that."

There had to be more.

He looked past her and frowned. "Lord Wulfrith does not like your hand upon me, my lady. Pray, spare me his jealousy and remove it."

Annyn looked into Garr's fierce eyes where he sat half a dozen up from her. Was it jealousy that shone from him? Jealousy when he did not want her?

"Lady Annyn?" Sir Merrick reminded her of her hand.

She looked back around. "May we speak again?"

"I shall be leaving soon."

Then he was returning to Wulfen. "Before you leave?"

"Perhaps, though there is naught more to tell."

Feeling as if she released a lifeline, Annyn drew her hand from him.

Garr stared. He did not like it, especially the unsettling emotion it caused to beat within his breast. Of what had the two spoken that Annyn thought to lay her hand on Merrick? What required that her head be so near his? He did not like it at all. She should have remained abovestairs where it was easier to clear his mind of her, but she had come down with her chin up and Gaenor's bliaut sweeping curves his hands remembered.

He tightened his hold on his meat dagger. There was something about Annyn Bretanne that stuck to him and would not be brushed off. He wanted to slide his fingers through silken strands so black they knew no sliver of moon and teach her soft mouth to give as it took.

By faith! I lust! And for a woman promised to another. Once more reminded of Duke Henry's demands, he ground his teeth. Though the first demand was decided, all three were required.

He rose and, when those in the hall looked up with dismay at the possibility their meal was at an end, said, "Continue." Ignoring his mother's gaze as he strode past her, he glanced again at Annyn and Merrick. There was little space between them, but he was pleased to see they no longer conversed.

Though Annyn's back stiffened when he passed behind her, she did not look around, and for that he was grateful. He was uncomfortable enough without having her blue eyes further stir him.

He crossed the hall, ascended the stairs, and entered the chapel.

Annyn longed for her chamber, but she knew she would find no escape there from Rowan's revelations though she endeavored to lay them at God's feet. Too, neither would she find insight into what Sir Merrick would not reveal. Thus, she forced herself to remain seated on the bench before the hearth in hopes that Sir Merrick might free himself from the men who had gathered to boast of swords and destriers. Would he ever? And what of Garr? Might he return to the hall?

She looked to Lady Isobel who sat opposite with a daughter on either side. Though the woman had been somewhat abrupt this evening, doubtless due to the deception worked on Josse, she persisted in her attempt to pull Annyn into a discussion. But Annyn knew little of needlework to which the three Wulfriths applied themselves. She had always found hunting and weapons more interesting. Not that she couldn't run a stitch to cloth. Or could she? It had been so long.

"You are sure you would not like to work a piece of cloth, Lady Annyn?" Lady Isobel offered again, the foreign lilt of her voice soothing.

And enjoy herself as much as they? Truly, none of them appeared to delight in the task of plying needle and thread. It had to be something they did because it was expected—while men enjoyed themselves.

Annyn shook her head. "Needlework is the lesser of my talents."

Gaenor's head came up from the sleeve of a bliaut to which she applied flowers and vining leaves. "What are the greater of your talents, my lady?"

Her mockery made a fine point on the air, causing Beatrix to giggle. "I hear, Sister"—she grinned—"'tis the things of men at which she excels." She slid her gaze to Annyn. "Is that not so, *my lady?*"

"Beatrix!" Lady Isobel admonished.

Though touched with embarrassment, Annyn told herself it was not for her to feel. She had been wrong in avenging Jonas, but at least her life had more purpose than poking and prodding a needle, tugging and jerking a thread, and suffering snags and snarled stitches. She smiled. "Most assuredly, Lady Beatrix."

Disappointment at missing her mark caused the young woman's pretty mouth to slouch.

"Then we make for poor company, Lady Annyn?" Gaenor tried again. "No doubt you would prefer the talk of men to the gaggle of women over needles."

True.

"That is enough!" Color suffused Lady Isobel's face.

Her older daughter lowered her gaze and shifted her graceless figure on the bench.

Though stung by Gaenor's attempt to humiliate, Annyn took pity on the young woman who reminded her of herself of years past. Still, there was promise in Garr's sister. Given a few more years, she could be most becoming—if she ceased stooping her shoulders in an attempt to subtract from her height and smiled rather than scowled.

"Actually," Annyn said, "what I would prefer is a game of dice."

A snort sounded from where Squire Samuel stood at her back, but it did not compare to Lady Isobel's wide-eyed dismay. "Dice, Lady Annyn?"

Realizing she had delivered Gaenor from her mother's wrath only to turn it on herself, Annyn regretted her choice for lightening the mood. Of course, she *did* like dicing, a game Uncle had taught her, though he had muttered over and again that he should not. It was one thing for a man to play the "sinful" game in opposition to the preachings of the Church, but far another for a woman to do so.

Annyn knew it would be best to say she jested but she decided against retreat. Decried for having disguised herself as Jame Braose, then Josse, henceforth she would simply be herself. And Lady Annyn Bretanne of the Barony of Aillil liked the casting of dice. "Aye, Lady Isobel, dice—also known as God's game."

"God's game?" Gaenor and Beatrix exclaimed.

Isobel dropped her needlework. "Surely I did not hear what I think I did."

Annyn sat forward. "Does not chance belong to Providence, my lady?"

Garr's mother seemed to consider it but shook her head. "I shall not abide this talk of dice being of God."

What was it Uncle had used to quiet his own conscience? "But surely you know from Bible readings that the Apostles cast lots to select the successor to Judas?"

Again, her words gave Lady Isobel pause, and again the woman shook her head. "The choice of a successor is far different from the wagering of coin that all know to be the daily ruin of nobles and villeins."

"On that I agree, but coin does not need to be wagered to enjoy the game. Indeed, many times I have played for the plumpest apple, the sweetest tart"—she eyed the needlework in Gaenor's lap—"so that another would undertake the task of sewing and mending."

Like a torch brought to darkness, Gaenor brightened and, in that moment, fulfilled some of the promise of the woman she would become. "Tell, Lady Annyn, how is dice played?"

"Gaenor!" Lady Isobel protested.

Lest the young woman's light blow out, Annyn stood. "Why tell you when I can more easily show you?"

"What?" Lady Isobel shrilled.

Putting all from her—Jonas, Garr, Rowan, the loom of Duke Henry and Lavonne—vowing this night she would find some enjoyment, Annyn smiled at Squire Samuel as she stepped around him.

"I require three dice," she announced as she advanced on the dozen men gathered before the dais.

Their ranks parting, they stared disbelievingly at her.

Annyn looked from one to the next. She skipped over Sir Merrick, Squires Charles and Warren, and paused on Garr's brother. "Surely you carry dice, Sir Abel."

"Surely he does not," Lady Isobel said. "There is no gambling at Stern."

Men were men regardless of the rules, and something told her Sir Abel was far from the exception. As Garr's mother drew alongside, Annyn looked to Abel's belt. "Kindly open your purse, Sir Abel, and lend me your dice."

All around, it was so still she thought she heard the color spot his cheeks, but he spread his purse strings.

"Abel!" his mother rebuked.

He smiled apologetically. "Surely you do not mistake me for your eldest son, Mother." He picked three dice from his purse that likely held a total of six to play the other games of dice.

"Thank you," Annyn said when he dropped them in her palm. She returned to the hearth where Gaenor and Beatrix were failing in their attempt to look less than eager. "Now what shall you wager your sister, Lady Gaenor?"

The young woman's gaze went to where her mother surely shone her disapproval, but at least Lady Isobel was not calling a halt to it. Because she was also curious?

"Tell, Lady Gaenor," Annyn prompted.

She looked to Beatrix. "If I win, you shall finish my embroidery. If you win, I shall set the sleeve of your chainse."

It hardly seemed a fair wager, but Beatrix proved shrewd. "Both sleeves and the hem."

"You agree, Lady Gaenor?" Annyn asked.

"Aye."

"Then let us try a few casts." Annyn cleared the rushes. "We shall begin with a game called raffle. The winner is the one whose dice—all three—land alike."

"All three?" Beatrix exclaimed.

Annyn waved the sisters forward. "It may take some time, but it makes for excitement."

Thus, with Lady Isobel and the men looking on, Garr's sisters first cast lots.

He would not have believed it had he not come upon it himself. But there it was—dice played at Stern—and presiding over it was Annyn Bretanne. On her knees before the hearth, surrounded by a score of men and women that included Garr's mother and sisters, she scooped the dice from the floor and looked to Squire Charles who rested on his haunches across from her.

"They roll best if you blow on them." She cupped her hands to her mouth and blew while those all around chuckled. Even Lady Isobel allowed a small smile.

Though outrage was Garr's first reaction to this violation of his family home, something kept him from bellowing a halt to it. Annyn's smile? The glee that lit her face following her roll? Beatrix and Gaenor who hovered near, countenances illuminated as he had never seen them? The air of revel over the hall that was usually grave? Whatever it was, it appealed to something he did not dare try to understand.

Annyn sat back on her heels. "Do you think you can do better, Squire Charles?"

The young man puffed himself up. "A man can always do better."

Her smile showed beautiful teeth, turning her more comely than Garr had thought her. "Then you say Sir Abel is not a man?" she baited.

Meaning Everard was not the only one to whom Abel lost. Amid Charles's sputtering, Garr searched out his younger brother. He stood near Isobel, arms crossed over his chest and brow furrowed.

"Of course not," Charles finally managed, having lost much of his puff. "What I meant was—"

"Roll the dice, Squire Charles," Abel snapped.

"Aye, my lord."

The dice did not fall well for the young man, as evidenced by a murmur and titter. He stood. "You win, my lady. I shall no longer scowl at you."

That was their wager? And what if Annyn had lost the roll?

"I am much obliged, Squire Charles. Who is next? Sir Merrick?"

The levity rarely seen on the knight's face departed. "I am content to watch, my lady."

Annyn rose. "But a simple wager, Sir Merrick. If you win the roll, I vow to no longer bother you with silly questions. But if I win, you shall indulge me with an answer to that which I put to you this eve."

What had she put to him?

The muscle in Merrick's jaw quickening, he said, "I do not wager women."

She turned to those gathered around. "Mayhap one of these men will play my wager for me."

"Still I will not accept."

She put her hands on her hips and swung back around. In doing so, her gaze swept over Garr and, an instant later, returned to him. Eyes large and round, her expression caused the others to follow where she looked and vent muffled groans.

Garr stepped from the stairs. "'Tis you who are responsible for this abomination in my hall, Lady Annyn?"

She clasped her hands at her waist. "No other, my lord."

He strode through the space made for him. "Were you not told gaming is forbidden at Stern?"

She moistened her lips. "I assure you, not a coin has passed hands this eve. It has all been in fun."

As he stared at her, he felt a stirring that mocked the long hour spent on his knees in the chapel. If he lost his soul, it would surely be over this woman.

He considered the three dice that had rolled a one, a four, and a five, and found himself wondering what Annyn would wager him. Though he fought the urge, he scooped the dice to hand and turned them.

"A wager, my lord?" Annyn asked, pulling a murmur from the others.

In her eyes, Garr saw her expectation that he would refuse. "I accept."

"Oh. Very well. What shall it be?"

He looked to her lips and immediately tossed out the unseemly. Distance was what he required of Annyn Bretanne, not a meshing of mouths. "If I win, you are to conduct no more gambling in my hall."

Was that Gaenor who grumbled at his back?

Annyn's lips tightened. "I accept."

"Your wager, Lady Annyn?"

"If I win, you shall take the guard from my person that I may move freely about the castle."

He nearly smiled. There was nothing to lose, for he had decided just that before leaving the chapel. "I accept. One roll each, the highest being the winner."

She held out a hand. "A lady always rolls first."

He raised an eyebrow. "Whence comes such rules for a game expressly forbidden women?"

She beckoned for the dice. "My game, my rules, Lord Wulfrith."

"Indeed." He dropped the dice into her palm.

She knelt and shook the dice. The resulting spill landed a six, a five, and a three.

"Fourteen," Beatrix called.

Garr bent, swept up the dice, and cast the ivory cubes. They settled to a four and two fives.

"Also fourteen," Gaenor called.

"Lo!" Abel piped. "You and the lady are well matched, Brother."

Garr knew what he implied. Happenstance only, he told himself and scooped the dice from the floor.

Annyn averted her gaze when he passed them to her, but this time she blew on them. A one, two, and five tumbled face up.

"Eight," Beatrix called ahead of her sister.

From Annyn's turned mouth, Garr knew she thought she was about to be bested. He claimed the dice, then did something even he did not expect. He reached his closed hand to her. "I hear tale they roll best when blown upon."

It seemed all held their breath, Annyn Bretanne notwithstanding. With raised eyebrows, she cupped his hand between hers and drew it to her lips.

It was a mistake. The feel of her mouth and the warm breath she pushed between his thumb and forefinger thrilled him. What a spell she spun!

She released his hand and sat back.

Acutely aware he was watched, Garr threw again. It hardly seemed possible, but up came two twos and a three.

"Seven!" Gaenor called.

Amid the chatter and mirth, Annyn's smile nearly melted him. "'Twould seem, Lord Wulfrith, the blow works only on one's own dice."

Garr glanced at Abel who shrugged. "I did not say *perfectly* matched," the youngest brother derided.

Garr stood and reached a hand to Annyn. "You may move freely about the castle, my lady."

"And play dice."

"So long as coin does not pass hands." He pulled her to standing and released her.

Her exaggerated frown cleared away the last of the smile he would like to know better. "I do not recall that limitation being set at the time of wagering."

"It goes unspoken, Lady Annyn."

"Then I must abide."

Garr looked to the others. "The night is old. Find your beds."

Though clearly disappointed, they began to disperse.

When Garr looked back at Annyn, he saw she had started for the stairs. And following her was Samuel. However, before Garr could call the young man back, Annyn turned around.

"Did I not win the wager, Squire Samuel?"

He peered over his shoulder. Garr's nod caused relief to sweep the young man's face.

Knowing Annyn might now escape, Garr started forward but halted when a hand touched his sleeve.

Lady Isobel's chin was high and haughty, but her eyes sparkled. "Methinks you did not wager what you truly wanted from the lady."

Irritation flushed Garr. "I am surprised you allowed dicing in our home, Mother."

"As am I." She skirted him.

Garr stared after her until she disappeared around the bend in the stairway.

"My lord?"

It was Sir Merrick whom he had denied an audience these past days. Though the night was late, he could no longer deny him. "Sir Merrick?"

"After consideration of what happened in the wood, I have determined it is best that I leave your service."

Garr was not surprised. "Aye, methinks 'tis best, though I would ask that you remain until our return to Wulfen."

The knight's expression told he preferred sooner than later, but he nodded. "If that is what you wish, my lord. Good eve."

"Sir Merrick, what answer does Lady Annyn require of you?"

He looked away, denying Garr the reading of his eyes. "She believes I know something of her brother's death and would have me speak of it, my lord." He raised his palms up. "But what more is there to tell?"

Garr stared at him, and when he could not summon the man's gaze back to him, said, "Good eve, Sir Merrick."

17

"Come see, Lady Annyn!"

Grateful for something to distract her from her task, Annyn looked up from the loom before which Lady Isobel had settled her an hour earlier.

Beatrix stood inside the great doors, grinning as she motioned for Annyn to follow.

"What is it?" Lady Isobel asked where she sat at the high table posting to Stern's journals.

"The merchants, Mother! They have come."

"Ah. They are early this month."

"Blessedly so." Beatrix looked back at Annyn. "You are coming?"

She longed to, but last eve she had lost a wager to Lady Isobel. And for it, she must complete a hand's width of tapestry that was to be part of Gaenor's dowry when she wed. If Annyn had known a sennight past that her wheedling of Garr would come to this, she would have lost to him. "I have hardly begun my work."

The girl's bottom lip pushed to a pout. "But you must see this. Why, even Gaenor agreed you ought to come."

She had? Though Beatrix had warmed considerably since the night Annyn had taught them dice, Gaenor was slower to accept the woman who had worked ill on her brother. Of course, the older sister's wager over the needlework had ended the same as Annyn's wager with Lady Isobel.

"Go, Lady Annyn," Garr's mother surprised her, "the tapestry can wait."

Had she wings, Annyn could not have sooner flown from the chair. "I thank you, my lady."

The woman waved a dismissing hand, dipped her quill in the ink pot, and returned to the journals.

Outside, the day was blue, not a cloud to blot the sky. Annyn drew a breath of the sweet air as she kept pace with Beatrix through the inner bailey, faltering only when her gaze found the tower in which Rowan resided. Though she had not asked, the physician said he had recovered—in time for Duke Henry's arrival a sennight hence.

Entering the outer bailey, Beatrix's excited chatter muted by the forging of arms in the smithy, Annyn clenched her teeth. A sennight. Seven days. How many hours?

She shook her head. She did not wish to think on it, having determined she would enjoy as best she could what was left before she was given to Lavonne. And she would be given to him, for it could mean the ruin of the Wulfriths if Garr remained at Stephen's side.

Still, the thought of being forced to wed Lavonne was nearly enough to tempt her to flee, especially as she was no longer watched by the squires. However, she would not have Garr and his family pay the price of her freedom. She had done them enough ill. Her only hope was that when Henry came she could convince him that she had given Rowan no choice but to accompany her. If she succeeded, her conscience would be clear of him as much as was possible. He, alone, must deal with what he had done to her mother.

"Look!" Beatrix exclaimed. "Did I not tell you?"

Past the raised portcullis of the outer bailey, beyond the drawbridge, wagons and brightly colored tents dotted the land before Stern. And though all the stalls were not yet fully erect, the merchants did a brisk business with the castle folk and villagers.

The sight was not new to Annyn, but it had never thrilled her as it did now. For once, she itched to see and touch and taste the wares, probably due to having spent so much time indoors. She was restless, and more so these two days since Garr had begun retraining his arm.

Though she had been tempted to venture to Stern's outer walls to watch his training in the field beyond, she had known she would not be welcome. Too, it was better to keep distance between them so this yearning of hers would not pain her more when she was gone from here.

"Hurry!" Beatrix urged. Young enough that none would think too ill of her, she lifted her skirts and darted across the drawbridge.

Annyn glanced around and found herself watched by the castle folk. What made her now care what any thought of her? As she lifted the hem of her own skirts, a shout pulled her regard to the training field. Garr was at its center, grunting and perspiring over a thick pel at which he swung his sword, his damp tunic molded to his chest and arms. He was not the only one at training, but she saw only him. And ached as she did not wish to.

"Lady Annyn! You are coming?"

Grateful her menses were past, the care of which would have slowed her, Annyn soon overtook Beatrix.

"There is Gaenor!" Beatrix pointed to a stand that boasted trinkets.

The two chased right and halted alongside her older sister.

"Do you think Mother would approve if I attach these to the ends of my girdle?" Gaenor showed them the tiny silver bells she cupped in her palm.

Annyn laughed. "Approve or not, do you wish all to know in advance of your arrival that you come?"

Gaenor wrinkled her nose. "I suppose not, but listen." She shook them and they sprinkled the air with sweet notes.

Annyn tapped the lowermost bell. "Mayhap you can attach them to your horse's bridle."

"That I shall!" Gaenor looked to the stout, rosy-cheeked woman behind the table. "How much for the bells?"

"Three shillings, my lady. And a fine bargain at that."

Gaenor opened her purse.

"Three?" Annyn placed a hand over Gaenor's. "A fine bargain? Surely you jest, dear lady."

The woman put her hands on her hips. "I do not. Them bells worth twice that. 'Tis a favor I do in selling them so cheap."

Ignoring Gaenor's mewl of protest, Annyn took the bells from her. "Of such favors we are not in need." She set the bells on the table, caught Gaenor's arm, and turned her away.

"But I want them," the young woman cried.

"And you shall have them," Annyn hissed.

"She shall?" Beatrix asked, hurrying after them.

"By the count of one...two..."

"How much ye willin' to pay?" the woman called.

Annyn turned. "Would you not agree one shilling is fair?" And it *was*.

"One?!"

Annyn sighed. "Come, dear lady, tell us yea or nay, for there are ribbons and cloth and meat pies to buy."

"Very well, one, but know that ye take from the mouths of my babes."

Gaenor ran back, pressed the coin in the woman's palm, and claimed her bauble.

"And for ye, my lady?" The vendor peered at Annyn. "Is there not something ye would like to steal from this poor old woman?"

Annyn scrutinized the offering and chose a ring. It was too large, intended for a man as it was, but she liked its design. She slid it easily onto her thumb and surveyed the miniature sword that wrapped fully around, blade tip meeting hilt. "Now this looks to be worth three shillings."

"That?" Beatrix exclaimed. "But if the bells are not—"

"Hush, Beatrix," Gaenor rasped and urged her sister toward the next stand.

"We are agreed on the price?" Annyn asked.

The woman nodded dumbly. "Aye, and a...fine bargain that."

From the meager contents of her purse, Annyn withdrew the coins. "For your babes, dear lady."

A smile spread across the woman's face. "Bless ye, my lady."

When Annyn turned away, her gaze once more fell upon the training field and the man who had every right to swing a sword, to defend family and home, to make choices, to be free. All denied her unless she escaped Lavonne when they left Stern. Unfortunately, it would be selfish to do so, for the Barony of Aillil and its people would be lost to Henry's whim if she did not return. Like her or not, she was their lady.

Painfully resigned, Annyn strained above the noise of the market to catch the clang of sword on sword. It was there, but too hard to hold to. If only she could heft a sword one last time before being chained hand and foot to a woman's duties.

"Lady Annyn!" Beatrix called.

As she hurried to where they awaited her, she considered the narrow band of silver on her thumb. Such a thing she had never worn, though her mother had left her several pieces of jewelry. It felt strange, and as she accompanied Gaenor and Beatrix about the market, she twisted the ring around and around. And longed for the training field.

Would she take this opportunity to escape? Garr wondered as he picked out the one whose laughter had reached him when he paused to quench his thirst. In that moment, he almost wished she would stay.

Annyn laughed again as a juggler bounced a ball nose to chin and back again. A few moments later, the man bowed and Annyn led the others in applauding his antics. Then she stepped to the platform, dug in her purse, and dropped coins in his palm.

For one who ought to be set on escape, she seemed unconcerned about having enough coin for the journey ahead. And coin she would need wherever she was going. Unless she was not going. After all, having known privilege her entire life, perhaps she had decided marriage to Lavonne was preferable to scraping out an existence that would surely be her lot if she fled Stern.

As with each time Garr thought of her wed to the miscreant, his insides twisted. Attempting to counter the discomfort, he swept up his sword and nodded to Squire Samuel.

"Harder!" Garr shouted as they crossed swords at the center of the enclosure. "Again!" Around the enclosure they went, exchanging blows that deepened the ache in Garr's shoulder, but he did not pause. When Henry arrived, he intended to be fully able to defend his people and lands if necessary.

It took some minutes to defeat Samuel who had become greatly skilled at swords, but finally the squire stumbled and landed on his backside.

"You are much improved." Garr cleared the sweat from his brow with the back of a hand. "Next time you shall do even better."

Samuel rose and slapped at his derriere. "Aye, my lord."

As Squire Warren ought to be recovered from their bout of a half hour past, Garr turned to where the others watched from atop the fence and was surprised to find the gathering of knights and squires had grown by three—Gaenor, Beatrix, and Annyn. Annyn who every day looked more the lady, though he avoided gazing upon her as much as possible.

Their eyes met, and in hers he saw what would be called a longing for the sword were she a man. But those days were past. Annyn in the disguise of Jame Braose was no more.

In searching out Squire Warren, Garr paused on Abel. He did not like the grin worn by his younger brother, the knowing in eyes that knew naught, the words he longed to speak.

"First, Squire Warren," Garr called, "then you, Abel." That put an end to his grin.

The squire hopped the fence, chose a sword from the dozen propped against a cart, and advanced on Garr.

Garr caught the squire's blow above his head, sent his opponent's blade running off the tip of his, then leveled his sword as if to part the young man's head from his shoulders.

Warren countered with uncommon strength and speed, the clash of their swords sending a pang through his lord's arm. Though the squire was more than capable at swords, this day he excelled beyond Garr's expectations. But it was unlikely that Annyn's presence was responsible, for still the young man resented the deceit worked on him. Gaenor, then? Beatrix?

Neither was pleasing, and Garr let his blade speak his displeasure with an upward thrust that sent Warren's sword flying.

"You are finished for the day," Garr said as the squire regained his footing. Though he ought to be finished himself, there was still much to regain that had been lost.

Becoming aware of a murmur at his back, he yanked at his tunic that clung shoulders to hips. Were he at Wulfen, he would remove it, but not at Stern, especially on market day. Now for Abel.

He turned, but it was Annyn who filled his eyes. Veil removed from shorn tresses, sword in hand, she advanced. This, then, the cause of the murmuring.

As for Abel, his face was turned aside to hide a smile. He could have stopped her.

Garr ground his teeth. What was so terrible about being a woman that Annyn could not remain one? Had no one ever told her of the boundary between the sexes?

Trying to appear calm, he lowered his sword and leaned his weight on the hilt. "Remove yourself from my training field, Lady Annyn."

Still she came, much to the amusement of their audience.

She halted before Garr, pricked the compacted soil with her sword tip, and rested both hands on the hilt. A peculiar sight, especially with her sleeves trailing halfway down her skirts.

Before Garr could summon harsh words, a glint of silver shone from her left hand. Upon her thumb was a ring he had not seen before, one made for a man. Had she bought it for Lavonne—as a peace offering of sorts? Or had she purchased the trinket for herself?

"Cross swords with me, Lord Wulfrith."

Feeling his breath blow hot through his nostrils, Garr bit, "I say again—"

"Surely you do not fear I will best you?" Her words made the others gasp. "After all, I am but a woman."

A woman who refused to behave as one. "Aye, and women do not cross swords."

Her eyebrows jumped. "Only when garbed as men, hmm?"

As those around them chuckled, Garr glared past her and rankled deeper to discover others were drawing near. And on the walls, men-at-arms leaned out from battlements to view the spectacle Annyn thought to make of them. If he did not put a quick end to this, all those at market would soon line the fences.

"Though you fooled," he said, "a woman you are. Thus, you may no longer trespass upon the name of Wulfrith." He jutted his chin toward the cart. "Return the sword."

"Lesson ten, Lord Wulfrith." She assumed her stance. "Let no man make your way for you."

He felt every muscle tighten. Never had his lessons been turned back on him, and in that moment, he loathed every one of them. "I do not exchange blows with any but men, Lady Annyn."

"No more, hmm? Pity, for you can scarce afford another injury." She sighed. "Now for lesson three: act when told to act." She swung her sword high.

When her blade caught sunlight, Garr reflexively brought his sword up to deflect her blow. "Enough!" he bellowed as she recovered her footing, but she fell upon him again.

"Lesson fifteen," he growled, "do not place your head in the wolf's mouth, Annyn Bretanne." He put all of his shoulder behind his next swing and caught her blade near the hilt. Surprisingly, his injury did not overly protest. Not surprisingly, the blow tore the sword from her hand and made her stumble back.

Shouts went up from around the fences, further evidence that she had made them performers, not unlike the juggler. But no more.

However, Annyn was of a different mind. When she moved to retrieve her sword, he lunged, gripped her arm, and pulled her around. "You are done," he rasped, "and, upon my word, the price you pay for this will not be small."

She raised her chin. "Lesson seven, make not vows you cannot keep."

Her words tripped fingers across his fury. If not that he struggled to contain the emotion that tempted him to toss her over his shoulder, he would immediately remove her from the training field.

"As for this terrible anger of yours..." She searched his face. "... surely there is also a lesson for that?"

One he had learned long ago, and which she too often tested.

When he gave no answer, she said, "Very well, I yield. 'Twould seem you are the better man."

"The only man!"

She tilted her head further back, catching the sun's light on her pretty face that no longer bore bruises. "Why are men so loath to share their pleasures with women?"

"Not *all* pleasures," he bit. "Only those that are the domain of men."

Her eyes flashed. "You have never sewn an accursed stitch, have you? Sat before a tedious loom? Wilted over endless menus? Been treated as mere chattel?" She caught her breath, and he glimpsed tears a moment before she dropped her chin.

Here, then, the root of her defiance—the knowledge that soon she would not only become a man's possession, but the possession of Geoffrey Lavonne who would likely keep her in bruises as easily as his coin kept her in finery.

Garr's anger faltered, but before he could claim victory over it, Annyn's head came up and she drew a deep breath. She wrinkled her nose. "What lesson was it that told of cleanliness?" She leaned toward him and sniffed. "Ah, yes, eleven."

Garr had had enough. As he pulled her across the training field, a cheer went up, but he disregarded those thronging the fences and walls, intent only on getting Annyn away. Unfortunately, he was far from being clear enough of mind to determine what her punishment would be.

Squire Warren appeared as they stepped from the training field and accepted the sword thrust at him.

Garr pulled Annyn over the drawbridge, bailey to bailey, and into the great hall where his mother stood so suddenly her chair toppled.

"What is this?" Isobel exclaimed. "What has she done now?"

Aye, *now*. No end to the mince Annyn Bretanne made of his ordered life. Indeed, regardless of her punishment, she would likely be undeterred.

He drew her up the stairs, down the corridor, and into the chamber his mother had given her. Only then did he release her, and only that he might close the door.

What in all of Christendom possessed me? Annyn wondered as Garr turned to face her. She had known it was a mistake to challenge him, but that—perhaps more than anything—had driven her to the sword. It might prove the last time she was able to make such a mistake without suffering Lavonne's cruelty.

"My only regret," she said, "is that it was over too soon." She crossed her arms over her chest. "What is to be my punishment, Lord Wulfrith? Will you return me to the dark tower? Will you once more set your squires upon me? Mayhap no supper for a fortnight—ah, but I shall not be here that long, shall I?"

His eyes narrowed but when his thinned lips parted, she shook her head. "You forget lesson fourteen: be slow to make decisions of great import."

"Annyn Bretanne!" He strode forward. "Why do you provoke me?"

"Why do you allow me?"

He turned his hands around her arms and pulled her near. "You ought to fear me."

She did not flinch. "Regardless of what I once believed, regardless of that anger of yours that causes men to quake, regardless of the power you wield as a Wulfrith, I cannot fear you. Nay." She shook her head.

"The trainer of whelps to warriors is not the same as the man I will be made to wed."

The fire in Garr's eyes flickered. "You are certain of that?"

"I am." Not that it would change anything between them. It could not. Under the threat of tears, she heard herself say, "Just one last time, I longed to embrace the thrill of owning my destiny, and for that I made a fool of myself by challenging you." She laughed bitterly. "But think, Garr, what had I to lose?"

His hands on her eased. "I know."

"Do you?"

His lids lowered, and when they lifted, it was her mouth he looked upon—as if he was tempted to it.

Was it desire he felt? Mere lust for not having had a woman recently? Or something more? And what of her own emotions, this longing in her breast? Was it—?

It could not be. Still, she lifted her hands between them and laid her palms to his chest. "Why did you twice kiss me?"

Slowly, he raised his gaze to hers. "I wished to."

"Do you wish to again?"

Without hesitation, he lowered his head and Annyn felt the pleasure of his mouth on hers, his hands on her back, and his arms sweeping her against his chest.

When he trailed his mouth to her ear, she turned her face to his neck and breathed in the male scent of him, then kissed him there and tasted the salt of his perspiration. It was strange that what had offended her on the training field should now cause such a stir within her.

"Annyn," he rasped, returning to her mouth. His lips teased and hands pushed through her hair.

In that moment, she knew what she wanted from him and what she would give him in return. It was wrong—more wrong than she dared think upon—but she wanted this memory to take with her when she left. Just this one thing and she would be as content as it was possible for one whose fate portended ill. No matter what Lavonne did to her, she would always have this.

"Feel how my heart beats." Garr drew her hand to his chest.

She thrilled to the knocking there. "I feel it. Now teach me how 'tis between a man and woman, Garr."

He stilled and, when she looked up, she saw regret on his face where there had been passion.

He released her and moved away. "Forgive me."

Heart aching, she said, "Why did you stop? Because I am not beautiful?"

He turned back. "I stop because 'tis a mistake I make in touching you so. Though women are not unknown to me, I do not lie with ladies, especially those promised to another."

She gasped. "Promised? Do you not mean enslaved?"

His face darkened. "It is what it is, Annyn. It can be no other way."

She took a step toward him. "But it can, even if only for this day."

"Nay. As you say that I am not Lavonne, neither am I Rowan or your uncle, pleasuring myself with a woman who belongs to another, making a harlot of her."

His words were like a slap, and Annyn looked away so he would not know how hard he struck. Regardless of her mother's sins, she did not wish to think of Elena in that way.

The silence stretched until Annyn found her old, bitter self. "How honorable of you, Lord Wulfrith," she said. "Would that I had words to express my gratitude that my esteemed betrothed shall find me intact."

He closed the distance between them and cupped her chin. "It *is* honorable, Annyn, and I will not be made to feel ashamed for it."

As the child in her wished him to feel. Struck with shame of her own that, for all her seeking of God these many days, she would have committed a sin she could never cast off for memory of this man, she pulled free of his touch. "You are right," she murmured. "What a pity more are not like you."

Silence descended again, and Annyn felt it straight through to her soul.

This time, Garr was the one to sweep it aside. "Come," he said, striding to the door, "you must have cloth to fashion a gown that fits."

She could hardly breathe for the sudden turn. After all that had happened between the training field and this chamber, he wished to take her to market? "But I do not require a fitted gown."

He looked over his shoulder. "Aye, you do—a bliaut worthy to receive the one you would have be king."

Henry, who would be here in a sennight. Though Annyn longed to decline, she knew Garr was right. If there was any chance of saving Rowan, she must gain the duke's favor, and that would be easier done in a gown that fit well and proclaimed her to be a lady.

She had returned, and appeared no worse for Wulfrith's anger.

Rowan closed his eyes on the sight of Annyn following Wulfrith across the outer bailey. The clamor of half an hour earlier had drawn him to the window of his prison. Unfortunately, the din had arisen from somewhere outside the castle walls, and not until he saw Wulfrith dragging Annyn over the drawbridge into the outer bailey had he known the cause of it. Had she tried to escape?

Fearing for her as a father would a daughter, though he certainly was not and did not deserve to be, he had pounded on the door and called to the guard. His jailer came, but no matter how Rowan raged, the accursed man refused to open the door. With naught left but prayer, which he had attempted, he had returned to the window, the width of which might allow a child through but never a man.

Not that it mattered now. Annyn was well, furthering her case that Wulfrith was not one to murder an innocent young man.

The relief over her well-being threatened by the never-ending ache of Jonas's death, Rowan watched the two step beneath the portcullis. A moment later, they were lost to sight, and he returned to pondering the conversation overheard between his jailer and a man who had brought

Rowan's dinner a few days past. Duke Henry was coming, not only to garner Wulfrith's allegiance, but to be delivered Annyn and the one who had aided in her escape.

Though his own fate did not matter, he agonized over Annyn's. What would Henry's punishment be? Worse than wedding her to the one who had struck her so hard as to leave a bruise? If only there was some way for him to aid her.

There was not. Somehow, she must do it herself. But how, with Wulfrith always at her back?

Rowan almost wished the renowned trainer of knights might come to feel something for her that would cause him to help her, but lust was not enough to risk the wrath of the man who would be king. As for love, Wulfrith was not so fool. It would take a miracle to see Annyn delivered free of Henry. And from Rowan's experience, there were no miracles laying about.

18

IT WAS NOT as he would have it, but that was the way of things. Nor would he have had himself be the one to stroll among the stalls with Annyn in search of cloth, especially as they did so beneath the curious regard of those who had witnessed their contest on the training field. But he would see to the task and know it was done.

"This." He reached past the eager merchant who smelled of chewed parsley. From beneath a fold of red and white striped cloth, Garr pulled forth a vivid blue.

"Silk of Almeria," the merchant crooned. "The finest, my lord, befitting a lady."

Garr looked to Annyn and saw her attention was on the woods bordering Stern. As if deep in thought, she twisted the ring on her thumb. Perhaps the cloth would not be necessary. "Lady Annyn," he clipped.

She looked around. "My lord?"

Resenting the awkward task, he held out the cloth. "What do you think?"

"It is lovely." She turned away.

Lord, why am I, a warrior, coaxing a woman to appraise cloth?

"How many ells?" a voice came from behind.

Garr looked around at his mother. What was she doing at market, she who shunned such frivolity? For the items required in her household, she always sent another. Of course, her curiosity must have been piqued when he came belowstairs with Annyn. She had asked if all was well, and he had told her it soon would be, then left the donjon with Annyn in tow.

"Five ells in that piece, my lady," the merchant answered. "Far enough to cut a fine bliaut."

She snorted. "Providing it is sleeveless and shows her legs."

Annyn turned, blinked as if only then realizing Isobel had joined them. "My lady."

Isobel scanned the selection on the table. "Surely you can do better than this, merchant."

"I've some Imperial." He bent behind the table. When he straightened, a fold of rich purple silk was over one arm, red over the other, both interwoven with gold thread. "Seven ells this." He raised the purple. "Eight ells this."

"Let us see which best suits her color."

The merchant came around the table and held the red against Annyn's cheek.

"Nay," Isobel said, "it does not go with her skin." She eyed Annyn. "And you will not take flour to your face?"

"I do not like it, my lady."

Garr was not surprised, nor would he care to see her pasty and pale. He liked her unmade face that made for a look fresh as rain. Doubtless, when she was an old woman she would still possess that simple radiance. He almost wished he might be there to see it.

"Let us try the purple, then," Lady Isobel said.

The color contrasted nicely with Annyn's fair skin and black hair, the gold thread lending a sparkle to her despondent eyes.

"The purple it shall be." Isobel leveled her gaze on the merchant. "And do not think to price it too high, for there are others who would as soon take our coin."

"I would not think to, my lady!"

She looked to Garr. "*Now* all is well?"

Hardly, but she need not know of his struggle over Annyn. "Well enough." He pivoted. Though he had not intended to return to the training field, he needed to cut down a pel.

"I would speak to you," Isobel stopped him, then turned back to the merchant. A few minutes later, the man laid the cloth over Annyn's arms.

"Return to the donjon, Lady Annyn," Isobel said, "and tell Josse she is to assist you in fashioning a bliaut befitting a noblewoman."

Garr stared after Annyn as she started for the drawbridge and could not help but sympathize, nor think that if she stole away from Stern—

His mother's arm slid through his. "Walk with me."

He was not accustomed to such a request, content as she was with her self-imposed confinement within the donjon. Nor was he comfortable with her arm joined to his as if they were close as they had not been since he had left Stern at the age of four.

She drew him away from the merchants and the castle. "A bath you shall require this eve," she said as they neared an ancient oak beyond the training field.

He did smell like an animal. It was hard to believe Annyn had allowed him so near, that she would have taken him to her if her plea that he teach her had not reminded him she was untouched. It had been wrong, and he had felt God's displeasure.

"When you pulled her abovestairs," Isobel said, "I feared..."

"You had good reason to, Mother."

She did not speak again until they reached the shade of the oak tree. Pulling her arm from his, she tilted her head back to stare up through the leaves. "The tree has grown much." She crossed to the trunk and leaned back against it.

Garr was surprised at how young she looked standing there, but when he closed the distance between them, the deepening lines around her eyes, nose, and mouth were more visible.

"You do not understand it, do you?" she said.

"Mother?"

"It makes no sense, but then perhaps, 'tis not meant to."

Riddles! Why so many words when fewer sufficed? "I do not know of what you speak."

"I speak of your feelings for her." As though something of import might be had in his reaction, she peered closely at him.

Garr longed to feign ignorance, but he knew it was Annyn to whom she referred, and it made him long to walk away. If not for the appearance of tears in his mother's eyes, he would have.

"'Twas the same for me," she said. "With Robert."

"Who?"

"The man I loved. The one I could not have."

Though Garr had never heard the man's name spoken, he had known there was one who had tried to steal his mother from Drogo—just as he had nearly stolen Annyn from Lavonne a half hour earlier.

"Not that I knew it was love that first day." Her voice lowered. "Indeed, it was not, but something in me knew it would become love. And it did, though it was a love not meant to be."

"Not meant to be because you were betrothed to my father?" he pressed too harshly.

Her wet gaze met his. "Not meant to be because your father killed him."

"What?"

"The day I was to wed Drogo, I stole from Stern and hid on the other side of this tree." She laid a palm to the gnarly bark. "It was here that Robert came for me, but ere we were a league gone, Drogo overtook us."

Garr could imagine his father's anger—carefully controlled, though its hot breath fanned all.

"He and Robert met at swords, and Robert fell. None could match Drogo."

The man she had loved killed by the man she had loathed, and from that a marriage made. It explained much.

His mother pressed a hand to her mouth.

Fearing she might crumple, Garr put a hand to her shoulder and urged her to sit.

She eased down the tree trunk to its base.

Garr waited. For some reason, he longed to know what had passed between his parents to make them such bitter partners. What had caused Drogo to take his four-year-old son far from his mother and put him to training intended for those twice his age?

Isobel clasped her hands in her lap. "Afterward, your father returned me to Stern and we were wed—that day."

Regardless of what fell to Drogo's path, he had always pressed on.

Isobel touched Garr's hand. "I was not a good wife. Pray though I did to get past my hatred, every time I looked at your father I saw the one who had murdered Robert. Had Drogo loved me, mayhap I could have healed, but he did not. I was young, pretty, of good size for breeding, and had all my teeth. That is what he bought, so I determined that was all he would have."

She shook her head. "And now I grow old with regret. Regret that Robert was lost to me, regret that I did not move past that loss, regret that my hatred for your father caused him to take you from me young, regret that I refused his offers of peace. Now all that is left to me are daughters, and too soon they will also wed men they do not love."

A tear rolled down her cheek. "But you, Garr, have been gifted with the rare opportunity to wed a woman unlike your mother. Lady Annyn—"

"Wed!" Garr stepped back so suddenly the birds in the tree took flight. "Has your mind gone astray, Mother?"

She rose. "She feels for you, and if you are truthful, you feel for her." As he opened his mouth to deny it, she shook her head. "Wasted words. Lies."

"You are wrong. Though I may want Annyn Bretanne in my bed, that is all."

"Then, it seems, my mind *has* gone astray. But tell, what of when Henry comes to Stern? Do you think you can give Lady Annyn to be wed to that man—the same that Abel said was responsible for her bruised face?"

Garr forced himself to stand firm. "You heard what Henry requires of the Wulfriths, and one of his demands is that I deliver Annyn Bretanne. If I must choose between a woman whose deceit nearly cost me my life, and my family, the latter shall prevail."

Isobel stepped near and brushed back the hair fallen over his brow, reminding him of the small boy who had known that touch. "Garr Wulfrith, son of Drogo, trainer of England's worthiest knights, feared and respected warrior, do not let your distrust of women make you less than what you are." She smiled. "There is only one weapon you must needs wield against Henry—your allegiance. And it should not be without cost to him."

She dropped her hand to her side. "Now I must return to the donjon and set to the task of overseeing Lady Annyn's gown." She stepped from beneath the tree but, once returned to sunlight, looked around. "You will not give her to Lavonne." She said it with the certainty of one who spoke of death as the only absolute in life, then she left him.

Garr stared after her. Annyn Bretanne's vengeful foray into his life had opened too many graves. But though the man his father had made him longed to put aside his mother's suffering tale, he could not. He had accepted that marriages were best made of alliances, love reserved for those foolish and weak of heart, but here before him was the pitiful result of such matches. And his mother was not alone in her folly, for Annyn's mother had also gone the way of her heart and left casualties in her wake.

Garr growled. Had he been wrong? Had his father? And his father's father? Was all the world wrong for impelling its children to make families with those for whom they did not care? But then, what would be the state of mankind ruled by the heart?

He shook his head. He would think on it no more. As he looked to the castle, he drew a breath that assailed him with the harsh scent of his labor. In one thing his mother was right. He needed a bath.

19

A FOUL WIND blew in the messenger, causing him to stumble as he entered the great hall behind two men-at-arms.

From the high table, Garr stared at Sir Drake—one of two men sent by Henry eleven days past to tell of the duke's impending arrival. Why did he come again when there were yet three days before Henry was due? Three days in which Annyn might still make good her escape?

He glanced at where she sat with his mother and sisters before the hearth, the last of the day's clouded light slanting through the upper windows to pool around her where she held the sleeve of her purple bliaut as she stared at the messenger.

Garr returned his attention to the villagers seated on benches before the dais. Their dispute, for which they sought intervention, would have to wait. "We shall return to this matter." He swept a dismissing hand toward the doors.

The men murmured their agreement and rose.

Garr also stood, vaguely aware of Squire Warren stepping from behind the chair to draw nearer.

"Sir Drake," Garr greeted, "What brings you once more to Stern?"

The man turned from the hearth where he had surely noted Annyn's presence. "Tidings from Duke Henry." He mounted the dais and pushed his mantle off one shoulder, then the other so that the garment draped down his back to show his full complement of weaponry.

Garr laid his palms to the table and leaned forward. "When do you intend to deliver these tidings, Sir Drake?"

A flush stole across the man's cheeks. "Forthwith, my lord. I am to tell you that the future king of England shall arrive early."

Garr heard Annyn draw the sharp breath he did not allow himself.

"If not this night," Sir Drake continued, "then by early morn the duke will come before your walls and be well received."

Well received. An order, doubtless spawned by Garr's earlier message that granted Henry leave to come unto Stern Castle. "Shall he?"

"If you seek an alliance, he shall."

Garr straightened and glanced at the windows that were filled with darkening thunderclouds. All day long rain had threatened to loose a torrent. This, then, what made Henry's arrival uncertain.

Loose the rain, Lord, Garr silently prayed. It was not for lack of a response from the earl, John Newark, that he did so. Indeed, within days of having sent the missive that advised an alliance with Henry, Newark had agreed. It was for Annyn he asked it.

Muddy this land, overrun its banks. Was He listening? *Curse all!* The silent oath slipped from him and he immediately rebuked the blasphemy that would hardly turn God's ear to him.

Lesson one, his father's words came across the years, *never allow anger to command your actions.*

Still, it turned his insides. Feeling backed into a corner, he struggled for control. Finally, he said, "Your tidings are well met, Sir Drake."

The man inclined his head. "My Lord Wulfrith."

What to do? If only those accursed clouds would open up. If only—

A pox on Henry! he once more blasphemed. *A pox on Stephen and Eustace! A pox on this crippling war!* Fight the answer though he had done all these days, he knew what must be done to assure Annyn was not forced to wed Lavonne. There was no other way, especially now that Henry approached Stern.

"Well met, indeed," he repeated. "We are pleased you have come to serve as witness for Duke Henry."

As the man's brow furrowed, Garr strode the length of the table.

"Brother?" Abel spoke low from where he had sat at table's end this past hour, feet on the tabletop, though with Sir Drake's entrance he had dropped them to the floor.

Garr met his brother's questioning gaze. "Be ready." He descended the dais.

"Of what do you speak, my lord?" demanded the knight.

He would know soon enough.

As Garr advanced on Annyn, she looked up, her pale eyes questioning, lips pressed, throat muscles straining to contain emotion.

Ignoring his mother's beckoning gaze and his sisters' murmurings, Garr halted before Annyn.

She fingered the purple bodice. "I—" Her voice caught, but when she found it again, it was flat as of one too weary to fight any longer. "I fear my bliaut is not yet finished."

"A pity," Garr said more harshly than intended. "I would have liked to see you wear it to speak vows."

"Garr?" his mother said, forgetting that, publically, he was "Wulfrith."

He waited for Annyn to react, but she kept her head lowered and a drop of glistening light fell onto the unfinished bliaut. The betraying tear darkened the cloth and spread outward.

Either she did not understand, or she found the prospect of marriage to him distasteful. Of course, considering what had nearly happened between them four days past, and for which he had spent hours on his knees, she could not be completely averse.

"What vows, Lord Wulfrith?" Sir Drake halted beside Garr.

"Those that Lady Annyn and I are to speak this eve."

Her disbelieving eyes slammed into his. She had not understood, then.

"You jest, my lord," Sir Drake exclaimed. "Lady Annyn's betrothal was given to Baron Lavonne."

Just as Isobel's betrothal had been given to Drogo. The realization that what he intended would make him no better than the man who had tried to steal Isobel from Drogo, gave Garr pause. But only for a moment, for though his father had been a man incapable of showing love, he had never raised a hand to Isobel as Lavonne had done to Annyn. And would not do again.

As Garr stared at Annyn, she pressed her lips inward as if to keep from speaking.

Grateful she understood the urgency that she remain silent, he turned to the knight. "You are mistaken, Sir Drake. Inquiries have revealed that, in all of King Stephen's England, no such betrothal was made."

Anger suffused the man's face. "Duke Henry, who will soon be your king, Lord Wulfrith, has decreed it."

As Abel moved behind the knight, Garr said, "Be it so, Sir Drake, Henry is not yet king, and I am not yet his man. Thus, neither I, nor Lady Annyn, answer to him. And I have determined ours is a satisfactory union."

"You cannot do this!"

"Of course I can. The bride is willing. Are you not, my lady?"

Annyn was hardly quick to answer, making him long to shake her, but at last she inclined her head. "The bride is willing."

As Gaenor and Beatrix took up tittering, a thrill shot through Garr, but he damped it. Likely, she was willing only because this evil was not as evil as the other.

"Nor by this union shall any laws of consanguinity be broken," he continued. "The lady and I share no relation to at least the ninth degree." That he did not truly know, but what was one more untruth? "As for a priest, he awaits abovestairs." Or so Garr prayed, for at this hour of late afternoon, the man might be out among the castle folk.

"What of the banns?" the knight foundered for argument. "They cannot have been read."

"They were, and none has come forth to oppose the marriage." An outrageous lie considering they had not been long enough at Stern for banns to be read the appointed three Sundays, but the wedding bed would be marked by consummation before any could prove otherwise. And therein lay the greatest obstacle—to speak vows and undo Annyn before Henry's arrival.

Sir Drake shook his head. "If you think I am so great a fool to believe any of this, you are mistaken."

Garr reached to Annyn. "'Tis time."

Her gaze flitted to Sir Drake, but there was naught that the man could do but spew and sputter over what his arrival had set in motion.

Annyn passed the bliaut to Josse, placed her hand in Garr's, and allowed him to draw her to her feet. The silver ring on her thumb winked at Garr as it had four days past, and now that he was so near, he saw the band was fashioned as a sword. Though a not-so-discreet inquiry put to Gaenor revealed it was but a trinket bought at market, jealousy had gripped Garr over the possibility it might end on Lavonne's hand. Now it would not.

"We are ready," he pronounced. Or nearly so, for he did not have a ring to give Annyn.

He looked to his mother and saw she had risen with his sisters. Isobel inclined her head, answering her son's unspoken request, and turned to the stairs.

Garr drew Annyn to his side. Though he wished for a moment alone with her to ease her worry, they would talk once they were bound until death. "Come, Lady Annyn."

As they started forward, Henry's man placed himself in their path. Immediately, Abel and Warren flanked him, hands on daggers.

"This is outrageous, Lord Wulfrith!" Though Sir Drake's voice was pitched too high for a man not to cringe, he did not seem to notice. "I vow, 'twill not be tolerated by the duke."

"Fear not, Sir Knight, I shall deal with Henry. Now, if you wish, you may serve as witness to the ceremony." He strode forward, forcing the man to step back to avoid being trod upon.

"I shall not be a party to this!" Sir Drake called as Garr and Annyn ascended the stairs.

Garr did not blame him, for his witness would only strengthen the validity of the marriage.

Squire Warren once more at his back, Garr said over his shoulder, "Hasten to the chapel and rouse the priest if he is there. Tell him what has happened and what is required of him."

"Aye, my lord." Warren took the stairs two at a time.

Once out of sight of those in the hall, Annyn pulled free of Garr and pressed her back to the wall. "We cannot do this. 'Tis all wrong."

"We can and shall." Garr laid his hands on her shoulders. "There is naught else for it."

Annyn held his intense gaze for as long as she could, then looked down. After all she had done, why did he offer this? Why when it would bring Henry's anger down upon his house? Might he care for her? Return something of what she felt for him, and over which she had agonized? But if so, he would not be so resentful, would he? And his resentment she had certainly felt when he told Sir Drake of his intention. *Naught else for it*, he had said.

Aye, he did it only out of a misplaced sense of obligation. Garr Wulfrith was, indeed, honorable, but such a sacrifice she could not ask of him, no matter how her heart cried that she accept.

"'Tis not necessary that you do this, especially as I do not wish to wed you." *Lord, the lie!*

His grey-green eyes darkened like the clouds gathering over Stern. "If you had only taken one of many opportunities given you to escape, it would not be necessary." He pulled her from the wall, and all she could do as she pondered the unexpected revelation was clamber after him.

She had seen the opportunities for escape, but had not recognized them for what they were. Garr had taken his squires off her, but had he wished to hold her, others could have been set to watch from a distance. Ironic that she had eschewed escape for fear of what Henry would do to the Wulfriths, and Garr had offered it for—it seemed—fear of what Henry and Lavonne might do to her. It was no small wonder he resented being forced to wed her.

They reached the first landing, but as Garr urged her up the next flight of stairs, Lady Isobel called out. Followed by her daughters who smiled as if they did not mind their brother wedding a woman who had tried to kill him not so long ago, she hurried down the corridor toward them.

"I have the ring." Isobel proffered a gold band set with a large sapphire and small rubies.

Annyn could not be certain, but she thought Garr hesitated before accepting it.

Isobel looked to Annyn. "'Tis the ring by which all brides of the Wulfrith heir wed," she said, then to Garr, "It shall be different for you. I know it shall."

Now Annyn understood. Isobel had worn the ring upon her marriage to Garr's father, a most unhappy marriage, it seemed. And Garr was not pleased for it.

He started to turn away, but came back around. "Change, Mother."

"What?"

"You shall not wear black at my wedding."

"But 'tis all——"

"Wear sackcloth, if you must. Any color but black. And make haste!" Leaving her gaping, he ushered Annyn up the stairs and down the corridor to the chapel before which Sir Warren stood.

Why did he care what color his mother wore? After all, it was not to be a proper wedding. No great gathering of family and friends, no pageantry, no trousseau, no garland of flowers for her hair, no special gown.

Annyn looked down. Indeed, this day she wore another of Gaenor's bliauts, brown and unadorned. As for the custom of wearing her hair long and loose as a mark of maidenhood, *that* could not be helped. None would ever say she had married in her hair.

"The priest?" Garr asked, continuing to hold Annyn to his side as if for fear she might flee.

"He is within," Squire Warren said, "preparing for the ceremony."

"Tell him to be quick."

The squire turned and slipped into the chapel.

Alone in the corridor with Garr, Gaenor and Beatrix no doubt assisting their mother with her change of clothes, Annyn met Garr's gaze.

"It is well," he murmured and released her arm. To her astonishment, he caught her hand and intertwined their fingers.

The sweetness of it nearly stole Annyn's breath. "Is it?"

"It is."

A flutter went through her, but it did not last long beneath the weight of foreboding. *Would* all be well? What hope had a marriage begun thus? How would Duke Henry receive the news? What cost to the Wulfriths?

Boots on the stairway caused Garr to pull his hand from Annyn's and turn it around his sword. But it was Abel who appeared, followed by Squires Samuel and Charles.

"What of Sir Drake?" Garr demanded.

"I have put men-at-arms on him," Abel said as he advanced. "Surely you know that for naught would I miss your wedding."

"Surely," Garr grumbled.

Abel halted before his brother, "Where is the old man?"

"I am here." Stepping from the chapel, the priest tugged at newly donned robes. "And do not call me old man."

Abel lowered his gaze. "Apologies, Father Mendel."

Squire Warren exited the chapel behind the priest and joined Abel where he stood behind Garr and Annyn.

Plucking again at the robes that fell from his bent shoulders, the priest looked to Garr. "Do you know what you do, my son?"

"I do."

"And still you ask this of me?"

"I do."

"'Tis foolish, not at all what I would expect from you, Garr Wulfrith."

Nor would Annyn have. It seemed there were pieces to Garr that none knew existed.

"As you know," the priest said, "ere the marriage ceremony can commence, banns must be read for three Sundays." He raised his hands, one of which gripped the Holy book. "You are not that long returned to Stern."

"I am not, but there shall be a wedding."

Father Mendel stepped nearer. "You know this marriage may be pronounced clandestine, judged adultery and fornication?"

"I do not care what others call it, Father. All I care is that there be a wedding this day in the presence of God who is the only witness we require."

"Do you not mean this night? And that is another thing: vows are to be spoken in the light of day."

Annyn watched Garr's face darken. The priest's belief in God would have to be unwavering for him not to cower. And he did not.

"There is yet daylight," Garr growled.

"A prick of it, but in a quarter hour it will be gone."

"Then make haste, Priest."

"Very well, but it is on your head if you are excommunicated." Father Mendel drew himself up to his full five feet and some inches and there, before the chapel, said, "If any know just cause why this man and woman may not be lawfully joined in marriage, declare it now." He waited, and waited again.

"On with it!" Garr snapped.

"Hold!" Wearing a gown of green, the cloth decidedly homespun, Lady Isobel bustled down the corridor. And looked no less regal for the simple garment that likely belonged to Josse. She, Gaenor, and Beatrix stepped around Abel and took up places before the others.

"You object to this marriage, Lady Isobel?" Father Mendel asked, hopeful.

"Of course I do not. 'Twas first my idea."

It had been, hadn't it? Did Garr know?

"Continue, Father," Lady Isobel urged.

The priest sighed. "Then I ask you, Garr Wulfrith, shall you take this woman to be your wedded wife, to live together after God's ordinance in the holy state of matrimony?"

Overhead, the skies rumbled, portending the thunderstorm all had known would come.

Garr looked at Annyn. "I shall."

Realizing she held her breath, she eased it from her lungs. There had been no anger when he spoke the words.

"Will you love her, comfort and honor her, keep her in sickness and health, be faithful to her?"

Would he love her? *Did* he? At his hesitation, Annyn was jolted by the reality of what they did. Or *was* it real? Did they truly stand beside one another? Speak vows that would bind them forever? Mayhap it was a dream from which she would too soon awaken.

"I shall," Garr said.

"And you, Lady Annyn Bretanne, shall you take this man to be your wedded husband, to live together after God's ordinance in the holy state of matrimony?"

How she longed to slip her hand into Garr's, to feel his warmth again. "I shall."

"Will you love him"—

More than she had ever believed she could love another.

—"comfort him, honor him, keep him in sickness and health, be faithful to him, obey and serve him?"

Obey and serve. That had not been part of the vows spoken by Garr. Still, she begrudged, "I shall."

Thunder rolled again, this time with such force it was felt through the floor.

Father Mendel leaned toward Garr. "Trust me, my son, this is best done on the morrow."

"'Tis best done now."

The man drew back. "Who gives this woman to be married to this man?"

Who would step forward? Sir Abel? He seemed the only choice, but as Annyn looked around, an achingly familiar voice resounded down the corridor.

"*I* give this woman."

Annyn felt Garr stiffen beside her as she looked over her shoulder at Rowan who advanced with a man-at-arms on either side.

The sight of him, unshaven and bedraggled, weight loss most pronounced in his face, made tears prick her eyes. These past days, she had time and again put him from her when he rose to memory, told herself she hated him for what he had done to her mother, that he was no better than Lavonne. But it was not true. He had done a terrible thing, but for it he had devoted himself to her and Jonas. Could a man make reparation for such ill, he had. God would be his judge, not she who had only ever reaped the kindness of Rowan's repentant heart.

"We shall speak on this," Garr hissed, drawing Annyn's gaze to Abel whose flush of guilt told he was responsible.

Rowan stepped through the path that opened before him and leaned near Annyn. "You will allow me to give you to him?" he said so softly she doubted any others heard.

Most remarkable was that he wished to pass her to the man he had thought responsible for Jonas's death. Or had he also realized the terrible mistake? He must have. Garr had not left him to die in the dark tower as the one who had heartlessly taken Jonas's life would have done. And finally he accepted it.

"I will allow it."

A sad smile creasing Rowan's mouth, he looked to the priest. "I give this woman to be married to this man."

Father Mendel joined Annyn and Garr's hands. "Now you will pledge your troth. This, say after me: I, Garr Wulfrith, take thee, Annyn Bretanne, to be my wedded wife."

Garr repeated it, and all that followed.

The priest turned to Annyn. "This, say after me…"

She repeated, "I, Annyn Bretanne, take thee, Garr Wulfrith, to be my wedded husband…to have and to hold, for fairer for fouler…for better for worse, for richer for poorer…in sickness and in health…"

"...to be meek and obedient in bed and at board," Father Mendel continued.

Nor had "meek and obedient" been part of Garr's vows. But in this man's world it would not be.

Garr squeezed her hand, urging her on, and she repeated the vow and all those that followed.

At the end of it, Father Mendel extended the Holy book, but no sooner did Garr lay his mother's ring atop it than a thunderclap sounded that elicited shrieks from Gaenor and Beatrix. Soon rain would be upon them.

Not until Garr's thumb caressed the back of Annyn's hand did she realize how tightly she gripped him. She smiled at the kind light in his eyes.

"We should continue?" the priest asked, again hopeful.

"Without delay," Garr answered.

Father Mendel spoke over the ring, then handed it to Garr. "Place it on her fourth finger."

He lifted her left hand, slid the ring on, and met her gaze. "With this ring I thee wed—" The sound of rain pummeling the roof halted him.

"'Tis not too late to think better of this," Father Mendel whispered.

Garr's jaw convulsed. "With my body I thee honor, with my body I thee worship."

Desperately, Annyn wished they could be more than words.

"In the name of the Father," he ended, "and of the Son, and of the Holy Ghost, Amen."

Then it was her turn to speak the words that included no mention or passing of a ring to the man who would be her husband, and she found herself wondering why it was that only the bride wore a wedding ring. To mark her as a man's possession? However, as tempted as she was to slide her worthless sword ring off her thumb and onto Garr's hand, she suppressed the impulse and finished the vows required of her.

"Kneel," the priest said.

They lowered to their knees, and he begged that the blessing of God be given them. "Those whom God hath joined together, let no man put asunder." Then, to those gathered, he proclaimed the marriage legal and valid and pronounced them man and wife.

"Now we shall take Holy communion." All followed him into the chapel where he instructed Annyn and Garr to kneel before the lord's table. What followed was a blur, excepting the man at Annyn's side and the sound of rain thrown against the walls.

When it was time to prostrate themselves in prayer, a pall was stretched over them with Abel, Squires Warren, Samuel, and Charles each holding a corner.

As the priest droned above, Annyn ventured a look at Garr. His face was pressed to the floor, eyes prayerfully closed. Feeling his reverence, she wondered if he concurred with Father Mendel that their marriage be blessed—that the yoke of peace and love be upon them.

His eyes opened and met hers, then he covered her hand with his and smiled—tightly, but a smile nonetheless. And the things it did to her!

As he looked into her face, Garr felt a tug. *It is well,* he had said, and he realized it was. As deeply as he had resented the unexpected turn of Duke Henry's arrival, as angry as it had made him, this was meant to be. He wanted Annyn Bretanne—now, Annyn Wulfrith. And he had wanted her for longer than this day, just as his mother had known. Determined to make this marriage as unlike his parents' marriage as the earth was the heavens, he turned his face to the floor again.

At long last, the mass was done and Father Mendel beckoned Garr forward to receive the kiss of peace. Once done, Garr returned to Annyn. "I will not make it long," he murmured and drew her into his arms. He pressed his mouth to hers, but when he started to pull back, she leaned into him and returned his kiss.

"Now we celebrate!" Abel landed a blow to his brother's back.

Inwardly bemoaning the sweetness lost to him, Garr lifted his head. "First, Rowan," he said, glancing at the man who stood at the chapel doors, the men-at-arms holding watch over him.

Abel grimaced.

"As for the celebration," Garr continued, "have a goblet of wine in honor of the bride and groom." Not that there had been time to prepare a banquet as was customary on so joyous an occasion.

Abel frowned. "You intend to forego the celebration?"

As Garr ushered Annyn from the chapel, he felt her gaze. True, the rain would likely keep Duke Henry from Stern throughout the night, but he would chance nothing. "And what man would not when a marriage bed awaits?" He stepped onto the stairs.

Above the excited chatter, he heard Annyn's sharply indrawn breath.

But she was not the only one to attend the discourse, as Father Mendel let be known where he trailed Garr. "What do you say?" he demanded.

Garr paused two steps down and looked to the man who was nearly at eye level where he stood on the landing above. "My bride and I are most eager to settle our marriage bed."

He did not need to see Annyn to know her disquiet. The air resounded with it—and the murmurs of those who had halted below and above to catch the priest's response.

Father Mendel turned the red of an apple. "Unheard of!"

Garr shrugged. "Until this day."

"This is most improper."

"Why?"

"I…" The priest's jowls quivered. "The marriage bed has not been blessed!"

Though Garr pitied the man for all that had been asked of one as proper as Father Mendel, he arched an eyebrow. "Then bless it as is your duty." He turned to his mother. "I ask that you accompany my lady wife to the solar and see she is properly put to bed."

Isobel nodded while Gaenor and Beatrix giggled behind their hands.

Garr stepped down, setting the wedding party to motion again. At the next landing, his mother and sisters stepped into the corridor to await Annyn.

Without a word, Annyn swept past him and started for the solar.

"Garr?" his mother said softly, halting his descent to the hall where he would speak with Abel about Rowan.

"Mother?"

She glanced down her bliaut. "You are pleased?"

He smiled. "Never have I seen you look lovelier."

The maddeningly reserved Isobel Wulfrith blushed. "It hardly flatters."

He leaned forward. "Look again in the mirror, Mother." When he kissed her cheek as he had rarely done for a score or more years, it surprised him as much as it did her. Scowling at the heat that warmed his neck, he left her and the priest to make their way to the solar.

Abel awaited him at the bottom of the stairs. "And all said you were incapable of love," he jeered.

Love? *All,* whoever *all* were, were not wrong. He felt for Annyn, but as his father had told, only fool men loved. "'Twas done to keep her from Lavonne."

"Only obligation, then?"

"Naught else."

"You are certain?"

"Naught else!"

Abel grinned. "You protest too much, Brother."

"And you have a fierce imagination, *little* Brother." Garr started toward a sideboard where wine was set out, but he remembered Rowan. A scan of the hall revealed the man was at a lower table.

Garr turned back, but rather than rebuke Abel as intended, he said, "Sir Rowan may make his bed in the donjon, though he is to have a guard on him at all times."

Abel grinned.

Garr glowered at him, then crossed to the sideboard. *Five minutes,* he told himself, *then I shall go to my wife.*

20

"She refuses to remove her chainse," Father Mendel griped as Garr entered the solar.

Garr looked to the bed, alongside which Isobel and his sisters stood. Annyn sat propped against the headboard, white chainse visible above the sheet and coverlet drawn up beneath her arms. Though she surely knew he had come, she stared at the wall opposite.

"Fear not, Father, I shall shed it for her."

"Humph," the man grunted.

Eager to clear the solar, the goblet of wine adding to the quickening of his heart, Garr pulled off his tunic and tossed it on the chest.

As his mother and sisters turned their backs, Annyn dropped her chin to stare at her hands. When he swept back the bedclothes and slid in beside her, she startled, and again when his thigh settled against hers.

The priest stepped forward. "*This*," he said with a stern countenance, "we shall do proper."

Thus, Garr's longing for his wife had to wait through five blessings. At long last, cool holy water was sprinkled over them.

"Peace upon you." Father Mendel stepped from the bed and extinguished the torches, leaving only the glow of the brazier and the candles on a nearby table to light the solar. Then Isobel, Gaenor, and Beatrix preceded him from the solar, the latter stealing a last glimpse of the marriage bed before the door closed.

No sooner did Garr turn to the woman he had made his wife than she scrambled off the bed.

Garr groaned.

Halfway across the solar, Annyn swung around. "I have yet to catch my breath."

And receiving his body unto hers would not help toward that end.

She pushed a hand through her hair, then lowered her hand to stare at her ring. "But two hours past I was to be given to Lavonne, now I am wed to you."

"Is it so bad, Annyn?"

She shook her head. "Sudden would be the better word." She took a step toward the bed, pivoted away, and came back around. "What is this matter of unclothing one's self before the priest?"

It seemed none had told her what to expect on her wedding night. But then, her mother had died when Annyn was young and, it seemed, Rowan and her uncle had been content to raise her among the things of men. The good tidings was that she did not cling to her chainse as a barrier between them. At least, he hoped it was not also that. "It is ceremony, Annyn."

"So Father Mendel told. But why?"

Could they not have this conversation later? "Consummation," Garr said, a bit too harsh, "the fulfillment of marriage. For how can a man and woman lay together unclothed and not know one another?"

Her eyes were large in the flickering light.

Garr reached out a hand. "You want this as I do, Annyn, as we have denied ourselves. We are husband and wife now, and it is good that we lie together."

She hugged her arms over her chest. "Is it merely lust you feel for me?"

Was it? Nay, he determined, but delved no further. He felt for Annyn as it was good for a man to feel for his wife. That should suffice. He tossed the covers off and dropped his legs over the mattress edge. "Come near and I will show you what I feel for you, Annyn Bretanne now Annyn Wulfrith."

She did not look away. Indeed, after the initial flush of embarrassment, she peered closer at him. "You are well made, Husband," she breathed, only to gasp when her gaze fell to his shoulder. "There will be scarring?"

"But one more scar among many. Now I would see you."

She bit her lip, lowered her gaze, and stared at her wedding ring. "Am I now a possession, Garr?"

He frowned. "If you are asking if you belong to me, you do."

Her eyes flicked to his. "And what of you? Do *you* belong to me?"

Where was she heading with this? Or was she heading anywhere at all? Perhaps such talk was merely a means of avoiding the marriage bed. If so, that would not do with Henry closing in on them.

"I am as much your husband as you are my wife," he said, struggling to keep impatience from his tone.

She nodded slowly. "And yet there is no sign that you belong to me, is there?"

He momentarily closed his eyes, and when he opened them, he did so with a sigh. "Pray, Annyn, speak. I know you are well capable of doing so."

She drew a deep breath, crossed to the bed, and pulled the sword ring from her thumb. "As I wear your ring, would you wear mine?"

Garr eyed it and mused that, not so long ago, he had silently rejoiced that it would never ride upon Lavonne's hand. "I have never heard of such—a wedding ring for a man."

"Will you wear it?"

What would Drogo have—?

He did not care what the ruthless warrior would have said or felt about a man who proclaimed himself as wed to his wife as she was to him. He raised his left hand. "I will."

Annyn looked momentarily surprised, then she smiled. With effort, she worked the ring over his large, resistant knuckle and settled it at the base of his finger. Continuing to hold his hand, she met his gaze. "I know it is but a market trinket and hardly fit for pledging one's life to another, but—"

"I count myself fortunate that it graces my hand and no other's," Garr interrupted.

"Truly?"

"Truly." He looked down her and up again. "Now, wife, will you let me see you? All of you?"

She released his hand and, to his relief, tugged her chainse off over her head and dropped it to the floor. "Do I disappoint?" she asked, though not coyly. After so many years of playing the boy, she needed to be made to feel a woman.

"Nay, you please." He drew her to him and slid his arms around her waist. "We will go slowly," he vowed and eased her onto the bed.

"Why?"

He groaned. Too much she had missed growing up among men. "A woman's first time brings pain."

Her gaze flickered. "And the next time?"

He brushed his mouth across hers. "Pleasure, Annyn. I promise."

Later, as they lay amid the shadows of night, Annyn gloried in her husband, a man she loved as had been denied her mother. A man who loved her, she realized. Now if only he would speak it.

When he rolled to the side, the loss of his body against hers was staggering, but then he turned her toward him and pulled her near.

Annyn pressed her cheek to his chest. It took more courage than she would have guessed to ask the question of her heart, but the sound of his deepening breath spurred her. "What is it you feel for me, Garr?"

"Did I not show you?"

She pushed up on an elbow and sought the sparkle of his eyes. "I would know its name."

"Mayhap it has no name."

"Mine has a name. Would you have me tell it?"

He did not answer.

"Very well." She leaned down and, against his lips, said, "I love you, Garr Wulfrith."

After a long moment, he said, "It is good that a wife feel such for her husband. It makes for a more pleasant union."

The distance his words put between them causing her to ache, Annyn lifted her head. Might she be wrong about his feelings?

"Let us sleep." He lowered his lids.

Annyn stared at his shadowed face—so handsome, though once she had told herself it was without appeal. As if a sculptor had one hundred times over formed his every feature, he was more handsome than any man she had looked upon. And he had chosen her.

She turned away, but as she stretched out beside him, he drew her back into the curve of his body.

"It is well, Annyn," he whispered into her hair. "Let us be content in that."

She could not. If it was true he did not love her, she would find a way to change that.

"You do not snore, Husband," Annyn mused, eyebrows gathered as she considered something on the chest at the foot of the bed before which she stood.

How had she known he had awakened? During these past few minutes in the earliest hour of morning, he had watched her move about the dim solar, lingering over the tapestries, frowning at the fine linen curtains gathered back from the bed, turning the ring that proclaimed her his wife, tempting him as she paced in nothing save the coverlet beneath which they had met last eve.

He sat up. "I am pleased to hear I do not snore. Did you think I might?"

She reached to the clothes he had discarded atop the chest, lifted his belt, and removed the misericorde awarded him upon his knighting, the same he had passed to Jonas only to have it returned by this woman who now professed to love him.

Love…As disturbing as her words of the night past were, and though he could not speak them himself, it felt as if they occupied every empty space within him—and even those he had not thought empty.

Annyn turned the misericorde. "You snored the night I came to render this unto you."

"That is because I wished you to believe I slept."

Her gaze flew to his. "You knew?"

"Only that someone had come within."

"But you let me…You did naught until I was upon you!"

He arched an eyebrow. "Lesson sixteen, lady wife, guard well one's knowledge of one's opponent."

She swept up a hand. "Pray, no more. I am no longer a squire in need of lessons."

"Aye, but now you are my wife, and for that there are also lessons."

Her lips tilted. "Far different, I expect."

"In some things."

"Tell."

Wanting her as he had not wanted any woman, he crooked a finger. "Come nearer and I will show you."

Blushing, she lowered her gaze to the dagger she had yet to set aside, and her humor cleared. "I would have you know that I could not do it."

"What?"

"The night I came to your chamber, I could not do that which brought me to Wulfen."

Could not kill him? But she had—

"I did not understand it then, but I must have known you could not have killed Jonas. You were not such a man, and surely no man can so greatly change."

"You are saying you would not have cut my throat?"

"'Twas as I intended, but when I drew the dagger back, I realized my mistake." She shook her head. "Ere I could withdraw, you seized me."

He *had* sensed hesitation when the intruder stood over him, but death had been too near to discover the truth of it.

"I ask that you believe me in this."

He searched her eyes. Though his father would have rebuked him for believing what he found in a woman's eyes, he said. "I believe you, Annyn."

She sighed. "Thank you, Husband."

That simple title from her lips made him want to make love to her again. In the next instant his passion faltered. Love? Only an expression.

"This belief I tried to kill you," she said, "is it the reason you continue to carry Jonas's dagger?"

"As a reminder?" He shrugged. "In part, but more because the misericorde was first mine."

She startled, as he inwardly did for having said what did not need to be told. What a lack wit he was in her presence! But it was no less than his father had warned—*always* a woman turned a man from his purpose.

"Yours, Garr?"

"Aye." He motioned her to the bed.

She came around and laid the misericorde in his hand.

He turned the weapon and tapped the steel beneath the hilt. "Those are my initials."

Annyn leaned forward and peered at the fine scratchings. "G. W." She shook her head. "As I did not know your Christian name, I believed the initials were the mark of the blacksmith who forged it. I feel the fool."

Garr lowered his gaze over her bared neck and shoulders, pulled her down beside him, and tossed the dagger to the far side of the mattress. "Now for another lesson."

However, as he bent to claim her mouth, she said, "Why did you give Jonas your dagger?"

Berating himself as he had done often since Annyn had come crashing into his life, he fell onto his back beside her.

Why *had* he given Jonas his dagger? Memory swept him back to Lincolnshire all those years ago: anger lengthening his stride through the wood, Merrick struggling for breath to stay near, movement ahead, a body swaying among tree limbs, Jonas's face mottled and contorted above a noose. The sight had nearly made him retch, not only for the shame of such a death, but that his harsh words and judgment had moved the young man to take his life.

He had known what he must do. And that no others must know, excepting Abel and Everard whose aid he had enlisted, and, of course, Merrick. While the squire had wheezed with his back to the scene, Garr had cut down Jonas, thus setting in motion a plan gone terribly awry.

"Garr?"

He raised his lids to find Annyn leaning over him. He reached up and fingered the black strands sweeping her cheek. "I cut him down."

Her gaze wavered.

"But I could not return him like that. Though he betrayed—"

"He did not—"

"Hear me and I will tell you all I should not."

She nodded stiffly.

"Though few die while in training, and usually only in battle, they are returned home wearing the Wulfen misericorde of knighthood to which they aspired." He drew a deep breath. "I knew I should not gird one on Jonas, but I could do no less for him. As there was no time to return to Wulfen, I fastened my own misericorde on him that his death would appear honorable." She did not need to know it was the same blade that had put the false wound to her brother's chest.

Annyn looked away.

"And you know the reason I made his death appear honorable?"

"Because you knew Jonas could not have taken his own life."

"By faith, woman!" He pushed onto his elbows, bringing their faces so near she jerked back to avoid what might have meant a bloody nose for one or both. "As I told before, I did it to spare your family shame, but also"—finally it would be spoken, and no more could he deny it—"I did it to ease my guilt over the judgment that pushed Jonas to a place that made death a better choice. Guilt I should not have felt for such a betrayer."

"Betrayer! I knew him better than ever you could, Garr Wulfrith."

"You *think* you knew him."

"I did!" She slapped a hand to her chest. "He was my brother."

"Listen to me——"

A knock shattered their private world. "My lord!" Squire Warren's voice came through the door. "Sir Abel bids me to tell you that Duke Henry approaches Stern."

Though Garr was grateful for last night's reprieve that had ensured consummation of his marriage, he bitterly wished for an hour more so that he and Annyn might put Jonas behind them.

"Send to my brother and tell him to hold Henry outside the walls until I come to the hall."

"I shall, my lord." There were murmurings in the corridor, then Warren called through, "The maid, Josse, has come to attend your lady wife, my lord."

Garr dropped his feet to the rushes, strode to the bed's end post, and pulled his robe from the peg. As he pushed his arms into it, he glanced at Annyn in her coverlet and followed her horrified gaze to the lower sheet that was marked with blood.

She whipped her head up, eyes turning more stricken when she saw he also saw. She wrenched the top sheet over it. "I do not understand. 'Tis not my time. Indeed, it is well past."

It took Garr a moment to understand the embarrassment that bubbled from her, and when he did, he nearly smiled. She thought it was her menses. What else had she not been told about being a woman? Did she know whence babies came?

He sighed. "I am relieved I shall not have to cut my hand after all."

"Why would you do that?"

He cinched the belt of his robe, stepped forward, and tossed back the top sheet. "Virgin's blood, Annyn. All the proof needed that a woman was chaste when she spoke her vows and the marriage was consummated."

Her frown deepened. "This is usual?"

"I do not know if 'tis usual, but it is as the church wishes it."

She looked back at the marked sheet, then once more whipped the top sheet over it. "You are saying that had I not...virgin's blood, you would have provided evidence yourself?"

"Aye, and I am pleased 'twill not be necessary."

"But who other than you and I would know?"

She was not going to like what he told. "Annyn—"

"My son!" his mother called through the door. "Make haste. Henry approaches."

"Enter!"

It was Samuel who opened the door. His face averted to afford his lord and lady privacy, he stepped aside as Lady Isobel and Josse entered. A moment later, the door closed behind them. One look at Annyn on the bed, the coverlet clutched to her, and both women smiled.

"Come, Daughter." Isobel bestowed the intimate title without strain or falsity. "We shall prepare you in Garr's chamber so that Squire Samuel may tend his lord."

Eyes large in her pretty face, Annyn drew the coverlet nearer and swung her feet to the floor.

Mayhap she did not need to know about the blood, Garr entertained, but then his mother exclaimed, "The sheet!" and hurried toward the bed. "Come, Josse, we must hang it out."

Annyn halted, causing the rushes to scatter. Had she heard right? She looked from the women as they descended upon the bed, to Garr. "They must do what?"

He crossed to her and laid a hand on her shoulder. "As is custom, the morning-after sheet is hung out."

Her face coloring deeper, she looked to Isobel and Josse. And cringed at the satisfied murmurs that rose from them as they assessed the sheet. The humiliation! "Never have I heard such."

Garr sighed. "Had you not been too busy with the things of men, you would have."

The outrage! "Mayhap I should have stayed with the things of men."

"I fear my taste only runs to women, Lady Wife."

There was nothing humorous about it! She glowered as the women pulled the sheet from the mattress. "This is primitive."

"I quite agree." Lady Isobel glanced over her shoulder.

Though she afforded only a glimpse of her face, Annyn was struck by the fatigue about her eyes and mouth.

"Unfortunately," Isobel continued, "'tis necessary, Daughter."

Daughter, again. The pleasing sound eased some of Annyn's embarrassment. "Where is the sheet to be hung?"

"Methinks the center window is best." Isobel held one end of the sheet and Josse the other as the two crossed the solar. The cool morning air rushed in with the opening of the shutters.

"For all to see?" Annyn choked.

"Most especially Henry," Garr said, "and Lavonne if he accompanies the duke." He leaned near and lowered his voice. "Regardless of whether or not our marriage is deemed clandestine, Annyn Wulfrith, that sheet proves it *is* a marriage. It says to all that you belong to me. And no man— no king—can take you from me."

His intensity stole her breath. Though what he said she knew to be true, it did not preclude excommunication. It tore at her that he, a man of such reverence, would risk it for her. And in that moment she was gifted with the certain knowledge of what he did not allow to pass his lips. He did love her. Garr Wulfrith, once her enemy, now her husband, loved her in spite of all.

For the moment putting the argument of Jonas aside, she laid a hand to his cheek. "I tell you true, Husband, I love thee. And though some may try, neither can any take you from me."

To her surprise—and hope—he pressed a hand over hers where she cupped his cheek. "We stand together, Annyn," he denied her the words she longed to hear. "Husband and wife."

It was not enough, but for now it would do.

"'Tis done." Lady Isobel stepped from the window. "Now come, Daughter, there is much to do ere you are presentable."

Annyn winced at the sight of the sheet in the window. Now all would know. Of course, what had happened in the solar on the night past was certainly expected of those who were newly wed. But that knowledge helped little. Though the solar was cooled by rain-scented air, the heat of embarrassment kept the chill from her.

"Be of good speed," Garr murmured as she turned to follow his mother and Josse from the solar.

Annyn hefted the coverlet higher to prevent it from dragging and stole a final glance behind. "And you, Husband."

His brief smile sending a shiver up her spine, she left him to prepare for his meeting with Henry.

21

"That is not me." Annyn stared at her transformation in the mirror that Josse held. "I do not know who that is."

Lady Isobel clapped her hands. "It is Lady Annyn Wulfrith, my daughter, my son's wife, the mother of my grandchildren."

Grandchildren. Would there be any? Might there now be one growing inside her?

She touched her face. Though she had refused powder, Isobel had coaxed her to apply a bit of rouge to her cheeks and lips and a light shadowing to her eyelids. But it was more than that which held her transfixed, more than the voluminous white head veil with its jeweled circlet of gold wire, more than the wisps of dark hair pulled forward and made to look feminine against her pale skin.

It was the bliaut woven of purple and gold silk on which Isobel and Josse had worked far into the night so that Annyn might wear it to receive Henry—the cause of their weary faces, and over which Annyn had cried when they had presented it. With its delicate embroidery at neck, hem, and wrists, its sleeves that fell open past her knees, its low waist and long train, it was more beautiful than any of her mother's gowns that had sufficed at Castle Lillia. And it fit her every curve, showing she did, in fact, possess some.

She stepped back to see more of herself in the mirror and thought one might even call her pretty.

"Who could deny you anything, hmm?" Lady Isobel's reflection joined Annyn's.

Annyn met her gaze in the mirror. "Never have I owned a gown fashioned just for me."

"I thought not."

"Thank you. And you, Josse."

"'Twas an honor, my lady." Josse dipped, causing the mirror's light to shudder around the chamber.

"Your husband awaits belowstairs," Lady Isobel said.

Annyn patted her skirts and was strangely thrilled by the slip of silk beneath her palms—and shocked that she should find pleasure in something so womanly. Would Garr be pleased? Would he even recognize her? Pushing back her shoulders, she hitched up the train of her bliaut.

Isobel preceded her down the corridor, then the stairs, beyond which voices were raised.

Had Garr let Henry in? Annyn prayed not, wishing to be at her husband's side when the duke descended.

A few steps up from the hall, Garr's mother looked around. "Do not forget that you are now a Wulfrith."

"I never shall."

When Annyn stepped into the hall, she became the dearest object of attention. A murmur rippled through the gathered knights, squires, pages, and servants—though not from Henry, for he was not yet within, as witnessed by her husband who was alone on the dais except for Abel.

Garbed in a tunic of red girded by a silver belt hung with a sword and misericorde, silver hair brushed back off his forehead, Garr stared at her.

What did he think? Annyn gripped her hands at her waist as she crossed the hall with carefully measured steps as Uncle had taught her—a waste of steps when half as many would suffice, but to stride the hall would detract from the image that Lady Isobel and Josse had taken such pains to afford her.

Garr's mouth curved, and he descended the dais. "My lady wife is most becoming." He caught up her hands and pressed his lips to them.

For this, the ladies swooned, but not Annyn. Though her clothes might make it appear she had been bred such a lady, and she more and more felt one, she could not so easily put out the things of men that had given meaning to her life when there had been none. And even if she could, she would not. Garr Wulfrith had not seen his last swordplay with Annyn Bretanne now Annyn Wulfrith.

"You are ready?" he asked.

"I am."

"Let Henry in, Abel."

The youngest brother's usually droll face now disturbingly grave, he nodded.

Garr led Annyn around the table, seated her to his right, and lowered to the lord's seat. Lady Isobel and her daughters also took their seats at the high table.

The hall fell silent, save for unintelligible whispers. In that silence, Annyn found Rowan where he stood near an alcove, flanked by men-at-arms, face gaunt even from a distance. As this was her day of judgment, so it was his.

Had he eaten anything this morn? she wondered when their eyes met, and only then realized her own belly was empty. But she was not hungry. Not when Duke Henry was without—and soon within—Stern's walls.

She considered Sir Merrick who leaned against the wall alongside the stairway. Several days back she had heard he would be leaving the service of the Wulfriths and wondered if it had anything to do with her questioning. Somehow, she must get him alone before he departed.

As she returned her regard to the table, she was struck by the absence of Henry's messenger, Sir Drake. He was nowhere among the many, meaning he had gone out to meet Henry. Meaning Henry did not need to look upon her humiliation hung from the window to know Garr Wulfrith had taken a wife.

Shortly, the pound of hooves reverberated through the hall as Henry and his men came into the inner bailey.

Annyn looked to Garr whose gaze was fixed on the open doorway. Jaw set, he was once more the warrior.

The clink of metal, scrape and thump of boots, and grunts and curses preceded the entrance of Henry and his men. Sir Drake on one side, Abel on the other, the young Henry who did not look like one who would be king, came first. With his quick and loose stride, his careless garments speckled and streaked with mud nearly up to his waist, his cropped red hair and beard, he looked more like a commoner.

He knew of the marriage, his color so livid he appeared only a shade off the purple of her bliaut—as did Lavonne who came behind him.

Beneath the table, a hand briefly covered Annyn's. "It is well," Garr softly assured, continuing to hold his gaze to Henry.

Lesson four, was it not? Keep your eyes on your opponent.

He stood to receive the duke, and Annyn and the others stood with him.

"Duke Henry!" Garr called. "We are most pleased to receive you in our hall."

The broad man stepped up to the dais. "Such a lie is better told by a woman, Baron Wulfrith," he spat in his cracked, hoarse voice, then stabbed Annyn with his blue-grey gaze.

Eyes upon your opponent. She held to him and was glad she did, otherwise she would have missed the startle in his eyes. It seemed she was, indeed, transformed, and not even the mighty Henry could hide his surprise. But would it soften him?

He returned to Garr. "'Tis an enemy you wish to make of me, Baron Wulfrith?"

Though Garr stood before a man who might soon call all of England his own, he did not flinch. "An enemy I would not allow within my walls."

Henry's freckled nose flared. "Then why do you defy me by taking what does not belong to you?"

THE UNVEILING

Whatever Garr's emotions, he did not show them. Still, Annyn felt his ire and foreboding for this man who was many years younger than he. "My lord, as you know, the lady Annyn and I were wed yesterday. In all things, we are now man and wife. Hence, on the matter of to whom she belongs, I must differ. Lady Annyn Wulfrith belongs to me."

Annyn was not offended by Garr's claim on her, for on the night past, she had as thoroughly claimed him as her own. She glanced at the ring that shone silver on his left hand.

In Henry's pause, Lavonne snarled, "She was promised to me!"

The future king swung his head around, and before he spoke a word, Annyn almost pitied Lavonne. "Get you back!" the duke roared.

As the baron retreated, Henry returned to Garr. "All know that your marriage is clandestine." His tone was slightly milder, perhaps for having eased some of his wrath upon Lavonne. "You would risk excommunication for a woman who disguised herself as a man that she might set upon you?"

A muscle in Garr's jaw spasmed, but when he spoke, his voice did not betray him. "Surely, Duke Henry, you did not come to Stern to speak of things that cannot be changed."

Henry's eyes bulged.

Garr laid his palms flat on the table and leaned forward. "Especially as there is something far dearer to your heart that can be changed, and all the sooner if you make me your ally."

Henry stared, then, by degree, turned thoughtful.

As if everyone held their breath, the hall resounded with a silence so deep that the soft snore of a dog could be heard.

"Your earl is in agreement?" Henry asked.

Then Rowan might also be delivered of the duke's wrath? Annyn prayed so.

Garr straightened. "He agrees he shall go whichever side the Wulfriths go."

Was that how it was? Though it was known that the Wulfriths were highly regarded by their overlord who often bent his ear to their counsel, it was surprising that he allowed one of his barons to decide all of his lands for him. Was the man truly so weak?

"Feeble fool," Henry muttered, then shouted, "Clear the hall! Baron Sevard and Baron Cheetham, you shall remain."

The two older men stepped forward.

"As shall my brother, Sir Abel," Garr said.

Henry shrugged. "As you will."

"I yield the high seat, my lord."

With the hall emptying around them, Henry skirted the table. At his approach, Annyn looked to Garr.

"Go," he said softly, then softer still, "Say your farewell to Rowan. He leaves Stern this day."

Before Henry remembered him? Were they alone, Annyn would have kissed her husband. "I thank you." She turned, but Henry blocked her path.

Though a stout man, he was not tall. Indeed, he topped Annyn by little. Gaze hard, he said, "Pray your *husband* keeps bargains better than you, *Annyn Bretanne*."

She dipped her head. "I am now Annyn Wulfrith, my lord."

His upper lip curled.

Suppressing a smile, she stepped around him.

"Annyn Bretanne, *now* Wulfrith!" he stopped her.

She turned and struggled to hide her surprise over the sharp contrast between the duke and Garr where they stood together. Not only was her husband nearly a head taller than Henry, he was as a beacon to the other man's candle light—handsome of face and form, distinguished with that shock of silver hair that she longed to push her fingers through. "My lord?"

He swept his gaze down her. "In one thing I am pleased—you heeded my advice on footwear."

She followed his gaze to the peep of a slipper beneath her skirts. Remembering the boots she had worn at Castle Lillia, a bubble of laughter passed her lips. "'Twas good advice, indeed, my lord." She put her foot out to better show the slipper. "Far more comfortable than boots."

"And more womanly."

Annyn caught Garr's questioning gaze before he turned his attention to a serving wench. "A pitcher of our best wine!"

As Annyn crossed the dais, she looked out across the hall that was empty but for a handful, among them Rowan and his guards, Sir Merrick where he lingered near the door, and Lavonne who strode toward the latter.

Annyn started toward Rowan, but then she saw Lavonne pause before Merrick. Their words whispered the air without form, and whatever was spoken, it caused Sir Merrick's face to darken. Lavonne's profile showed he was no more amiable.

Remembering when Sir Merrick had caught her on the stairs at Wulfen and warned that Lavonne was not to be trusted, she halted and struggled to rearrange the pieces of Jonas's death that she had once fit to include Garr.

Stride stiffer than moments earlier, Lavonne stepped outside, and Merrick stared after him before also starting for the doors.

Annyn glanced at her husband and Henry. As they and their men were too absorbed in this day's talks to pay her heed, she picked her skirts high and hurried outside. In the dank of after-rain, she overtook Sir Merrick. "I must needs speak with you."

He continued his descent of the steps.

"I beseech you, Sir Merrick, but a few minutes is all I ask."

Only when she stepped ahead of him into the inner bailey did he halt. Sleepy eyes wider and brighter than she had ever seen them, he said, "I cannot help you, my lady."

She caught his arm. "You know the truth of my brother's death. I know you do."

"The truth is that Jonas was found hung from a tree in the wood." Still, dark shadows, as of dread memories, flickered in his eyes. "And that is all the truth there is."

"You were there, weren't you? When your lord found my brother?"

His mouth twitched. "My lady, 'tis inappropriate that you stand so near me."

"Then speak and I shall step back."

He drew a deep breath. "I accompanied Lord Wulfrith in the search for your brother, and was there when Jonas was found, there when my lord made his death appear honorable."

Rowan came out onto the steps above, and with him his escort. Questioningly, her old friend looked from her to Merrick.

Annyn released the man's arm. "Who else was there?"

"Sirs Everard and Abel."

"And?"

"None others, my lady. None others could know."

But others *had* known. According to Lavonne, who had taunted her over her brother's death while at Wulfen, all had known Jonas had hung himself and their lord had put a wound to him to cover the truth of it. Unless it was a lie he told.

Beginning to tremble, she breathed, "It was Lavonne."

Sir Merrick's breath snagged, and he glanced right and left. "We must needs speak elsewhere."

"Where?"

"The stables in the outer bailey. Come in five minutes."

Five minutes seemed a world away as she watched him stride from her.

"Lady Annyn?"

She turned and was wounded by sorrow at the sight of her man. How had he grown so old so soon? "Sir Rowan?"

"All is well, my lady?"

She longed to reveal what Merrick had confirmed, but could not do so in the presence of the men-at-arms. She caught up Rowan's hands that seemed to lack the strength that had long ago helped a young girl pull her bow string. "Pray, do not leave until I speak with you."

As his brow knit, she stepped past him and traversed the inner bailey. Knowing five minutes was not yet gone, she lingered before the gatehouse. Every second feeling a minute, every minute an hour, she held there though she drew curious glances from Henry's and Garr's men.

Guessing five minutes had passed, Annyn hastened across the drawbridge.

The clang of metal on metal, testament to swords being beaten to life, rang clearly from the blacksmith's shop as she hurried across the bailey. Not even with Henry come to make him an ally did Garr pause in the defense of his home.

Entering the dimly lit stables of the outer bailey, Annyn called, "Sir Merrick?"

At the far end where a torch flickered, a figure appeared and beckoned, then returned to the stall from which he had emerged.

Annyn hurried past the other stalls, most of which were occupied, and stepped into the end stall that was larger than the rest, as of one used for birthing colts.

Sir Merrick stood in the light that shone through a small window.

"It was Lavonne who murdered my brother," she said. "Was it not?"

He stared at her.

"For this you sought me out at Wulfen and warned me to be cautious of him. Tell me it is so."

His eyes momentarily closed. "It is so, my lady."

Dear God. The man for whom she had revealed herself at Wulfen that he would not stand accused of her crime, had done far worse than she. Such bitter irony that she had gone to the aid of one whose death was warranted.

Annyn reached a hand out to steady herself, but there was naught to hold to where she stood at the center of the stall.

"My lady?" Sir Merrick grasped her arm.

When he started to urge her to the floor, she shook her head. "I did not break my fast this morn."

"Forgive me for telling you. 'Twould have been best had you never known."

"You are wrong. I had to know."

Continuing to brace her, Sir Merrick said, "I give you my vow that Jonas will be avenged."

Vengeance that was not hers, but God's. Just as it was not Sir Merrick's, though he made it sound like it belonged to him. "What do you intend?"

"Lavonne will not see another sunrise. He has agreed to meet me here in the half hour, and it is then I will do to him as he did to your brother." He nodded to the left of the threshold.

Annyn peered into the shadowed corner where a noose hung from a rafter. Her skin creeped. "You shall hang him," she whispered. Though it was as she would have once wanted, and a part of her still longed for, God once more spoke to her of vengeance. This time, He did it through Garr's voice.

"I shall hang him," Sir Merrick said, "and in that, Jonas will be partly avenged."

"Partly?"

His gaze faltered. "Your brother was strong of will and body, Lady Annyn. One alone could not have done to him what happened that night in the wood."

Chill bumps rose across her limbs. "Who was the other?"

He released her arm and crossed to the stall window. Bracing his hands on the sill, he dropped his head to his chest.

"Sir Merrick?"

He did not move, did not even look to breathe.

Annyn hurried forward and laid a hand on his shoulder. "Pray, tell me who the other one was."

He turned. Tears glittering in his eyes, revulsion tugging at his mouth, he bit, "'Twas me."

She stumbled back. "Nay, you would not!"

A tear crawled down his cheek. "Alone, I would not, no matter my anger and feeling of betrayal, but Lavonne is most persuasive. Aye, my lady, I did it, and violated the most inviolable of lessons. I let another make my way for me."

"Why?" She trembled, her hands nearly numb. "Why did you do it?"

"Jonas betrayed. Jonas, whom I had come to admire and love as a brother." He wheezed as he pulled in air. "Most esteemed and trusted of all squires, he stole a missive from King Stephen to Lord Wulfrith that he might deliver it to the enemy—Henry."

As Garr had told.

"In my presence and Lavonne's, he admitted it to Lord Wulfrith and defended that, after stealing the missive, he realized his error and intended to return it."

Annyn stared at her brother's murderer. "You believed him?"

"I might have, but like a fool, I allowed Lavonne to goad me to anger. Half the night he spat and raged over Jonas's betrayal, pushing me, testing me, tempting me to do what I would not have done." He dragged a hand down his face. "'Twould be but to put fear into Jonas, he said, to teach him a lesson he would not soon forget. Still I did not want to do it, but I did, my lady." Bitter laughter rent the air. "And now to see whose side Lavonne has gone. Forsooth, methinks he was always there, that he used me against Jonas whom he believed had betrayed *him!*"

Somewhere in the stables, a horse snickered and another whinnied, but the ache rolling through Annyn rendered the sounds as insignificant as the buzz of a fly. "You killed my brother. You stood there while he kicked and tried to open his throat. You let him die."

"I wanted to cut him down. I told Lavonne it was enough." He shook his head. "But a few moments more, he said, and then…I lost my breath." A glistening drop fell from his nose to the dirt floor. "I am weak and foul…dishonorable…not worthy."

"How true," another voice entered the stall.

Annyn swung around and saw Lavonne where he stood on the other side of the threshold. If not for his sword in hand, its blade propped against his shoulder, she would have set herself at him, but the lessons Garr had taught her prevailed. At her back, she heard the metallic whisper of Sir Merrick's sword as it was drawn from its scabbard.

"Forsooth"—Lavonne stepped forward, giving her no choice but to retreat deeper into the stall—"you are as weak and unworthy as Lady Annyn's beloved brother whom I persuaded to steal the missive for Henry." He smiled. "Jonas, who thought himself above all, was ruled by me."

"Stand back, my lady," Sir Merrick entreated.

Annyn did as told.

The baron surveyed the shadow-ridden stall. The noose made him frown, then cluck his tongue. "For me, old friend?"

"By the sword or by the noose, this day you shall die."

"Mayhap were I fool enough to come at the half hour, but see, I am here." Lavonne sighed. "Surprise is a powerful weapon, Lady Annyn, a lesson taught to me by your dear husband."

"Cur!" she spat.

"Ouch! Thee wounds!"

Sir Merrick chose that moment to lunge, sweeping his sword so near Lavonne's face that, if the baron had a beard, it would have been shaved from him.

Lavonne countered, seemingly unhindered by the wound that Garr had done his arm at Wulfen. A pity it had not been his sword arm.

The swords crashed again, turning the horses in their stalls restless, causing Annyn's hand to itch for a hilt as she watched her brother's murderers—each set on ending the life of the other. She edged toward the threshold.

"Nay, my lady," Lavonne scorned, "you stay." He deflected a blow from Merrick's sword, then knocked her to the far side of the stall. If not that she threw her hands up, she would have hit the wall headfirst.

Palms splintered, she turned to see Sir Merrick's hose rent by Lavonne and his blood spill forth. But the injury to his lower thigh did not stop him, nor his rattling breath. He launched himself at Lavonne again.

Annyn considered the window. Surely someone would hear the meeting of swords? In the next instant, hope fled. The sound would not be heard above that of the swords being forged in the smithy. And for this, Sir Merrick had likely chosen this place to stand against Lavonne.

He stumbled against her, the wheeze of his breath and high color evidence he struggled to overcome some ailment. More, it told that he could not long hold against Lavonne whose sword slashed without cease. When next they met, blood was drawn from Merrick's left arm.

The knight staggered against a side wall and Lavonne followed.

Knowing he would now put an end to Merrick, Annyn threw herself against Lavonne, causing him to lurch.

"Witch!" He thrust her off and she fell to the dirt floor. Forgetting the one whose death he had been near to dispensing, Lavonne swept his sword up and came for her.

Annyn scooted backwards. *Heavenly Father, deliver me. Be my help, my shield!*

With a bellow, Merrick charged with his sword high in a two-handed grip.

The man who was to have been her husband halted, twisted his sword behind, and smiled as Merrick hurtled onto the blade.

"Nay!" Annyn cried.

"Weak." Lavonne denounced and jerked his sword free.

Merrick landed at an awkward angle on the beaten dirt floor and, from the quiver of his chest, it was certain he would soon be dead.

Why Annyn should ache for the one who had aided in murdering her brother, why she should wish to go to him, she did not understand, but with Lavonne standing between them, it was not possible.

The baron drew a finger through the blood on his blade. "That is one," he said, "and you, Lady Annyn, are two."

Fear bounded through her. She did not want to die, especially now that she was loved by Garr.

Fortunately, Lavonne seemed in no hurry to render her his second murder of the day. With less than a foot separating them, he looked down on her as if she were a hare without hope for another day, then he dropped to his haunches. "I cannot tell how I anticipated our wedding night when I whispered"—he leaned near and touched his mouth to her ear—"'twas I who killed your brother."

Wishing she had a belly full of food to retch upon him, Annyn said, "Why did you do it?"

He drew back. "For the same reason you believed Wulfrith killed him—betrayal." His sour breath stung her nostrils. "In refusing to deliver the missive, he betrayed Henry for loyalty to a man who stood the fool's side of this war."

As she had known, her brother *had* realized the wrong from the right and, in the end, had not betrayed Garr.

"Too, I could not have him revealing I was Henry's side, could I?"

"Was it Henry who ordered my brother's death?"

Lavonne snorted. "There was no time to consult him, but I am sure he would have approved."

Would he have? Lord, she prayed England's king was not so hell bound.

"Now for two," Lavonne reminded her of the fate she shared with Sir Merrick. He stood and beckoned with his crimson blade.

Did he intend to gut her as well? To part her head from her shoulders? She stole a glance at Sir Merrick's sword that lay beneath his slack hand. "One last question I beg of you."

Lavonne stepped over Sir Merrick, putting the knight's body between them. "You think it will buy you a way past me, my lady?"

"I would not presume to better a warrior such as you, my lord. After all, you *were* my husband's pupil."

A reminder that splashed his cheeks with uncomely color.

"Did Henry know my brother sided with him?" It was as the duke had alluded at Castle Lillia when he claimed to have had Jonas's loyalty, but how had he known?

Lavonne bared his teeth. "Once Jonas agreed to deliver the missive to Henry, I sent word to the duke."

"As you also sent word of my brother's death? How he died?"

A near drunken smile turned the baron's lips. "I told him shame had caused Jonas Bretanne to hang himself upon being found with the missive." He chuckled. "Some things are best held close, my lady."

"Another of my husband's lessons?"

"One of my own." He looked to the fallen knight. "Pity I did not kill him years ago. I would have slept better."

Could she gain Merrick's sword before Lavonne brought his own down upon her? "Which is the reason you must now kill me."

"Thou art most perceptive. Now for that hanging."

Annyn shifted her regard to where the noose swayed, her thoughts to Sir Merrick's sword. If she lunged right, she might just reach it.

"You will not like it any better if I have to drag you."

Now he would kill her as he had killed Jonas, would—

You can do this, Garr's voice came to her.

She could do it. *Would* do it. As she lunged for the sword, Lavonne hurtled toward her. Gripping steel, she rolled, jumped to her feet, and swept her blade up to deflect his blow.

"Witch!" He spewed sour breath past the crossing of their swords.

"Murderer!" She thrust back and swung again.

This time it was he who deflected the blow. When their swords next met, the force caused her head veil to skew and block her vision. Blindly, she pushed off his blade, with her free hand tore the veil from her head, and just barely countered his next swing.

Around Merrick's body they met, Lavonne cursing her for all things foul in this world until he laid a blow so hard to her blade that she fell against the wall. Thrusting off, she aimed for his exposed belly.

He retreated enough to spare his innards, but Annyn's sword opened his tunic, scoring the skin beneath. He roared and swung wide.

Annyn sent his blade up off hers, but then he was on her again. Though he next sought to cut her legs from beneath her, it was the skirt of her bliaut and chainse that fell victim to his sword.

"Now you die!" He came again.

She spun away and her foot caught in her torn skirt. If not that she threw out her arms, she would have fallen on her sword.

Slamming his booted foot to her hand that held the hilt, Lavonne ground it into the dirt.

Annyn cried out as her fingers spasmed open, cried again when Lavonne took hold of her hair and dragged her across the stall. She screamed, kicked and clawed, and reached for Sir Merrick's arm as she was pulled past, but to no avail.

In the corner of the stall, Lavonne halted, and there, above his wretched grin, hung the noose.

Fear denying her air as if the rope was already fit about her neck, she stared.

"I shall enjoy this." Lavonne slid his sword into its scabbard. "Such fond memories."

Annyn screamed and flailed as the noose neared, and then it was falling past her eyes and flopping to her shoulders. The horror of it stilled her long enough for Lavonne to retrieve the other end of the rope. As he began to take up the slack, she reached to the noose. *Dear Lord, help me!*

The rope cinched tight, forcing her to her feet. And, bit by fearsome bit, he raised her to her toes.

22

GARR STARED THROUGH Henry's face and wondered at the fear in his breast. Though he was wary of Henry, this feeling was not caused by the man. Whence did it come?

"What do you say?" Henry asked for the answer Garr had yet to give. As fear deepened, he pressed a fist to his chest. Was his heart failing?

"Brother?" Abel asked.

Where was Annyn? Had she followed his mother abovestairs?

"What ails you, Wulfrith?" Henry asked.

Garr looked to Abel. "Where is she?"

"Who?" Henry demanded.

"My wife! Where is my wife?"

Abel looked around. "She is not here—"

"I know she is not here!" Garr shoved his chair back. He started for the stairs, but something turned him away. How he knew it, he could not say, but she was not in the donjon. Ignoring his brother who called to him and Henry who demanded an explanation, Garr ran to the great doors.

The porter hastened to open them, barely managing to step out of the way as his lord thrust past.

The inner bailey that stretched before Garr was empty of Annyn. But there, before the inner gatehouse, was Rowan, his arms held by one of the men set to guard him, and gathered around him was a score of knights.

Annyn's man shouted something as he strained for release.

"Pray, what is it?" Abel asked, coming up behind his brother.

"Annyn." Garr took the steps two at a time to the bailey. "Back!" he bellowed as he ran toward the gatehouse.

The knights opened a path for him, and before he was even upon Rowan, he demanded, "Where is she?"

Relief flashed across the man's face. "Gone to the outer bailey. She followed Sir Merrick there, but I do not know where. Your men would not allow me——"

"Release him!" Garr stepped forward, pulled the soldier's sword, and thrust it at Rowan.

With a look of wonder, the man accepted it.

"Come with me!" Garr sped over the drawbridge.

In the center of the outer bailey that sounded with the cry of beaten steel and the pound of those who followed, he halted.

The granary? The mews? The stables? The millhouse? *Lord, let me not be too late. Not now that I love.*

Holding the end rope taut enough to keep her on her toes, Lavonne spat, "If not that you first whored yourself on Wulfrith, and were you more comely, I would take you myself."

Never had Annyn been so content with her appearance than she was at that moment. Both hands dragging on the noose about her neck in her struggle to catch a breath, she stared at him. Her lungs were rewarded for her efforts, but not enough to satisfy their straining.

Lavonne leaned near. "When you are dead, I shall have your lands. 'Tis the least Henry can give for the betrothal stolen from me."

Movement, so slight she thought it was of her imagining, drew her regard past him. There it was again—larger. Though there was no more breath to be had, she looked back at Lavonne for fear he would follow her gaze.

"Finished with your prayers?" he said with a twisted grin.

Sir Merrick rose at his back, and Annyn did not have to look near upon him to know he was crimson-stained—nor that he was swordless and had no chance of returning his blade to hand before Lavonne turned on him.

Fearing he would be heard, Annyn pulled from her depths what little strength she had left and crammed a knee into Lavonne's groin. A silent howl opened his mouth and his eyes wide as he lurched back. But rather than give up the rope, he leaned on it.

The noose snapped Annyn's chin to her chest and swept the ground from beneath her. She clawed at the noose and sucked hard, but her throat would not open. *Lord, pray, not like this!*

Then she saw Sir Merrick fall upon Lavonne's back and heard the men's grunts and shouts as they crashed to the ground.

Annyn fell back to earth. Landing hard on her hands and knees, she rolled to the side and found air in the noose's ease. As she threw off the vile rope, she gulped her lungs full.

Knowing every second that passed drew her nearer the noose again, she brought the loathsome baron to focus and saw he straddled Sir Merrick who struggled beneath him. A moment later, Lavonne drew back his arm to deliver a death blow.

"Nay!" She scrambled to her feet.

But still Merrick bled again. A dagger protruding from his chest, he settled his darkening gaze to Annyn and mouthed, "Forgive me."

She stared, hurting for this man who had aided in murdering her brother.

"Fool!" Lavonne shouted and heaved the dagger free.

Reminded that her own death was near, Annyn whipped her head around. There lay Merrick's sword that Lavonne had ground from her hand.

Act! 'Tis your only chance.

She grabbed the sword before Lavonne could rise from Merrick. As she charged toward him, his hand went to his sword. However, before he could wrap his fingers around the hilt, she thrust the blade tip to his chest.

He stilled and stared at it, then raised his eyes to where she stood over him—eyes that mirrored her own disbelief at what she had done. "I fear you have me, Lady Annyn," he spoke as one might comment on a blade of grass. "But can you do it?"

She could not, though not so long ago she had believed she could take the life of so foul a being. But she would not have him know that.

With a jab of the sword that surely pricked him through his tunic, she said, "Four long years I have lived for this day. Aye, miscreant, I can."

"Yet you do not. Why, when there is no more to be told of your brother's unfortunate death?" He laughed. "Nay, Annyn Bretanne, you cannot. You may play at swords, but you are no warrior."

He was right. She was not a warrior, this woman who found unexpected pleasure in donning a dress that fit, this woman who loved Garr Wulfrith.

"Give me the sword," Lavonne ordered.

"That I shall," she threatened.

"Some time this day? Or would the morrow better suit? Better yet—"

The widening of Lavonne's eyes alerted her to the sound of others entering the stables. She glanced toward the threshold and, as Lavonne reared up, all she could think was that she had violated lesson four that told to keep one's eyes on one's opponent.

She jumped forward to put him to the sword again, but he lunged to the side, slammed his forearm into her sword arm, and propelled his body hard into hers. The clamor in the stables swelling, answered by the thrash of distraught horses, Annyn and Lavonne fell together against the far wall.

Though the impact nearly loosened her hand from the hilt, she held to the sword above her head and struggled to bring it down. She was pinned. Worse, Lavonne drew his own sword.

As she followed it up from its scabbard, Garr hurtled across the space with a roar that made her and the baron startle. Then he was there, his sword spinning Lavonne's out of his grasp.

Looking the wolf with his shock of silver hair and lips pulled back in a snarl, Garr slammed a hand around Lavonne's throat and lifted him off his feet as if he weighed less than a skinned chicken. A moment later, the baron bounced off the wall and landed beside Sir Merrick.

A killing in his blood, Garr started to follow, but then halted. Though beneath years of incessant training was a terrible anger of which many spoke when he took up a sword, what he felt went beyond that to a rank hatred that threatened to devour him. He must not allow it—for God and Annyn.

Shoulders heaving, he called himself back to the woman who needed him. As the others crowded the threshold of the stall behind Sir Rowan whose face contorted as he looked upon the scene, Garr turned.

The sight of Annyn—flecked with blood, continuing to grip the sword where she stood with her back pressed to the wall, skirts torn and dirtied—caused his hatred to surge anew. Had Lavonne ravished her? Fury boiled his blood, but then she whispered, "Garr."

He went to her, eased the sword from her hand, and cupped her face in his palm. "You are hurt?"

"I do not think so."

"Did he…?"

She jerked her head side to side and fell against his chest.

Garr wrapped an arm around her to support her, closed his eyes, and sent thanks heavenward. Dear Lord, he did love her. Regardless of his father's lesson that a man love nothing save his destrier, sword, and shield, he loved this woman who was now his wife. It went against all to which a warrior must aspire, but there was nothing he wanted more than to love her and be loved by her.

A shout sounded at his back. Holding Annyn, he swung his sword around.

It was not needed, for Rowan was there. With a thrust of the sword that Garr had given him, he put Lavonne through where he had come up on his knees. A bloodied dagger to hand, the baron looked at his torn center before crumpling atop Merrick.

Garr returned his sword to its scabbard. Whatever had happened here was done. As he swung Annyn up into his arms, she looked down at the two men and shuddered.

"'Tis over," he soothed.

"Aye." She searched out Rowan. "By your hand, Jonas is avenged."

Garr's step faltered. This had all to do with Jonas? But of course it did. Had she been right all along that her brother was murdered? It seemed so, and by Lavonne. Though the questions burned, now was not the time to ask them. As he carried her forward, he saw the rope in the corner from which a noose was fashioned. The chill hand of death clawing at him, he held her nearer and carried her from the stables, only to find the duke advancing on him.

"What is this?" Henry demanded.

"Your man, Lavonne, is dead." Leaving Henry sputtering, Garr continued to the donjon where the morning-after sheet fluttered in the breeze.

Shortly, he laid Annyn on their marriage bed. "Out!" he ordered those who had anxiously followed. His mother ushered her daughters, Josse, and the three squires Warren, Samuel, and Charles from the solar and softly closed the door.

"They did it," Annyn whispered and crept a hand to her neck. "They were the ones."

Lavonne *and* Merrick? Surely—

Glimpsing the abraded skin beneath her fingers, he peered nearer. Rope burns about her neck. *Dear God!*

He would have torn from the solar to the stables to sunder Lavonne's corpse limb by limb, but Annyn's voice reached through the fire.

"Hold me, Garr. Pray, hold me."

All was told—all that made him feel a fool for not having believed.

Continuing to curse his blindness that had brought this day upon Annyn, Garr dipped the towel in the steaming bath water. Though no blood remained on her—blessedly, little of it her own—he once more swept the cloth over her shoulders, across the back of her neck that was nearly untouched by rope burns, down the other shoulder, and lastly her palms from which he had eased the splinters.

Despite the certainty of Henry's impatience, Garr had held Annyn for what seemed hours, and bit by aching bit she had told of her encounter with Merrick and Lavonne, explaining so much he had thought he understood. Finally, she had fallen into a restless sleep from which she had awakened as the last of day's light went out. But not a word had she spoken this past half hour.

He wrung the towel, draped it over the tub's edge, and came around to the side. As he dropped to his haunches, Annyn lifted her head.

Suppressing his reaction to the abrasions ringing her neck, Garr said, "I am sorry, Annyn."

"For what?"

"That the warrior I was—that I am—was so unseeing that Lavonne and Merrick could do what they did and go unpunished for four years. And punished now only because you could see what I could not."

"You did not know my brother as I did."

"I knew him well enough to know I had his loyalty—his eyes told me so. For that and his facility with weapons, I made him First Squire."

She shifted nearer, causing the water to slap against the sides of the tub. "His eyes?"

The intensity with which she regarded him when, moments earlier, she had been content to remain inside herself, was unsettling.

"Aye, that seat of emotion where truth cannot hide. Jonas took the missive, but when he told he could not betray after all, my anger would not allow me to believe him though his eyes were true." Garr shook his head. "Had I not let anger rule, I would not have begun to distrust what I saw in others' eyes. I would have seen what was in Lavonne's and Merrick's and known." The irony was that even now his anger swelled. Never would he have believed the unveiling of Annyn and her revenge would lead to further unveilings—Rowan's deception and fathering of

Jonas, Isobel's tale of love and death, Merrick and Lavonne's murder of Jonas.

He thrust to his feet and nearly trampled the remains of the purple bliaut that Annyn had first donned this morning—would never don again.

"By faith, Annyn! For his guilt, Merrick allowed Rowan to take you from me in the wood, and still I did not see the lie in his eyes when he blamed his negligence on lost breath! For all my father labored to teach me, I am unworthy!"

The water sloshed and Annyn rose and stepped out of the tub. Her body glistening in the light of torches, she laid a hand to his cheek. "Nay, Garr Wulfrith, you are more worthy than any man I have known. I am honored to be your wife."

As much as he longed to pull her to him and bury his face against her neck, he stepped back. "Then you are a fool." He retrieved his robe and thrust it at her. "Cover yourself."

She put her arms through it and belted it around her small waist, then came to him on the sweet scent of rushes that released their essence beneath her feet. "Shall we be fools together, Husband? Shall we love one another, forgetting all the ill gone before?" She pressed her palms to his chest. "Shall we make children and grow old together?"

How wonderful she made it sound, as if it was possible. "You nearly died."

"But I did not. You came for me." A smile touched her lips. "How did you know where to find me?"

Though the warrior that Garr's father had demanded of him balked at revealing what had pulled him from his negotiations with Henry, he said, "I do not understand it, but I felt your fear as if the Lord Himself whispered it to me."

"Truly?"

"Aye." He clenched his hands at his sides. "You ought to detest me, Annyn."

"That I could never do."

"You once did."

Her gaze lowered to the left side of his face that bore evidence of the hatred her fourteen-year-old self had felt for him. Where her eyes went, her fingers followed, and she gently traced the four scores those same fingers had clawed into his skin. "That was when I wrongly believed you responsible for Jonas's death."

"And am I not?"

Her hand stilled on his jaw. "Jonas did betray, and though he could not finish what impulse led him to do, only a fool would have disregarded that betrayal, regardless of what the eyes told." She took a step nearer Garr, so near he could smell the warmth of her skin. "He let another make his way for him, and for that he died." Tears brightened her eyes. "Nay, you are not responsible. Jonas and Lavonne and Sir Merrick are to blame. Regardless of your anger, you could have done no different."

Could he not have? Mayhap. "Still, that does not excuse me for being blind all these years. So blind I could not see the murderer in my midst. Near every day since, Merrick has been in my company, and all that he revealed in behavior and the depths of his eyes I named all but the guilt it was."

Annyn shook her head. "You were wrong about Jonas's death, but no more wrong than I was in believing you murdered him—far less wrong than I who sought your death."

Though Garr longed to accept what she spoke, he struggled with all Drogo had taught him.

She cupped his face between her hands. "'Tis over. No more will I allow my brother's death to cast me in darkness. I want light, I want laughter, I want tomorrow. I want you, Garr Wulfrith." She leaned in and put an ear to his chest. "Even when your heart whispers, it speaks most loud." She peered up at him. "Will you say it, Garr? Though I feel it, I long to hear it."

He knew what she wanted—one last unveiling. Words for which he had received no training. A declaration of emotion that, until Annyn

Bretanne, had been but something at which to scoff. It was true he loved her, but surely it would make him vulnerable to speak it. And a warrior—

By faith! Despite having had a sword to hand since the age of four, he was first a man. A man who loved this woman. But before he could speak the words that shied from his tongue, Annyn lowered her gaze.

"One day you will tell it to me."

Garr caught her chin. "I will not." Putting his father behind him, letting himself feel what was real and true and good, he said, "*This* day I will tell you. I love you, Annyn Wulfrith. If you will have me, I will pass all my life with you."

Eyes sparkling, she touched a finger to his lips. "I will have you."

Though it was too soon to ask her to be one with him again, Garr touched his mouth to hers. *A kiss will suffice*, he told himself, but when she sighed into him, he pulled her nearer and deepened the kiss. Later he would go slowly. Later—

He drew back. "Do you want this, Annyn? Mayhap 'tis too soon."

"I do want this."

"As do I." He freed the belt of her robe and slid the garment off. It fell to the rushes, revealing the woman that Annyn was. Perfectly formed.

"You do not mind that I am not comely?" she asked.

"Not comely?"

She averted her gaze. "'Twas not difficult for me to play the man."

Considering her upbringing, he was not surprised that she doubted her femininity. Forsooth, one did not have to look too near to know she was less than comfortable with the things of women. "A man you played, but a man I more than once bemoaned for being too pretty."

"You did?"

He drew her to the table on which the basin sat and retrieved the mirror there. "Look." He stepped to her back and lifted the silvered oval before her face. "There was but one thing you lacked, Annyn, and now you have it."

She searched her features, touched her mouth, nose, and cheeks, and saw what Garr saw. She was not and would never be Lady Elena, but she did not need to be now that she possessed that of which Garr spoke. "Love," she said softly and met his gaze in the mirror.

"Aye, love." He pulled her around. "There is none more comely than my lady wife. And never will there be." He returned the mirror to the table, swung her into his arms, and carried her to the bed where he made love to her.

How much time passed before he turned with her onto his side, Annyn could not have said, but it was with obvious regret that he did so.

"I must go to Henry."

She had forgotten about the duke who would be angered at having been kept waiting all these hours.

Garr must have sensed her dismay, for he said, "All will be well, Annyn. Henry needs me nearly as much as the Wulfriths need him."

"And Stephen?"

"If England is to ever again prosper, Stephen must surrender the crown. There is naught else for it."

"I am sorry."

"Do not be." He kissed her brow. "It brought us together."

She threaded her gaze through his. "Am I worthy, my lord?"

He pressed a hand to his chest. "So worthy, my love."

Epilogue

Stern Castle, November 1153

"I AM SUMMONED." Garr looked up from the missive delivered minutes earlier.

Praying the tidings were favorable, that at long last there would be an end to this war, Annyn crossed the solar to where he stood alongside the table. "And?"

He let the missive roll back on itself and pulled her into his arms. "Stephen has agreed to negotiate."

She dropped her head back and met his gaze. "Then 'twill be over soon."

"Does the Lord will it."

She smiled. "Most assuredly He shall." Of course, she had thought the same at summer's end when word came of the death of Stephen's son and heir, Eustace. The count having choked on an eel while dining at Bury St. Edmunds with his father, it was whispered that it was the Lord's vengeance upon Eustace for plundering those abbey lands the week before.

"I would have you go with me," Garr said, "but 'tis best you do not."

Especially now. Hopeful, she slid a hand between them and splayed her fingers across her abdomen. "Where do you go?"

He looked to the hand she laid upon herself. "The negotiations are to be held at Winchester. I leave on the morrow."

So soon? And for how long? He had spoiled her terribly since their marriage, rarely leaving her side. Though she had expected to see little of him once he returned to Wulfen to resume training boys to men—and where he had sent Rowan to replace Sir Merrick—he had not returned. Indeed, within a fortnight of their marriage he had determined to give the castle into Everard's care that he might be husband to her and father to their children when they were so blessed.

She caressed her abdomen. Though she knew the answer, she asked, "You really must go?"

"I have forsworn my allegiance to Stephen, but he tells he will come only if I am present." He tilted her head back and kissed her. "Upon my vow, I shall return anon."

She arched an eyebrow. "Do not make vows you cannot keep—lesson seven, is it not?"

"Aye, and I shall keep it." He laid a hand atop hers on her belly. "Still your menses have not begun?"

It was the same he asked at least twice a day since she had told him her flux was late. Unfortunately, there were yet no other signs to confirm her pregnancy, so it might not be at all. "They have not begun, but neither does there appear to be any swelling."

He laughed. "As my mother told, 'tis often months ere a woman's belly boasts its prize." He tucked a tress behind her ear, her hair having grown these past months such that it now fell past her shoulders. "Patience, Annyn. We shall know soon enough."

She drew her hand from her belly and laid it to his chest where his heart beat with hers. Aye, soon they would know. Soon they would be three, mayhap four.

Excerpt

THE YIELDING

Age Of Faith: Book Two

SHE HAD KILLED a man. Or so it was said.

During the ten days since her awakening, Beatrix had tried every locked door within her memory. Some creaked open wide enough to allow her to peer inside such that she now remembered her flight from Stern Castle with Gaenor, Sir Ewen's death, and Sir Simon's face when he sought to violate her. Though she remembered little beyond the hands he had laid to her, she was fairly certain he had not stolen her virtue. But there was that gap between her flight from Sir Ewen's side to the fall.

Suddenly light of head, she lowered to the chest at the foot of the bed and breathed deep until the feeling passed. Then, as she had done time and again, she struggled to fill the gap preceding her return to conscious-ness in the ravine when she had rolled the knight off her. But once again, the memory she needed to defend against the charge of murder was denied her. However, that was not all she needed. She required words to tell what had happened, words that too often teased her tongue, the absence of which made her seem a simpleton.

Four days past, when she had first recalled Sir Simon's attempt to ravish her, she had begged an audience with Baron Lavonne. He made her wait two days and, when he finally appeared, it had been for naught. Like a moth straining to light, she had tried to voice the terrible memory, but the head injury had bound her tongue and incurred the baron's impatience. That second visit to her chamber was his last.

Thus, she would soon be brought before the sheriff, but even if she could tell what had happened, there seemed no outcome other than death—unless her family delivered her. Each day she set herself before the window to watch for them, certain they would come, but they did not. Why? The castle was not barricaded, the folk allowed to move freely within and without the walls. Surely she would not stand alone before the sheriff and her accusers?

She touched a finger to her lips in anticipation of what she would say, but even when she thought the words through before speaking, her tongue and lips faltered as if she were empty of mind. She was not. Of course, one would not know it to be near when she opened her mouth.

She felt the place where her hair had been cut away to stitch up her scalp. Though she might never again be as she was, she was alive thanks to the elusive Sir Michael D'Arci who had yet to appear though he had surely been apprised of her recovery.

Dreading his arrival that the curt chamber maid who attended her had told would be this day, Beatrix stood and once more crossed to the window. Shivering in the cool air that her removal of the oilcloth allowed within, she watched the lowering sun draw shadows across the castle walls. As always, her gaze was tempted to the wood and, leaning forward, she stared at the bordering trees and wished she could reach them. Of course, what then? She might once have been capable of finding her way back to Stern, but now...

She lowered her gaze to the inner bailey. It bustled with those whose work for their lord was done for the day. Now they could return home, break hunger, and bed down for the morrow when they would again rise to serve their lord.

As if the thought made the baron appear, his immense figure emerged from the stables. He was not alone. Beside him strode a man of obvious rank. Michael D'Arci? It had to be. And now he would ensure justice was done. His justice.

Beatrix considered the dark-haired man. As he and the baron neared the donjon steps, the latter said something. Though his words aspired to Beatrix's window high above, they arrived in unintelligible pieces. But there was no mistaking her name that fell from his lips, nor that it caused the dark-haired man to stiffen and look around.

His revealed face made Beatrix's breath stick. Even at a distance, she knew his countenance, for it was that of Sir Simon—albeit crowned by black hair rather than blond.

She clenched her hands at the realization that soon she would stand before one whose resemblance to that miscreant would surely cause her words to fail. Though he was not as big a man as Baron Lavonne, from the dark upon his face, he might as well be a giant.

He looked up, and though Beatrix knew she could not be seen among the shadows, she took a step back. The frown that crossed his face darkened it further. And as surely as she breathed, she knew he knew it was upon her chamber he looked.

She turned, retrieved her psalter from the bedside table, and pressed it to her chest. Such relief she had felt upon discovering it the day of her awakening. Telling herself God's word would sustain her, she opened the psalter and settled down to await Sir Simon's vengeful kin.

Hours passed, her supper was delivered, more hours passed, and still he did not come.

When her lids grew heavy, she slid beneath the bed covers. "Lord," she whispered, "you allowed me to survive a f-fall I should not have, but surely not for this. Pray, re-reveal to me what you would have me to do."

'Tis said you are a devil, Michael.

Not in all things, but some—namely, women. But he had good reason. And now, more so.

Michael returned to his memory of the lonely youth who had followed him to the roof of their father's donjon years earlier. He saw the night breeze lift Simon's fair hair and sweep it across his troubled face.

Would that I could be like you, Michael.

Had he known what it was like to be Michael D'Arci, a man unwelcome at most nobles' tables, he would not have wished it so.

Drawing breath past the bitterness, Michael opened his fists and began beating a rhythm on the window sill. He loathed waiting on anything or anyone, especially a murderess whose face ought to be set upon an angel.

No fair maid will ever want me.

And for that, Simon ought to have been grateful. Still, Michael had been pained by his brother's plight, especially when he saw moonlight sparkling in the boy's tears. Tears for fear he might never know a woman.

Michael looked to the postered bed where Beatrix Wulfrith's still figure was played by the light of a dimming torch. Though her face was turned to the wall, denying him full view of her beauty, the slender curve of her neck was visible, as was the turn of an ear and the slope of a cheekbone swept by hair of palest gold. Deceptive beauty. No woman was to be underestimated, not even his stepmother who had been as a mother to him.

I would be a man and mother would have me remain a boy, Simon's voice found him again.

The boy's mother had loved him too well, refusing to see past her own heart to what was best for her son.

Trying to put away the memory of Simon's bent head, slumped shoulders, and the sobs jerking the youth's thin body, Michael returned his focus to the bed, something of a feat considering the amount of wine he had earlier consumed. Too much, as evidenced by his presence in the lady's chamber when he had vowed he would wait until the morrow. But she had only been two doors down from the chamber he was given, and he had been unable to sleep. To resist the impulse to seek her out, he had donned his mantle and walked the outer walls for an hour, but when he returned to the donjon and drew near her door...

Would she awaken? It was as he wished, for he had waited too long to delve the guilty eyes of his brother's murderer. If not for the delay in delivering him tidings of her recovery, she would have been brought before the sheriff by now, but it had taken a sennight for Christian Lavonne's men to locate Michael in London where he had gone to assist with an outbreak of smallpox. However, Simon would have his justice as Christian had promised—and so, too, would the old baron, Aldous.

Recalling the two hours spent in the company of Christian's father, tending the man's aches and pains that should have ended his suffering long ago, Michael shook his head. For years he had urged Aldous to not dwell on Geoffrey's death, to accept it and continue as best he could in his ravaged body, but it was as if the old man's life hinged upon working revenge on the Wulfriths.

With Simon's death, Michael now understood Aldous's pain. Indeed, this day the old baron had wagged a horribly bent finger at his physician and goaded him for finally knowing such terrible loss. The bile in Michael's belly had stirred so violently he had been grateful when Christian appeared. Christian who allowed his father his acts of revenge but had not refused to take a Wulfrith bride despite Aldous cursing him for acceding to King Henry's plan. Christian who was now the baron but had once been a man of God. Christian who was in many ways still a man of God but hid the threads of his former life behind an austere front. And among those threads was the notion of forgiveness.

Remembering the supper and conversation he had shared with his lord, Michael tensed. Though Christian had promised justice, any mention of it this eve had caused the man to fall silent or speak elsewhere. Michael feared he wavered and suspected it was not only due to the tidings that King Henry still expected a union between the Wulfriths and Lavonnes but Christian's training in the ways of the Church. Regardless, the baron would wed Gaenor Wulfrith as agreed. Of course, first she must be coaxed out of hiding.

Though it was believed she was at Wulfen Castle, the Wulfrith stronghold dedicated to training young men into worthy knights, it could not be confirmed due to the impregnability of the castle. But eventually the Wulfriths would have to yield her up, for King Henry would not long suffer their defiance. It was likely he did so now only because it was believed his edict had resulted in the death of Lady Beatrix. Though the Wulfriths were as much vassals to the king as any other baron, they were allies worthy of respect that King Henry afforded few. But if that respect precluded the dispensing of justice—

Nay, his brother would have justice!

You are the only one who has a care for me, Simon's voice once more resounded through him.

Often it had seemed he *was* the only one who cared. Unfortunately, too much time had passed between his visits home for him to do more than play at training his half-brother into a man. It had boded ill for Simon whose mother found excuse after excuse to avoid sending him to a neighboring barony for his knighthood training. Thus, when she was forced to relent, Simon had struggled to keep pace with what was expected of one his age. However, after a long, arduous journey toward knighthood, he had attained it, unaware that his accomplishment would soon be stolen from him. By this woman.

Michael increased the thrum of his fingers. Reckless and willful his brother might have been, but he could not have warranted such a death. Might the lady seek absolution from her crime? Might she say the murder was the result of a bent mind, as it was not uncommon for those of the nobility to claim in order to escape punishment? Might she put forth that her head injury prevented her from properly defending herself at trial? The latter would likely serve her better, as there was proof she had suffered such a blow. Indeed, according to Baron Lavonne, her speech was affected, though he submitted it might be more pretense than impediment. What if she *were* absolved?

Michael seethed over the still figure beneath the covers. As his movement about the chamber and thrumming upon the sill had not moved her, mayhap he ought to shake her awake. But that would mean laying hands on her, and he did not trust himself. How was it she slept so soundly, without the slightest twitch or murmur? It was as if she feigned sleep.

That last thought settling amid the haze of too much drink, Michael stilled and considered it more closely. Indeed…

Beatrix stared at the wall and strained to catch the sound of movement. Though the man's fingers had ceased their thrumming, and there was only the soft pop and hiss of embers that were all that remained of the brazier's fire, she knew Sir Simon's kin was there as he had been for the past quarter hour. Once more reminded that she was alone with the brother of a man who had tried to ravish her, and that he was likely no different, she suppressed a shudder. Why had he come in the middling of night? And what was she to do?

He strode so suddenly around the end of the bed that there was no time for her to close her eyes. Wearing a mantle as red as new-spilled blood, a tunic as black as a moonless night, he slowly smiled.

"Lady Beatrix awakens." He angled his head, causing his dark hair to skim his shoulder. "Or mayhap she has been awake some time now."

Waiting for him to leave, devising a way to deter him if he tried to do to her what his brother had done. But the only thing near enough with which to defend herself was the pewter goblet on the bedside table.

"I am Michael D'Arci of Castle Soaring. You know the name, my lady?"

Too well as well he knew.

"Have you no tongue?"

Aye, but the bridge between it and her mind was in poor disrepair. If a reply was forthcoming, it would surely come too late.

He pressed hands to the mattress, leaned forward, and narrowed his lids over pale gray eyes so like his brother's and yet somehow different. "Mayhap you are simply frightened?"

As he wished her to be.

"Or perhaps you are as witless as I have been told."

Anger built the bridge to her tongue. "I am not witless!"

"Ah, she speaks. What else does she do?" He bent so near she could almost taste the wine on his breath. Though he did not appear unsteady, she sensed he had imbibed heavily, a dangerous thing for an angry man to do—especially dangerous for her.

His eyebrows rose. "She assists her sister in escaping the king's edict"—

Had Gaenor escaped? Though Beatrix had asked after her sister when Lavonne last visited her chamber, the man who was to have been Gaenor's husband had not answered.

—"puts daggers to men as easily as to a trencher of meat, and survives a fall that should have seen her dead."

A tremble, as much born of anger as fear, moved through Beatrix. Struggling to keep her breath even, she reminded herself of the goblet. If he tried to defile her, she would bring it down upon his head. *If* she could get it to hand. *If* she could harm another.

"You wish to know the reason I tended your injury?" Michael D'Arci continued. "Why I did not allow you to die as is your due?"

She did not need to be told. Her words might be slow to form, but she knew he sought revenge.

"Justice," he said.

Revenge by a lesser name was still revenge, especially where unwarranted.

"Though you may be clever, I vow you will be judged and found wanting."

In the past, she had been called clever. Would she ever be again—lacking D'Arci's taint of sarcasm?

When she gave no reply, he said, "Could you, you would kill again, hmm?"

Again, her tongue loosened. "Most assuredly I would defend my person against any who seeks to violate me." Was that her voice? Strong and even without break or searching? Whence did it come?

"You speak of ravishment?" D'Arci bit.

Though she longed to look away, she kept her gaze on his face, noting his full mouth, straight nose, broad cheekbones, and heavily lashed gray eyes—so like his brother's she strained to hold back the panic that would have her scurry for cover.

Of a sudden, he cursed, his unholy use of the Lord's name making her flinch. "Is that what you will tell the sheriff? That you murdered my brother because he ravished you?"

Beatrix blinked. Though ravishment had surely been Simon D'Arci's intent, it seemed the Wulfrith dagger had stopped him. Determined to correct Michael D'Arci—to assure him she was fairly certain his brother had failed to commit the heinous act—she searched for words. However, his darkening face once more caused her tongue to tangle. Could the devil assume human form, he would surely be pleased to do so in the image of Michael D'Arci.

But for all of her fear, hope slipped in. Of that day at the ravine, he surely knew only what Baron Lavonne had shared. What if she told him the truth, even if most of the truth she could only surmise?

"I did not…" She swallowed. "I tell you true, I…"

"Did not murder him?"

"I could never murder. I but d-d-defen—"

"Defended yourself?"

How she detested his impatience! "'Twas surely hap—"

"Happenstance?"

That word she had not lacked. "Aye, happenstance."

"You do not know for certain?"

"I do. I just cannot…remember it all."

"What fool do you think me, Lady Beatrix?" he growled.

"I am not a m-murderer."

"You expect me to believe the young man I knew well was a ravisher, and you whom I know not at all are no murderer? I should have let you bleed to death."

Anger streaked Beatrix's breast, and her next words sprang free as if she were quick of tongue. "Your brother would have!"

D'Arci drew a sharp breath, then splayed a hand across her throat. "You lie, witch, and I shall see you dead for it."

Though certain he meant to strangle her, his fingers did not tighten. Still, her own fear denied her breath. Was he playing with her? First torment, then death?

She glanced at the goblet. Providing she did not alert him, she could reach it. Providing he had imbibed as much wine as his breath told, she could escape him.

He slid his hand further up her neck. "When you stand before the sheriff"—

She was not to die this night?

—"I will savor your fear."

She swallowed hard against his palm and reached. "Nay, you will not," she said and swept the goblet to hand.

As he jerked his chin around, she slammed the vessel against his temple. For a breathless moment, he was still, and then he collapsed atop her.

Staring at his head on her chest and the trickle of blood coursing his brow, she quaked in remembrance of his brother who had similarly fallen across her.

Had she killed Michael D'Arci?

Nay, he breathed, but that did not mean she had not damaged him terribly. She, better than most, knew what could result from a blow to the head. Recalling her return to consciousness in the ravine when she had seen crimson on her gloved fingers, she began to shake. That day, her young life had come as near to ending as one could come without actually dying.

She squeezed her eyes closed, but when she opened them, the crimson remained. This time it bled from Michael D'Arci.

Knowing he might soon regain consciousness, she wriggled out from beneath him and dropped to her knees alongside the bed. Now how was she to escape?

Think. Think hard, Beatrice. She shook her head. *Then pray hard, for you cannot do this without help.*

Though she knew she risked much, she delayed her escape to call upon the Lord. And when she said, "Amen," she knew what must be done. As her only covering was the chemise the chamber maid had delivered the day she awakened at Broehne Castle, and the baron had taken her bloodied gown and mantle for evidence, she would have to impose on Michael D'Arci.

She slid a hand under him and released the brooch that clasped the red mantle at his throat. Blessedly, the lining was black, which would allow her to merge with the night. She turned the inside of the garment out and dragged it over her shoulders. As she secured it with the brooch, she saw the dagger and purse on D'Arci's belt. Beseeching God's forgiveness, she appropriated both and retrieved her psalter. Not until she reached the door did she realize she lacked footwear, but there was nothing for it as D'Arci's bulky boots would only hinder her.

She eased the door open and peered into the dim corridor. Unlike the first sennight since her awakening, there was no guard present. Obviously, Baron Lavonne had grown confident she would not—or could not—escape. Now if she could make it through the hall, into the bailey, and out the postern gate.

Though she had known the latter would prove difficult, if not impossible, since so much of a castle's defenses depended on the gate being well disguised, she quickly located it and slipped through.

Not until she was outside the castle walls, driving one leg in front of the other beneath a cold sliver moon, was the hue raised. Entering the wood she had so longed for, she paused and pressed a hand to her throbbing head.

Which way? She peered through the darkness and, clutching her psalter in an attempt to pry free the icy fingers of fear, made her decision. The only way that mattered was away from Broehne, though not so far she could not watch for her family who would surely come for her.

A good plan, for Lavonne and D'Arci would never expect her to remain on the barony of Abingdale.

About The Author

TAMARA LEIGH HOLDS a Master's Degree in Speech and Language Pathology. In 1993, she signed a 4-book contract with Bantam Books. Her first medieval romance, *Warrior Bride*, was released in 1994. Continuing to write for the general market, three more novels were published with HarperCollins and Dorchester and earned awards and spots on national bestseller lists.

In 2006, Tamara's first inspirational contemporary romance, *Stealing Adda*, was released. In 2008, *Perfecting Kate* was optioned for a movie and *Splitting Harriet* won an ACFW "Book of the Year" award. The following year, *Faking Grace* was nominated for a RITA award. In 2011, Tamara wrapped up her "Southern Discomfort" series with the release of *Restless in Carolina*.

When not in the middle of being a wife, mother, and cookbook fiend, Tamara buries her nose in a good book—and her writer's pen in ink. In 2012, she returned to the historical romance genre with *Dreamspell*, a medieval time travel romance. Shortly thereafter, she once more invited readers to join her in the middle ages with the *Age of Faith* series: *The Unveiling, The Yielding, The Redeeming, The Kindling,* and *The Longing.* Tamara's #1 Bestsellers—*Lady at Arms, Lady Of Eve, Lady Of Fire,* and *Lady Of Conquest*—are the first of her medieval romances to be rewritten as "clean reads." Look for *Baron Of Emberly,* the second book in *The Feud* series, in early winter 2015.

Tamara lives near Nashville with her husband, sons, a Doberman that bares its teeth not only to threaten the UPS man but to smile, and a feisty Morkie—named Maizy Grace, by the way—that keeps her company during long writing stints.

Connect with Tamara at her website www.tamaraleigh.com, her blog The Kitchen Novelist, Facebook, and Twitter. To be added to her mailing list for notification of new releases and special promotions, email her at tamaraleightenn@gmail.com.

Made in the USA
Monee, IL
25 November 2019